EDEN
CONQUERED

EDEN
CONQUERED

JOELLE CHARBONNEAU

An Imprint of HarperCollinsPublishers

Library of Congress Control Number: 2018933349
ISBN 978-0-06-245388-4

Typography by Jenna Stempel-Lobell
19 20 21 22 23 PC/LSCH 10 9 8 7 6 5 4 3 2 1
❖
First paperback edition, 2019

For my Nana, Marion Zimmerman.
The walls are now gone. I hope you are flying free.

1

Something whispered.

Carys stared at the hills surrounding her traveling party. Nothing moved. The only sounds were the crunch of the snow beneath her quivering horse's feet and Garret's irritated voice as once again he insisted they were going the wrong way.

No branches rustled on the trees that dotted the landscape. The air was still.

But Carys heard whispering.

The wind. It was calling.

She shivered, wiped the trickle of sweat off her forehead, and burrowed deeper into the coarse gray cloak that Lord Errik had wrapped around her on their escape from the Palace of Winds. The biting cold both inside and out had made the first several days a blur of bone-aching pain, a desperate fight to stay on her white-and-brown mount. The voices of Lord Errik, Lord Garret, and Larkin grew increasingly angry. All three felt they knew what was best for Carys, after all, now that she was dead.

Carys would truly *have been* dead if her twin had gotten his way.

Years of drawing punishment onto herself—diverting attention from Andreus and his secret—should have ensured their trust was unbreakable. She had always been there for her brother. Defended him. Yet, when it most mattered, he had abandoned her.

She clutched the reins tight in her hands. The whispering inside her head grew louder.

The trees rustled. Her horse danced beneath her as a branch snapped and fell to the ground to her left.

"We need to go faster," Lord Garret complained from atop his limping gray mare. "Someone could be following the tracks we're leaving in the snow."

"No one is following us," Lord Errik countered. "We traveled in that stream to ensure there were no tracks. Or maybe you forgot that's why the horses are so worn. If we push them to go any faster, they'll give out and we'll be stuck traveling on foot. Something I'm certain you have never done in your life."

"If you had found better mounts instead of these plow nags, we wouldn't have to worry about them giving out."

More arguing. It got them nowhere.

"Next time I have need to steal several horses without raising suspicion from the guard and anyone else inside the city, I will have you take the lead. You're lucky you even have a horse. You, Lord Garret, were not supposed to be a part of this journey."

"Garret." The word scraped her dry throat. A breeze tickled her neck.

"I'm here because Princess Carys wishes it."

"You're here because Princess Carys had no choice but to bring you," Errik snapped, then shook his head. "Of course, Lord Garret, if you are feeling tired of this journey you have only to say the words and . . ."

"Call him *Garret*." Carys straightened her shoulders. "*Only* Garret."

Despite the effort, her voice still sounded weak to her ears. But it was stronger than yesterday and stronger still than the day before. Six days in all had passed since the Kingdom of Eden was told of her death, thus ending the Trials of Virtuous Succession. Prince Andreus, being the only "surviving" competitor, was now the occupant of the throne.

Her twin was now His Majesty King Andreus. Guardian of Light. Keeper of Virtues.

And she was nothing.

She was outside of the confines of the walls that surrounded Garden City and the Palace of Winds, but she was still not free. Not the way she had once dreamed. Instead, she could feel the pull of the walls and the people inside them growing with each mile she put between them. Calling her back to face the darkness.

Calling her back to bring them the truth.

"What did you say, Princess?" Larkin called.

"I said that Errik should call him Garret." Carys tugged on her reins, bringing her trembling mount to a halt. "Titles command attention." People—especially commoners—notice them for fear of the consequences if they don't. "I can't risk word getting back to the Palace of Winds that there are nobles traveling the roads with a mysterious girl. No one must know I'm alive."

No one. Not until she discovered who in Garden City had killed her father and older brother and was plotting against Andreus at this very moment.

She shouldn't care about Eden or her brother anymore.

She knew it marked her as weak that she did.

Her twin had tried to kill her. He intended for her to die and probably celebrated now that he thought she had breathed her last. She hated him for that. She wanted the Gods to strike him down for turning against her—against the trust they had forged in the womb. And still . . .

Carys pulled her cloak tight as Errik and Garret brought their horses to a stop. Larkin struggled to bring her own mount under control. The mare bucked and pranced before finally coming to a halt fifteen feet away from the others. As someone who typically rode in the cart alongside her father on trips, Larkin never had need to learn how to do much more than sit a horse. Carys would have to teach her childhood friend that she had to take control if she wanted the horse to follow commands. Just as Carys would have to take control now.

Her brother had weakened her body and soul. She had no choice but to follow Errik and Garret away from the Palace of Winds if she wanted to stay alive and gain the power to return. Now the Tears of Midnight she'd relied on for so many years were almost purged from her body. Her body was still pained and weary, but she would be stronger than before when she saw her brother again. She would be free of the drug's cursed withdrawal. She would do whatever it took to make that so.

"I am sorry, Your High . . ." Errik stopped himself. He shook his head, causing the gray hood to slide off and down his back. His dark hair fluttered. He gave a slight smile that warmed his rich brown eyes. "*Carys*. You were right then and you are correct now. You are not only in danger from those in Garden City, but from the company you keep until your return. Any threat to that safety must be swiftly dealt with."

"I am not a threat to . . . Carys," Garret snapped. His red hair gleamed in the dying light of the sun. "If I were, do you think I would be here with you now trying to help her get away from my uncle and the rest of the Council of Elders? I could have remained in the Palace of Winds and helped my uncle to gain more power or gone home to take my place as High Lord of Bisog. Instead, I'm risking my title, my lands, and my life out here in the cold on this nearly crippled horse."

"If you'd like to go back to Garden City, I won't stop you," Errik said with a laugh. "But I will insist you leave your much-maligned steed."

"And leave Carys with you? I have waited too long and worked too hard to leave her in the hands of someone . . ."

"Quiet!" The word echoed through the trees. Carys's cloak billowed. Another branch snapped in the wind.

Her mount danced anxiously, and she yanked on the reins.

"I'm sorry, Your . . . Carys." Errik's eyes caught hers and held them. "It was not my intent to upset you. I know you aren't feeling well."

"I'm fine." Her head rang. Her back throbbed from the lash marks that had yet to heal. More than anything she wanted to find a place to curl up and wait for the pain to end—both inside and out. "I would be better if you stopped bickering like children." And if the whispering at the edge of her thoughts would stop. The whispers compelled her to listen, but spoke no discernible message. It pushed at her mind as her frustration built. She felt as if she were going crazy.

Seers talked of calling the wind. Of having the power to bend the air to their purpose. To travel on its back. To compel it to level armies.

While she was growing up, Seer Kheldin claimed to have stopped a wind tunnel from destroying Garden City and the palace. It was a tale so heroic it was akin to the children's fables of seers from hundreds of years ago. But in none of the stories about the seers did they speak of *hearing* the wind. Of feeling the pressure of the element in their mind and its urgency and . . .

"I didn't start it," Garret said. She frowned at him, and he let out a chuckle. "Sorry, I couldn't resist. Andreus used to say the same whenever Micah and I stumbled upon you and he squabbling. Do you remember?"

Micah's stern expression and Dreus's answering grin echoed in her mind. The memory clamped onto her heart and squeezed. She shook off the sorrow that threatened to pull her under.

"Andreus never liked anyone believing he'd done anything wrong," Carys said. "He still doesn't."

"That's something we can use to our advantage when you return to the Palace of Winds to claim your rightful place on the Throne of Light," Garret said. "The sooner you return, the better it will be for the kingdom. We need to start gathering forces."

"I hate to admit this, but Garret is right." Errik frowned. "If you do plan on returning, we will need to start planning for that moment. I know you are still weakened from the competition, but each day that passes will increase your brother's confidence and power."

And each passing day would give whoever had been working with Imogen the chance to stab Andreus in the back and take the throne. The seeress was dead now, but in the months she had exerted influence in the Palace of Winds, she had fooled them all. Because of her, Carys's father and oldest brother had paid with their lives. Andreus had paid with his heart.

Whatever Imogen had set in motion, Carys had to stop. Otherwise, there would be no way to avoid a war that would tear Eden apart.

"Then that settles it," Garret said with a nod. "We will ride to Bisog."

"There is no way Carys is going to Bisog." Errik laughed.

The whispering grew louder. Swirling through her head as the men faced each other. Her anger built with each accusation they hurled.

"The houses in Bisog are bound by oaths to the High Lord of the district," Lord Errik argued. "Now that my father's dead, they are sworn to me. I will take control of their guardsmen and lead them into Eden under the princess's banner."

Her heart pounded. The wind pushed against her chest, drowning out the words.

"And once she's in your district surrounded by your swords, you'll take control of Carys as well. Over my dead body."

Garret reached for his sword. "That can be arranged."

"Stop!" she shouted as Errik drew his sword. Fighting each other about who could be trusted—when she didn't know if either could be.

Wind gusted and swirled on the top of the hill in front of them. And that's when she saw them. Six men on horseback with steel brandished, cresting the hill and bearing down toward them.

"Run, Larkin!" Carys unfastened her cloak so she could reach into the pockets of her gown. The wind caught her cloak and pulled. Her fingers closed around the hilts of her stilettos. Errik and Garret moved in front of her with their swords drawn, ready to fight the four charging men.

Carys cocked her right arm back to throw when she heard the twang of bows. She lifted her eyes and spotted two of the men at the top of the hill notching new arrows in their longbows. They fired again—in the direction Larkin had run. Urging her horse forward, Carys picked her target and let one stiletto fly. Despite the cold and her weakness, her aim was true. The man dropped the bow in his hand as the stiletto buried its long, sharp point deep in his neck.

Steel scraped against steel not far from her. Someone let out a war cry that ended abruptly. Carys couldn't turn. She kept her eyes on the man before her—who had just let another arrow fly.

"Look out!" Errik shouted as his blade slashed through one attacker.

A horse screamed. She heard Garret call to Errik as she drew back the other blade and let it fly. The wind gusted. The stiletto missed the attacker's throat and dug deep into the hollow of his cheek. Carys saw his eyes widen just before he fell from his horse.

"Carys!"

She turned. Her friend was standing under a tree. Her horse was nowhere to be found. Garret fought with one of the two remaining brigands on the ground. Two others were dead by Errik's hand. The other attacker was still mounted and thundering toward Larkin. And Carys had no other weapons with which to protect her friend.

Wheeling her horse, she urged it forward, desperate to reach Larkin before the man with the sword.

Then Errik was there atop his own horse. His steel flashed. The man clad in brown and gold parried, then looked up at Errik's face and shouted, "It's you!"

The attacker dropped his blade to the ground just as Errik swung his sword again and buried it in the man's neck.

"Larkin," Carys yelled, sliding off her horse. She caught her friend in a tight embrace before pulling back to look at her. "Are you okay?"

Larkin swallowed hard as she nodded. "I'm fine." She looked down at the ground near where she'd been standing. At her feet were several arrows—their shafts cracked in two. "I thought I was going to die. But—none of the arrows hit me. They just . . ." She looked at Carys with wonder. "It's like they just stopped. They're broken."

Anger swirled in Carys's thoughts. Then it was gone. She shook her head and wrapped her arms around herself. "The arrows must have been in the cold for too long. The shafts must have splintered."

Errik cocked his head to the side and studied her before sliding his bloody sword into his sheath and dismounting. "Bad luck for them. Good luck for us."

"I'll take that kind of luck any day," Garret said, crossing to Carys and Larkin. Not once did he look at the men whose blood was draining into the snow. He pulled off his cloak and draped the thick garment around Carys's shoulders. "But you and I both know we have another force to thank for our lives." He whispered into her ear, "We have much to discuss, Your Highness." A shiver went up her spine as he turned to the others. "And our luck continues because these men are no longer in need of their horses. Would you care to join me in taking charge of our new mounts, Errik?"

Errik smiled. "Lead the way."

The minute the two were gone, Larkin stooped down and picked up a broken arrow shaft. Fear filled her face. "This wasn't luck. Was it, Carys?"

A lie sprang to Carys's lips. After years in the Palace of Winds, surrounded by people scheming to gain influence and power, speaking untruths with conviction was, for Carys, akin to breathing. But this was Larkin—someone who had her own life turned upside down just because she dared be Carys's friend. Larkin should, at that moment, have been traveling to her wedding. Instead she was on the run.

Carys owed her the truth, even if it meant scaring her even more. Hearing the stories of the powers of the old seers was one thing. Seeing them—*living* them—was quite another.

Carefully, she said, "It wasn't luck, but I . . ." She felt the confusion inside her build anew. The whispers returned. Carys clenched her fists and her breath caught in her throat. The trees bent as she pressed a hand against her stomach—and took a deep breath to clear her mind. "I don't understand what's happening. The wind is . . . in my mind. It saved my life during the Trials, but I don't understand what it is or how to control it."

Or if it can be controlled. Stories claimed that it could, but her brother hadn't believed the seers had this kind of power. His faith, for lack of a better word, rested only in what he could see with his own eyes and test with his own mind. He convinced her the stories were complete fabrications. She never studied them. She had no idea what wisdom they might hold.

"You're scared," Larkin said.

It wasn't a question, but Carys nodded anyway. "Since the trials, I've heard voices I can't comprehend. I keep thinking I'm going crazy because I can't understand what they say. The wind cannot speak.

Not to me. I'm not a seer. So how can this be?"

"How do you know?" Larkin asked. "What makes you believe it's the wind that calls to you?"

"How could it be anything but? How could I mistakenly believe I had some kind of affinity?"

Larkin gave her a long look. They didn't discuss Carys's secret, but it sat between them just the same. The Tears of Midnight and all they had done to her, body and mind. Larkin held out a broken arrow shaft. "I don't know what is happening, but I believe there is a reason for it. Just as there was a reason for us becoming friends."

"Maybe . . ." Carys frowned as Larkin slipped the broken shaft into her pocket. "I'm just grateful you are safe. And as long as we get you to your betrothed and his family in Acetia, you will stay that way."

Acetia was far to the north, but if they found a group of merchants, it might be possible . . .

"No," Larkin said firmly. "Your brother is convinced that I was involved in a plot to assassinate him. If he hasn't learned of my betrothal yet, he will soon. How long do you think Zylan and his family would live if they protected me?"

"Then I'll find somewhere else for you to hide until it's possible for you to be reunited with him. You are not going to be safe if you stay with me."

"I did not become friends with you because it was *safe*," Larkin snapped. "And winner of the Trials or not, you are my Queen. Whether you wish me to or not, I will stand at your side and defend you with my last dying breath—as I know you would do for me and for the rest of Eden." As if to prove it, Larkin dropped into a deep curtsy and in a voice filled with certainty said, "Your Majesty, I pledge myself to your service. When the night is darkest, I promise to be a light to help you find your way."

Tears pricked Carys's eyes. The words weren't the typical ones spoken to swear fealty, but the passion behind them sealed the vow as certainly as if it was said in the Hall of Virtues before the Throne of Light. Yet, they made clear Larkin's intent to be her champion. To be, in her own way, a knight in Carys's service.

Swallowing the lump in her throat, Carys took Larkin's arm and helped her stand. "I'm supposed to vow that I will never ask you to betray the seven virtues of our kingdom. But considering I'm going to return to Garden City in order to unmask traitors and take the throne, I'm not certain I can do that."

Larkin stood and gave a hint of a smile. "I'd be happy to push your brother into a dung heap if given the chance."

"No offense," Carys said, feeling the anger that had been growing with every passing day vanish like smoke. "But that's something I might have to do myself."

Larkin nodded with mock sincerity. "As you wish, Your Majesty. Would you like me to retrieve your stilettos?"

"I have already done so," Errik said, sliding off a chestnut brown stallion and starting toward Carys. "But feel free to take anything else from our fallen friends that you think we might have use for."

As Larkin hurried off, Errik pulled the long, silver blades from beneath his cloak. "Things might not have gone so well for us had the bowmen not been stopped so quickly. It's a relief to be traveling with one so skilled."

Carys looked down at the blades, then into the handsome face of the foreign dignitary who had helped her when she needed someone to trust. And she *had* trusted him, but that was before he assisted her escape through the tunnels below the Palace of Winds.

He should never have known about the tunnels' existence. How had he discovered the passage out when she, who had spent so much of her childhood roaming those lost tunnels, never had? Her body's craving for the Tears of Midnight had made it impossible to demand answers before. But she was growing stronger, and now that the danger had passed, she could see the attack on them with greater clarity.

"Are you feeling all right, Your . . . Carys?" Errik asked, stepping closer.

In the distance Carys saw Garret speaking to Larkin as her friend examined another of their enemy's bows. "I'm . . . not sure." Carys wrapped her hands around the hilts of her silver weapons and took them from Errik's grasp.

"Is there something I can do?" He took another step forward and put his arm around Carys's shoulder. "You must be tired."

Carys leaned against him, felt the warmth of his body relax against hers. Then she pictured the man Errik had killed. A man who laid down his weapon because he recognized Errik.

She took advantage of his ease and jabbed the point of a stiletto into his side. His body went still as she quietly said, "I'm tired of the people I trusted with my life lying to me. So it's time to tell me how you found the escape tunnel under the palace, and after that you will explain how you knew the man you just felled."

"Carys, you have to trust me . . ."

"No." She dug the tip of the stiletto through his shirt and felt him gasp as the steel pricked his flesh. "I don't. But you did aid me in my escape so I will allow you to explain. You are not a Trade Master."

"No. I am not from Chinera."

"Then where? Who are you and how did you come to the Palace of Winds?"

"Technically, I have no true home. My family has shed blood, broken oaths, spurred others into war and betrayed one another to regain the power they believe is rightfully theirs."

"You speak in riddles."

"I speak the truth." He paused. "I grew up in the castle of Dragonwall, but it was never my home."

"Dragonwall. You mean *Adderton*?" The kingdom to the south had been at odds with Eden since long before Carys was born.

"There is more." He sighed heavily. "What was left of my family took refuge in Adderton a hundred years ago when they fled through those same passages that carried you to safety. *My* ancestors fled— while their brothers and sisters were being slaughtered by *yours*. My name is Lord Errik of the Family Bastian."

Bastian.

Carys's head spun. Her great-grandfather had cut down the Bastians in order to be King. The Bastians had sworn revenge against them at all cost and had, through Eden's last fraudulent seer, killed her father and brother and turned Andreus against her. If given the chance, the Bastians would kill him, and her, too.

Her cloak fluttered as she turned. "I will do you the honor of looking you in the face as I dispatch you for this treachery."

"There is no treachery. If I wished to betray you, Carys, I could have done it long before now. I could have left you to die as your brother did or killed you quietly when you begged in your sleep for someone to end your pain. I am not like my cousin, the seer. Imogen came to reclaim the throne for her father, my uncle, and return the Bastians to power here in Eden. I am not with them. I want none of that."

Don't listen, she told herself. *Kill him now.* But his words and his face held no fear, no sign of deceit, only conviction. It stilled her hand from spilling his blood then and there onto the frozen ground.

"What do you want?" she demanded. "If not the throne, why did you come to Eden?"

"I came hoping to find a way to make peace. Instead, I found something more important." His eyes met hers and held them fast. "I found you."

2

The lights in the stone hallway dimmed. It was only half a second. If he had blinked, he might have missed it.

Andreus paused to see if it happened again, but the lamps scattered in between the colorful tapestries that lined the hallway glowed bright and strong. Andreus glanced at the guards at the end of the hall, but their stoic expressions said they hadn't noticed the change. Yet Andreus was certain he had, just as he had seen the lights flicker in the Hall of Virtues—not just now, but earlier today and yesterday.

He grimaced at the ache in his leg as he started down the corridor again. If there was something wrong with the lights . . .

"Your Majesty, if I could have one more minute."

The sound of Elder Jacobs's voice snaked down the hallway, and Andreus wanted to scream even as he slowed his pace. In the days since his coronation, the Council had rarely left him alone for more than a few minutes at a time. Taxes to be determined. Orders to be sent to the High Lords begging for more troops and supplies for the war. Favors to be granted and time provided for his father's and brother's friends to fawn over him.

"I knew you would be triumphant in the Trials, King Andreus."

"Your brother always said that in his stead, you would make a brilliant king."

"Your father would be so proud."

He wanted to believe all of them—and knew he could believe none.

Straightening his shoulders beneath the weight of the sweltering blue-and-gold-stitched ceremonial robe, Andreus turned and nodded. Elder Jacobs was the sole Council member who had helped Andreus during the Trials. As much as Andreus appreciated the Elder's aid then, now he wished for just one day with Jacobs not at his side.

But like the brace he wore—the one that was supposed to heal the wounds inflicted by Xhelozi claws—the Council, and Jacobs, had to be endured. Andreus's leg was still too weak to walk without the metal contraption, and his authority was still too fragile to push anyone aside, especially an Elder who might be an ally. "Elder Jacobs, did you notice the lights dim just moments ago?"

"I did not, Your Majesty." Elder Jacobs shook his head. His long, black braid undulated in a snakelike fashion, and Carys's voice came unbidden into Andreus's head. *Fitting for one as underhanded as he.*

Andreus shook his head.

"Forgive me, Your Majesty, but do you doubt the report we received yesterday from the Masters of Light?" the Elder asked. "They assured us the windmills and the lines were all functioning as they should."

Andreus had no doubt the Masters reported what they believed they should as they stood in the Hall of Virtues surrounded by court, Council, and King. The report was politically savvy, but that did not make it true.

If there were weaknesses, and they were disclosed, word would spread. And as the days plunged them deeper into winter, panic would have followed. Public meetings would never give Andreus the answers he sought. Nor would any encounters that involved the Elders and their private agendas. Unfortunately, each time Andreus had tried to go to the battlements to seek out answers on his own, a member of the Council, unfailingly, appeared.

"The Masters have my trust." Andreus gave Elder Jacobs the carefree smile his mother had instructed him to use ever since he was old enough to remember. "But I cannot help my concern. After all, the lines were sabotaged not long ago, and the culprit for that sabotage has not been captured. Neither has the accomplice of the assassin who tried to kill me during the Trial of Humility. And I am not certain that finding those behind the plot is at the forefront of Captain Monteros's mind."

Indeed, only one suspect had been questioned. Larkin's father swore his daughter had nothing to do with the attempt. The old tailor was currently being watched, but other than his statement, Captain Monteros had had little to report about the woman Andreus saw, or those who colluded with her.

Elder Jacobs frowned and looked down the hall before lowering his voice to barely a whisper. "Captain Monteros has left the Palace of Winds with a contingent of guards at Chief Elder Cestrum's order."

"Our chief officer leaves the palace, and I am not informed of it?" Andreus demanded.

"The Council *did* inform you—of their intent to ensure a new Seer of Eden is installed in the palace. You said you trusted the Council of Elders to handle the matter and dismissed the topic. Elder Cestrum took that as a sign the Council was free to direct matters as they wished."

Andreus clenched a fist at his side and shook his head. It was his own fault. Any discussion of a new seer brought back memories of Imogen. Her dark eyes filled with passion and her ebony hair brushing against his chest. She should be at his side right now, preparing to become his Queen. Instead, she and the love they shared were dead—lost to him because of his sister's jealousy and betrayal.

The village, where the seers studied and trained, was in the southwesternmost district of the kingdom. "Captain Monteros is on his way to Village of Night to escort a new seer to join us?"

"Acquisition of a new seer is the goal he was given by the entire Council, but in addition Elder Cestrum spoke privately with the captain before he left. I believe they were discussing Lord Garret."

Garret. The Chief Elder's nephew and his dead brother's best friend.

Garret had a habit of making unexplained disappearances. First two years ago when he left the palace after a fight with Andreus's older brother. Then again on Andreus's coronation day. The High Lord was to swear fealty and suddenly could not be found. The Chief Elder feigned ignorance over his nephew's absence, but Andreus had not been convinced by his display.

"Has Lord Garret been located?" Andreus asked. Until his sister's death, and the declaration made that he had won the crown, Garret's every move had been followed by the only other person

Andreus could trust—the boy he had rescued, Max. But before the coronation, Garret slipped away. Andreus worried. Did the lord's absence mean he was planning to stake his own claim to the throne? If so, Andreus wasn't sure whether the oaths of fealty the Elders of the Council swore to him would hold.

"Elder Cestrum clings to his claim that his nephew must have returned home to Bisog to deal with matters in his district, but none that I have spoken with believe that to be true."

"Then where is he?"

"It is my belief Elder Cestrum has sent Captain Monteros and his men not only to act as escort for the new Seer of Eden, but to discover the answer to that very question. I am sure you understand that Lord Garret is of great import to Elder Cestrum."

Because Chief Elder Cestrum wanted Lord Garret to sit on the throne. Andreus kept that thought to himself. "I trust you will come to me with any information you learn about my missing High Lord. Maybe when the new seer arrives, he or she will be able to *divine* his whereabouts."

"Troublesome as he is, Lord Garret is not the concern I wished to speak with you about." Elder Jacobs glanced back at the guards at the end of the hall. "Perhaps it would be best if we continue our conversation in private."

"Very well." Andreus spun toward the steps that led to the King's private chambers. "Follow me."

Elder Jacobs's tread was light. Andreus ached as he climbed the brightly lit steps to the floor of the easternmost tower. The rooms were supposed to be a sanctuary for Eden's ruler, but Andreus had rarely stepped foot in the series of chambers since his coronation.

Despite his lack of use, a fire crackled in the stone hearth.

Fruit, bread, and cheese were laid out near the high-backed chair etched with the orb of Eden that his father had favored. Large windows looked out on the mountain range—a reminder, perhaps, of the dangers that during the cold months ventured down from the mountains and threatened to destroy all inside Garden City's walls.

In front of the windows was a massive wooden desk filled with maps and war plans. His father had studied them for hours with Captain Monteros as they plotted ways to defeat Adderton and secure Eden from attack on the southern border once and for all.

Had they succeeded, Father would still be alive. Imogen would still be seer and Carys . . .

Andreus's head throbbed from the weight of the crown of virtue and from the day filled with the Council's squabbling. Turning toward the fire, Andreus asked, "What is your true concern, Elder Jacobs?"

"None have come to me directly. They know that I am loyal to your cause. However, I have heard whispers from my sources. Several members of the Council of Elders have been observed speaking with a number of . . . *ladies* over the past week."

Andreus laughed. "And that is cause for worry?" As far as Andreus was concerned, anything that distracted the Council of Elders from advising him as to *what choices his father would make* was most welcome.

"It might be, Your Majesty. From what I have been told, these are ladies who believe they have a claim against the throne—or more specifically, that the infants they will bear have claims."

"Infants?" Andreus spun back around. "They're saying King Ulron fathered other children?"

"Not your father, Your Majesty." Elder Jacobs clasped his hands in front of him. "Nor your brother, Micah."

The silence hung heavy between them. Andreus's chest tightened even as he gave the Elder his mother's practiced smile. He picked up a glass of wine from the table near the blazing fire. Gods, the robe he wore was hot.

"These women—they say they are pregnant and the father of their children is me? You must know that's preposterous."

The pounding in Andreus's head grew louder as he thought about all the girls—from the ones he'd met in the stables to the ladies of the court—who had willingly been seduced in dark corners of the palace. Could one of them be carrying his child?

"I am certain you are right," Elder Jacobs assured smoothly. "And it would be impossible for any claim to be proven. But . . ."

"But what?"

"Your interest in women is well-known. Your father had the same interest, but he had an heir and had been King for years before any claims surfaced. Having these women speak against you so soon after your coronation and your sister's death . . ." The Elder sighed. "The Princess captured the imagination and the hearts of many during the Trials of Virtuous Succession. Stories are being told of her skill and dedication to the people of the kingdom."

"My sister is dead."

Andreus turned toward the fire. An image of his sister's white-blond, blood-matted hair flashed in his memory. Her screams clawed through his mind as they did every night in his sleep or when he saw people in the streets of Garden City wearing blue armbands. The bands once showed support for Carys becoming Queen, but they now served as a way to honor her memory. No one he saw in the streets wore yellow bands on their arms. There was no reason the people would feel the same need to honor him. He was, after all, not the one who was dead.

And still . . .

He shook his head to clear it. "I am the one that survived and won the Trials and the crown. My sister does not rule, no matter what some might wish."

"There are people with power who would never have allowed your sister to take the throne," Elder Jacobs insisted. "And the people of Eden are grateful you are now their King. However, after years of war and weeks of mourning and upheaval and uncertainty, they are looking to the throne for inspiration." Elder Jacobs paced in front of the fireplace as sweat dripped down Andreus's back. "It is why I came to you today about the claims that are being made. I worry some on the Council might be encouraging these women to come forward in order to weaken your position. Elder Cestrum . . ."

"What about Elder Cestrum?"

"I did not mean to speak of him specifically, Your Majesty. But I have been told our Chief Elder has spoken with each woman a number of times and has instructed his pages to search for others who might have similar stories to tell. The gold he has given to them is most certainly designed to buy their silence so your enemies cannot use that information against you. With the people still mourning your sister, it would be easy for some to point to your lack of virtue in one area and give voice to the idea that you are also lacking in others."

"So what do you suggest I do about these women?" And the children they claimed belonged to him. They could not belong to him. He wanted children, certainly, but not like this. By the Gods, he was King.

"There is little to be done, Your Majesty." Elder Jacobs shrugged. "I cannot say for sure who convinced them to make these claims or to what purpose."

Andreus set the goblet down with a thud. "Then why tell me of this at all?"

"To give you the advice your father once gave your brother from that chair." Elder Jacobs's braid undulated as he turned toward the high-backed seat near the fire and pointed. "There are always those who will try to distract your attention with one hand so you do not notice what they are doing with their other. I have done nothing but support you, yet you do not fully trust me. I hope someday you will. I am loyal to your mother the Queen and to you. I cannot say the same of the others who sit on the Council. There are some who will use your every move to undermine you, even as they claim to be your ally."

"You think I don't understand that?" His chest tightened. "Despite what you might think, Elder Jacobs, I am not stupid."

"No, you are not, Your Majesty, which is why I supported your claim to the throne from the first." The Elder bowed his head in apology. "The orb of Eden and the lights that keep the city safe from the Xhelozi are stronger because of you. Your understanding of the windmills is that of a Master. However, you must realize that people are not like windmills. They do not follow your design. They do not act according to logic. Your sister understood this."

"And I don't." Guilt and anger crackled in his words.

Elder Jacobs stroked his long braid. "I fear I am bungling this, for that is not what I intended to imply. What I am attempting to convey is that you have lost a number of those you care for in recent weeks and are now looking for counsel as to how to best lead. I know you wish for the people of the kingdom—your people—to see you as a strong leader. For the good of Eden, make sure you choose to listen to those who have your best interests and those of Eden at heart."

"As you do."

"There is much I have and can help you with, Your Majesty, especially if you were to publicly show your confidence in my counsel."

Here was the endgame. Elder Jacobs wanted a demonstration that he alone had the ear of the King. To what end, Andreus wasn't certain. "And what private advice would you give me if I asked, Elder Jacobs? Surely you have something more you'd say."

"Years ago your father was supposed to marry a princess of Adderton to ensure cooperation between our two kingdoms. He broke that treaty by marrying your mother, the Queen. That single action led to the war we have been embroiled in for years. By marrying one of the Adderton princesses, you could honor the treaty, and bring the peace our kingdom requires. Give the people a queen they can love, end the war in a strong show of leadership—and confound all of your enemies at the same time."

A bitter taste filled his mouth. "You want me to . . . get married?"

Elder Jacobs's lips curled. "If you keep people looking to the future, they will forget the complications of the past. I will leave you now. I know it has been a long day. You have much to contemplate before the Hall convenes again on the morrow." The Elder bowed deeply and didn't wait for Andreus to dismiss him before he pulled open one of the large gold doors and disappeared through it.

The door closed and Andreus grabbed up the goblet and smashed it into the fireplace. Glass shattered and flames leaped.

Damn it all. He was *King*.

He had won the Trials of Virtuous Succession.

He was wearing the crown.

He was supposed to be the one in charge, yet Elder Jacobs and the rest of the Council were determined to push and prod—to shove him into doing things he didn't want to do.

Married.

The word turned everything empty and cold.

Imogen was gone. When she died, his interest in taking a queen died with her. He'd insisted she be buried in the Tomb of Light when the court buried Carys. The Council of Elders had fought him. Even Elder Jacobs tried to talk him out of the idea. None but those who were members of Eden's royal family had been laid to rest in the tomb. Elder Cestrum had warned Andreus the unusual command would cause questions to be asked and perhaps uncomfortable answers to be revealed.

It had been a threat.

Andreus saw that now.

He grabbed another glass, cocked his arm back to throw it, and could almost hear his sister warn him not to take out his anger here.

The guards stationed outside the door would hear the sound of the crash. The maids would whisper to each other about how they had to clean up the goblets hurled in a rage by his majesty.

Carys always saved her personal outbursts for the dirt-packed tunnels beneath the Palace of Winds. Her public ones were a farce—performances only undertaken when Andreus needed attention distracted from him.

The attacks he suffered—his curse—if known, would cause turmoil in the kingdom. When Carys saw one coming, she would make a spectacle of herself so none would notice his struggle.

A part of Andreus wondered if she was secretly glad of the chance to scream and rage at all those she held in contempt. Then he remembered the lash. How she would be punished, all so his secret would never be revealed. Had the pain Carys suffered in his defense been what finally caused her to turn against him?

He limped to his father's desk and looked down on the maps and messages. Andreus had reviewed at least a dozen times these plans for a war his father and brother had been determined to win. Victory was just as far out of reach now as it had been when the war began, only now it was Andreus's responsibility to stop the fighting in a way that would make Eden look strong. Anything less would paint him as weak. If there was one thing he'd learned from his father it was that the crown could never look weak.

Gods.

Pressure built as everything he now faced as King swirled in his head.

Living in the shadow of his father and Micah, even in death.

The Xhelozi awake, and from recent reports, they were hunting in greater numbers than ever seen before.

A new seer on the way despite Andreus's belief that all seers, even the one that he had wished to make his Queen, were charlatans.

Women claiming to be pregnant with his children.

Elder Jacobs pushing for him to wed and bring peace.

The sight of his sister's bloody, broken body that chased him each night to the dawn.

He was King because he let her die.

He was King for that reason only.

He moved to the stack of scrolls on a large wooden table along the wall. They were filled with things on which the Council wanted him to focus. Things his father would have found important. But the sabotage of the wind-powered lights the night his father's and brother's bodies had been returned to the Palace of Winds still had not been explained. That was important, too. *More* important, since the lights going out could spell disaster for Garden City.

The Masters said the lights were fine now, but Andreus knew there was something wrong. If no one would tell him, then he was going to have to find out for himself. He might not know how to discuss new trade routes for grain or win the war against Adderton in the middle of winter, but he knew how to keep the orb above the Palace of Winds, and the lights that lined the city walls, glowing. In that way, he would keep the city and the kingdom safe.

Andreus unfastened the fur-lined, ceremonial robe and dropped it on his father's chair. Then he removed the heavy gold-braided crown edged with sapphires that his father had worn only on formal occasions. Andreus had donned the crown, a visual reminder of his authority, almost every waking moment, but now he placed it on the center of his father's desk and turned his back on it.

He told the two guards outside his doors to remain at their stations and strode down the hallway. Several startled servants dipped into deep curtsies as he passed. He slowed for a second when he recognized the dark-haired girl that he encountered just a few weeks ago in a dark corner of the stables. She had smiled an invitation at him that he had been more than willing to accept. Now she kept her eyes downcast as he strode by and didn't move until he turned in to the stairway and made the three-story climb to the battlements.

His injured leg throbbed as he pushed open the door and stepped into the biting winter cold.

Yes, his calf ached, but he felt the tension in his shoulders ease for the first time since he sat on the Throne of Light. He looked up at the glowing orb stationed atop a tall pedestal high above the easternmost tower. His father would never have approved his design modifications had the Masters presented them as such. Instead, they claimed them as their own, so his father never knew. But it was the truth. The orb was Andreus's. Not only had he secured its light, but he had identified a flaw in the design of the wind-power flow. It was a fatal flaw—one that allowed the orb and the lights on the walls to be severed with one cut.

Someone exploited that discovery. Back at the beginning of it all. Carys had been certain that the power outage was designed to strike a blow against them—to discredit Andreus or their family in the eyes of the people.

At the time, Andreus thought his sister's imagination had gotten the best of her. Now . . .

The gears of the windmill creaked. Two guards huddled near the base of it startled when they saw him, but he waved them back into the alcove. He crossed the battlements listening to the sound of the slats churning the air. The blades moved slowly. Far slower than was normal. But the lights currently appeared to be working as they should.

He peered over the white stone battlement wall to the city below.

The lights shone with a steady, bright light along the perimeter. No dimming or flickering. He looked back at the battlements and—he saw her. His sister dressed in fitted black pants on the platform that was no longer there. He saw it as clearly now as he had then. Her face pale and sweating despite the bitter cold.

He'd done that. He had vowed to do worse after she took Imogen away from him. And he had.

Still, he could see her standing on the platform, shivering and weak, with eyes somehow filled with strength.

"My life has been pledged to you since the day I was born, and no matter what you decide—I will be here for you."

Something darted out from the darkness, and the vision dispersed. Andreus grabbed the hilt of his sword and pulled it from the scabbard as the small figure stepped into the light.

"King Andreus! It's me."

"Max." Andreus let out a relieved breath as the boy crossed the stone battlements toward him. He stopped several lengths away and kept his eyes down at the ground.

When Andreus had found the boy in the streets, Max had been left for dead—his family believing his illness was caused by evil spirits. Thankfully, Madame Jillian's concoctions ensured Max was healthy, so long as he didn't do anything to create problems. Being out in the cold was a problem.

"I thought Madame Jillian told you to stay out of this weather."

The boy kicked at the stone beneath his feet. "I haven't had any problem breathing for days. One of the 'prentices said the Masters were gathering so I had to come."

"The Masters are holding a meeting?"

"The Masters are meeting at the Northwest Windmill," Max

said, his dark curls bouncing as he nodded. "I was going to sit near the door and try to listen, but I had to hide when Elder Ulrich showed up."

Andreus's smile faded. "Elder Ulrich is meeting with the Masters?"

Max nodded again. "He did. For a short time. He left and . . ."

"You can tell me about it later." Andreus put a hand on the boy's shoulder and felt him flinch. Two weeks ago, Max would have grinned up at him wildly, but the choices Andreus had made during the Trials had been frightening for a boy his age. Andreus was determined to put him at ease again. "I'm going to talk to the Masters, and you are going to go to my rooms and sit in front of the fire so Madame Jillian doesn't have reason to fret and fuss. Once I'm back, we'll have dinner and you can tell me everything that's happening in the castle. Do we have an agreement?"

He held out his hand to the boy with mock sincerity. Slowly, Max took Andreus's hand. "Can we have apple tarts? Madame Nadila made a batch earlier today."

Andreus smiled. "Get going. I don't want Madame Jillian scolding me for your going out into the cold."

"She'll never know, long as you don't tell her, Your Highness." Max flashed a gap-toothed grin and hurried off. Andreus couldn't help but notice the boy took the longest path to get to the proper tower. Maybe, Andreus thought, he'd ask Max tonight whether he wanted to study the windmills since he always seemed interested in . . .

"Let me go!"

Andreus spun at Max's scream.

"Leave me alone!"

31

Andreus ignored the flare of pain as he raced across the battlements. He peered into the shadows and . . . there! There was a cloaked figure and Max struggling against the wall in the shadows of the Northeastern tower.

"Let him go! I command you!" Andreus screamed. He ran faster, but the iron brace slowed him down. He reached for his sword and felt his heart stop as the cloaked figure picked up the kicking boy and shoved him over the battlements.

3

She should have killed him.

I found something more important. I found you.

Carys tried to shake Errik's words away as she tethered her new horse—a large gray mare—to a squat bush just outside the cave Larkin had directed them to.

She should have killed him, only the words kept repeating in her head.

She had seen deception up close all her life. She had watched for it. Measured it. Guarded against it. And everything in her heart told her Errik had been telling the truth when he said those words. He believed in her. And now she was uncertain how to proceed.

The opening of the cave was narrow and hidden behind a grove of pine trees. Larkin was the only one who could stand up inside without cracking her head on the stone and dirt above. It was small, but it gave them cover from the snow that was starting to fall in earnest from the night sky.

"So, tell me again how you found this place?" Errik asked as he secured his own mount, a brown stallion that pranced in a way that said the animal still had energy and wished to run.

Larkin shrugged. "I accompany my father on his trade routes. Before the war, one of them was to the south. When I was a girl, he told me that if we ever needed emergency shelter, I was to watch for the three-pointed rock formation."

"And you remember those rocks after all these years?" Garret asked, pulling his travel pack off his new mount. "That's remarkable."

"What part do you find remarkable?" Larkin asked, taking a bundle of the clothing she'd stripped off the dead men to the cave. "That my father bothered to tell a mere girl about the cave or that a tailor's daughter is smart enough to remember what he said?"

"I was trying to pay you a compliment," Garret said, following after her.

"Oh, well if that's what you were doing," Larkin called, ducking inside the cave, "you will have to try harder."

"Or *you* will have to . . ." Garret disappeared into the cave, which muted the rest of his words. Carys considered going after them to broker a peace, then decided against it. This wasn't court. Without the inequality of power that would normally hold her at a disadvantage, Larkin could handle herself.

"Do you think we should brush the horse tracks in the snow?" Errik stepped beside her.

She thought of the way he cradled her in his arms when he took her back to the Palace of Winds to help her manufacture her death. The drink he gave her to keep her fast asleep had taken hold. Her eyes had been so heavy she couldn't keep them open. Before she plunged into nothingness, she heard him speaking to her, telling her not to fear. That he would keep her safe while she slept. That he would give his life before she lost hers.

Errik had smuggled her out of the castle. He had helped keep Larkin out of Imogen's hands and ensured she avoided the death sentence that would have surely followed had she been captured.

Errik claimed he wanted peace, and that he believed in her.

But he was a Bastian. Even now his family was plotting to take back the Throne of Light. His own cousin had tried to kill her. Carys shouldn't trust him. She shouldn't care about him.

She didn't want to . . .

"No," Carys answered Errik's query. "Tracks in the snow might command interest, but most will think they are made by someone like them—trying to get out of the cold. Brush marks will make certain that anyone who passes wonders why someone wished to keep their passage a secret."

He nodded. "For someone who rarely left Garden City, you are proving to be a good travel companion."

"Because I have common sense or because you still have your life?"

"Do I have to pick one or can I be grateful for both?" He smiled. "While I am obviously thankful you didn't use me for a pincushion, would it be too forward to ask what stilled your hand?"

"Self-preservation," she snapped, her answer no less true than any of the others she could give. His dark eyes met hers. The pull was there between them as it had been from the first. "I am not fully recovered from my . . . illness. And Larkin is not able to help defend us. Your sword arm, for now, is required." Admitting any more would be a risk she wasn't willing to take. Not when she didn't trust her own feelings. Her brother, whom she had faith in and whom she had loved, had turned on her. How could she take the chance of caring for someone else?

The wind whispered again. The spark of anger that lived deep in her heart flared hotter.

"My sword arm is yours." Errik stepped forward. She automatically slid her hand into her pocket to grasp one of her daggers, and Errik sighed. "I would draw my sword and give an oath of allegiance to you if I thought you would accept it."

"Why?" she asked. "Why me? I am not agreeable or sweet or malleable like most ladies in court."

"You're right. And if you were, you'd be dead. *Actually* dead." Errik took another step toward her. "Instead you are getting stronger by the minute. And you *can* trust me."

The whispering grew louder. "What if I no longer desire to trust you?"

"I don't believe that to be true—and neither do you." Errik moved close enough that Carys could feel the warmth of his breath in the cold of the night. "If you did, you would have already told Larkin to be wary of me, and she shows no sign of caution when I am near. I lied to gain entrance into the Palace of Winds because I believed someone needed the truth of what was happening in Eden. I had to see for myself why all attempts at peace ended in more blood and death than before."

"Attempts at peace?" Carys straightened her shoulders and stepped back from Errik. "Which ones? Do you refer to the four times your King sent the heads of my father's messengers? How silly of us. We should have recognized it as *rapprochement*."

Three heads had been displayed on pikes near the tournament grounds. The last had been delivered just months ago in a satchel by a farm boy who had no idea what he carried. Someone in a brown cloak had paid him to pull his small wooden wagon several leagues to Garden City to deliver the sack to the King's Guard. Had it not been for Andreus, the boy would have been thrown in a cell as a traitor. Instead, her twin took charge of the boy and accompanied the guard when they escorted him home and questioned his family about the story he had told. The boy and his family were terrified all, but they had their lives in the end.

"The King of Adderton did not order the deaths of your father's messengers, Carys." Errik frowned.

"I saw their heads myself."

"I don't doubt they died," Errik insisted. "But King Lukha did not have a hand in it."

"Defending him is not helping your own case."

Errik grabbed hold of her arm before she could turn. "King Lukha sent messengers to your father with two treaties that I know of, which would have ended the war. Both were rejected out of hand."

"I know of no messages received by my father."

His fingers eased their grip, but he didn't release his hold as he said, "That doesn't mean they didn't exist."

That was true. Messengers on both sides could have been intercepted and the situations manipulated to further someone's agenda. Or Errik could be lying to further gain her trust. To prove she needed him.

Errik's fingers trailed down her arm and touched her hand. "If we travel into Adderton, I would be able to prove I speak the truth. King Lukha's fatigue with the war is well-known."

Carys jerked back. "You wish me to travel with you into a

kingdom that views me as the enemy? A kingdom whose subjects killed my family?"

"It is the last place anyone would ever look for Princess Carys of Eden. And if we ride to the town near my uncle's stronghold, we could learn more about what my cousin was doing in the Palace of Winds. My uncle has always considered himself to be the rightful heir to the Throne of Light. Imogen had to be working to help him gain the crown. If you intend to return, you need to know who else was helping them and what the entirety of their plan might be."

"*If* I intend to return?"

Errik brushed his fingers against hers. "Everyone in Eden believes you to be dead. It is up to you whether or not they learn different. You could choose something else. You could choose to be free of the life you were born into and start a new one."

Freedom.

The word echoed inside her. The wind fluttered the jagged edge of her hair as if affirming she *could* choose between the walls she was born behind and what lay beyond.

The very idea was dazzling. The chance to be whatever she chose. The chance to . . .

No. She shook her head. There could be no freedom. Not like this. Not when Eden was in danger and her brother was . . .

"If you think you know how to do it better, then feel free to try." Larkin's voice cut across the night. Carys stepped away from Errik and turned as Larkin appeared at the mouth of the cave with a small torch flickering in her hand. Larkin spotted them and crossed the snow looking as if she wanted to throttle something—or in this case some*one*. "Garret is taking charge of setting up camp for the night. He would like me to mend his trousers, an honor I have declined."

"I am certain he is suitably crushed by your refusal." Errik gave a small bow.

Larkin plunked a hand on her hip. "If he is allowed to continue with setting up camp in the cave, we will all end up dead. He's decided to build a fire."

"A small fire could prove quite comfortable once—" Errik said.

"Not if it's built in the wrong place. It is winter. The dirt and rock could warm, soften, and crack. Would you like to get crushed as you sleep? Would you find *that* comfortable?" Larkin's eyes narrowed. Carys grabbed the torch from her friend's hand. "Larkin, come with me."

Snow crunched beneath her boots as she strode toward the opening in the rock, dipped her head, and climbed into the cave. Garret looked up from where he squatted at the far end of the large oblong space that stretched deep into the rocky hill. A smile lit by the torch he held spread slowly across Garret's face as he spotted Carys, then faded as Larkin took her place at Carys's side.

Being tall had always served Carys well at court. It was easier to intimidate other ladies into keeping their distance when you towered several inches over them. Now her height meant she had to stoop to keep from cracking her head against the ceiling of the cave. Larkin, fully upright, glared at Garret and the pile of sticks and leaves he'd placed in the center of the space.

"Have you ever built a fire in a cave, Lord Garret?" Carys asked.
"No, but . . ."

"Larkin." Carys turned to her friend who had her arms crossed in front of her chest. "Since you and your father have camped in this very cave, I am putting you in charge of keeping us warm without killing us. Garret and Errik will follow whatever instructions you give."

"You . . . want me to take orders from a commoner?" Garret stood. His hair in the torchlight looked as if it, too, were on fire. The whispering started again. Like mist at the edge of her thoughts. She was dead to all those who loved her, and Garret was upset about answering to her best friend? Her legs trembled, still weakened from the desire for the Tears of Midnight.

Her heart pounded.

The torch flickered.

Leaves scattered.

And the whisper of the wind grew more insistent, asking her to . . .

To what?

"You will take orders from the person I deem best suited for this task." The air stilled as she handed the torch back to Larkin, then headed for the exit.

"Where are you going?" Larkin and Errik both asked as Carys ducked out of the cave. The two of them followed with Garret not far behind.

"Hunting." She walked to her mount and pulled a bow and quiver recovered from the armed men from her pack. Her heart still pounded. Her breathing was coming fast and shallow, and the whispers in her mind were pulling at her. She had to get away. She had to think.

"You can't go alone," Errik said, pushing past Larkin.

Being alone was exactly what she needed. She needed to think without someone watching her. She needed the quiet. Maybe then she'd be able to figure out what the whispers wanted or why they made her want to scream with rage. "I won't go far and I won't be long."

"Let me go with you," Larkin offered. "After today it's clear I should learn how to shoot."

"I can teach you better when it's light, and the longer we argue about this the longer it will take. Take our things into the cave and get us set up for the night. Garret, follow Larkin's instructions. We will discuss what our next steps will be when I return."

Larkin frowned.

"Please."

Larkin turned and flounced past Garret. Had a chill not run up her back, Carys would have smiled at Garret's irritated scowl.

Carys trekked away from the cave. Behind her was the crunch of boots on the snow. "You would have a better chance of earning my trust if you followed my wishes."

"If I followed your wishes without questioning them, you would do well not to trust me."

She turned to find Errik right behind her, his own bow in his hands. "I will not accompany you. But I will be close enough to help if something . . . or someone attacks."

"And if I refuse?" she demanded.

"I don't see how you have much of a choice. Unless, of course, you want to finish what you started earlier." He stepped closer as he said, "Your life is important to me, Carys. I will do what I must to see you safe."

His hand touched her face with a gentleness that stole her breath and made her mind swim with confusion. Warmth swirled through her stomach. The anger churning inside her vanished like smoke. His eyes were clear of the calculation that had defined her life, and she froze under that gaze, uncertain how to respond.

"This feeling," he said in a voice that sounded as puzzled as she felt. "It is not what I wanted, but I will not turn away from it because you are afraid."

Carys straightened her shoulders. "I am not afraid."

"Really?" Errik leaned down so his mouth was a breath from hers.

Blood pounded in her ears. Wind whipped at her cloak. She heard the dare and saw the amusement in his eyes. She might still be weak and confused, but there was one thing she was certain of—she wasn't a coward.

Carys grabbed his head and crushed her mouth against his. Without the Tears of Midnight in her, feelings exploded. Anger pulsed. Desire leaped. Everything inside her crackled with want. Never had she been allowed to want for herself. Duty came first. Duty meant everything. Now, she reveled in the taste of Errik. Of his desire for her. Of the way it felt to be a woman instead of someone's weapon or shield.

Errik's hands pressed against the small of her back and desire was doused with pain. She gasped and Errik immediately pulled back.

"What's wrong?"

"It's nothing," she said.

"The lashes." His fingers tilted her face to look at him and he frowned. "You're in pain. You're still healing, and I hurt you."

"I'm fine," she insisted.

"Carys," Errik said, taking her hands and holding them between his own—keeping her fingers warm in his. "You can admit to me when you hurt. You are allowed to show your weaknesses. If you let me, I will lend you my strength until you are ready to fight again."

The kisses had fired her body. But the words cracked the walls she had built around her heart.

A sob built in her chest. Without the walls, who was she? Who would she even want to be?

She bent down and picked up the bow and quiver she had dropped. "I'm going to hunt," she said. "Alone."

"I will find you if you need me. Always."

She walked away listening for the sound of footsteps following her. There were none.

The moonlight was bright against the thin layer of snow as she navigated the uneven, rocky path leading around the hill. Until now, she had thought the walls surrounding her were a curse, as much as Andreus's illness. Something that controlled her life.

Now, she wasn't sure. Errik claimed she was free, but she had never felt more trapped.

Carys pulled an arrow out of the quiver and notched it in the bow as she walked—aware that Errik was behind her watching. When she reached a group of trees, she angled to the left and ducked behind a tall outcropping of the rocky hillside where she was no longer in sight of the cave.

Her legs buckled and she grabbed the rock for support. The taste of fear was bitter in her mouth. The whispers she had been hearing for days grew louder. She huddled deep inside her cloak. Tears she had refused to let flow welled. Under them bubbled fear and hurt and longing.

Longing for the Tears of Midnight and the oblivion they brought.

For the way Errik made her feel when she stood at his side.

For Andreus and the way things used to be.

Fear that she'd made the wrong choice by leaving the palace. By pretending to be dead. By leaving the walls that she'd hated, but understood.

For the first time, she had no orders other than the ones that she gave to herself. No clear direction other than the one she chose. Garret thought he knew how to proceed. Errik did, too. They both seemed so sure.

But they couldn't both be followed.

So, Bisog or Adderton?

Anxiety churned her gut and her mind. Cold sweat dripped down her back. If she made the wrong decision . . .

Carys pushed away from the rocks and with shaking hands raised her bow. Her body ached from the cold and her still-healing wounds, but she pushed herself forward. She didn't know what path to choose, but she did know how to pull strength from an empty well. She'd done it time and again.

She drew the bow. The flex of the wood, the tension in the string, the rote movements calmed her, as they always did. As a girl she would flee to the tunnels after one of Andreus's attacks. She could not undo the curse that sucked away his breath and stalled his heart, so she would practice with the bow, and with the sword, and eventually with knives.

Over and over, she would drill until her mind was at peace.

Carys slowly placed one foot in front of the other and focused on the quiet of the night, pushing away all worries and whispers. She concentrated on the sounds around her instead of the confusion raging inside her.

A twig snapped to her left. She searched the shadows for something moving. As a girl, she would stalk the rats that roamed the tunnels below the Palace of Winds. They moved fast and they screeched when her arrows skewered them. Andreus hated the high-pitched sound. He preferred targets to the vermin scurrying along the walls.

Carys saw nothing scurrying now. Her fingers were stiff with cold. Her legs shook, but she refused to go back to the cave without something to show for her efforts. Just as she would not return to Garden City until she had learned something that would help her unmask the ones behind the darkness lurking inside the Palace of Winds.

Garret wanted her to use the strength of his forces to take her place on the throne. She didn't have to see the strings connected to his offer to know they were there, just as she didn't have to travel to Adderton to understand Errik had not been honest about all that would be waiting down that path.

Two choices.

Two men.

Both believed they knew what was best, but neither had hunted the rats under the palace. Like Andreus, they aimed at the target in plain sight.

But whatever rodents had helped Imogen kill Carys's father and brother—and the men in the dungeon who could have pointed her to those behind it—were walking the halls of the palace under the cloak of the seven virtues. As Imogen had. They claim to walk in the light and yet . . .

A shadow moved up a tree. Carys inhaled, held her breath as she stretched back the string of the bow, then exhaled as she let the arrow fly. The arrow punched through the shadow and it fell from the tree onto the moonlit snow.

Carys approached the gray-furred creature she had felled. It had a white face and black feet. She slit along the white of the creature's neck to make sure it was dead before lifting it by its long pink tail. Though it weighed at least two stones, the creature reminded her of the rats she had stalked and removed from the palace tunnels. Because she'd had patience to watch them—to learn the way they moved—she had learned the best way to hunt them.

Imogen had been a rat. She'd wormed her way into a hole in the palace defenses. She'd made it her home even as she ate away at the foundation of the kingdom.

How?

Carys had been so focused on Andreus's betrayal—and the danger Imogen had put them in—that she hadn't asked that question before.

How *had* Imogen been given the position of Seer of Eden? Carys remembered her arrival at the steps outside the Palace of Winds not long after the old seer's death. She had been accompanied on her journey by palace guards and said her guild had foreseen the death of Seer Kheldin. The Queen had flown into a rage when Carys's father shut her out of the meetings to decide whether the young seeress was acceptable. A week after the old seer was buried, it was announced Lady Imogen would take up residence in the Tower of Light.

Imogen had trained in the Village of Night for years. Which meant Imogen's father, Errik's uncle, must have been plotting even longer—for decades perhaps—for Imogen to gain admission to the Palace of Winds.

Carys looked down at the kill in her hands. The whispers at the edge of her mind returned.

Her enemies had patience. They knew how to hunt.

Well, so did she. And now she knew where the hunt would start.

4

"No!"

Max disappeared over the side of the battlements. The hooded figure bolted toward the entrance to the tower stairs.

Andreus couldn't breathe.

Rage burned. Footsteps sounded. Andreus's chest clenched as he stumbled forward against the stone wall.

He forced himself to look over the edge.

Max whimpered. The boy's fingers desperately clung to the narrow ledge. His small face was pinched and desperate. His eyes closed tight.

"Hang on, Max," Andreus yelled, grabbing Max's hand. The boy's eyes flew open and the grip Max had on the wall slipped.

"Help!" Max screamed. Andreus dug his fingers into Max's wrists as the boy's sudden drop almost yanked him off his feet. But he didn't let go. He wasn't going to lose the boy.

"Andreus!" Max cried over the churning of the windmill above.

"It's going to be okay," Andreus shouted. "Just hang on to me and try to stay as still as you can." He gritted his teeth and pulled.

The boy rose an inch . . . two . . . three.

Andreus's chest tightened again.

Max's feet flailed in the empty space beneath him, making it harder to haul him up. Making it harder to hold on.

"Max, stay still!" Andreus's grip began to slip.

"I've got him!"

Another hand clamped onto Max's forearm, keeping him from dropping. Then a second hand grabbed hold. "Pull, Your Majesty."

Andreus shifted his hold on Max, took a deep breath, and pulled. It felt like an eternity before finally Max's tear-streaked face appeared over the ledge. He whimpered as he landed on the stone.

Safe.

Heart pounding, Andreus wrapped his arms tight around the slight figure and sank to the ground. The boy buried his face in Andreus's cloak. Sobs racked Max's body. Andreus's own tears choked him as he held the boy in his arms and rested his chin atop the boy's head.

Max was alive.

And Andreus was going to make sure whoever had tried to kill him would die a slow painful death.

"Perhaps we should get the boy inside, Your Majesty." The guard who had given aid knelt on the ground next to them. His hand was on the hilt of his sword. His vaguely familiar face searched the battlements for signs of danger.

Max's skinny arms tightened around Andreus's neck, making it impossible for him to rise to his feet. Andreus sank back down, gently pried Max's hands off him, and looked directly into the boy's tear-streaked face. "We need to get you off the battlements and out of the cold. Guardsman . . ." Andreus looked up at the youth who had come to Max's rescue.

"My name is Graylem, Your Majesty."

"Graylem, did you get a look at the man who . . ." Andreus couldn't say the words, but Graylem didn't need to hear them.

"I'm sorry, Your Majesty. I was too far away. I heard the cry, and I ran toward it." Guardsman Graylem bowed his head. "I saw you struggling to pull the boy back up and didn't think to give chase."

"You made the right choice." Andreus wiped his palm against his cloak, remembering how he had been losing his grip before Graylem arrived. "Max." He waited for the boy to open his eyes. The tears had stopped. Max was pale, but his breathing didn't appear to be labored. "Can you tell me what happened?"

Max gulped air and bobbed his head. "I was doing what you told me. Honest."

"I know you were," he assured him. "But you didn't take the most direct path."

Max sniffled. "I thought I saw Chamberlain Oben near the far tower. I wondered if he was meeting Elder Ulrich, but then . . ."

"Wait a second." Andreus stopped Max's rambling words. "Elder Ulrich was here?" He looked toward Graylem. "Did you see him, who he spoke to, or which direction he or my mother's chamberlain went?"

Graylem swallowed hard and shook his head. "I'm sorry, Your Majesty. I . . . I was just taking a walk."

"You were just taking a walk?"

Graylem's eyes flicked downward as he nodded.

Slowly, Andreus let go of Max with one hand and reached under his cloak for the hilt of his sword. "You had the urge to take a walk in the cold at the same time both the Masters of Light are meeting *and* an Elder of Eden's Council decided to get some fresh air?"

"I . . ."

Andreus drew his blade as he sprang to his feet and pushed Max behind him. "What were you really doing up here? Are you one of Ulrich's men or aligned with another?"

"No, Your Majesty. I was not here because of Elder Ulrich or the Masters or any of the other members of the Council. I was . . . following you."

"Me." Andreus raised his sword and searched the guard's freckled face. As the blade neared him, the guard's eyes went wide and his cheeks paled under the light of the orb. "You are not a member of the King's Guard. Only a handful have been chosen and all are my elders by at least ten years. So why were you following me?"

"I . . . it . . ."

"Who are you working for?" Cestrum? Ulrich? The Kingdom of Adderton?

"No one, Your Majesty. I just thought the Princess . . ."

"What about the Princess?" Andreus asked.

"Princess Carys was concerned with your safety." Graylem swallowed again and shuffled his feet. "Now that she's gone, I wanted to honor her by doing what she no longer could."

Andreus's sword dipped downward as he stared at the guard who looked so much younger than Andreus's seventeen years. "You knew my sister?"

Graylem nodded. "I was one of her guards. I was with her on the night the lights went dark."

When Andreus said nothing, Graylem continued, his words so quiet Andreus could barely hear them over the pulse of the windmills above. "We were at the entrance to the palace when . . . *it* happened. My legion captain gave me the task of protecting the Princess. She grabbed my knife and ran off. I didn't know what to do, so I followed her. She was fast."

She'd been faster before the Tears of Midnight or the withdrawal he'd forced her to go through.

"She didn't slow, not even on the stairs. Not until she got to the battlements and found you."

With everything that had happened since the lines to the orb were cut and restored, Andreus had forgotten that moment on the battlements when his sister appeared, weapon in hand. He could tell the minute she spotted him. Her shoulders had slumped, and relief filled her face.

"And because my sister stole your knife, you are now shadowing me?" It didn't make sense.

"No, Your Majesty. It wasn't just that." Graylem frowned. "I was there when King Ulron's and Prince Micah's bodies were . . . returned. Everyone else was watching the sword when the Princess took it from your hand. I was watching her face. I've seen that expression several times before, and she wore it when she took my knife and ran to find you. Princess Carys did what she did to protect you, my King. She was willing to risk her own safety for yours. I know what that feels like. I had a sister, only . . ." Graylem shook his head. "Princess Carys succeeded where I failed. I wanted to honor her strength and bravery by continuing what she is no longer here to do."

"Andreus?" Max coughed and Andreus let the tip of the sword tilt to the ground as he glanced at the boy, who seemed to be struggling to catch his breath.

He glanced back at Graylem, who was standing with his

shoulders straightened as if resigned to the harsh punishment that his actions would demand. Suddenly, it wasn't Graylem that Andreus saw, but Carys standing with her head high, sword in hand, knowing what she was doing would exact a heavy price, but doing it anyway because she believed it was right.

Andreus shook the image away. Whatever the reason Graylem was on the battlements, he had saved Max's life tonight. The guardsman had a lot of questions to answer—like what he knew about Andreus's curse. But on the question of whether Graylem would protect Max, Andreus already had information. "Guardsman Graylem, take Max to my old rooms and stay with him until I arrive."

Graylem frowned. "Of course, Your Majesty, but the person in the black cloak still might be nearby. Would it not be best if I stayed with you?"

"What would be best is if you followed your King's command," Andreus barked in the way his sister often had to cut off complaint or dissent.

And it worked. Graylem snapped to attention and said, "Yes, Your Majesty. Max, let's get you out of the cold."

Max grabbed Andreus's cloak as Graylem tried to lead him toward the steps. "What if something happens to you?"

"A King has to put the good of the kingdom above the good of himself." Andreus looked down at Max's tense face. "But I promise I have no interest in dying tonight. I will take care. Go inside. I will come check on you as soon as I am done speaking with the Masters of Light." Andreus turned to Graylem. "Speak with no one until I arrive."

He gave the boy's shoulder a squeeze. Then, sword at the ready, he strode across the battlements to the turret windmill where the

Masters of Light were currently meeting. After a few steps, he glanced over his shoulder to watch Graylem escort Max into the stairwell.

The guardsman Graylem was young and clearly untried, but he had guts. Did he know Andreus lived with a curse? Was he aware of the old seer's prediction and what it could mean for Eden now that Andreus was King? How much had Carys—wittingly or not—revealed to him?

With war raging and his Council weaving their own plots, Andreus couldn't risk his secret being used as a tool to undermine his authority. Removing Graylem would rid him of that threat. Elder Jacobs would surely advise that course of action if Andreus sought his counsel.

But Graylem seemed relatively harmless. Even innocent. And the guard had saved Max's life. Andreus wondered, would he be able to harden his heart to order Graylem's death? Uncertainty gnawed. He studied the shadows as he crossed the battlements. Mere weeks ago, the place he felt happiest in the castle was at his sister's side or up here with the windmills. Now his muscles tensed with every rattle of the slowly turning gears and shift of the shadows.

He spotted two guards in the distance at a lookout post near the southwesternmost tower. The men scanned the grounds beyond the wall for the Xhelozi or other possible attackers. The Masters, if they hadn't adjourned, would be inside the northwesternmost tower Andreus approached now.

The men in gray jumped to their feet as Andreus threw open the door to the windmill. The musty space was filled with pieces of line and insulating wool and tar. The room was lit only by a single wind-powered orb, which dangled from above.

"Your Majesty." Master Triden shuffled forward and bowed his head. "We were just finishing our business for the night. The Council of Elders did not inform us that you would be attending."

"The Council of Elders did not invite me to this meeting," Andreus said, glancing around at the men he had worked alongside for years. None of them could meet his eyes. "In the past few days I've detected minor flaws in the flow of the wind power."

Master Triden glanced at the other Masters before nodding. "We have . . . been working to reroute some of the lines to make sure the lights on the walls remain bright."

"Has there been additional sabotage?"

"No," Master Triden assured him. "There has been no further attempt to attack the lights. We promised the Elders they would be informed if we noticed anything."

"You promised the Council of Elders?" Andreus asked. "Why not discuss the matter directly with me?"

Master Triden's eyes widened. "You are now the King. The Elders have made it clear to us that your interest in the wind and the lights could distract you from other, more pressing problems that require your attention."

"We are going into the heart of winter. The Xhelozi seem to be awake earlier than normal and are roaming the countryside in greater numbers than ever before. If the lights fail us, the entire city could be in danger. The lights, Master Triden, if compromised, are our *most* pressing problem."

It had been years since the Xhelozi had last breached the walls of Garden City. When they did, the Palace of Winds escaped unscathed, but the people of the kingdom paid a terrible toll. Especially the poorest, who lived on the outer rim of the city, closest to the barrier wall, and farthest from the protection of the castle. Coins and titles bought influence in addition to a safer residence in the chance of attack.

As long as the lights held, there was little reason for anyone to fear. But Master Triden was casting nervous glances at the other assembled Masters, and Andreus knew there was something not being spoken.

"Master Triden," Andreus said. "I cannot fix what I do not know is wrong."

"Unfortunately, Your Majesty," Master Triden sighed, "what is wrong technically cannot be fixed. The windmills and the lines are working as they should, but the wind . . ."

"What about the wind?" Andreus asked.

Master Hulkar stepped forward. "The air has oft been quite still in recent days. People in the city have taken to making sacrifices at the shrines, as if burning their favorite ribbons and hunks of bread will help."

"We have reworked the power allotment to compensate," Master Triden reported.

"Have you adjusted the position of the windmills?" Andreus asked.

"Aye," Hulkar answered, "we have. But the wind has not been this still since the days before you and your sister were born."

Master Triden frowned. "We have tried everything to capture the air. And we have been working on other options in case the lack of wind continues."

Heart pounding, Andreus concentrated on the creaks and groans of the mill. Normally, the sounds comforted him, but now that he was listening with greater care, he could tell the grinding of the blades was slower. Fainter than it had been even yesterday.

"Masters, we must continue to conserve as much power as possible until the wind patterns return to normal."

"We are doing what we can, Your Majesty. We have lowered the power allotment to the merchants in the city for a second time not long ago, but it might not be enough."

"You lowered it twice? When?" Andreus asked.

"Just before King Ulron and Prince Micah rode to the battlefields to the south. And then again the night the orb went dark."

The same day his father's and brother's bodies were returned by the then surviving members of the King's Guard.

"You should have told me. I would have insisted we use torches in the palace." Instead, he and the court had been draining resources that they would need to keep the Xhelozi at bay. "How much wind power do we have in reserve?" How long could they go without the wind gusting until the darkness of the night brought danger to them all?

"A week," Master Hulkar said, drawing looks of anger from the rest. "If we are very careful."

Seven nights. Maybe less.

"Why did you not come to me sooner," Andreus shouted, panic rising as he tried to come up with a solution.

"We were told that—"

"Were told? By whom? Master Hulkar, I say one last time, the Council of Elders does not speak for me!"

"It wasn't the Council," Master Triden said quietly. "It was your mother. The Queen."

5

Carys sat down on the cold cave floor next to Larkin. "Have you ever been to the Village of Night?" she asked. Her friend's surprised expression was lit by the flicker of the small fire. "Can you find it for me?"

"You can't be serious," Garret said from the other side of the cave. He climbed to his feet and cracked his head against the rocky ceiling. He swore as dust and bits of rock fell at his feet. "If a new seer hasn't presented himself at court, your brother and the Council will be sending a messenger along with a guard to bring one to Garden City. The Guild of the seers has always served those who sit on the Throne of Light. You are naïve if you think they will stay silent about your presence—or let you leave once they have you in their grasp."

"Naïve is the one thing I am certain I am not. There is little chance I will be able to live as if I am dead for very long."

Garret stooped his head and stepped forward. "That is why the only choice is to follow my lead to Bisog. My guard will be the strength you need to take back the kingdom from Andreus. "

"There is more than one kind of strength in the world, Garret," Carys said, studying the flames. "I will need a great deal more than swords if I am going to reclaim my kingdom. Andreus is not my only enemy, and swords cannot defeat what cannot be seen."

"But Andreus has the guardsmen of the Palace of Winds and Garden City at his command," Errik offered from the entrance to the cave. "You will need swords. Not that I agree with Garret."

Carys shook her head. An outright attack would force the people of Garden City to take sides and die in a war for which they shouldn't have to shed blood. And whoever was working against Eden inside the Palace of Winds would welcome the distraction of battle, using it as the perfect opportunity to strike.

"No. You have offered me your way. I have found my own." Carys pulled her eyes from Errik and turned back to Larkin. "Can you find the Village of Night?"

"I have traveled much in the southern districts. My father and I never visited the seers . . ."

Garret scoffed.

Larkin's eyes flashed. "*But* there was a town we traded in that claimed to deliver supplies to the Village. I will be able to find the town again."

"Then it is decided," Carys announced. The weariness she'd been holding at bay seeped through her, helped along by the warmth of the crackling fire. "We will eat. Then Larkin will lead me to the home of the seers."

"But . . . ," Garret started. Carys cut him off.

"You can always leave if you have no faith in the choices of your Queen."

"I will not leave you," Garret said quietly. "You will take your place in the Hall of Virtues. It is inevitable. It is fated, and I will be with you when you ascend to the throne."

Carys wished she had his faith as Larkin stood up and brushed the dirt off her skirts. "Since no one cleaned Carys's kill before bringing it in, I guess that chore will be left up to me. This whole journey is starting to feel more and more like traveling with my father than I would have expected."

"I'm sure I can handle skinning the rous," Errik said as Carys closed her eyes and sank into the warmth of the cave. The fire wasn't large, but after the shuddering brought on by the cold of the elements and her body being denied the Tears of Midnight, the meager flames felt like a blaze.

"Carys?"

She jerked her head up toward Larkin, who was standing in the entrance with the rous in her arms.

"Would you like to keep me company as I work?" Larkin asked. "You can watch me, like you did when you decided to learn how to use a needle and thread by watching me sew."

That never happened. Larkin's father would not have allowed her to do anything of the sort when she attended fittings at the palace. Which meant Larkin needed a moment—a private one, and this was her way of asking.

Carys pushed to her feet. She winced at the ache of the still-healing wounds on her back, but forced a smile as she said, "It was the only time we could talk without Andreus around."

Larkin's laughter rang in the cave. "Your brother was never interested in activities when he couldn't be the center of our attention."

"Well, I expect that animal will be the current focus." Carys brushed past a stony-faced Errik as she followed Larkin toward the chill coming from the entrance. "Make sure you keep the fire going," she called behind her. "If Larkin is as quick with a knife as she is with a needle, I'm sure we won't be long."

She shivered as she stepped out of the cave. Larkin finally dropped the rous to the ground when she reached a large tree at least twenty lengths away.

She glanced behind Carys and said, "My father taught me that it is always best to clean the kill far away from where you are making camp. Otherwise, the smell of blood and entrails could lead predators to you while you sleep." Then she knelt down on a patch of ground free of snow next to the animal and pulled out her knife.

Garret was standing in the cave's entrance watching them.

"We wouldn't be friends today had you tried to teach me how to sew. What's wrong? Do you think you won't be able to find the Village of Night?"

Larkin sliced through the gray fur. "It is not the seers I have worry about." Her knife stilled. "You brought Garret with us. There is much happening right now that I do not understand. But Garret . . ."

"What about him?"

"He doesn't want you near me or Errik." Larkin's knife sliced efficiently through flesh and tendon. "For the last week, he has been trying to convince me to leave your side, first with promises of a marriage to a wealthy lord of Bisog. He seemed to think I would jump at the chance to become a lady."

"Garret has much to learn about you."

"It is you he is interested in. While you were . . . ill . . . he implied that it was his duty to care for you, as if you belonged to him. And once I awakened during his watch to find that he was not anywhere near the camp. He claimed to have climbed a tree to better see if there were any palace guards giving chase."

"But you didn't believe him."

"I am not sure. What I am sure of is that he is jealous of any attention you pay Errik. If he could run a sword through him, he would in order to gain what it is he desires."

"You think he desires . . . me?"

"I know it."

Carys had no use for such attention. Not now. It just added to the confusion surrounding her.

"Errik does as well," Larkin added.

Carys simply nodded. "And do you trust *him*?"

Carys hated that Larkin paused. She wanted Larkin to automatically answer yes. Instead, her friend said, "Lord Errik saved my life. He helped save yours. And the fact that he refused to leave your side when you were shaking with fever speaks to the feelings he holds for you. And yet . . ."

"What is it?" Carys asked.

Larkin frowned. "Since we've made camp, I've seen him staring southward as if he is waiting for something to appear."

Or some*one*, Carys thought. Like his uncle. And if they all journeyed south, the way he suggested, she might walk right into their trap.

"I think we would be well advised to be cautious around both of them until we understand their motives," Larkin counseled.

Carys's stomach swooped as thoughts of Errik's kiss flooded her. The warmth of the memory pulled at her heart, and she shoved it away, knowing she could not be so foolish again. Not with so much uncertainty around her and so much at stake.

"Now that I'm feeling more myself, you will no longer be alone in your caution."

Larkin's knife stilled and she slowly looked up at Carys. "Are you well now? Errik and Garret both swore you would recover, but you were so ill and if there is a remedy we should seek . . ."

"I am better," Carys said. She wrapped her hand over her friend's, and even as she said the words, she felt the yearning inside her for the Tears. The ache of the wounds on her back throbbed, and shame filled her as she squeezed Larkin's hand tight.

Larkin believed in her. She believed she was strong enough to keep Carys safe. Carys wished with all her heart that her beliefs were based in truth.

Larkin deserved honesty. Or at least as much honesty as was Carys's to give. "My illness was *caused* by a remedy. My father warned me the next time I showed the crown disrespect I would be lashed." He thought she would heed his warning and fall into line. Had it not been for her need to help hide Andreus's illness, she might have.

"I remember the shock in the city when you were taken to the North Tower for punishment," Larkin said quietly. "I wanted to come see you, but my father said it would only make things worse for you."

"There is nothing you could have done," Carys assured her friend. But she wondered if anything could have changed the course that her life had taken, or if it was all in the stars as the seers suggested. "My mother brought me a remedy—something she promised would ease the pain. It did." It dulled the ache of her body and the hurt she tried to bury in her mind. It took the edge off the anger and unhappiness that were so much a part of her. "So I took it until the wounds were healed and then kept taking it because I couldn't stop." No. That wasn't the whole truth. "I didn't want to stop." The bitter words taunted her.

Carys swallowed it down and said, "*I* took too much when I was ailing and I continued to take it long after the pain of the wounds was gone. It became as necessary to my body and mind as water, or as air. I told myself not allowing myself the drink would make things harder—especially during the Trials of Virtuous Succession. But then I stopped taking it."

"Why?"

The trees rustled. "The choice was not mine. My brother made it for me."

Larkin's knife cut deep into the rous and ripped in one strong stroke down its back. "Did Andreus know what that would do? Did he know how sick you would become?"

Carys nodded. "That was one of his reasons."

"And now he is one of mine for doing whatever it takes to return to Garden City." Larkin said as her next stroke severed the head. It rolled and bounced onto the cold, hard ground.

"No," Carys insisted even as the whispers in her head began to swirl. "He is my brother. If any hand will strike at him, it should be mine."

Larkin looked up, her hands slick with blood. "As long as your life is not in danger, I will not intervene. I'm not sure I can say the same for Errik or Garret. It is my guess that they both know what made you ill."

Errik knew enough to have guessed the truth. Garret, meanwhile, had always seemed to know about her mother's remedy and the hold it had on her. Years before, he had insisted she get free of the drug. He had warned about what might happen once her body was no longer under the drug's spell. And also, he seemed to know about the wind when no one else, not even her own twin, did.

"How long do you think it will take to get to the Village of

Night?" Carys asked as they walked back to the cave.

"When Father and I traveled by wagon, we avoided cutting through the forest. Then it took about a week from this location to the village I mentioned. If we travel the more direct path and ride hard on horseback, we should be able to reach it far more quickly. Perhaps three or four days."

Once the rous was cooked, it tasted far better than it looked. Garret grimaced and poked at his portion, which annoyed Carys, but at least it gave her something to focus on other than the pull of the whispers in her mind.

As Garret questioned Larkin about what direction she planned to take them in, Errik whispered, "Princess, you should get some sleep." He removed his cloak, rolled it into a ball, and placed it on the ground. "Here."

Carys started to reject the offer, but Errik held up a hand and said, "Don't worry, Carys. I will not take your willingness to use my cloak as a sign of anything more than a lack of fondness for resting your head on rocks."

Turning his back, Errik settled on the ground several feet away. Carys did the same, nestling her head into the coarse material of Errik's bunched-up cloak.

Poor Larkin. Garret continued to insist he knew a better way to get across the district than the route she proposed. Carys attempted to cover her ears to drown out the sound. Errik's scent clung to the fabric—filling her senses as she was pulled into sleep.

"Carys, wake up. They're gone!"

She opened her eyes to darkness.

"They're gone," Garret repeated. "Errik and Larkin are missing. So are their horses."

"Missing?" Carys sat up and blinked, trying to get her bearings. The fire was out. Everything was black. "Larkin? Errik?"

"Carys, they're gone." Garret put a hand on her shoulder. "I had first watch. Everything was quiet. I woke Errik for his turn and turned in. I woke up a few minutes ago and realized both Errik and Larkin were missing."

"Larkin wouldn't just *leave*." She put her hand on the cloak she'd been using as a pillow. No matter what he might want from her, Errik had gone to such trouble to get her to this point it was simply illogical that he would vanish now.

"Perhaps they were lured away or maybe . . ."

"Maybe what?"

"I know you have trusted Errik in the past, and Larkin is your friend, but while you were ill, they always had their heads together. How do you know he has not convinced her to betray you to whatever kingdom or Elder he has allegiance to?"

"Larkin would never betray me."

"And Errik?"

Her heart thudded hard in her chest. Errik was a Bastian—Imogen's cousin. A member of the family that wanted to reassert its claim on the Throne of Light. "He helped me survive."

"For which I am grateful, however . . ." Garret looked toward the entrance of the cave.

"What?" she demanded.

"Errik has been directing our travel since we left the Palace of Winds. He claimed it was the least likely direction anyone would think we would take, but what if the attack we fought off today was not by chance? What if Errik has been trying to deliver you to Adderton?"

"No," she insisted even as her stomach twisted with dread and the whispers began inside her mind. "He wouldn't do that."

"Do you think it is coincidence that this occurs the very night you announce that we will travel west—away from those with whom Errik might be trying to rendezvous. And don't you think it is strange that the guide for your travel has disappeared along with him?" Garret placed a hand on top of her arm. "Princess, your loyalty is hard-won and steadfast. You stood by your brother even as he demonstrated over and over that his allegiance was only to himself. The price for that was nearly your life. Can you risk making that same kind of mistake again?"

She pictured Errik's eyes—warm and teasing and filled with secrets. Was one of them that he had always intended on betraying her? That he was willing to put Larkin's life in danger to get the power his family desired?

She grabbed Errik's cloak from the ground and scrambled toward the cave's entrance. The moon was fading in the sky, but the sun had yet to rise. Everything was still as Carys bundled her cloak tight against her and hurried toward the horses.

Two mounts were missing and whatever footprints they'd made in the snow had been brushed out. Just as Errik had suggested they do earlier.

"We have to go after them. They couldn't have gone all that far." Carys turned to go back to get her travel bag, but Garret had already grabbed it and was striding forward to secure it to her horse.

"Why don't I go?" Garret insisted. "You stay here. I can cover ground more quickly by myself, and you can be here in case Larkin finds her way back."

He could either cover more ground or pretend to. Garret was at odds with both Larkin and Errik. With both of them removed from her side, his opinions would not have as many detractors.

"Besides, you are still recovering your strength. You should stay and let me . . ."

"I'm going," Carys said. The more he insisted she should remain behind, the more worried she became. Besides, trusting Errik had been her decision. She had to deal with him if he had betrayed her. "Make sure the horses are ready."

Before Garret could irritate her further, she hurried back to the cave and ducked inside. The blackness enveloped her as she felt her way toward the center of the space to where the small fire once crackled. If Garret was wrong about Errik, and Larkin returned and found her missing, Carys needed to leave a message for her friend to find. She pulled a piece of charred wood from the small pile, and drew three letters—VON—on the rock just inside the opening. Then, brushing her hands on her skirt, she headed out to where Garret was waiting with their horses.

The moon shone as they galloped south. The wind whipped through the scraggly trees and raged inside her head as she scanned the horizon. Her friend and Errik had to be out there somewhere.

Only there was no sign of them. Just trees and shadows and snow as Garret and she pushed their horses to go faster across the frozen ground.

A rusty shriek cut through the air.

Carys's heart jumped. Her breath caught. She reached for her stilettos and looked over her shoulder.

There was nothing but snow and trees.

Another cry scraped the night.

And then she saw them. Three shapes in the distance coming fast. Large. White. Hooked claws extended as they loped on their tall legs toward Carys and Garret.

Xhelozi.

"Run!" Carys dug her thighs into her mount and headed to the open ground to the west. Garret's horse matched hers stride for stride as they flew across the icy earth. Angry screeches chased after them. Carys clutched the reins tighter and leaned over the neck of her horse, urging it to go faster.

"Head for the woods!" Garret yelled over the swoosh of the wind.

"No!" Carys yelled. "We have to stay in the open." The Xhelozi thrived in the darkness and shadows. As much as she wanted to hide, their best course of action was to keep running—because dawn was approaching. And with dawn came the best weapon they could use against the Xhelozi—the sun.

Their horses' hooves thundered.

The Xhelozi screams cut the air.

The wind howled in her mind and bent the bushes and trees behind them.

Branches cracked.

The monsters from the mountains' cries sounded fainter than before.

Carys clutched her cloak tight.

"Look!" Heart pounding, she pointed to the sky that was tinged with pink against the gray of the night. The sun was starting to rise.

The Xhelozi shrieked in protest of the dawn. They stopped their attack, turned, and began to run in the opposite direction. In the blink of an eye, the immediate danger ended.

Breathing hard, Carys pulled on the reins and brought her horse to a stop. Panting, Garret pulled up next to her. "Are you okay?"

"No. The Xhelozi never stray this far from the mountain. Especially not this early in winter." The skies were lighter for longer now than they would be in a few weeks' time.

He studied the horizon with a frown. "Clearly, it is not just the wearer of the crown that has changed in Eden. Something has altered for the Xhelozi as well."

A wave of fatigue threatened to overwhelm her. Larkin was out there. Somewhere. Carys had no clue where to start looking, and now the Xhelozi were hunting in places they should not be. "You're right," she agreed. "Something has changed for the Xhelozi since the last cold season. The question is what?"

6

His mother.

Andreus pulled his cloak tight with one hand and clutched the hilt of his sword with the other as he strode across the battlements. The air was almost still. He should have noticed, but his focus had been on other things. The wind was something Andreus had always been able to count on. The air consistently blowing down the mountains was one of the reasons the palace had been given its name. Only now the wind was faltering, and because of his mother's command, one that kept all the lights in the palace shining instead of conserving that power for the past few weeks, there might not be enough light to keep the city safe until the wind blew strong again.

His mother had put them in danger. Why?

Andreus grimaced as he hurried into the stairwell of the northeast tower, then stopped and listened for the sound of anyone who might be following.

Nothing.

He flexed his throbbing leg and cursed the wind-powered lights shining bright as he hurried down the halls. He should have insisted the Masters set up torches and shut down the lights tonight, but the abrupt change would cause members of the court and servants alike to panic. He could almost hear his sister warning that it would take but a matter of hours for that spark of concern to turn into a full-fledged hysteria in the city below. Fear, of any kind, would only make matters worse. He had to project calm and control. There would be no safeguarding against the Xhelozi or Adderton's forces if Garden City devolved into chaos.

Andreus limped down the hallway that led to the rooms he'd lived in since he was a boy. Two guardsmen snapped to attention as he ignored the door that led to his sister's empty rooms and hurried to his own.

Graylem scrambled to his feet as Andreus stepped inside. Max was curled around a pillow, sound asleep on the deep blue rug that was set in front of the fireplace. Max was safe. No matter what it took, Andreus would make the choices required to see that he stayed that way.

"I ordered food for him while he waited for you to return, Your Majesty," Graylem whispered. "Only he fell asleep before he had the chance to eat. Other than the kitchen maid who brought the tray of food, no one has approached me or the boy."

Andreus studied the guard's earnest face. The freckles and shock of rust hair made him look more boyish than fierce. More dance instructor than warrior. It was a perfect face for an Elder to select with orders to gain Andreus's trust. Perhaps that was the wrong conclusion to jump to, but Andreus had only to look at the sleeping boy to steel his resolve as he reached for the hilt of his sword. A King could not afford to spare those who might know his weaknesses and potentially use them against him.

"Now that you have returned, Your Majesty," Graylem said, looking down at the ground, "I will surrender myself to North Tower and await whatever punishment you decree."

"Do you believe I should imprison you?"

Graylem took a deep breath then looked up. "I confessed to following first Princess Carys and now the King of Eden. No matter my reasons, I was, in essence, acting as if I was an intelligencer. You know what I must have seen and you would never allow me to return to my guard duties with that knowledge."

Andreus went still. "What do you think you know?"

"You have the same breathing illness as the boy you saved, or something like it. Your sister was helping you keep it secret so no one could exploit that weakness."

Fear and anger churned. The whisper of his sword coming free echoed in the room. "Treason is punishable by death." And death would end this knowledge of his secret. If others knew, he would deal with them as time passed.

Graylem swallowed hard. Fear lit his eyes. Andreus gripped his sword and waited for the guard to beg for his life or sink to his knees. Instead, he said, "I am prepared for death, but the boy should not see and think he is to blame."

Andreus glanced at Max and hated that Graylem had to remind him of the boy's presence. "You saved Max even though you knew doing so could mean that I would order your death?"

Graylem straightened his shoulders. "I failed my sister . . . I knew in my heart she was in trouble, and yet I didn't act until it was too late. I was not as strong as Princess Carys was. But after her death I joined the guard and in doing so vowed that I would not fail another who needed my protection again."

It was the crack in the guard's voice when he said the word *sister* that compelled Andreus to lower his sword. It was the sound of the love Andreus once had for his twin. He knew the kind of loyalty that love evoked. "Did you speak to anyone of what you learned from following me or my sister?"

"No, Your Majesty," Graylem said emphatically. "When I am dead, your secret will die with me."

Andreus looked at Max's sleeping figure again. With Imogen gone, there was none save the boy Andreus could trust inside the palace. He needed other allies.

"I have use of you so let's hope you don't keel over dead any time soon." Sheathing his sword, Andreus ignored Graylem's gaping surprise and said, "I have something I must see to. I am not sure how long I will be gone." He removed his cloak and dropped it on the chair next to his desk. "Guard the boy until I return. We will speak of your new role as my personal intelligencer then."

"Yes, Your Majesty." Graylem bowed as Andreus turned and headed back out the door to the stairs that led to the floor below.

It was time to pay a visit to his mother.

Andreus stood outside the massive double doors of what was once his parents' solar, although his father had rarely, if ever, spent time in these rooms.

Ever since Andreus could remember, this area of the palace had been his mother's sanctuary. It was where the women of the court came to curry favor and where his mother ruled over Carys and him with an iron fist—always reminding him of the curse that he was born with and schooling Carys on her obligation to help keep his secret safe. Perhaps it wasn't any wonder then that he and his twin spent a great deal of their lives avoiding these rooms, or that he hadn't come to visit his mother since before the crown of light was placed on his head.

He had told himself that he was too busy.

That the demands of ruling required focus.

But he knew the truth. He couldn't take the sight of his mother in her current state.

Before, she had been more than formidable. Now, since the King's and prince's deaths, she was no longer the strong woman who had manipulated the court and the Elders. The deaths of his father and brother had broken something, leaving her uncertain and haunted—the opposite of the woman he had known all his life. Seeing her now would be like looking into a mirror at the cracks in his own reflection.

Andreus grasped the ornate handle to his mother's chamber. The last time he came to these rooms, Carys was alive. Inside, he had made a choice that he knew could kill his own twin, and, in essence, had.

Pushing open the doors, Andreus stepped from the cool, brightly lit hall, into the stifling warmth of his mother's sanctum. Only the fire blazing in the large, stone fireplace and several candles glowing on a small table set for tea illuminated the large space. The yellow rug looked almost tan in the dim light. The blue-velvet, high-backed chairs that his mother preferred to have filled with ladies of the court looked almost black.

Despite his mother's lack of fondness for the court, she had until recently always spent her days surrounded by its members. She was skilled at manipulation. She understood the rules. His father had relied on his Queen to tell him of schemes that would upset his power. Dozens of lords and ladies had ended up in the North Tower after his mother whispered what she'd learned in his father's ear.

"You never know what someone will say or do that will give you the advantage you didn't know you required," the Queen had instructed him and Carys. Perhaps if he had remained in her rooms more, he might be better equipped to deal with the Council of Elders now.

"Your Majesty." The Queen's longtime chamberlain, Oben, stepped out of the shadows near the entrance to his mother's bed-chamber. His deep purple robes and dark hair made his mother's faithful attendant almost blend into the shadows. Andreus straight-ened his shoulders to stretch to his full height, as he found he often did around the inscrutable man whose expression was as unreadable as ever.

"I did not expect to see you," Oben continued. "Chief Elder Cestrum and Elder Jacobs did not mention that you were planning to visit when they stopped by on your command to check on the Queen's condition."

"The Elders were here." Andreus shouldn't have been surprised. "When?"

"Elder Jacobs left not long ago. The Chief Elder was here about an hour before that."

"What did they wish to discuss with the Queen?"

"All the Elders have found reason to stop by at least once a day since the King's and Prince Micah's death. They claim to be con-cerned about the Queen's health."

"And you don't believe them."

Elder Jacobs must have come here immediately after his

discussion with Andreus. Was he looking to enlist the Queen in his efforts to see Andreus wed? As for the Chief Elder, Andreus could only wonder at his motives.

"My duty is to see to the safety and health of Queen Betrice. It is not for me to dispute the Council or their intentions, Your Majesty," Oben said.

"I hear you were on the battlements earlier. Did you see any of the Council members then?"

Oben shook his head. "I fear whoever gave you that information was mistaken. I was not on the battlements tonight."

"Are you certain?" Oben was taller than anyone in the Palace of Winds. Max had been hiding, but it seemed unlikely he would have mistaken Oben for anyone else.

Oben gave him a grim smile. "I believe I would remember going out into the cold, Your Majesty."

Andreus wanted to press the issue, but the stonelike expression of the chamberlain made him doubt there would be any point. Oben had never said more than necessary, even under the best of circumstances. Andreus had known him his entire life, but knew little about him save his devotion to the Queen. "I thought perhaps she might have had you meet with members of the Council if she could not. Mother has never liked to be away from court business for long if she could help it."

"Any questions you have about the Queen and the Council of Elders will have to be taken up with her."

Andreus frowned. "The last time I saw her she was . . . not herself."

Oben nodded. "Madame Jillian and her herbs have helped the Queen a great deal. There are times she seems restored."

"And the other times?"

"Perhaps, Your Majesty, that is another question you should answer for yourself." Oben walked to the bedroom door and pushed it open. "Your mother is awake. She has been hoping her only surviving child would come to visit."

Andreus's chest tightened. He stared at the dimly lit doorway wondering what he would find on the other side. Would it be the mother who insisted he learn how to charm the court or the Queen who laughed as she looked upon Carys's bloodied, disfigured face?

Whichever he found, he would face it. He would do whatever was necessary to learn why she gave the Masters such a dangerous command.

The ornate bed in the center of the room was empty. He turned and spotted his mother, dressed in a flowing white gown. She was standing in front of a full-length mirror brushing her long, ebony hair with slow, deliberate strokes.

"Mother."

Instead of answering, she began to hum.

"Mother, we need to talk. Eden is in danger."

Andreus looked back at Oben, but the older man standing in the doorway looked unconcerned by the Queen's actions. Either she was fine and toying with Andreus or this was what Oben considered an improvement from her previous state.

"Mother, we need to talk."

With deliberate movements, his mother put the silver brush on the small dressing table in front of her before turning to face him. Her dark eyes met his and she frowned. "The last time you and I spoke of the danger facing this kingdom, you smiled and brought me a flower."

"Much has happened since that day." Andreus chose his words carefully. He studied his mother for signs that she had returned to herself—had reemerged from her grief as the cunning woman who once calmly instructed him to seduce his own brother's betrothed.

When she did not respond, he asked, "Mother, what did you say to the Masters about the wind power shortage and why? They claim you talked to them before Father and Micah were brought back to us."

She smiled. "Queens speak with a great number of people. That is my job. To talk and to listen. Those who listen hold great power. Because it is not what we want to hear that aids us, but paying attention to that which we would rather not acknowledge. You have never liked to listen, my son."

"I'm listening now."

"Are you?" His mother cocked her head to the side and studied him. "Then what is it that you hear?"

"It sounds as if you have recovered from your ailment."

"Ailment." She shook her head and laughed. "Such an interesting word to choose for the shattering of a lifetime's work. For discovering that rather than claiming victory, you have been outplayed by fate."

"Mother," he snapped. She had to stay focused if he was going to get answers. "I have just come from the Masters of Light. They said they told you there was a problem with the winds. They warned you that we would not have enough power to keep the lights shining throughout the winter, and you told them not to do anything about it."

"I warned you Imogen was not skilled as a seer. You did not wish to listen."

"This isn't about Imogen, Mother."

"Of course it is." His mother's eyes narrowed. "I told you she was not capable. She could not become Queen. Not without destroying Garden City and the Palace of Winds. I saw her for what she was. I warned Micah. I warned you. Neither of you understood how to listen and now—"

"Imogen is dead, Mother!" His heart slammed hard in his tightening chest.

"Not soon enough." She laughed. Her eyes narrowed. "Yes, the Masters told me about the wind power, and I insisted they allow the power to be used and the lights to burn. When the power ran out, you would all finally see what I knew from the first moment Imogen came to the Palace of Winds. She was a fraud determined to destroy us."

Andreus gaped at his mother. She looked sane, yet— "You *wanted* the lights on the walls to fail?"

"Yes." His mother smiled across the room—this time with a terrible kind of delight—and looked beyond him toward the doorway to where Oben was standing in the threshold. Watching her. "Imogen's pretty face and cunning words would not have helped her then. Your brother would see past her façade—the beautiful face she used to bend him to her will."

No. Imogen hadn't seduced Micah. She had confessed to Andreus that she had felt she had no choice but to acquiesce to the Crown Prince's wishes. The only one she had loved had been Andreus. It was only with him that her passion had flared. His mother continued before he could defend the woman he had loved and lost.

"I told Micah to use her body as he wanted, but not to trust her." She let out a small sigh. "What we were doing was too important.

79

Your brother swore he wouldn't give her his faith, but I could see him faltering. He began to think he might actually be in love with her. Foolish. He was foolish! I had no other choice but to force Micah see her for the danger that she was."

"So you put Garden City and everyone in the Palace of Winds at risk? Mother," Andreus snapped, "don't you see what you've done? Most of our guards are fighting the war with Adderton and now the cold season is here. The Xhelozi are awake and in greater numbers than ever before. As soon as the lights falter, they will attack. If I don't find a way to fix your mistake, people will die."

The candlelight cast a halo behind his mother as she shrugged. "They were always going to die. I finally understand that now."

Andreus stared at his mother, his mouth agape. "Understand what? That you are willing to consign your subjects to violent deaths?"

"My dream." She walked to the small table next to the head of the bed, picked up a delicate teacup and lifted it in a mock toast. She took a drink and sighed. "The tea keeps the dream away. It's the only thing that does. My first memories are of the faces in my dream. Blood streamed from their mouths as their eyes went blank with death. Dozens of them. It was a vision."

"A vision." Andreus shook his head. "Mother, you are not a seer."

"As much as I wished to stay with them in the Village of Night, you are right. I was never one of them. I was born with a single dream that visited me when I slept. No more. No less. But over the years I have recognized many of the faces from that dream. They've walked the streets of Garden City and strolled the halls in this palace. Even as I watched them laugh or struggle to gain power I understood they were meant to die, but I was certain I knew what would cause their deaths and that I alone could change it."

"You . . . you aren't well, Mother." Andreus took a step backward, away from the terrifying certainty in his mother's eyes and the insanity that still lurked behind them. None of this made any sense. His leg throbbed and his chest tightened. There were no other answers to be had here.

"And once again you aren't listening. Imogen . . ."

"This isn't about Imogen," he yelled. Blood roared in his ears.

His mother threw the teacup across the room. It shattered like a thunderclap against the wall. *"She was but one snake in a garden!"* She paused, her breathing heavy. "How many more are there? And who is playing the tune that makes them slither? She had to be working with someone. She wasn't that clever on her own."

Andreus shook his head. "No. She was—"

"I saw it in her eyes the first minute she stepped into the Hall of Virtues. I saw the way she studied your brother as if searching for the right key to slide into a lock. It was the same way I thought of Ulron even before we met—as a path to gain what I wanted most—power. Imogen wanted that power. She schemed to convince your brother that she was worthy of his trust. Micah must have been foolish enough to believe her and then she killed him."

"Imogen was nowhere near Micah when he died. Micah and Father died in an ambush to the south of Garden City."

"How stupid men become when a woman presses her body against theirs. Did she profess love to you as well? Do you think she meant it, my son? Just because a person does not wield the sword doesn't mean she didn't strike the death blow. You of all people should understand that." His mother slowly walked toward him. "What blood did you spill to gain the crown you wear?"

The white, gauzy dress fluttered as she reached up and stroked his face. Then her hand whipped back and cracked against his cheek, sending him staggering back, his knee buckling as pain swelled in his wounded leg.

"Imogen learned of my plan. She used it against me—and there is no stopping what she started. She could not have been working alone, and now they will be coming for you. They will want what you gained." Her mouth curled. "You are King now. If not for that all my years of planning would have been lost. If Carys had won . . ." She shook her head and stepped forward with her hand outstretched. "You will have to be wary. Stop them if you can. I took the steps and put the pieces in place so that Eden would finally walk in the virtues. So that I could be free."

"What steps? What pieces?" Andreus moved toward his mother and grabbed her hand as she raised it again. His face still stung as he squeezed her wrist and demanded, "Free from what, Mother?"

His mother went still and looked him dead in the eyes. "Free of the vision, and the last person with control over my life. From a man who insisted that I remember that I served him and who would have put you to death had he discovered your curse. The only way to stop the vision was to remove him. Micah picked men he thought he could trust. It was all arranged. Micah understood that Ulron had to die so we all could survive."

Andreus released his mother's wrist.

Ulron.

The King.

His father.

His heart stilled and his breath caught in his throat. It was as if he had fallen out of the stable hayloft and onto the ground below and his lungs had forgotten how to breathe.

"*You* killed my father?" he whispered.

"No," his mother smiled. "I killed a king. Imogen killed the rest."

Andreus lunged forward and wrapped his hands around his mother's neck. He squeezed as she gasped with pain. "And Micah and Carys and Imogen . . ."

She clawed at his shirt. Her eyes wide. Her mouth bright red, almost like the blood she had spilled—that he wanted to spill. His *mother's* blood.

He let go and staggered backward looking down at his hands. This wasn't him. And it wasn't her. She didn't know what she was saying. She was ill. None of this was real and he was leaving.

Turning, he headed toward the doorway where Oben stood still as stone.

"Carys never mattered. Micah did. You do. Stop them. Do what you must to stop them all, because they are coming." His mother's raspy voice floated to him on the shadows. Andreus tried to block her out as he pushed past Oben, but there was no ignoring the words. "Inside the walls. Outside the walls. The orb is a beacon and they are coming. Like moths to a flame. And when they arrive everyone will burn!"

"Move!" Andreus commanded Oben. The man stared at him then slowly stepped to the side. Andreus's heart pounded as he limped past the solar's fireplace and headed for the double doors. More than anything, he wanted to flee the sound of her voice and the words she had spoken. They could not be true. His mother had not orchestrated his father's death. It had to be the illness speaking because the words made no sense.

And yet, allowing the lights to falter was exactly something his mother would do in order to oust Imogen—a rival for power within the palace—from her position of authority. The action made a warped kind of sense. Scheming to murder his father, the King, her husband, however, did not.

He heard a door click closed and the shuffle of feet behind him. Not turning around, he said, "My mother is still . . . confused."

"The tea the Queen takes to quell her nightmare doesn't always react well with the remedy Madame Jillian has given her. The combination loosens her tongue and her heart."

Andreus turned. "Are you telling me that what the Queen said was true?"

"I do not speak for the Queen," Oben said as he moved toward the fireplace. The flickering flames made it harder than ever to read the chamberlain's expression.

"But you know what she is doing and what she has done."

Oben slowly nodded, and Andreus's throat went dry. His chest clenched and his stomach turned as he realized what action his role as King dictated. If his mother's words were true, she had committed treason. And for treason, there was only one option. "The Queen must not leave these rooms. You will keep her confined until she stands trial for her part in King Ulron's and Prince Micah's deaths."

He moved to leave as Oben's deep voice replied, "If the Queen wishes to leave, I will not stop her."

"That was not a suggestion. It was a command." Andreus turned and straightened his shoulders. "From your King."

"Yes." Oben nodded. "You are King. But how long will that last if others know what your mother has done?"

"I had nothing to do with her plans."

"Do you think the Council of Elders will care?" Oben strode forward. "Think! How many in this castle wished to keep you from claiming the throne? Do you believe they will give up the opportunity to remove you now?"

Uncertainty swirled as he thought of the Elders and the guardsmen. Men who technically answered to Andreus, but who might have any of a dozen conflicting alliances. All the Elders had guards from their districts who served the crown, but whose loyalty was given to them.

Andreus shook his head. "I am the King. I have to follow the law."

"As if the law ever matters to kings. Don't be foolish. You have enemies in every shadow and few allies. Do not start something unless you know where it will lead. You did that with Lady Imogen and look what came of your actions."

"I did nothing with Imogen . . ."

Oben reached out and grabbed Andreus's upper arm. "Denials are pointless. You are no longer a boy who has only to worry about getting scolded, and Carys is no longer here to stand in front of you to deflect attention and take your punishments. Your mother tried to warn you. You wouldn't listen to her then. But by the Gods, you will listen to me now. You say you are the King? Be the King!"

Andreus yanked his arm, but Oben held fast.

Oben's eyes held his with an intensity that burned like a fire. The chamberlain insisted, "Become the man I have always known you could be."

The words settled on Andreus in the silence. The fire in the hearth popped. The flickering candlelight made the shadows dance as his mother's muted voice called from the other room.

"I must attend the Queen." Oben bowed his head and started toward the bedroom door.

Andreus swallowed hard. "How do I know this isn't another of my mother's plots?"

Oben turned. For a second, Andreus thought he saw regret flicker across the chamberlain's face. Then the expression was gone as Oben said, "You don't."

The man disappeared, leaving Andreus alone with the candles and the fire and the roar of questions pounding in his head. He pushed through the double doors. The wounds of the Xhelozi pulsed with pain. His breathing was shallow as he walked the brightly illuminated halls that tomorrow would be lit only by torches. He would have to explain about the dwindling wind power. People would be scared. They would not be alone in their fear. The Council was plotting against him. His mother had confessed to plotting to kill his father. And Imogen . . .

His belief in Imogen's love for him had been the only true constant since his father and brother died, but from the seeds of doubt his mother had sewn grew questions he could not ignore. Had any of what he believed about her been real? Had she loved him? Had she convinced Micah to trust her and used that trust to kill him? If so, the men who returned Micah's and their father's bodies would have known.

Carys said they did know.

Andreus stopped walking.

If Imogen was what his mother claimed . . .

He shook his head.

That couldn't be. Carys was a liar. She had pretended she was no longer using the Tears of Midnight. She kept her continued friendship with Larkin hidden for years. Carys and Larkin were behind the assassination attempt on his life.

Or so he was led to believe by—Imogen.

Could the woman he had loved and trusted be what his mother claimed? Could every choice he made have been built on a lie?

He started walking again, this time faster despite the pain aflame in his leg.

Oben was right. Andreus wore the crown, but if he wanted to be a king he had to start acting like it—whether the Council of Elders liked it or not.

7

"Are you all right?" Garret stopped his mount next to hers. "We can go back, and I'll keep up the search if you wish."

She blinked away the fatigue and studied the landscape. For the first hour after dawn, Carys had insisted on continuing to look for Larkin. But as the temperature rose, Carys felt hope fade. The wave of warmth made it easier to travel, but the melted snow destroyed all chance of locating her friend's tracks. Larkin was out there somewhere and Carys was powerless to help her.

"No." Carys straightened her shoulders. "I thought I saw something in the distance, but I was mistaken. We should keep going."

"You need rest, Carys," Garret said quietly.

"I'm fine," she lied. Her body ached with fatigue, but there was no time for sleep. The Xhelozi presence this far to the west meant it was only safe to travel during the day. She had to reach the seers and learn what she could about Imogen's rise to power as quickly as possible. There was no telling when Imogen's co-conspirators would strike in the Palace of Winds. Carys had to return before that happened. And if Larkin got away from Errik, she would ride with all haste to the Village of Night. Carys was determined to be there when her friend arrived.

"Larkin isn't the only one who knew of your plans to visit the seers," Garret said quietly. "If she does manage to get there, Errik and whatever forces he might have won't be far behind. If we take a few extra days to ride to Bisog, I can gather men to defend you . . ."

"No," Carys snapped. Her cloak fluttered. She would not spend several days traveling to Garret's district and his source of power. If Errik was rounding up troops to come to the Village of Night, Carys had to beat him there or risk him destroying any chance of her learning the truth behind Imogen's rise to power. "We will continue riding southwest to the Village of Night."

Since Garret claimed he didn't know this area and had no idea how to get to the place of the seers, Larkin's vague description of the route was the only navigational tool Carys had. The forest Larkin had spoken of had been easy to find, but the trees stretched for leagues, and, now that they were on the other side, Carys had no way of knowing if they were going in the correct direction or if they were too far north or south.

She would not show uncertainty around Garret. He had helped her escape and seemed to know her secrets, but she didn't trust him.

"Come on." Carys nudged her horse forward, but Garret reached out and grabbed her arm.

"Look."

Carys looked to the muddy ground where he pointed.

Wide prints were set deep in the wet earth. They measured at least as long as the tips of her fingers to her elbow with three marks as long as her hand jutting out like toes. The deep scrapes in the mud next to those toes made it clear what had made those prints.

"The Xhelozi," she said as her stomach churned.

"Have you ever heard of a time when the Xhelozi came this far west?" Carys asked.

Garret looked down at the prints scarring the earth. "Only in a story that seemed impossible when I heard it."

Carys frowned. She hadn't heard many stories growing up. Her brother had hated the storytellers, who always seemed to weave the power of the seers into their tales. He refused to believe in the seers. Because believing in them would be admitting that his illness—his *curse*—could lead to the downfall of Eden. So, while the rest of the court listened with rapt attention to the traveling storytellers, she and Andreus had been in the tunnels of the palace pursuing other entertainments. Now, with the wind whispering in her mind, Carys wished she had paid more attention.

"My grandfather used to say the storytellers were wrong about the Xhelozi." Garret cocked his head to the side as if trying to hear the words his grandfather spoke. "That the Xhelozi were not spotted outside the mountains until a few years before the Bastians lost the throne. I assumed it was because there were more hunting parties searching the mountains for kills then. My grandfather liked to regale everyone with those stories, too."

"Perhaps," she said. Or maybe there were forces—things besides the cold and dark that called the Xhelozi to hunt in greater numbers.

"After what happened the past few weeks, it is hard to be surprised by much of anything and my guess is there are more surprising things to come before you ascend your rightful place on the throne."

"You speak in riddles, Garret." Carys reached under her cloak for the hilt of one of her stilettos as her horse danced beneath her and dead leaves swirled from the ground up into the air. "I am tired of your knowing nods and secretive smiles. It is time to share with me what you know about your uncle and what the Council has been plotting. And why you insisted on coming with me when I feigned death and fled the Palace of Winds."

"I wanted to make sure you returned and used your power to help Eden as I promised my uncle you could," Garret said smoothly. "I know you are the reason the arrows broke before striking Larkin. I've suspected what you can do for quite some time."

Carys stilled. "Why would you think I had anything to do with that? And your uncle thinks I'm dead." The Chief Elder of the Council would never have allowed Andreus to be installed as King had he thought there was a chance she was alive.

Garret smiled. "Perhaps. Or perhaps he has understood the advantages of turning a blind eye. As for the other, I have watched you more closely than you think. I have studied what I believe you can do. You don't trust me, but once you do I will be able to help you . . ."

A scream pierced the air. A woman's scream.

Larkin!

Carys wheeled her horse toward the rocky hills to the south and squinted into the sunshine. The shout echoed again. Carys drew her stilettos with one hand and urged her horse toward the sound at a gallop. The clattering of hooves behind her said Garret had done the same.

Her mount slipped on a patch of mud and Carys almost lost her grip as it regained its footing. Another shout echoed—a long, chilling sound that raked down Carys's spine—as they crested the top of the hill and she could see the source of the screams.

Far in the distance, a girl was struggling with two men. Another man with a broadsword was standing over a white-haired body crumpled on the ground.

The restrained girl spat and one of the men reached back and slapped her across the face. Still, she continued to kick and bite, trying to free herself as the men laughed.

Garret pulled his horse up next to Carys. "It's not Larkin."

"We have to help her," Carys said as the laughing man flipped open the girl's cloak, grabbed the neckline of her dress and yanked it downward.

Carys nudged her horse forward and Garret's hand clamped over her arm. "Don't be foolish," he hissed. "Look over there." Carys followed his gaze to where seven horses carrying travel packs were tied near a small stone outbuilding not far from the farmstead's windmill.

"Some of the brigands must be in the house," Carys realized.

One of the men slapped the girl again. Even at this distance Carys could hear the contact of flesh against flesh and see the blood dripping from the crack in the girl's lip. Blood pounded in her head. The whispering that had quieted returned louder than ever as the girl stopped struggling and the man with the broadsword strutted in her direction.

Carys started her horse forward and Garret grabbed the reins. "We're outnumbered and there is a chance that you could be recognized. No one can know you are alive until you are ready to reclaim the kingdom."

"I don't care!"

A muted scream came from the direction of the squat farmhouse.

"A queen has to put the good of the kingdom ahead of any individual."

The girl's head, which had been hung in defeat, came up as she kicked the man who had laughed square in the groin. The man with the broadsword swept her feet out from under her and she hit the ground. Carys yanked her arm free of Garret's grip and pressed her knees into her mount's flanks.

The wind howled with rage as the horse shot forward down the incline, leaving the rest of Garret's plea behind. A man pulled at the girl's clothes while the other two, with their backs to her as she approached, cheered on the assault.

The first of her stilettos left her hand and buried itself in the back of the man climbing on top of the screaming girl. She clutched the other hilt tight as her horse closed the distance toward the other two, who had stopped cheering as their fellow brigand toppled to the ground. Two men with weapons. One stiletto.

The brigands spun, shouted as they saw her and her stallion bearing down on them. They fumbled for their swords. Shouted for reinforcements as Carys rode her horse directly toward a blond bearded man struggling to get his weapon free of its sheath.

The other dirt-streaked, dark-haired brigand raced, sword in hand, toward her. The girl on the ground scrambled to her feet.

Carys let the stiletto fly as her horse reared. She grabbed the pommel, squeezed her legs, and hung on with all her might.

Her horse whinnied. The wind roared, and the man spun in the air. He cried with fear and begged. "Stop! Please stop!"

Begged. Like the girl he had been attacking. The man wanted mercy, but he would get death.

The wind twisted. Rage burned in Carys, hot and thirsty for blood.

The man screamed in horror.

Carys smiled at his fear.

His head snapped and the scream was gone.

The air went still and the man dropped to the ground with a thud. Carys's horse reared again and there was a sickening crack of hooves connecting with flesh.

Anger was replaced with a different feeling. Gone was a fatigue and the deep ache of withdrawal and the lack of control she had felt her entire life. The chill that had plagued her vanished in a flash of heat.

Sastisfaction, that was what she felt. The whispers roared approval as she turned to look for something else to destroy.

Then she heard the whimper and turned to see the girl looking with horror at the broken man on the ground. His arms and legs were bent in abnormal directions like a doll that had been stomped on in a tantrum.

And his neck.

Its flesh was twisted and ripped—gaping from the force of the wind and her anger.

The air went still. Carys gasped. The whispering disappeared as bile rose in her throat. She had meant for the man to die. But she hadn't meant to do *that*.

Shouts rang out from one of the buildings.

"Are there others?" Carys asked as the girl climbed to her feet.

"There are at least four more. Inside the house."

The wind rustled her cloak and the whispers began again. Carys shook her head and pulled her bow and quiver out of one of the side travel packs. She flung her leg over the saddle and leaped to the ground.

"You have to hide."

The dark-haired girl shook her head. Her winter cloak was unfastened. The front of her dress was torn to her waist, but the girl didn't try to cover herself. Instead she reached down, grabbed the large, bloodstained broadsword from the ground with both hands, and slowly raised it. Her arms shook from the weight that she would never be able to swing with any force. "They have my family."

The girl's eyes flicked to the house. Muted shouts floated on the air. Something clanged. There was a clatter of hooves to the right of her as a man emerged from the house holding a sword dripping with blood.

Anger sparked anew. Carys breathed deep and pulled back the string of the bow. The man's eyes widened a moment before a point drove deep into his forehead and he toppled off the steps of the house, leaving the front door standing wide open.

Garret slid off his horse and drew his sword. The girl swung toward Garret, fear and defiance lighting her face.

"He's with me," Carys called. She yanked one of her blades from a man's back and the other from the attacker's throat, then assessed the third—the girl's grandfather. His hands were coated in blood from where the sword had punctured his stomach. The white-haired man's eyes were open but saw nothing. He was dead.

"Stop it!" A boy's frantic scream echoed from somewhere inside the house. "Leave her alone!"

"My brother!"

Carys gripped the hilts of the stilettos in her hands and turned toward the house as a young boy started screaming.

"Carys!" Garret hissed and fell in step beside Carys as she started across the courtyard toward the house.

Something crashed.

The wind whispered again, fanning the kernel of anger that seemed to burn hotter and stronger. Wanting to break free. Desperate to hurt as she and the girl and the girl's grandfather had been hurt.

No! She couldn't set the wind free. Not when she couldn't control it.

Men shouted. A child sobbed for his mother.

"Shut that brat up, now!"

Garret blew out a breath and whispered, "I'll go first. They'll think I'm the threat and by the time they realize they have to worry about you, it'll be too late."

Carys nodded and followed Garret to the doorway. Her mind swirled. She fought against the anger that threatened to break free with every beat of her heart. She held her breath and shifted her hold on her blades as Garret stepped through the door.

"You men are here uninvited. I order you to leave," Garret said smoothly.

"Who the devil are you?" a gruff voice yelled as Carys stepped into the dimness of the house.

It took a second for her eyes to adjust to the change of light. Metal clanged against metal. A young boy wailed and scurried toward an older woman huddled on the floor in the corner of what must have once been a homey kitchen. Garret slashed over a broken wooden table at a black-bearded man with missing teeth. The man leaped out of the way of the blade and slashed back. Two others came running into the kitchen.

Carys barely raised her voice. "Hey—"

He turned and her stiletto found his chest, punching through an all-too-familiar yellow and blue insignia, before he spoke another word. Seeing the emblem of Eden—an indication that these were *her* kingdom's soldiers—made her ill. She refused to think of them as anything but enemies as her second blade pierced into the other man's gut a moment later.

The toothless attacker dropped his own sword arm just a hair as his comrade fell. Garret jabbed his long, wide blade into the man's chest and out through the other side. The man's sword fell from his hand. Garret yanked his sword out of the body and the man crashed to the ground. Garret then walked toward the two men Carys had felled. He slit the throat of the man with the stiletto in his stomach as Carys retrieved her weapons.

"Mummy!" A curly-haired boy who looked to be about four struggled against the gray-haired woman who held him tight in her arms. "Grammy, I want Mummy."

"We'll find her," the woman said, the anguish in her eyes telling Carys the woman feared the attackers had not left her daughter alive.

"We'll look for her and help you get the bodies out of your home," Carys said, wiping a line of blood from her face.

"Thank you," the old woman said dully as she hugged the squirming child.

It took time for Carys, Garret, and the girl to drag the three men out of the house and find the other members of her family whom the brigands had restrained in the other room—the boy's mother thankfully alive and among them. The only fatality was Naila's grandfather, who had died before Carys and Garret had arrived to lend aid.

"My father and Viktor went to town today," Naila said, looking down at her grandfather's face. Garret had moved the grandfather's body to the barn so that he could be prepared for burial, and was now watering and feeding the horses as he waited for Carys. But she couldn't leave. Not yet. "Father didn't want to go, but we were running low on supplies and he was worried the snow would come again soon and make travel too hard. Grandpa told Warin to watch for travelers while he milked the goats and mucked out the stalls, but Warin must have gotten bored and snuck off."

Naila kicked a bale of hay and put her hands over her face. "I should have made sure he was still watching. I didn't hear the horses until Grandpa told me someone was here and to stay hidden. But I couldn't, you know? Not after what happened a month ago at Briggins Manor."

"I'm sorry, but I don't know what happened at Briggins Manor. I live . . . farther to the north," Carys admitted. "There have been other attacks like this? Or, have the Xhelozi come this way?"

"My mother says the Xhelozi are a fairy tale—used to make children afraid of wandering out at night." Naila gave a ghost of a smile despite her swollen lip. Carys didn't have the heart to correct her. Then the smile faded. "I would rather the Xhelozi than the deserters we've had roaming the southern districts."

"Deserters. This has happened before?"

"Father says when a war has gone on so long, men don't remember why they are fighting. When they don't remember, it is easy for men to lose their way. At least a dozen packs of deserters have come to this area since winter last ended. Eden guardsman and foreign ones, too. A few have asked if they can work for food. The rest . . ." Naila placed a hand on her grandfather's shoulder, then sighed. "They are trained soldiers with weapons given to them by their kings. You either hide and let them take what they want, or they kill you."

Naila lifted her eyes and clutched her cloak together in the front. "And sometimes before they kill you, they make sure that you want to die."

Carys had heard her father talk to Micah about food short-ages, attacks on supply wagons, and the need for more fighting men. Never about deserters from Eden's own guard.

Carys cocked her head to the side. "You say foreign soldiers have passed by your farm? Those men. What were their colors?"

"Most of them wore brown and gold."

Not the colors of the kingdom they were warring with. Instead, those were the colors of the Bastians. The same worn by the soldier who stopped his attack short when he recognized Errik. "When? When did you see them? Recently?"

Naila nodded. "My father says he saw the first not far from the forest when he rode to town three weeks past. I spotted the last group just days ago. They were going northeast."

Northeast—toward the Palace of Winds. Were they part of the Bastian attack force? Perhaps they had deserted, or maybe they were traveling in small groups because it was easier to avoid notice. If the Bastian forces were now within Eden's boundaries, Errik could, at this moment, be delivering Larkin to them.

"I'm sorry for your family's loss," Carys said. Naila draped a worn blanket over her grandfather's body and covered his face. "I wish I could have done more."

"Without you, we would all be dead." Naila turned to her and bobbed a curtsy. "This is not your fault, Your Highness."

The title and the genuflection stilled Carys's heart. "I think you have me confused with someone else. Do I look like the kind of person with a place in the royal court?"

Even if Naila had seen her at a distance at a tournament, or in Garden City before the trials, now, dressed in the tight-fitting trousers Larkin had crafted, with unevenly cut short hair, Carys looked nothing like her old self, and certainly appeared nothing like royalty. Royalty maintained their façade at all costs—no matter what side of the wall they were on.

"The lord called your name. He said, 'Your Highness.'"

"He likes to tease . . ."

"Also, a merchant from Garden City traded with us last week. He spoke of a princess, skilled as if by magic with long knives that were as silver as her hair." Naila lifted eyes that were no longer filled with tears, but blazed with a fierce light. "I think you are her. But even if you say you are not, I would still call you Lady. For all that you have done."

The words brought back the memory of the Trials, of standing on the battlements as she spoke to the crowd below.

The people. *Her* people. For years she had denied the connection to them, choosing only to focus on her twin and keeping him safe. Then they lifted the banners of blue and for the first time she realized she was not the disappointment to them that she had always thought.

They believed in her no matter the flaws they had seen and the walls between them.

"If you wish to honor me," Carys said, "you will speak not of your suspicion about my identity. Not even to your family. Do you understand?"

If her survival reached Andreus's ears, her brother would give the order to hunt her down himself.

Naila straightened her shoulders, gathered her skirts, and performed an awkward but deep curtsy. "I won't tell anyone, Your Highness. I swear on my life."

Certain the girl meant what she said, Carys asked, "Naila, have you ever been to the Village of Night?" With Bastian men infiltrating the countryside, it was even more important that she learn about the traitors inside Garden City and return to the palace with the utmost speed.

"I have not, Your Highness."

Not a surprise, but Carys couldn't help the stab of disappointment.

"But several people seeking the place of the seers have stopped here to ask my father for aid in finding it. He always sends them to Hopeshire Village to speak with the blacksmith."

Then that was where Carys would go.

Garret tapped his foot and crossed his arms as Carys, the hood of her cloak now covering her shorn hair, said good-bye to Naila in the courtyard. She warned her that the Xhelozi were more than fairy tales and instructed her to keep as many lights on as possible in the dark winter nights to come. "Burn the bodies of the deserters, but keep their weapons and carry them at all times"—Carys smiled—"even if it makes you look less like a lady. Things like that don't matter as much as some would like you to believe."

Naila looked as if she wanted to say something else, but before she could Carys turned and mounted her horse. As she rode toward the gate, she looked down at the stained ground where the body of the beaten man once lay. The wind had torn him apart. A chill went down her back as she remembered how the body had dropped, broken, to the ground.

She had barely set off when the whispers returned. Disgusted as she was by what she had done, deep inside where the hurt and anger burned, she knew she would have the chance to do it again. A dark part of her welcomed that chance. And when she looked at Garret smiling at her, she knew he would welcome it, too.

8

Andreus wiped his brow, looked up at the Palace of Winds, and frowned. "Why is the orb shining?"

Standing at the base of the steps carved into the plateau, which led to the palace, the Masters looked at him with bleary eyes. It had taken two sleepless days for the Masters to outline and finish the changes that were required to shut off the wind power to all but the essential lights that bordered the walls. Andreus had spent several hours of both days lending his hands to the cause. The work had to be completed as quickly as possible, leaving him little time to think of anything else.

The Council of Elders had been outraged by the idea of a torch-lit Palace of Winds. Elder Ulrich suggested a more gradual approach, darkening sections of the palace to allow the court and those in the city to grow accustomed to the idea.

"It's like wading across a cold river, Your Majesty," Elder Ulrich had explained, training his one seeing eye on the other members of the Council. "You ease in a little at a time to brace yourself against the shock. Your subjects cannot take much more upheaval before their unrest devolves into chaos."

"Weak kings believe the only people they can control are those who are cowering in fear," Elder Jacobs added quietly as he stroked his long dark braid. "Your father was not weak."

"Nor is King Andreus," Elder Cestrum said smoothly. "He made his abilities clear during the Trials of Virtuous Succession. I am sure many here in the palace, including the Masters, fear crossing him. Fear can be a useful tool."

Andreus wished he could use that tool on the Council of Elders. He instructed them to inform the court and post notices in Garden City about the blackening of the orb and the change in the rest of the lights. If all went as planned, he would keep the fear at a manageable level. At least until the wind began to blow again or the stored power ran out.

The orb had been darkened. The city stayed bright.

Only now the orb was glowing again, drawing on precious power stores—against his command.

"Were the orders I gave to block the energy from the orb not carried out?" he asked the Masters.

Master Triden flicked a glance at the Council, who were also assembled at the base of the steps. "We need . . . more time to alter the orb, Your Majesty. Once we finish the inspection, I will find a solution."

"Night is approaching quickly, Your Majesty." Elder Jacobs stepped forward. "If we are to do the inspections, we should start now, when the people will be able to see you riding the city streets. It will be a sign to them of your vigilance. An assurance that the city is safe."

Andreus studied the Master. Master Triden lowered his gaze, and Andreus clenched his fist at his side. The Masters themselves had told him how much energy the orb required and had been insistent that it be shut down in order to keep the lines on the wall supplied with power for as long as possible.

And now the Masters defied him and accepted the word of the Council?

He—not the Council—sat on the throne. *He* was the King. *His* commands were the ones to be followed.

He turned toward Master Triden, prepared to demand the truth. Everyone within earshot would understand that he couldn't be countermanded. Then, out of the corner of his eye he saw Elder Jacobs leaning forward, eyes bright as if awaiting Andreus's rage.

Elder Jacobs had worn the same look during the Trials of Virtuous Succession when he claimed to be on Andreus's side. But Andreus had no idea what side he was actually on other than his own. Carys had frequently said that whenever someone on the Council wished him to do something, it was a good enough reason to do the opposite.

Thinking of his sister's words, Andreus swallowed his emotions, and nodded to Elder Jacobs. "The security of Garden City is paramount. Let us start our inspection. Our return is soon enough for the Masters to continue their work on the orb."

The tour of the walls took hours as their party and a dozen of the King's Guard traveled the perimeter of the city making sure all sections of the wall were receiving the power necessary to keep the Xhelozi at bay. As they rode, people lined the street to get a glimpse of Andreus—first in the fading light of day and later by torchlight.

Here and there he spotted someone wearing a blue ribbon or piece of blue fabric tied on their arm.

For Carys—the one they lifted their banners for when she spoke to them atop the wall.

The kingdom had started the competition cheering for *him.* Now there were no ovations. Just looks of worry—and the remaining bands of blue.

They will cheer me again, Andreus thought. He would keep the Xhelozi from attacking and discover the truth behind his father's and brother's deaths. When he did, they would be glad. Then his people would see his worth as King.

"It appears the lights are all working as they should, Your Majesty," Chief Elder Cestrum said as they reached the final section of the wall. "The Masters of Light are to be commended for their efforts."

"Yes, everyone deserves a good night's rest after all the work that has been done," Elder Ulrich agreed. "It was important work. Captain Monteros was given instructions to see that the new seer be escorted back to Garden City with due haste, he may be delayed."

Elder Jacobs nodded. "If all works out as planned, the wind will begin to blow as it always has and these precautions will be rendered unnecessary. But until then, the people of Garden City will know they are safe from attack—and that the King places their well-being above the comfort of those in the Palace of Winds."

Commendation or condemnation? Andreus couldn't say.

They turned from the wall and headed back toward the plateau and the palace.

"Your Majesty, may I have a word?" Elder Jacobs called.

Andreus sighed, slowed his horse, and turned. "Of course, what can I . . ." A flicker from the wall behind Elder Jacobs caught his attention and he pulled his horse to a halt.

"Is everything all right, Your Majesty?" Elder Jacobs asked.

The light dimmed, then brightened again.

"Did you see that?" Andreus asked.

Elder Jacobs glanced around with confusion.

"The lights," Andreus said. "Did you see one of them flicker just now?"

Elder Jacobs shook his head. "I don't believe so, Your Majesty. Is there a problem?"

"I think one of the new connections might need to be tightened."

"I will go look at the connection now, Your Majesty," one of the Masters said from nearby. "If there is a problem, I am certain it is minor."

Elder Jacobs leaned close and whispered, "If there is an issue, it would be best to make sure the trouble is corrected as soon as possible, Your Majesty, or the people might blame you for the failure."

Andreus glanced up at the orb still glowing in the sky, then back at the Master who was clasping and unclasping his hands. "No. Return to the Palace of Winds and get some sleep," he ordered the anxious Master. "I believe I can handle any issues with the connection on my own." Before the Elders could object, he smiled and added, "The men who taught me what to do trained me well."

Master Triden gave a weary smile.

"Go back to the palace with the others. I will be along shortly." Andreus turned his mount and headed back toward the wall, followed by several members of the guard. Andreus had always thought his father's guards were a sign of how powerful and important he was. He had never imagined that one or more of them could pose a threat. Now, Andreus couldn't help but wonder if the six men currently riding with him were truly sworn to serve him or if they served another.

He shivered and pulled his cloak tighter to ward off the chill of the night. He was looking forward to finishing this task and returning to his rooms, where a roaring fire and hot tea would await him.

Andreus climbed off his horse outside a narrow alley and left it with four of the guards, who he ordered to stand watch at the opening. Then, with the other two unmounted men, Andreus walked down the dark, narrow path between a glassblower's establishment and a weaver's shop that led to the portion of the wall he needed to study. When he turned the corner, he nodded at the two apprentices, who jumped to their feet and hastily bowed.

"One of you come with me to the top. The other stay here," he ordered the two members of the guard, who walked with him toward the metal rungs on one section of the wall. One snapped to attention. The other waited for Andreus to start climbing before following behind him.

He took the rungs slowly on his way up the wall. Here the stone barrier stood over three times his own height. Madame Jillian had been pleased this morning to see that her new salve had finally beat back the infection that had been keeping the Xhelozi claw marks from healing, but the leg was still raw and unsteady. The last thing he wanted to do was fall to the cobblestones or onto the apprentices below.

His breath was coming hard and fast as he reached the top of the rungs. He pulled himself onto the rim of the thick stone barrier. Carys always said the walls represented a double-edged sword. The founders of Eden built the kingdom near the mountains to harness the wind's power, never believing the threat in the mountains could, one day, overcome their precautions and lay ruin to all that had been built.

Ruling, his sister had observed, was also a double-edged sword, where a decision that solved one problem inevitably caused another.

Hauling himself up to the top, Andreus rubbed his aching leg. His twin might have been right, he thought as he climbed to his feet and waited for the guard to join him.

"Make sure no one comes up the ladder," Andreus ordered. "I'll be right back."

As the guard drew his sword and stood at attention in front of the ladder, Andreus squinted into the blinding beams and carefully made his way past the narrow, illuminated cylinders. They stood several lengths tall and were placed every few paces along the wall to make sure no section was left in shadow. Each main connector controlled eight lights. Four on each side. It was a configuration Andreus had suggested to improve the distribution of power. The lights dimmed slightly and flared to life again as he reached the connector. He squatted down and pried open the stone that covered the lines.

Strange . . .

One of the wires had been loosened from the bolt, and then placed so that it was touching the conductor, but it was no longer secured. He wasn't imagining anything. The light *was* flickering, and this was the cause.

Andreus sat back on his heels so as to not cast a shadow on the connections and studied the problem. The bolt had clearly been worked away with a prying tool of some kind. He could see the fresh scrape marks on the metal bolt and the casing around it. The

Masters and apprentices all had tools that allowed them to loosen and tighten the bolts easily. Even if they had forgotten to fasten the wire after finishing the adjustment, they would never have done it in the method he observed here. No, whoever had caused this had to have done it after the Masters and the rest of the Guild of Light finished their alterations. Otherwise even the newest apprentice would have noticed the problem and alerted the Masters to correct it.

Pulling his own tools out of a pouch on his belt, Andreus flipped the switch that cut off the power and the light, rendering it safe to work. Quickly, he fixed the wire and tightened the bolt so the lights would not malfunction again and flipped the switch. He smiled with satisfaction as the lights flared, then placed the stone cover back atop the connector box. Pushing to his feet, he studied the brightly lit wall stretching around the city. He could see the outline of several guardsmen as they watched the lands beyond the wall for signs of the Xhelozi. None of the lights flickered. Everything appeared as it should.

Still, instead of turning to head back toward the guard he could see standing still as stone near the rungs Andreus had used, he limped down the wall to check the next connection. Just in case something similar had happened.

The connection in the next series of lights was fine. No pry marks. No wires waiting to malfunction and cast the wall in darkness. Whoever had sabotaged the one connection had done so in a way that made the lights not dependable, but still operational. That had to have been intentional. But why? What good was making the lights flicker for a few seconds? Why create a problem that would cause a set of lights to lose power at an unexpected time instead of when someone wanted darkness to obscure their actions?

It made no strategic sense.

He heard a thudding sound and turned to look down the wall in the direction from which he had come. The guard who had been waiting at the end of the wall just a moment before was no longer there.

Andreus started to call out, then spotted the guard's body lying motionless at the top of the wall. The guard was either unconscious or dead. No doubt the one stationed below was as well.

The flickering light had been a trap, and Andreus had climbed right into it. Whoever had laid it had removed his guards and would be waiting for him in the direction that he had come from.

He slid the stone panel back into place, crawled to the edge of the wall, and peered down. Only a handful of places in the wall had rungs to aid someone in climbing up to the top. This wasn't one of them. He would have to walk past another ten connection points atop the wall before he reached the next set of iron rungs. His still-injured leg wasn't going to travel that distance very fast.

"Do you see him?" he heard a voice call.

In the distance, Andreus saw a man's head crest the top of the wall not far from the guard's body. "I'm almost to the top," a different voice hissed, the sound carrying on the quiet of the night. "He couldn't be far."

Hopefully he was far enough to avoid suffering the same fate as his guards.

Andreus glanced down. He spied a small tree, low bushes, and several open-top barrels of rainwater in the courtyard next to this section of the wall. At twenty feet above the ground, Andreus wasn't dumb enough to jump. Twenty feet was too far for both his leg and his neck to survive. If he was going to take an alternate route to the ground, he'd have to find a better option and he'd have to move fast. The first man had already climbed atop the wall and had turned in Andreus's direction. The lights would blind him for at least a minute or two. Andreus had to make that time count.

Studying the ground below, Andreus scrambled along the wall looking for a way down. There. He spotted a cart loaded with several rolls of hay sitting next to the wall. "King Andreus," a voice called. He looked up and saw a small, narrow shadow flying toward him just in time to flatten himself to the stone as an arrow zipped over his head.

He was too easy a target up here. He had to get off the wall.

Andreus slithered toward the edge, and shifted position. He dug his fingers into the cursedly smooth stone and eased himself over the edge. If he could dangle above the cart first before letting go, it would make the drop less . . .

His fingers slipped and he crashed onto the hay cart, his shoulder cracking hard against the wood rails. Chickens squawked and flapped, and a horse whinnied. His head rang. Gasping for air, he ignored the pain shooting down his arm and rolled toward the edge of the cart. Footsteps sounded above him high atop the stone wall. Whispers and shouts inquired as to where he could have gone.

He listened hard to the voices, trying to place whether they were familiar, as he flung himself off the cart. The voices were too deep for any of the Master's apprentices and they sounded too gruff to be counted among the younger members of the guard. As much as he wanted to know the identities of the traitors, he wasn't about to lose his life. With his leg in its current condition, he wasn't up to fighting off more than one skilled swordsman at a time. But his leg wouldn't be injured for much longer. Once it was healed, he would track them down and make them pay for the murder of his guards.

For now, Andreus grabbed the trace poles on the wagon like he was a horse and wheeled the cart several lengths away from the wall. He then dropped the traces and limped as quickly as he could toward the side of the nearest buildings. Then he headed for the street beyond them.

Everything ached.

His heart raced.

Chickens clucked from the nearby pen giving whoever was on top of the wall clear directions as to where he had come down.

Andreus reached the buildings, plunged into the pathway between them and was blinded by the dark. He blinked several times, hoping to adjust his sight to the shadows as he carefully limped along the building, feeling in front of him with his hands to keep from running into anything.

The sound of the chickens faded, and the rest of the sounds of the city came to life—laughing, horse hooves against cobblestone, the clang of metal, and the slamming of doors. His eyes adjusted as he hurried around the building, pushed open the gate, and reached the street.

Now what?

He looked in both directions, trying to decide where he was.

Working with the Masters of Light, he'd spent time in parts of the city in which most members of the court would never dare to tread, but with only a few flickering torches posted here and there outside doorways, he was having trouble deciding if he had been in this section of Garden City before, or where this particular road led. The only thing he was certain of was that he was a long way from the Palace of Winds and that his leg throbbed. He doubted he was going to be able to walk all the way to the Palace of Winds on it before the Council and the King's Guard were alerted to his disappearance.

He heard the chickens squawk again and headed down the street he hoped led to where he'd climbed up the wall.

Gods it was cold. His throat was dry. The stone road was uneven. His head and his leg ached. And his chest was getting tighter with every breath.

Listening hard to the night behind him, he reached under his cloak and felt for the small vial in his pants pocket. Relieved to find it hadn't shattered when he cracked his hip against the edge of the cart, Andreus pulled the vial out of his pocket and yanked out the cork.

After having taken at least one dose of the strong herbal concotion for each day of the past three weeks, he should have been used to the remedy his mother had had the castle healer concoct. But the acrid, bitter taste of the brew still made him grimace, which he took to be a good sign. Years ago, his mother had related a warning the healers had given to Oben, who they had been told was the holder of the affliction they were treating. They said that using the brew too often would render it less and less useful until there would be no stopping the symptoms when they stole his breath, and his heart strained hard enough to explode. Andreus would have to limit his use of the remedy once the threat to Eden was over. Until then, he would take his chances.

Hand on the hilt of his sword, and keeping to the shadows, Andreus hurried as fast as his leg would allow along the stone street. He took the turn to the left when another road intersected it. Then he ducked into the shadows and waited for several long moments for any sounds that might indicate the men who had been on the wall with him were following. Yet the fiddle and flute and tambourine playing coming from a nearby tavern made it hard to hear anything. All Andreus could do was keep going and try to stay a step ahead of the men who had set the trap for him.

Even though he was careful to avoid the areas with the most torchlight, Andreus still drew notice. Several men watched him from a doorway. Boys just older than Max raced down the street as a man walking down the street yelled, "Get inside, before the King's Guard gets ahold of you."

"They don't care about us," one of the boys shouted back.

"And they can't arrest us if they can't see us," another said, laughing.

The King's Guards. He couldn't be sure which among them were compromised, but if he could find them in a group, odds were there would be enough of them with true fealty to the crown to keep him safe on the return trip to the palace.

Raising the hood of his cloak, Andreus made his way down several narrow streets. He approached a gray-haired merchant dressed in a cloak decorated with the symbol for the Silversmith Guild, and quietly asked, "Excuse me, Goodman. Could you tell me if there are members of the King's Guard nearby, and if so, where I might find them?"

The silversmith's hand hovered over the sword at his side and his eyes narrowed. "You want to find the King's Guard?"

Andreus nodded, careful to keep his face turned from the torches, making it harder for the man to recognize him. "I heard there were several members of the guard in this area after the King and the Council of Elders finished their tour of the wall."

The silversmith cocked his head to the side and leaned toward

Andreus. "Very few people actively seek out the King's Guard who aren't looking to cause trouble for others. The last thing we need in this city is more trouble. We have trouble enough as it is."

"No trouble," Andreus said quickly. The man thought he was looking to turn someone in. Andreus's father and the Council under his rule had been known to reward those who helped ferret out unrest in the city and the rest of the kingdom. His father said throwing those who were looking to act against the crown in the North Tower discouraged others from doing the same. Treason had to be rooted out. Considering that any treason committed would now be against him, Andreus understood the sentiment. But he had noticed that more than once a man who was thrown in jail just happened to have a young wife who suddenly was comforted by the man who was behind the report.

Andreus shifted his feet and shook his head as he searched for an excuse that would not give his identity away. "I was hoping maybe I could show them my skill with a sword. I thought I could join their ranks. My family is struggling and I thought—"

The man nodded. "Follow this street to the end and turn left. If they are still there, you will find them at the end of that road, but I would encourage you instead to go home. Be ready to guard your family if the lights fail and Garden City falls."

A cheery thought.

The man glanced up at the palace and the windmills turning far too slowly and started down the street without another word.

Cursing the pain that was worsening with every step, Andreus followed the man's directions down the narrow, smoke-filled street until he reached the end. He passed a noisy inn. Laughter and music flooded out the door when it opened and several patrons came out onto the street.

Andreus adjusted his hood and continued walking until he reached the two-story stone glassblower's shop at the end of the road. He was close to where he had climbed up to the top of the wall. The guards who had escorted him to this location had to be near. He listened hard to the sounds of the night, doing his best to filter out the laughter and singing from the inn and the crackle of torches scattered along the street.

There was the clatter of hooves on the stone and the nicker of at least one horse. He thought he heard the murmur of voices, but he couldn't be sure.

Slowly, he drew his sword, wincing at the hushed hiss the metal made as it freed itself from the sheath. Then, taking a deep breath, he peered around the wall and spotted two of the guards standing about ten lengths away in the center of the road with their backs to him. He was about to alert them of his return when he heard one of them say, "What do you think is going on?"

"How should I know? The others are going up on the wall now to look for the King."

"They said Nigel must have lost his balance and fell, but that can't be right. We were told to report if the King did anything unusual or spoke to anyone. What if this is something Elder . . ."

"Keep your voice down! If you want to go sticking your head in a rock wolf's mouth, you go ahead. Nigel is dead. We were told to hold our position while the others look for King Andreus. I don't know about you, but an Elder's coin isn't worth getting tangled in whatever is happening right now. I want to keep my head attached to my neck."

The guardsman started to turn and Andreus dove back around the corner and pressed his hand to his stomach. He kept still as stone. Every breath he took sounded loud and harsh in his ears. He waited for footsteps coming his way, yet none materialized.

Slowly, carefully, he straightened, adjusted his hood, and tried to decide what to do next. His leg was trembling more with each step. He steeled himself against the pain and willed himself to keep upright. This was *his* city—*his* kingdom. He was not going down without a fight.

The conversation had confirmed that the guard who had followed him up the wall had been killed. And now he knew at least one Elder had guards acting as intelligencers and reporting on him.

But which Elder? And who would have set this kind of trap? Anyone looking to assassinate him surely could have found a better way to isolate him than to hope he saw a flicker in the lights and decided to fix it himself.

Yet the plan had worked and he *was* isolated and uncertain as to whether the guards he should trust with his life were working for him or for a foe. Suddenly, it seemed the only guard he felt certain he could trust was one who had admitted to spying on him. Unfortunately, Graylem was not here.

He needed to buy himself time and pretend to be unaware of the trap he'd sprung. As long as his enemies thought of him as a rabbit oblivious to the rock wolf stalking, ready to pounce, the element of surprise would be in his favor. Then, the next time they tried to strike, he could catch the perpetrator unaware.

Turning, Andreus limped down the street toward the noisy, run-down inn and almost smiled when a group of three men and two women burst out of the front door.

One of the men slid his arm around one of the girls and tried to kiss her only to get shoved back into a post for his effort. Andreus shivered in the cold even as sweat dripped down his back. He concentrated on walking without a limp. As he got closer, Andreus realized the girls were near to his age and the men only a few years older. All were dressed in well-made, sturdy cloaks lined with fur. Not noblemen and -women, but from wealthy families. Likely merchant class who were slumming in this part of town. Clearly, they must have been drinking for some time, because the men were swaying as they walked.

They were perfect.

As they turned in his direction, he asked, "Is the common room closed so early?"

"No. The only thing done early is our coin."

Andreus pushed off his hood and took a step forward so he now stood in the flickering light of one of the street torches. The black-haired girl standing next to the man who spoke gasped and dipped into a curtsy.

"King Andreus!"

He put a finger to his lips, pushed aside the pain that was making it harder for him to stay upright and gave his best flirtatious smile. "Shhh. I don't want to announce to everyone that I'm here. I've had little privacy in the past few weeks and am desperate to talk to normal people instead of those desperate for favors."

"Of course, Your Majesty." The girl with long, red hair returned his smile with a wide one of her own.

"How is the wine at this inn?"

"Not much worth the coin we spent on it, your lordship," said a dark-haired young man as he staggered to the side, grabbed onto his friend to steady himself, and almost took both of them to the ground. But that hadn't deterred him. "This inn won't even allow us to buy on credit. Not even when I told them who my father was.

They should have more respect for their betters."

Andreus reached into the bag tied to his belt and pulled out several gold coins. "Maybe you can buy superior wine and gain a bit more respect with this?" He carefully placed the coins into the hand of the man who seemed to be the most in control of his faculties. "The next round is on me."

The men let up a cheer. The girls appeared less enthusiastic as they watched their escorts head back into the inn with shouts for the best ale in the place.

"You are very generous, Your Majesty," the redhead said with a seductive smile.

"It is easy to be generous when I am looking at such charming and beautiful women." Andreus caught the girl's hand in his own and lifted it to his lips. He reached for the hand of the ebony-coiffed girl, who looked flustered as he performed the same gesture with her. Still holding the hands of both women, he said, "I have to get back to the palace, but would love to learn more about both of you and hear your thoughts on what is happening in the city. Perhaps the two of you would like to join me somewhere more private to take our refreshment?"

Without a backward glance at the inn or the young men they had spent the evening with, the women tucked their hands in the crooks of his arms and giggled as they walked with him.

Clenching his jaw, he asked the girls their names and about their families and laughed at something the redhead said that he knew was supposed to be charming. He was too busy fighting the pain and attempting to look as if everything was normal to pay real attention.

"Your Majesty!" The guards turned and stood at attention as he and his escorts came around the corner and headed toward them.

"We thought you were still up on the wall. Some of the guards . . . we thought there was a problem. One of your guards might have lost his footing, and we were worried when you did not return."

"I hope the guardsman did not cause himself harm," Andreus said as the image of the man's crumpled body flashed in his mind. "As for me, I found myself farther down the wall and opted to come down in that spot." Andreus laughed. "Which was lucky since I met these two lovely ladies in the process." He winked at the younger of the two guards who was gaping with surprise. "They will be returning to the Palace of Winds with me."

Getting on his horse was a struggle, but he managed, then instructed the two guardsmen he'd heard speaking earlier to give up their horses to the ladies. Walking was a small price to pay for their willingness to sell information about his movements to one of the Elders, but it would have to do—for now. If they had something more to do with the attack, Andreus would make sure their penalty was steeper.

When his party reached the steps that led to the gates of the Palace of Winds, Chief Elder Cestrum, Elder Ulrich, and Elder Jacobs came hurrying out of the entryway with several of the officers of the palace's guard just steps behind. All of them wore expressions of dismay.

"Your Majesty," Elder Jacobs called. "We are relieved to see you are safe!"

"Why wouldn't I be?" Andreus asked with a practiced smile while studying each of the faces in front of him, searching for signs of disappointment at his appearance.

"We heard rumors that there were disturbances in the city and that at least two members of the guard are dead." Elder Ulrich turned his good eye on Andreus—with concern or calculation? "We were just ordering additional guards to find you. Eden could not survive if something else happened . . ."

"I'm fine." Andreus laughed. "I'm sorry if you were worried, but the light was quickly repaired and I am going to celebrate by having dinner with my new friends. Let me know if you have news about what happened to the deceased guards." He turned and beckoned the girls forward and once again had them take his arms.

"Andreus may be King, but he has not changed," he thought he heard Elder Cestrum mutter.

Yes, I have, Andreus thought as he stiffly made his way inside. And he was going to make those who were attempting to take his throne pay. He only had to unmask them, and now with the help of his escorts he knew exactly where to begin.

9

"It's me," Garret's voice whispered in the night. A moment later, Carys heard a snap of twigs and saw the shadow of Garret navigating his mount into the grove of trees where Carys had been waiting for him to return from the town. As much as she'd wanted to join him, she could not risk being recognized. Not again.

He swung down from his mount. Leaves crunched under his feet as he crossed the space between them. "I'm sorry it took me so long. Naila's blacksmith was harder to track down than I'd hoped. But he did provide me with directions. We should reach the Village of Night in less than an hour if we start riding now."

The whispering grew louder in her mind at his words, as if warning her not to go. Or maybe it was her own fears that caused her to doubt this course of action. The Village of Night would provide not only answers about Imogen, but about Carys herself. Answers she wasn't sure she wanted.

In the two days since leaving Naila, Carys had tried not to think about the quiet voice in the corners of her mind that called to her—beckoned her to embrace the force that had torn a man apart. Disgust at what the wind had done warred with the desire to wield the power again.

"We will wait to make sure no one from the village followed you before we start out," she said. Perhaps Larkin would be waiting when they arrived. Carys had watched for her friend as they rode, but there had been no sign of her. Or Errik.

Here was another string of thought she wished to avoid. Errik had taken Larkin, and yet, despite this, every morning Carys woke and looked first for him.

Foolish. It had to be fear that made her yearn for the warmth and safety she had once believed his touch represented. And still . . .

"You don't have to be afraid of what you feel, Carys," Garret said quietly.

Carys jerked her eyes toward Garret, wondering what he saw on her face. "I have no idea what you're talking about."

"I've known you for a long time, Princess." Garret stepped closer. "I know your expressions as well as I know my own."

Did he? She shook her head. "I am merely impatient to get the answers I seek and return to Garden City."

"You are scared of the power growing stronger inside you with every passing day." Before she could deny it, he put a hand on her arm and looked into her eyes. "Carys, I've known what you are capable of for a long time. You tried to bury it inside you, but your power is too strong to be denied. You had to pretend with the others, but you don't ever have to pretend to be less than you are with me. I saw what you did at the farm."

The whispering in her head grew louder. Her heart pounded. "We have to get going."

His fingers tightened on her arm. "You have changed the subject each time I have tried to talk to you of your gifts. You are scared of who you are becoming, but you don't have to be."

"You know nothing!"

"I know more than you think. I want nothing more than to help you, but I can only do that if you realize you can trust me."

"Your uncle declared my mother's grief-filled words insane and removed her from succession. He unearthed an obscure law in order to see *you* seated on the Throne of Light, and at the same time you just happened to arrive back at the Palace of Winds. And you wish for me to set all that aside and simply trust you?"

"My uncle's choices are not my own, and I had good reason to leave the palace and to return when I did."

"So you say."

"Yes! So *I* say. I am not my uncle just as you are not your family. I am my own man just as you are your own woman."

Carys frowned. She had never been her own person. She had never been allowed to be. She was the other half of Andreus. The other side of his reflection, whether she wanted to be or not.

"Then tell me why I should trust you," she demanded as the whispers inside her head returned. "Tell me what you think you know about me and why you came back."

"I left for the same reason that I returned. Because of you." The wind pushed back the hood of his cloak, and his hair gleamed like dying embers in the moonlight.

The whispering stopped. Her stomach tightened. Garret turned and looked at her with a hunger in his eyes that made her step back. This wasn't the gentle admiration that Errik's gaze had expressed. It was a need to consume.

"Why?" she asked. "Because you want the throne? Because you think you'll gain it through me?"

"I have no need of the throne if I have you." Garret held her gaze, then raked a hand through his hair as he explained. "When I was ten my father sent me to court with my uncle and one instruction. I was to befriend the Crown Prince and become indispensable to him, which I was happy to do."

"Micah was glad to have your friendship, but that's not . . ."

Garret turned and walked toward the edge of the clearing. "As I was Micah's closest confidant, every lord and lady of Eden courted my friendship in hope that I would use my influence to sway his decisions once he ascended the throne. I was given gifts. The furs and jewels I passed along to your brother claiming they were for him, but there were gifts I held back."

"What kind of gifts?"

"Secrets." Garret slowly walked toward her. "The Palace of Winds is filled with them. Alliances being made to consolidate power. Plots to gain more land. Speculation about the midwife who went missing after you and Andreus were born. Whispers about meetings held in dark corners with members of the Council of Elders, or those who had purchased the allegiance of the Captain of the Guard. All things I used to help Micah gain the fear and respect of those in the Palace of Winds even as I held back the most important things for myself. After all, your brother was my friend, but I was not foolish enough to think he would not turn against me if the opportunity called for it. That is the way of court and I was happy with that until a few years ago when I was approached by a minor nobleman looking for support in a land dispute with a much more powerful lord. For my assistance, I was given the gift of a woman's satchel."

"I don't understand what this has to do with why you are here with me now."

Garret continued as if she hadn't spoken. "The man who gave it to me said it belonged to one of your father's mistresses who disappeared years ago."

The idea of her father's infidelity was not shocking. Carys had heard whispers about the women who visited the King's private quarters. Some members of court spoke loudly of it when Carys was among them, no doubt to see what the brooding princess would say or do. She said nothing. She did nothing. As far as she was concerned, as long as her father was occupied, he would have less time to consider Andreus, to puzzle out his curse. "Which mistress?" she asked. There had been many. No doubt more than even she knew about.

"It was Lady Diandra of Vigoral Keep," Garret said quietly. Before Carys could react, he added, "She was my uncle's wife—my aunt. She went missing when I was four years old. My only memory of her is of her drawing pictures for me when she and my uncle came to visit our keep. She was a skilled artist."

Garret walked over to his horse and reached into one of the saddlebags. "I found a notebook inside with pictures drawn by her hand and notes that made little sense. There was nothing about her affair with the King or anything that could give me additional leverage so I put the book to the side. Then the wind tunnel struck the palace and I pulled the book out again."

There was the now-familiar sound of flint striking rock, the crackle of flame, and when Garret turned he was holding a lit torch in one hand and a small leather-bound book in the other.

He opened to a page marked with a blue ribbon, crossed the distance between them, and held the book out to her. "My aunt had drawn this."

The drawing took up both pages. A wind tunnel. It was drawn with skill that took Carys's breath away. Beneath the tunnel, a man cowered. The man's face wasn't visible, but there was no mistaking the distinct star atop the staff he clutched in his hands. It was the same staff that Seer Kheldin—the seer who predicted that either she or her twin would be cursed and destroy the kingdom—had never been without. He had had that staff when the wind tunnel appeared in the sky.

"Years before the tunnel hit, my aunt knew what would come and drew it."

"Your aunt was a seer." Carys looked up from the book. "I still don't understand . . ."

"Look at the bottom corner of the page."

Garret held the torch higher, illuminating the section of parchment that had previously been obscured by shadows. And Carys gasped. The whispers in her head grew louder as she studied the miniature girl, hair streaming behind her, crown perfectly placed atop her head. The girl's arms were stretched out to the wind—palms up. And on each outstretched hand was a tiny wind tunnel that matched the one in the sky.

The picture was of her.

The image was small and she was younger in the drawing than she was now, but there was no doubt the face was the one she had seen every day in the mirror—although rarely did she smile the way the girl was smiling here.

Carys had been on the battlements when the wind tunnel struck. She had followed Seer Kheldin to watch him attempt to call the wind that had been quiet for weeks. She saw the tunnel appear seconds before it struck one of the palace's towers. The next thing she remembered was waking up with bandages on her head and her mother placing a small red bottle in her hands—to help with the pain.

"After I saw this picture, I understood what had happened on the battlements. I understood the power you held and how you could conquer the *world* in the name of Eden. And then I found this." Garret flipped to the back page and held the torch high.

The page had water stains on it, but the wall surrounding Garden City was still recognizable as was the woman standing atop it. The girl had grown up. He hair hung just beneath her ears. The crown atop her head was larger than before—and appeared to weigh heavy on the frame of the one wearing it. On one side of the image was the blackness of night. On the other was light. She still held her palms out, but this time she was holding the wind in one hand and the orb in the other.

"My aunt foresaw your power before you were born. She knew the wind tunnel that crushed the turret windmill and almost destroyed the palace. She saw that you would hold the fate of Eden in your hands."

"So you returned because you wanted the power you thought you had gained by being close to Micah."

"No." Garret extinguished the torch on the wet ground, and darkness rushed into the space the light once possessed. "I am attracted to power. I won't pretend otherwise. In Bisog, strength and power are revered. And there is something seductive about a person who holds the lives of everyone in a kingdom in his . . ." Garret closed the book she held and put his warm hands on either side of hers. "Or *her* hands. But you were not embracing your power. That remedy—those Tears of Midnight were keeping you from becoming the woman you were meant to be. You were weak, even though the kingdom needed you to be strong, and I knew you would require someone at your side to help you gain that strength."

Pressed between the book and Garret's hands, Carys's fingers were hot. Her heart raced as she looked at the man she had felt a girl's attraction to. Only she wasn't a girl anymore. "Is that why you left?" she scoffed. "Because I was weak and you were disappointed?"

"I was the weak one. I didn't trust you to turn away from the Tears of Midnight on your own, and there were none around you who could help you. Only your brother discovered my plan. He and Oben were waiting for me when I snuck into your chamber intent on stealing you away."

"You—tried to *kidnap* me?" How had she not known?

"Your brother was furious at my betrayal. He thought I had feigned my affection for him because I wanted you. Because I wanted to marry you and to move up a place in the line of succession. He gave me a choice—to leave the palace, or be thrown in the North Tower for treason. So I left, but I didn't abandon you. I sought out those who could teach me about the power inside you so that when the time came I could impart that wisdom to you."

There was only one place he could have learned what he claimed. "You've been to the Village of Night?" She pulled her hands back. "You've been lying about not knowing how to get there?"

"I have been to the Village of the Night, the place of the seers, but last time I came from the north and I came with a guide. I could not be certain I could find my way from the east in the time you needed. But," he continued quickly, "my time there was well spent. I learned you must give yourself entirely to your emotions. The more you feel, the more power the wind will have when it strikes."

She remembered the surge of joy that ran through her when the man was torn apart by the wind. The whispers grew louder—yearning for her to release them again. Looking into Garret's face, with his eyes shining with excitement, she realized a small, terrible part of her wanted to give in. She wanted to feel that power, to let the world see the hurt she could inflict on those who wished her harm.

The trees around her rustled.

Fear and anger and bitterness and desire for revenge churned. The wind swirled in her mind. She saw the Hall of Virtues—her brother seated upon the throne. The air gusted in the Hall. The crown flew from her brother's head as his neck snapped.

"No. I can't." She shook her head. This wasn't what she wanted. *Was it?*

"You don't have to be afraid," Garret insisted. "I am here to guide you. Together we will reclaim your throne and you will become the most powerful Queen Eden has known."

His voice rang with conviction that spoke to something deep inside her. The Council would listen to Garret. He would help her pave the way to taking back her kingdom. He would help her destroy her enemies.

"Andreus betrayed you, but I never will." Garret reached out his hand. "There is power in being needed by someone who appears to need no one. That is the power that I have sought all my life. You will stand for the kingdom and I will stand for *you*."

The wind swirled as she stepped forward and reached out to take Garret's hand in hers. The Council would accept her with Garret at her side. He'd help her push the limits of her power and together . . .

Errik's smile flashed in her mind and the air went still as she pulled back her hand. "I can't."

Garret's eyes narrowed. "Is it because of him?" he demanded. "Errik? Because you have feelings for him?"

"I don't know," she said truthfully.

"Errik betrayed you. He took Larkin—your closest friend. Right now, he could be using her against you, and when he and the Bastians are done, they will kill her. And yet you still trust him over me?"

"No." She didn't. Garret was right. Errik had betrayed her. He had taken Larkin in the middle of the night with no explanation. He didn't deserve her trust. But Garret seemed to. His eyes were hot on hers as she said, "I am trying. I simply need time."

Garret looked off in the distance, beyond the trees and nodded. "We will ride to the Village of Night. We will get the information you seek, and I promise that by the time we get back to the Palace of Winds, you will trust me." He held up the book. "And then, we will be unstoppable."

Unstoppable.

She didn't need his assistance, but Garret held her horse steady as she mounted, and stayed close to her side as they rode through the trees to the southwest. Garret's final words echoed in her mind, mixing with the ever-present whispers of the wind and the emotions that were so quick to bubble to the surface now.

The Tears of Midnight had dampened her emotions. Now, each time anger flared, Carys wanted to lose herself in her rage's white-hot embrace. Just as she used to lose herself in the Tears of Midnight. Perhaps that was the reason she could not trust herself to surrender to the emotions inside her and to Garret's need for her trust.

Trust Garret? Trust Errik? After her brother's betrayal, trusting anyone seemed a fool's errand.

She thought of Andreus, and the murmur of the wind grew inside her head. He had needed her. He had taken her entire life and she had given it to him because his life was just as important to her as her own.

Had he ever felt the same?

She had believed he had. Each time he teased her from a bad mood or stood up for her when their mother was harsh, Carys had felt the tie between them strengthen. Yet at the first real test of his love, Andreus snapped the connection between them. They were no longer reflections of each other. He wanted to shine on his own.

The wind howled around her. The anger that always seemed to be smoldering burst into flame. The wind called for her to unleash everything she'd always had to keep buried inside.

Garret wanted her to give in to that anger—to be a weapon.

But her mother had said she was meant to be a shield.

Deep inside, she feared that without her twin she was nothing.

She refused to be nothing.

They reached the stream the blacksmith had directed Garret to look for and headed west toward what had for hundreds of years been the home and training grounds for the Guild of the seers. Carys could feel Garret's resolve strengthen as they rode toward a small hill in the distance. It grew taller with each step the horses took. Anxiety and anticipation churned—the wind grew louder with every passing league.

They reached and rode around a tall stone wall that circled the hill. Another wall like the one around Garden City.

"The blacksmith said if we follow the wall, we will eventually come to the entryway," Garret said.

A bell chimed from somewhere in the dark. It sounded as if it was coming from atop the hill.

They were here. Finally she would get the answers about Imogen she craved, and those about herself that she feared.

Carys thought she could hear muted voices as they rode through the night. Finally, she spotted a stone archway emerging from the shadows and pointed. Garret nodded and they walked their horses toward it. Carys pulled her hood up and sank into the folds of her cloak. There were no torches to light the way or mark the entrance, but as soon as they rode under the arch, several people dressed all in white stepped out of the shadows.

"My Lords, welcome to the Village of Night." A dark-haired woman in a white cloak walked toward them, the bottom of her dress fluttering in the chilled breeze. "All who seek are welcome, but weapons are not allowed beyond this point. If you wish to enter, you must leave your steel and bows here along with your horses where the guardians will see they are safe and well-tended until your time of seeking has come to an end."

Garret looked at her, his eyebrow raised in question. Surrendering their weapons was the last thing she wanted to do, but she also could not protest without revealing that she was not a lord, but a lady. Nodding to Garret, Carys pulled the bow and quiver of arrows from her pack, slid down to the ground, and silently handed them to the woman. Garret sighed, dismounted, and followed suit by passing over his long sword with a frown. The small man who took the weapon seemed unfazed by the weight.

Carys reached into her pack and pulled out a knife she took from the deserting soldiers but did not reach for her stilettos.

"Without our weapons, we will not be able to defend ourselves if there is an attack," Garret said.

"If you do not intend harm, harm will not befall you," a broad-shouldered man said. "What do you seek inside these gates?"

"Understanding," Garret said smoothly so Carys would not have to answer.

"Understanding is not easily come by. It can only be found when the heart and the mind are willing to surrender to truth." The woman smiled. "The calling ceremony has just ended. If you follow the path up the hill to the stone circle at the top you will find food and maybe, my *Lords* . . ." She paused and turned to Carys. "You will also find the understanding that you seek."

She knew. How long before everyone realized exactly who she was? The seers were supposed to see the future in the stars. Had they seen her arrival? Did they know what was still to come? Could they really help her defeat those who would tear her brother and the rest of Eden down?

They followed the dirt path as it wound through what appeared to be small, squat, lifeless dwellings until they reached the base of the hillside. There the path began to glow with a pale, ghostly green light.

"Fungus," Carys whispered. The entire path was lined with mushrooms that gave off the faint, otherworldly glow. The light cast by the mushrooms wasn't bright, but enough to help guide her steps as they climbed the path to the stone circle atop the hill.

Several villagers dressed in white cloaks were coming out of the circle as they reached the top and stepped through the archway into what looked to be a feast. Mushrooms glowed here in the large stone space. Stars winked from the sky above, and everywhere there were men and women dressed in white eating food from the tables in the center of the circle and talking in hushed voices.

Heads turned their way. One by one conversation in the circle stopped and everything went quiet. Carys looked for Larkin, hoping her friend had made it here. She saw someone move near the side of the wall. Thought she saw a flash of Larkin's dark hair before a man with a beard approached. He lowered his hood, and the moonlight gleamed off his scalp as he nodded to her and Garret. "Welcome to the Village of Night. We have been expecting you."

"Did you see our arrival in the stars?" Carys asked.

"The stars didn't tell them you would be coming," a voice snapped from behind her.

Carys spun around.

Several men wearing mail shirts and the familiar blue-and-yellow cloaks that marked them as members of Eden's guard had come to stand in the archway blocking any escape. Captain Monteros, head of Eden's guard, strode through the crowd in front of them.

Smiling at Carys, he placed his hand on the pommel of his sword—a sword he wasn't supposed to be carrying in the Village of Night. "The stars had no idea you were coming. But I did."

10

Andreus closed the door to his rooms behind him, stumbled, and fell to his knees. Without the inadvertent support of his female companions who were currently waiting for him in the Hall of Virtues, he had barely made it on his injured leg back to his rooms.

Max jumped out of a chair near the fire and bolted toward Andreus. "The Xhelozi! Did they attack? Should I get Madame Jillian? I know you don't want me to be in the palace halls, but I can be quick. I promise."

For the past several days since Max had been thrown over the battlements, Andreus had insisted that Max stay confined to these rooms. Something Max had complained about before Andreus went on the tour of the lights.

"No, Max," Andreus said between clenched teeth. He sat on the ground and stretched his injured leg out in front of him. He forced himself to take several low breaths to ease the tightening of his chest. "The lights are all working. I put too much stress on my leg before it was healed," he said, careful not to mention how he had stressed it. Max was spirited and loyal, but he couldn't keep a secret no matter how hard he tried. "And let's not bother Madame Jillian. You know how she gets when she learns one of her patients has disobeyed her instructions."

Max nodded with vigor. "When Madame Jillian is mad, she's the doom."

"After dealing with the Council, I've had enough doom for one day." Andreus forced a smile. Sweat dripped down his back. His heart beat hard. He needed time alone, but the thought of sending Max out of his rooms to roam the palace halls gripped Andreus's stomach.

Andreus was almost certain Max was attacked as a diversion. Someone had simply needed to escape the battlements without anyone learning of his identity, and Max had gotten in his way.

He looked at the boy—his large brown eyes. His unruly curls that had grown long and tangled since the time Andreus had found him—dying on a patch of dirt. He'd seen himself in the boy, and what he might have been had his sister not done everything to shield his own curse from the world.

Unfortunately, Andreus didn't have the luxury of shielding Max the way Carys had shielded him. Not anymore. As King, he had to allow those who served him to take the risks he could not, and Max was one ally that Andreus was certain could be trusted.

Pulling the knife from his belt, Andreus held it out to Max and said, "I need you to go to the Queen's rooms and speak to Chamberlain Oben. Ask him for some of my mother's special tea." It would relax Andreus's muscles and dull a bit of the pain. "Bring it back here. Once you have done that, I want you to find Graylem. He said he was assigned to the stables tonight. Show my seal to his captain then bring Graylem back here with you. Keep to the servants' hallways whenever possible, and do not hesitate to use this knife if you think you are in danger."

"Yes, King Andreus!" With wide, excited eyes, Max took the dagger from Andreus, gave a hasty bow, and bolted toward the door. "I'll be back soon."

Andreus was counting on that.

As soon as the door closed behind the boy, Andreus gritted his teeth. He pushed himself up to his feet, taking care to keep most of the weight off his leg. He limped to the washbasin in the bedroom, unfastened his pants, and sat down to study how badly he had reinjured the wound.

The cagelike brace Madame Jillian had directed the castle blacksmith to fashion for him had broken in several places. It must have happened when he jumped from the wall into the cart of hay. Two metal strips that were supposed to help provide support when Andreus walked had snapped and scraped deep gashes beneath his knee.

The good news was that only one of the healing wounds made by the Xhelozi claws had reopened. Blood and a milky-white ooze were weeping from the injury.

He removed the brace and tossed it into the corner. Then he carefully cleaned away the blood from his leg and tightly wound a cloth bandage around the wounds. His leg still throbbed, but it was better, and with the cane Madame Jillian had instructed him to use just after the end of the Trials, he was able to wash. He changed into fitted brown trousers and a deep blue shirt with gold embroidery on the high collar and tight cuffs. By the time Max returned with the pot of the Queen's tea and Graylem, Andreus had firmed up the plan he'd concocted on the ride back to the Palace of Winds.

"There are clothes laid out for you. Change into them and leave your uniform on the wooden chest at the foot of the bed," Andreus instructed Graylem. The guard's face looked pale and his eyes fearful as he hovered near the door as still as a statue.

"Did you hear me?" Andreus asked.

Graylem swallowed hard. "Yes, Your Majesty. I'm sorry, Your Majesty." Then he hurried across the room, tripping twice on the carpet.

"Max," Andreus said, taking the pot of his mother's brew from the boy. "Could you help him before he hurts himself?"

Max grinned and bolted across the room to where Graylem was struggling to unfasten his breastplate. The guard's actions weren't exactly inspiring confidence in his abilities to help carry out Andreus's plan. But Andreus only had to look at Max to remember the guard's quick reflexes and strong grip on the battlements. They had saved the boy's life.

The guard might be untried, but underneath the shaking hands and freckled face were nerves of steel. Andreus just hoped they would show themselves again tonight.

As Max helped the guard into black trousers that were an inch too short in the legs and a bit baggy in the waist, Andreus limped to the serving table and poured his mother's tea into an ale stein. The familiar brew smelled of mint and lemon and tasted flowery with a hint of bitterness. He downed the entire mug and poured himself another. The drink would dull his reflexes a bit, but it was a risk he was going to shoulder since it was the only way to take advantage of the events of the day. And it was unlikely that those who killed his brother and father would wait for him to feel better before striking again.

The more time that passed, the more he was certain his enemies would strike soon. Unless he struck them first.

He downed the last of his mother's tea, rolled out his shoulders, and bent his knees. From experience he knew the tea would continue to work its magic for the next hour or two, smoothing the edges off his pain and the anger that was simmering deep in his gut.

"You have to let me brush your hair," Max complained, and Andreus turned to see the boy standing on the four-poster bed attacking Graylem's golden, almost orange hair with fervor.

"He looks fine," Andreus said, gaining a weak smile of gratitude from his unwitting ally. In the crisp white silk shirt and velvet, midnight blue vest, Graylem looked like a member of the court. "No one will mistake him for a guardsman in his current attire. You did a great job, Max."

Max frowned at the brush, then shrugged and gave Andreus a grin. "Can I have an apple tart?"

"You can have one *after* Graylem and I finish entertaining our guests for the night," Andreus agreed. "I want you to run one errand for me once we leave and then you need to stay out of sight until I return."

"Yes, Your Majesty." Max sighed, but he paid rapt attention to Andreus's instructions before asking, "If I do well, can I have *two* apple tarts?"

"Graylem," Andreus said, flexing his knees. "Let's go."

Andreus led Graylem into a narrow servants' hallway lit by only a single torch and quietly said, "I am counting on the loyalty you spoke of."

"Of course I'm loyal, Your Majesty," Graylem stammered. "I have taken an oath to protect . . ."

"Oaths are easily broken," Andreus said. "All members of the Council of Elders had taken an oath of fealty to my father and look how well that worked out. *You* claimed to be loyal to my sister."

Graylem straightened his spine. "I was loyal to her, Your Majesty. Just as she was loyal to you."

A knot formed deep in Andreus's stomach. Doubt tugged at him. Had his feelings for Imogen clouded his thinking? If so . . . The knot tightened.

"My sister is no longer here." He swallowed the bitter taste of those words. "I am, and I need your aid to find those who are plotting against Eden from inside this palace. As your King, I am asking for your oath of loyalty to *me*."

Graylem didn't hesitate for a beat before saying, "You have it, Your Majesty. Whatever the danger, I am honored to prove myself."

"Good," Andreus said, starting down the hall again. "There are questions that must be answered tonight, and the Council and their intelligencers cannot know I am asking them. You will distract them and be my shield, and we'd better hurry or we might face danger far sooner than I intend. There are two women in one of the Hall of Virtues antechambers who are expecting us."

"We are going to speak with women, Your Majesty? How is that dangerous?"

Andreus laughed at the confusion in the guard's voice. "Trust me, Graylem. And in my experience, there is one thing all women have in common. They don't like to be kept waiting."

The Hall of Virtues flickered with hundreds of candles. The white stone floors and columns reflected the light, making the towering white-and-gold hall radiate with a kind of warmth. A long table flanked by two servants was set with food and wine. It had been placed not far from the dais.

Two ladies jumped to their feet as Andreus and Graylem crossed the glistening floor and both dropped into curtsies. Andreus nodded and smiled, but his attention was focused on the throne atop the dais. The earliest memory he had was of his father seated on that throne. The light would gleam off the ornate gold arms and the inset sapphires glistening behind his father's head. He had looked untouchable atop the dais, gazing down at those who bowed before him.

Andreus remembered thinking the throne was magic. That it made the person seated on it perfect—powerful. Unbeatable. That night, Andreus's curse landed him in bed. Carys slept next to him, her hand in his as he stared at the ceiling holding his chest, thinking that if only he could sit on the throne the curse would go away.

In the past two weeks, Andreus had learned there was nothing magic about the ornate seat. It was hard and flat and impossible to sit upon with any hint of comfort.

He had come through so much, and still he was denied the thing he most wanted.

"Your Majesty," Graylem asked quietly. "Is something wrong?"

Andreus looked at the throne one last time as it glowed in the candlelight appearing almost to be lit from within—looking once again as if it were the answer to all his problems.

But looks were deceiving, and he had believed in deceptive appearances for too long. It was time to find out the uncomfortable truths that lay beneath the light and virtues of his kingdom.

Out of the corner of his eye, he saw a figure standing deep in the shadows of one of the Hall's antechambers. The figure shifted, and for a moment Andreus caught a glimpse of a scarred eye and a hairless scalp. Elder Ulrich. At least one of the Council was watching.

Good. Let them.

Turning his back on the throne, he smiled at the two girls looking nervous next to the banquet table. "With such lovely guests, what could be wrong?"

Andreus flattered the girls. He insisted Graylem sit next to the dark-haired one, and shook his head when Graylem started to correct her when she called him *my lord*.

"Lord Graylem's title is still quite new," Andreus said, looking over at the surprised face of his guard. "It was given to him because of service and sacrifice on behalf of my family and myself. I believe that rewards should not be saved for those who inherited their titles, but for those who have shown loyalty to the Seven Virtues of Eden."

The girl next to Graylem took his arm and said something flirtatious.

The Queen's tea smoothed away Andreus's aches, but not the impatience he felt as he laughed and flattered and kissed the redhead's hand and acted as if he had not a care in the world. Several times he caught sight of boys wearing the black attire that distinguished them as pages for the Council of Elders hovering in the antechamber doorways or near the entrance to the Hall. Each stayed for several minutes before racing off to make their report that the King was back to his old ways. That he was distracted. That he had completely forgotten that the orb was still glowing atop the highest tower, despite his commands to the opposite, and was oblivious to any plot that had been enacted against him tonight.

The easiest way to gain ground on an enemy was to make sure

they were looking in a different direction when you advanced. It was time to see if his plan worked.

Pushing back from the table, he stood and held his hand out to Demitria, the redhead with the devastating smile who claimed her father was a jewel master. Perhaps he was. To Andreus, her family didn't matter.

He turned Demitria's hand over in his, placed a lingering kiss on her palm, and looked up into her eyes. "Would you care to see the orb from the battlements?" he asked. "It might be a bit cold outside, but I think we can find a way to keep ourselves warm. Don't you?"

"The cold won't bother us at all, Your Majesty."

Elder Cestrum stepped through the main doors of the Hall as the four of them were heading out. The Chief Elder stroked his short, white beard with his iron claw. His eyes swept over Graylem and the two girls before settling on Andreus. "Your Majesty," he said with barely a hint of a bow. "If I might have a word?"

"The three of you go ahead," Andreus said smoothly. Elder Cestrum had not shown any recognition of the guard disguised as a noble, and Andreus wanted Graylem gone before that changed. "I will join you in a few minutes."

Graylem didn't have to be told twice. He held his arms out to the two ladies and escorted them from the hall. When they disappeared through the doors, the Chief Elder said, "Your Majesty, you should not have invited these women to the Hall of Virtues. Even your father would not have been this brazen with his mistress."

"Would you prefer I invited them into my bedroom?" Andreus asked.

"I would prefer they not be here at all. I am certain you have been warned. There are those using your past actions to sow seeds of dissent. Your actions tonight will cause those seeds to grow. Your father understood that he . . ."

"My father is dead." The words echoed in the Hall. "He planted his own seeds in this kingdom and what grew out of those seeds killed him."

"Adderton soldiers killed your father and brother."

According to his mother that was not the truth. But the Chief Elder said the words with conviction. If he knew the real reasons and people behind the King's death, he gave no sign of it.

"My father could have ended the war. He chose not to. And he chose to go to the southern border to encourage Eden's fighting men himself."

The Council had objected. Yet, one of them must have rejoiced in the decision even as he voiced the group's concern about the King's safety.

"Your father did what he thought needed to be done."

"And something I would never do," Andreus said. "I have tried to fill my father's shoes in ways that you would prefer, but I find they are a poor fit. Perhaps they will be better tomorrow, but for tonight I intend to be myself."

He turned, put too much weight on his injured leg, and caught his balance. It all happened in a blink of an eye, but Elder Cestrum noticed. "Your Majesty, I thought Madame Jillian said your leg was healing. You did not appear to have any problems during the inspection. Did something happen after you went back to reexamine one of the lights? Two guards are dead. We have been told they lost their balance atop the wall and that you suddenly appeared from an unexpected direction. Naturally, the Council is concerned by all of this."

"You're also concerned about the ladies I appeared with," Andreus quipped. Elder Cestrum studied him. His eyes narrowed. The iron-claw hand twitching at his side. If Andreus trusted the man's motives, he would explain how he fled for his life and that the guards died in the protection of their King. Instead, he said, "When I fixed the loose connection, the light went dark and then flared. I fear the guards must have been blinded in that moment and lost their balance. Please make sure their families are compensated for their loss. And now, I don't want to keep my guests waiting." Andreus winked, and reveled in Elder Cestrum's glower before he headed out of the hall to the staircase that would lead him to the battlements.

He sent up a small prayer of thanks to the Gods for his mother's tea as he climbed the low-lit staircase. The aggravated wounds hurt, but the pain was dulled enough that he would be able to continue with the rest of his plans.

Or maybe he had spoken too soon.

Andreus grabbed the wall as he wobbled and almost lost his footing. He started to curse the low light for his misstep, then remembered which stairwell he was in and what step he was on. It was *their* step. Carys's and his. The already-loose step that Carys pried away so the two of them could pass messages without being seen. Carys had not been able to be on the battlements with him all the time—not without others noticing her presence and wondering why she felt such a need to watch her twin.

In the initial days, the steps had been a good way for Andreus to let her know what windmill he was working on in case she wanted to catch a quick glimpse of him or station herself somewhere nearby. After a while, they came up with other ideas, and the step had fallen out of use. Until the Trials of Succession, when his sister suggested they use the old hiding place to communicate since they would need people to believe they were true combatants for the throne.

He had never sent his sister a message, though. And he never checked the step to see if Carys had tried to communicate with him. Not after he learned that his sister was tied to the ones who attempted to assassinate him on the tournament grounds.

Imogen's face, when she told him of his sister's connection to the attack, had been so filled with love. She had been so worried that Carys would do absolutely *anything* to gain the throne that he had believed it, too.

Now both women were gone.

He leaned his head against the cold stone wall in shame as dark as the shadows wrapped around him.

If Imogen had not come to him the night of his father's and brother's deaths and stood by his side during the Trials, would his distrust in Carys have spung up and grown the way it did? Would he have checked under this step? Worked together with her to bring an end to the insanity of the Trials?

He had wanted Imogen. He had wanted the crown. Given the chance to have both, Andreus had refused to believe the best in his sister. He had chosen to believe her dark and greedy and filled with betrayal. But now he had to wonder if when he looked at her he had only been seeing his own reflection.

Slowly, Andreus knelt down and pulled a dagger from his belt. He wedged the blade under the lose step, pried the heavy brick up, and felt underneath it. There was nothing there. Just cold damp stone and sand. It had been foolish to think Carys had left something for him. Still, he had . . .

The side of his hand brushed against something. His fingers

dug deep into the crevice beneath the rock and slid out a bit of parchment.

The parchment was folded and the edges torn. Andreus knew it had probably been there for years—from the time that he and Carys had first discovered the step. Still, he slipped the torch into a holder on the wall and unfolded the piece of his sister that she had left behind, and read the words that stopped his heart.

Dreus—you have not won. Be ready. I will return.

11

"What a delightful surprise to see you alive, Princess!" Carys's muscles coiled as the Captain of Eden's Guard strode forward. "I am sure the Council will be interested in knowing of your health! And that you are here as well, Lord Garret. I will be well rewarded by the new King when I return you both to the Palace of Winds."

"King Andreus might surprise you," Garret said as Carys reached under the cloak for the hilts of her stilettos.

Captain Monteros smiled. The metal of his sword scraped against the scabbard as he pulled it free. "I wasn't talking about Andreus. Guards, seize them!"

"You promised no violence if you were allowed to keep your weapon." The seer who had greeted them stepped in front the captain with his hands raised as the other guards raced forward.

"Out of my way!" Captain Monteros shoved the seer to the side and raised his blade. Garret lunged for the captain's arm. Captain Monteros turned and jammed his elbow in Garret's face. There was a sickening crunch as Carys pulled her stilettos free and looked for a way out. Four other guardsmen advanced. Two had knives. The others, cudgels.

There was only one exit to the round space lined with stone. She had to go through the guardsmen to get out the way she came in. There were too many attackers for her to throw her blades. Once she threw one, she might not be able to get it back.

The wind inside the circle began to swirl. Cloaks fluttered.

The men in yellow and blue approached as those in white raced for the exit behind them. Garret clambered to his feet.

A dark-bearded guard lunged, and Carys slashed with her blade. Sharp metal sliced through fabric and flesh. The guardsman dropped his knife as she spun toward the next.

A cudgel flew at her head. She flung herself to the side, felt the whoosh of air as the weapon missed cracking against her face and hit the ground. Flipping over, she scrambled back as the second guardsman with a long, hooked knife slashed at her.

"What are you doing?" Garret yelled. "This isn't what I agreed to. This isn't what my uncle and I ordered."

Ordered?

Carys leaped to her feet, turned, and ran directly at the guardsman with the hooked blade. Surprise made him pause for just a second. A second was all she needed to jab her own blade into the base of his throat. The man crumbled, and his hooked weapon clattered to the ground.

"I have new orders." Monteros spat the words.

Blood bubbled as she yanked the stiletto out. The man fell to his knees, and she whirled toward the next attacker who shoved a man in a white cloak to the side and began to advance on her.

"Garret! What is happening?" she yelled, parrying the guardsman's knife with her blade. She ducked under his other arm as he tried to grab her, spun, and buried the stiletto deep in the man's thigh.

The guardsman growled. She yanked the stiletto out and darted back as the man's dagger clipped her arm.

Pain flared.

The wind roared.

"Kill her!" Captain Monteros yelled, swinging his blade at Garret.

Garret dove for the hooked blade that had fallen from her attacker's hand, sprang to his feet, and yelled, "Carys, there will be more of them coming."

"How do you know that?"

"It doesn't matter. You have to run!"

More.

Garret knew there were others, just as he knew Captain Monteros was going to be here.

Carys clenched her blades tight.

He said he wanted to be trusted.

She had vowed to try. Only, he could not be trusted at all.

Anger burned hot in her chest and bubbled upward, desperate to be set free.

People shouted.

The first guard she injured lurched toward her. Garret blocked the captain's broadsword with the long, hooked blade. Metal clanged. The guard charged her. The rage inside her grew. Hotter. Wilder. The whispers became howls blocking out all other sounds.

She lifted her stiletto, but before she could release it, the guard flew back. The knife he had been holding spun from his hand and buried itself in the cheek of a woman cowering against the edge of the stone circle.

Gods, no.

Carys stumbled back. Horror bloomed as bright as the blood that dripped from the woman's wound and stained her white cloak.

That's not what I meant to do, she thought. *That's not what I wanted.*

The wind howled. Garret dodged another attack, and the force of the wind brought him to his knees. He struggled to get back to his feet and turned toward Carys. The wind filled her thoughts. Her heart slammed painfully in her chest as he mouthed the word *Run.*

Carys ran to the entrance and looked down the hill. There were at least a dozen more guardsmen with torches climbing the incline toward her. She looked back into the center of the stone circle. Garret raked the hooked knife along the back of a guardsman's thigh, sending the now crippled man to the ground. He swung back at Captain Monteros, who was once again climbing to his feet. Whatever treachery he had committed, Garret was fighting with her—for her. She had to help.

She lifted her blade as a hand latched on to her arm.

"You must come with me, now," a woman in a dark cloak yelled to her. As the cloak flapped in the gusts of air, Carys could see hints of the white dress that marked her as a seer. "I know why you're here. I can give you what you seek."

The dozen other guardsmen continued to climb the hill as those in white descended to the safety of the town below. Garret was still fighting the Captain of the Guard and the wind.

"He will only survive if you come now."

That decided it.

Hating herself for fleeing, Carys turned and bolted out of the stone circle. She followed the woman around the outside edge of the curved wall as the wind pushed them both off balance. It seemed to be growing in strength.

The woman yelled back, "Think of something that calms you."

Calms her?

Shouts rang out. Metal clashing against metal rang in the night.

More men with weapons were coming to kill her, and this woman wanted her calm?

"Think of something that makes you feel safe," the woman shouted. She turned and headed down a steep decline toward a group of squat evergreen trees. They bent in the wind that only seemed to be gaining strength. "Try! You must try!"

The hood of her cloak slipped from her head. Carys tightened her grip on the stilettos and looked back in the direction they'd come from. Her feet itched to stop—to quit running from the fight as she had been doing since leaving the Palace of Winds. To stop hiding and give in to her need to punish those who claimed to care for her and yet decided to betray her. First Andreus. Now maybe Garret. She needed to know what he had done.

The whispers howled.

A tree snapped. Screams floated up from the village. A tunnel of air appeared in the sky and was descending. The anger in the tunnel rang in her head. Filled her heart. Burned inside her gut.

"The underground passages," she yelled. She thought about the comfort of being alone with her twin where no one in the Palace of Winds could find them. It was the only time she could roam far from him and still be certain he was safe. It was the time when the need to be skilled enough to defend him was turned into a game. When she first decided to teach herself to throw knives, Andreus ducked whenever she lifted her hand and kept doing it long after she could hit everything she aimed at because he knew it would make her laugh.

In the tunnels, they laughed. They also sat in the quiet, happy to have only each other for company.

They had been a team.

"Very good!" the woman in front of her yelled. "Now hurry."

The whispers faded in her mind, and Carys realized the trees were no longer bending as if ready to snap. Instead the branches were swaying to a gentle breeze.

Carys's foot slipped on some loose rocks, and she half slid down the steep hillside. Her stomach swooped as she fought to stay upright.

"This way," the woman said, pointing to a small path at the bottom of the hill. It snaked around the rocky base and disappeared into a group of tall trees. Carys shivered in the icy air and followed, grateful that the snows had not yet come to this part of the kingdom. There were no footsteps to follow. They needed only to stay out of sight.

Finally, they reached a small grove of trees in the center of which was a small wooden cabin. It was the only dwelling on this side of the hill. In the distance beyond the trees, Carys could see the dark shadow of the wall she and Garret had followed to the entrance. The one that surrounded the hillside and the land of the seers.

The woman held the door open for Carys, then shut the door behind her, plunging them into a black void. There was the click of flint and metal, a flash, and the warm glow of candlelight lit the space.

The woman quickly lit a number of candles scattered throughout the room, which was barely more than functional, with a narrow wooden table and two low-backed chairs to Carys's right, a small cot and a chest on the far side, and a small fireplace on the wall between. In the center of the cot was a pair of blue-and-silver beaded slippers, which seemed far too small for the tall woman moving toward the hearth. Wood was carefully laid for a fire that started quickly when the woman touched the kindling with a candle's flame.

"Few know of this place. Even still, we won't be able to stay long." The woman removed her cloak and shook out her short cap of golden-red hair as she hung the dark garment on a peg near the door. "I am Kiara."

The woman sat, then nodded for Carys to take the chair closest to the hearth.

Carys stayed standing, watching the door, stiletto still in her hand. "How did you know I would be here? How did the Captain of Eden's Guard know?"

"The stars told me you would come as would the lord who rode into the Village with you. He sought to gain your trust with what he felt would be a harmless ruse. He met them in the town and directed them here so that he could fight for you. He did not know the captain had sold his allegiance to another."

"The stars told you this?" Carys shook her head even as the words rang true in her heart.

Kiara smiled. "It is amazing what you hear when you listen. Of course, had your lord listened to the stars, he would have seen that you cannot force trust no matter how clever the ruse or determined the heart. Your power consumes him. He wishes it to consume you. But it cannot."

"I don't understand. Is Garret working with . . ."

"You ask the wrong questions." The seeress interrupted. "They will be searching. There is little time. I must give you the answers in my way. It is why I returned to the Village of Night after being away for so long."

"Why haven't you been at the Village? I thought all seers lived here."

Candles flickered. The fire popped and flared as Kiara explained, "That is what you are supposed to think. Before, seers only called the winds, and described what they saw in the skies. They illuminated, without agenda, their visions. But soon, kings and emperors looked to us to circumvent the repercussions of their choices. They used us to avoid a blow from the harsh hand of fate. Our visions were warped by interpretation." She paused. "There were reactions. Some seers were determined to fix the wrongs caused by kings. Instead, we made them worse."

Carys thought of her own wrongs. The guard's blade buried in the old woman's face when the wind gusted in the stone circle. Innocent blood, shed because Carys had wanted to destroy those who meant her harm.

"Our sacred calling was corrupted and wars were waged. In Eden, the winds were unleashed to defeat those who marched against it. The Seven Virtues were shattered. The Xhelozi grew in number and strength as the balance between virtue and vice tilted. The Guild recognized the hand its members had in the chaos—the damage they had done. They saw in the stars the destruction that would follow if they did not heed the warnings and take their hand off the scale of fate."

"But the seers didn't heed the warnings," Carys shot back. "Seers still advise the throne."

"You see what you are meant to see. Power is a seductive force for those who wish to claim it for their own. Had we abandoned Eden, kings and those thirsty for our skills would have hunted us down. So, one by one we left the Village of Night behind, save a few dedicated souls who understand and champion in the true purpose of this place."

"True purpose?"

"Those with talent begin their training here, but this is not where they remain. If a candidate is determined to have a true gift, they are called away from the Village and ferried to the Isle. The rest remain here fully believing they are part of the Guild, but they are not destined to read the stars."

Carys shifted her hold on the stiletto as she looked from the seer toward the door. "You're saying that everyone here is a fraud, including the seers sent to advise the King or Queen?"

Kiara looked toward the fire. She was easily two decades older than Carys, but there was something about her that seemed ageless. "When the Seer of Eden died, the Guild made the decision to choose from our ranks one with a keen intellect, but little gift for the stars or the winds. They sent him with a single vision to use as he saw fit to aid the kingdom."

The *least* powerful seer. "Someone had to notice the difference."

"To them there was no difference. He was powerful because that was what the Seer of Eden had always been. No one doubted his ability because the winds continued to blow. If he read the same message in the stars over and over it was because of the path the stars wished the world to take."

Carys frowned. "But there is a test." Her mother spoke of it on more than one occasion. Her mother had been convinced the test and the power of the seers were real.

"The Artis root." Kiara nodded. "It is still given. None would believe that true seers exist without the test. Here, everyone drinks from the same well, eats from the same stores. One can cultivate an immunity to the root if one undergoes the proper conditioning. Meanwhile the truly gifted among us go to the Isle to study and perfect our understanding of our powers and wait for a time when the world will not exploit them."

The confession took Carys's breath away. It was the perfect deception. No one would seek out the missing seers because they believed the seers were still among them—helping them. And it explained how someone like Imogen was able to become the Seer of Eden. She had been smart. She must have manipulated those in the Village to guarantee her selection. And when she left here, she was armed with the one vision every Seer of Eden was given and the book in which she had found the law that led Carys and Andreus to the Trials of Virtuous Succession.

The whispers in her head grew. The fire in the hearth flared.

"Calm," the seeress said gently. "Take a deep breath. Wall off your emotions or you will destroy not only those around you but yourself. *This* is the reason the seers had to leave Eden. If we had stayed, we would have destroyed all."

She thought of the tunnels again and the fire settled.

Kiara nodded, and Carys paced the small space. "I need to know who helped Imogen become the Seer of Eden. Whoever it was helped her kill the King and the Crown Prince. That person is still inside the Palace of Winds."

Kiara folded her hands in front of her. "When you learn the answer to this question, what will you do then?"

"Whatever I have to in order to see that Eden is safe."

"You will fight if necessary."

"Yes."

"You will kill those who threaten you?"

"If I must."

"Will you forgive?"

Carys went still. "This isn't about forgiveness."

"Is it not?" Kiara stared at Carys for one heartbeat. Two. Then said, "Imogen arrived ten years ago at the gates of this village. I was in the place of the seers. I only returned recently because of what I saw in the stars, so I was not a witness, but the merchant who escorted her claimed she had recently been orphaned. I am told he said he brought her to the Village because she foresaw her isolation before her family's deaths occurred. They say the man visited her several times in the first few years, then the visits stopped. She was dedicated to her studies and became a favorite among the leaders of the Village."

Already plotting. Convincing them she was the right choice for the next Seer of Eden.

"Before Imogen was chosen as the Seer of Eden, the Village of Night was paid a visit by a member of the Council of Elders. One with a long braid and a soft voice."

Elder Jacobs. How many times had Carys seen him twisting that black braid in his hands?

"He came bearing a missive that held the signatures of several members of the Council requesting the next seer be young and beautiful to capture the imagination and heart of the kingdom and help give hope during such a trying time."

"Elder Jacobs was here?" Carys demanded confirmation, and the seeress nodded.

Elder Jacobs had been atop the battlement walls the night her father and brother had died. She had spotted him speaking to Andreus during the Trial of Temperance moments before her brother condemned an innocent boy to death.

"Many wish to change the course of Eden, but it is only you and Andreus who can determine which path the kingdom will take."

"Why tell me any of this?" Carys asked. "I thought seers did not want to interfere in the world anymore."

"We don't, but I changed the history of Eden once, years ago, without understanding what I had done, and the stars have told me that I have this one chance to set it right. You see, Betrice heard the prediction I had made. Without my words she might have never become Queen."

Candles flickered. The fire crackled. Then everything went still.

"You . . . know my mother?"

Kiara crossed to the cot. When she turned back, she held the blue-and-silver beaded slippers in her hands. "These belonged to Betrice before she became Queen. She gave them to me when she left this village behind. These are the key to your freedom."

Uncertain, Carys took the shoes from the seer. The firelight hit the beading, but something about the jewels seemed to absorb the light instead of reflect it.

"My mother was a seer?"

Kiara shot a look at the door. "Lady Betrice was born with a single vision that brought her to this place. No more. No less. You were born with far more, but it is up to you to learn how to use it."

Carys shook her head. The whispers grew more insistent. "I've tried to control it. I can't. It just . . ."

She saw a flash of the man twisted and broken and the woman

with the knife buried in her face.

"You cannot control what is not yours to command," Kiara said. "The air around us can do great things. But no matter how gifted you are, the wind will never be a subject that does your bidding. You must calmly surrender yourself to gain the control you seek. You must trust. To surrender to the wind in anger or fear is to unleash a power that can destroy not only your enemies, but yourself. There is no virtue when you lead with fear. There is only darkness and destruction and death."

Kiara cocked her head to the side and went still. Her eyes widened. "They are coming."

"But I still don't know . . ."

"You know all you must except this—your heart will be broken and when it is you will be given the keys to unlock the prison that holds you. Then only you can decide if you will be free."

The seeress opened the door and headed out into the cold without her cloak. Her hair and the bright white dress fluttered in the wind as Carys hurried after her.

"What does that mean?"

Voices shouted in the darkness. Carys heard someone calling her name. She held the stiletto tight in her right hand and clutched the bejeweled shoes in the other. Kiara led her through the trees, toward the stone barrier. The voices were getting louder with each passing moment. They were coming closer.

The whispering in her brain returned.

Surrender. Trust.

She didn't know how.

She ignored the wind and ran toward the stone barrier between the outside world and the hill of the Village of Night with her stilettos ready. In the distance, men emerged from the trees.

"Two paths stretch before you, Princess. One is covered in darkness. The other is in light. Your journey has been far, but you have farther yet to go. The Kingdom needs its Princess to return balance to the virtues. The darkness gets stronger without the light."

"And what if I fail? What if I don't make it that far?" She was tired of hunting and being hunted. Of people she trusted betraying her. Elder Jacobs and Imogen had caused her brother to turn against her. Why should it be her responsibility to *once again* step forward and save him from the punishment that was so rightly his?

"Then the Throne of Light will go dark, the virtues will stay unbalanced, and the Xhelozi will thrive. Death will ravage not only our kingdom, but others." Kiara grabbed her arm. The seeress led her to a clump of tall, thorn-filled bushes and pointed behind them. "You will find your way out there. Go to the cluster of stones a half league beyond the wall. You will find your horse and belongings there."

"What?" Carys asked. "How . . ."

"Not all knowledge comes from the stars. Sometimes it comes from those around you," Kiara whispered. The sound of crunching leaves and shouting voices grew louder.

"What about you?" Carys asked.

"I have fulfilled my purpose. Remember that those who betray are often betrayed themselves, and gardens have more than one serpent among the leaves. Now go."

Before Carys could stop her, the seeress hurried toward the rocks and trees to Carys's left. The voices grew louder. Another shadow emerged, this one closer than the other, and the sound of branches breaking said more were coming.

Casting a last look in the direction Kiara headed off in, Carys plunged into the thicket. Thorns clawed her face and pulled on her cloak. She held her breath each time the branches shook as she pulled herself free and kept going. She stumbled on a root, pitched out of the prickly bushes, and fell to her knees, dropping the slippers and her blade. She gathered her things, then examined the wall behind her for the opening Kiara had promised.

There.

She found a section of the wall where the two sides were built one in front of the other with a narrow space between them to slide through. It was a cleverly constructed illusion where the wall appeared to be whole from just steps away. And hidden behind the thorny thicket, it was the perfect escape path for someone who didn't want to be followed.

She heard a woman scream. The wind inside her howled, but she refused to give in to the anger and fear as she ran. The cold air stabbed her lungs with every breath. Her body ached. Her mind was fuzzy. More than anything, she wished for the red bottle and the Tears of Midnight that would smooth away the pain and plunge her into oblivion. Desperately, she looked for the landmark Seeress Kiara had directed her to, while every few moments glancing behind her to see if the guardsmen hunting her were on their way.

She spotted the rocks in the distance. Stones white as snow and black as night clumped together, reaching up to the sky.

Her chest and throat burned. Her legs shook with fatigue.

A rock skittered across the cold earth and Carys lifted her stiletto. Something leaped from the shadows. It rammed into her arm, sending the stiletto flying out of her hand and her crashing to the ground. She fumbled for her other stiletto but couldn't reach the hilt before someone pinned her arms and a face loomed above her.

Brown hair framing an angled face.

Dark eyes staring into hers.

Errik. He had found her.

So she did the only thing she could. She kicked him in the crotch.

12

I will return.

The script on the note was shaky, but he knew the handwriting. He would know it anywhere. But it could not be real.

His throat tightened.

His leg buckled, and he fell onto cold stone.

He had seen his twin's dead body. He had looked upon the disfigured face shredded by the claws of the Xhelozi. Blood and gore and bone framed by the almost white-blond hair—a color no woman in the court possessed save his sister, Carys.

Andreus read the words again.

He'd left her for dead.

He'd won.

But Carys was . . . alive?

Laughter bubbled up, echoing in the stairwell.

Someone had attacked him on the walls.

Council members were plotting against him, and he had no idea which ones.

He was beginning to suspect the woman he had loved had played him for a fool, and here he was—sitting and giggling.

The amusement faded.

At this moment, the note meant nothing. The throne was his, and it would not be wrested from him by those inside the walls or the Xhelozi beyond them. Even if Carys had somehow lived and escaped the castle, the withdrawal from the Tears of Midnight would have taken its toll on her body. She could not have gotten very far without help.

He thought of Trade Master Errik and Lord Garret. Neither of them had been seen since the night she disappeared. Maybe . . .

He shook his head. There was no way to know if this note was placed under the stone before or after that final Trial and, until there was proof otherwise, Carys was dead.

And yet, he had never *felt* her death.

When Carys broke her arm, Andreus swore he could feel an echo of her pain.

Carys always *knew* when he was having trouble breathing, even when no one else saw a hint of his secret.

After his sister's betrayal during the Trials, he had been determined to cast her from his mind. But despite his anger, they were twins. Shouldn't he have *felt* something when she died?

Shoving the complicated feelings aside, Andreus made his way to the battlements. The temperature had dropped since earlier in the evening when he had examined the lights on the walls. Graylem and the ladies stood just steps away, huddled in their cloaks. Andreus forced a smile and moved forward as the windmills rolled against the night sky.

Yesterday the mills had moved sluggishly. Today the creaking of the blades was slower still. The air felt stagnant. If he didn't move fast, he could soon be fighting a war on two fronts—inside the Palace of Winds and on the Garden City walls. And right now, he was fighting it all on his own.

His swirling thoughts made it hard to focus on Demitria. He feigned interest in her admiration of the orb and his climb down the wall and subsequent race to retrieve the crown from the Tomb of Light. She pressed her body against his as she talked—something he would have been delighted to take advantage of just weeks ago. But when he pulled her close and kissed her and she caught fire in his arms, there was no rise of passion. No spark.

He caught Graylem's eye, then took Demitria by the hand and led her to the shadows of the windmill. Pressing her against the wall, Andreus kissed her one more time and whispered, "I am more sorry than you know that I have to cut our time short. Lord Graylem will see you arrive safely home."

Graylem bowed, still holding fast to the dark-haired girl's hand. "It will be my privilege." The flush on Graylem's face was bright even in the low light.

Andreus placed a kiss on Demitria's hand as he led her into the stairwell, then walked to Graylem and pulled him to the side. "Take your time showing them out. Give them a tour and make the first stop my rooms. I need the Elders to think I am still occupied so they don't come looking for me."

"Yes, Your Majesty," Graylem agreed.

"I could also use a distraction in about an hour," Andreus added. If he hadn't found anything tangible that pointed him to the truth in that time, there wouldn't be anything to find.

"A distraction?"

"Anything that will pull the attention of the guards and whatever intelligencers the Elders have roaming the halls away—without burning the palace down."

"It shall be done." Graylem met Andreus's eyes and nodded.

After a lingering farewell kiss for a visibly disappointed Demitria, Andreus headed back onto the battlements, careful to stay in the shadows before ducking into the windmill that topped the southwestern tower.

The creaking of the gears was louder inside the mill. The octagon chamber was pitch-black when he closed the door. The interior of each windmill was used by the Masters for a specific purpose. Some housed the apprentices. There was meeting and building space. This one was storage. Rarely did anyone enter this particular mill after nightfall, which is why it was a favorite location for Andreus to visit with whatever amorous lady he was sampling on a particular day. It was also the reason Andreus had chosen it for the next phase of this hastily conceived plan.

He felt around the floor next to the entrance and smiled into the darkness as his fingers brushed across a large satchel. Max had come through. Tomorrow, Andreus would make sure the kitchen baked dozens of apple tarts for him to share with his friends.

An icy chill bit into his body as he pulled off his coat and shirt and shrugged into Graylem's guard tunic. The material was coarse and itchy, but not as bad as the improperly sized trousers that Andreus struggled to get over his thighs. After several tries, he finally fastened them. The ensemble was more tourniquet than uniform, but it would have to do.

He slid the sword into the scabbard, slapped the helmet onto his head, and threw the guardsman's cloak over his shoulders. Then he headed back out onto the battlements. He walked slowly, concentrating on disguising his limp, which would quickly give his identity away.

The walls around Garden City were brightly lit. Nothing moved in the darkness beyond them. For now, the Xhelozi were being pushed back by the lights. He could only hope the wind would blow again before the stored power was depleted.

Pulling the cloak tighter, he strode across the battlements and headed down the stairs on the northwesternmost tower. He spotted Master Triden in his gray robes standing beneath the tallest of the towers. He stared up at the orb as it glowed bright in the night. He was about to make a detour to speak to the Master of Light when he saw two men striding across the battlements toward the Master. The short white beard made Elder Cestrum recognizable from a distance. The other man had his hood raised.

Frustrated that there was nowhere he could hide and listen to their conversation without potentially giving his own deception away, Andreus turned and hurried into the stairwell. He paused at the bottom of the tower and listened for the sound of footfalls, then continued down the hall to a doorway that led out of the Palace of Winds.

Andreus stayed in the shadows as he crossed the courtyard of the palace toward the North Tower . . . the tower that was constructed at the plateau with the sheerest drop. It had only one entrance to make sure the prisoners inside would have less chance of escape. Andreus had never had cause to go to the North Tower. Carys, however, had been on several occasions—each because she had drawn punishment on herself to distract others from one of Andreus's attacks.

The last time was on the night of their father's death. She had spoken to one of the King's Guard. He warned her against asking questions, but Carys had vowed to return and get the truth of what happened to the King and the Crown Prince as soon as she recovered from the flogging she'd received. Only, the four King's Guard were discovered dead first. Poisoned. By whom, no one knew.

Carys had believed that the men were killed before they had a chance to reveal the truth behind the ambush that took the lives of the King and the Crown Prince.

Andreus had not found the guardsmen's deaths as menacing as his twin. It wasn't uncommon for a prisoner who displeased the guards to suddenly die before the end of their sentence. The North Tower was not a kind place.

Now, Andeus wished he had asked more questions when his sister had told him about sneaking up to the second floor where the King's Guard were locked away.

Andreus intended to retrace her steps now. The only place to find confirmation of his mother's accusations was where the King's Guardsmen died.

He pushed open the heavy iron door of the North Tower and winced as the hinges groaned. The musty smell of rotting fabric, rusty metal, and soot washed over him. Wind power was not wasted on those who committed crimes against the crown—not even here on the first floor where minor trials were held and corporal punishments were enacted.

He eased the door closed behind him. A snorting grunt echoed in the shadows, and he almost lost his grip on the handle in his surprise. He froze. Blood pounded loud in his ears as he waited for the guard sitting on a wooden chair near the stairs to jump up and recognize him.

The guard shifted in the chair and snorted again as he slept on. Now what?

A picture from that fateful night of Carys wielding a sword outside the palace entrance flashed in his head. She had boldly drawn attention to distract from her true purpose. Using that image as inspiration, Andreus let the heavy iron door slam shut and yelled, "On your feet, Guardsman!"

The guard scrambled to get up, almost knocking over the chair. Andreus kept his face in the shadows as he snapped, "I didn't know sleeping was one of the duties for guards in the North Tower. I will have to have a talk with Captain Monteros upon his return."

The guard shuffled his feet. "It was just . . . it was dark and I didn't mean . . ."

"Silence!" Andreus stepped forward. "I have been instructed by the Council of Elders to handle a delicate matter upstairs. While I do so, I would suggest you step into the cold outside to wake yourself up. If I can be certain you will not make the same mistake again, I will not report your actions. I remember what it was like to have to stand watch on a long, uneventful night."

"Yes. No. I mean, I will step outside. Thank you. I promise it won't happen again." The young guard barely lifted his eyes as he hurried toward the exit. Andreus stepped to the side and let out a sigh of relief when the iron door slammed shut.

Once he rooted out the treason in the palace, he would have to insist on better training for his guard. But for now, Andreus grabbed a torch off the wall, lifted a ring of iron keys off a hook near where the guard had been sleeping, and headed up the steps.

The smell of decay grew as he climbed. He could almost taste the stench of rotting food, unwashed bodies, and defecation.

Andreus stepped out of the stairwell onto the second floor and started down the hallway that, aside from his torch, was bathed in blackness. It appeared light was now denied to those who did not embrace the seven virtues, especially since the torches were needed in the halls of the Palace of Winds and throughout the city below.

Metal clanged against stone.

Someone wept.

And from down the hall, there was a sound of humming. Faint, but Andreus recognized the old folk tune. It was the air their nurse had sung when he and Carys were little. Then, it was a song of warmth and kindness. Now, it was the melody of hopelessness and decay.

Torch held high, Andreus peered into the first cell. The wooden door was thick, with an iron lock and bars that lined the narrow window near the top. The cell was empty except for moldy hay and a small bench. Something scrambled across his foot. Andreus jerked to the side. The keys in his hand clanged against the wall as the rat scurried down the hall into the darkness. Had Carys been here, the rat would already be dead.

Andreus straightened and realized the humming had stopped. But something rustled in the cell next door.

Andreus lifted the torch to the window. A dirt-smudged, gray-haired woman sat on the wooden bench. Eyes squinted at him before she looked back down at her hands.

"How long have you been here?" he asked.

"Three days," she answered. "I think it's been three days. Maybe four. My husband is sick. I was only trying to get him help. Do you know what happened to 'im?"

Four days. An eternity to her, but not long enough to help Andreus.

"I'm sorry." Pity swirled as he stepped back and moved along the hall. His stomach lurched at the now-overwhelming stench of unwashed bodies and urine.

He peered into the next cell. A man with bloodstained bandages wrapped around a stump that ended just above where his elbow used to be was sprawled on the ground—not moving. Dead—or soon would be.

Andreus continued looking into cells, trying to decide how to find something that would help confirm the identities of the traitors involved in his father's and brother's deaths. His mother might be fabricating her story of treason, but there was no way to be certain without proof. One way or the other, he needed to speak to someone who had been here when the men died.

The guard he'd intimidated would return to his post soon. Andreus needed to finish his search and get out of here.

He reached the last of the cells in the hallway—all empty—and started back toward the stairs. Perhaps Graylem could ask some questions. It was risky and . . .

The humming started again.

Andreus stopped and listened hard through the sounds of shuffling hay and shallow coughs. It sounded as if the humming was coming from behind him—from the line of empty cells.

He headed back in the direction he just came from and the music stopped.

"Hello?" he asked quietly.

No answer.

"I know you're there."

He peered in the windows of the cells again. Empty. Just as before. Perhaps he'd just imagined the humming. Or . . .

"Feel it in the mountain air," he sang softly, feeling beyond

foolish as his voice cracked. Still he continued to sing, *"See it in the streams. Virtues set the world alight."*

"Jealousy darkens dreams," whispered a voice coming from the second-to-last cell.

Andreus pressed his face against the bars of the window. There was still no one in view. But there was someone there. He sang another line of the song and heard rustling in the hay. A moment later a rail-thin woman with sunken eyes and tattered clothes appeared in the window.

"How long have you been here?" he asked.

"Summer and winter and summer and winter again . . . ," she sang in a gravelly, tuneless voice.

"Years?" Most prisoners stayed for a short time—many were punished and released. Some executed. But there were a few held longer. Sometimes for good reason. Some because they were forgotten.

She nodded.

"So you were in this cell a few weeks ago?"

She nodded again.

"You were here when the King's Guardsmen were poisoned?"

"Winter and summer circle each other . . . jealously guarding their prey."

"Is that a yes?"

"The stars in the sky . . ."

The clang of a door echoed through the hall. The woman jerked back, her eyes wide with fear. The guard downstairs must have come back inside. Either that or someone else had arrived in the North Tower. No one was coming up the stairs yet, but his time for this masquerade was running out.

He looked back through the window, but the woman had

disappeared from view. "If you know anything about why the men died, tell me. I can help you get free if you tell me what you know."

Silence.

"Do you know who killed them?"

There was rustling from inside the cell, but nothing more. He waited for several long seconds for her to return, but she didn't appear, and the guard below would begin to ask questions soon. Frustrated, Andreus turned.

"They said that she promised. She said it was fated they would succeed. They would be rewarded. They said she would not abandon them."

He spun back around. The words were ghostly. Barely audible, but real. "Who said?"

"The snakes. They whispered. They thought no one could hear them. They don't know how to whisper. I know how to whisper. You have to whisper if you want to live. The snakes didn't live."

"Why? Do you know why they died?"

The door below slammed shut again. Someone else had come into the tower.

"They were promised summer. It was winter they ate."

"What did they say?"

"They'd traded the Queen for the seeker of stars and the man of black heart and the moon they promised. New King. The seer promised summer if they gave her the old crown's death."

They promised to give the seer death. Bitterness churned in his stomach and filled his mouth.

"Lady Imogen?" he asked.

"They thought she would step into the darkness for them. But one said she would never come. He was right. It was a man who came."

Andreus glanced toward the stairs and asked, "Did they call the man by name? Do you know who the man of black heart is?"

Voices rose from below. It was time for him to go.

"Iron for blood. Iron for heart. Clawing for summer when winter does start."

"Do you know who killed them?"

"He knew how to whisper."

"Did he work with Lady Imogen? Did he work with the stars?"

"No. He wasn't of the stars. They said they did as they were told, and saw the palace plunged into darkness."

The darkness. They returned after the wind-powered lights were sabotaged! Was it a signal that those inside the Palace were ready to move on to the next phase of their plot?

"Who was the man who visited them?"

"Skin of snow. Eye of night. Scratching in the dark after the gift of death. Scratching. Lots of scratching until there was nothing."

He didn't understand, but he had run out of time because he could hear voices downstairs—and they were getting louder. "I must go."

"Don't accept gifts," she whispered from the dark. "I don't accept gifts. I'm alive. No scratching for me."

Scratching, he thought as he limped down the hall. Was that crazy talk or had she truly heard scratching after the guards took the "gift" and before they died? Perhaps one of the guards left a clue behind . . .

Footsteps sounded on the stairs. Andreus adjusted the helmet so it sat low on his forehead and put his hand on his sword as the footsteps grew closer.

The clang of a gong echoed. Then another.

"The signal! The Xhelozi must be coming!" a voice called.

Maybe. Or maybe Graylem had provided the distraction Andreus had requested.

Andreus was betting on the latter. The footsteps on the stairs retreated and Andreus hurried to the empty cells. He pulled the first door open, and searched—the walls, the hay on the floor—looking for something. Anything other than rats and mold.

The gongs went silent as he moved into the second cell. Still nothing.

He lifted his torch in the third cell. Nothing on the walls. Nothing under the hay. He was about to give up when he spotted uneven letters etched into the leg of the rickety wooden bench.

BEWARE IMOGE

The last letter was only partially carved—the guard must have succumbed before he could finish his task, but the intent was clear. Carys had spoken to the guards. She promised them she would return. If Andreus was to guess, one guard had left the warning for her to find. Only Carys hadn't returned. And now, between the confession of his mother, the ramblings of the gaunt, dirty woman in the last cell, and this final confirmation, Andreus understood, to his own deep revulsion, the truth of what had happened.

The men in these cells had exchanged working for the Queen to serve the stars. His mother had said herself that she had plotted with Micah to have the King, his father, murdered. The strange words of the old woman and this etching served as proof of his mother's horrible confession. It also gave credence to his mother's belief that when Imogen learned of the scheme, she altered the plan and convinced the assassins to murder not only the King, but Andreus's brother and much of the King's Guard as well.

Andreus wanted to sink to the ground under the weight of the truth. Instead, he limped out of the cell and downstairs, very much aware of the silence. The distraction Graylem had provided was over. He had to get out of the tower in a hurry.

He placed the torch in a sconce, yanked open the door, and plunged into the cold. In the distance, he could see men coming his way. Keeping his head down, he ignored the tightening in his chest as he made his way across the courtyard and into the palace.

His head spun as he yanked the helmet off, removed the cloak and the mail vest, and stashed all of them in the servants' stairwell outside the hallway that led to his rooms. Sweat beaded on his forehead and ran down his neck. He forced a smile as he swaggered toward his rooms, stumbling several times from the pain growing in his leg and expanding in his chest. He stumbled and hoped if anyone was watching they would interpret his uneven gait as the drunken King returning after a night of carousing.

When he had switched clothing, he had forgotten to take with him the remedy that would ease the curse. Each step made it harder to walk—harder to breathe.

He reached his rooms, and his knees went weak. He thought about the black vials he had hidden in the adjoining bedchamber, and knew he didn't have the energy to make it that far. Or maybe he didn't want to reach the remedy. Maybe he deserved for the curse to take him.

He stumbled into the chair next to the crackling fire. He hadn't cried when his father and Micah were dumped onto the palace steps. He hadn't cried when he stood over the body he thought belonged to his twin or when he buried Imogen. But he cried now.

Imogen had used him. And he had let her.

He could have seen through her soft touch and seductive words.

Carys had warned him, but he hadn't listened. He hadn't wanted to. From the first, he had wanted Imogen. More, he wanted what she said she believed him to be.

Perfect.

Perfect like his brother who had been born first, without the curse. Who had secured the promise of Imogen's hand and body because he was the Crown Prince.

When given the chance, Andreus had unhesitatingly embraced a woman who claimed he was perfect and turned his back on one who never expected him to be.

His lungs burned. It was like he was underwater, taunted by the view of a surface he could never hope to reach.

Carys had protected him. She had loved him, and even as he returned her affection, he had hated her for being born without the curse. He resented that she had to stand for him because there were times he could not stand for himself. And most of all he had hated the scars she was forced to bear because he was alive.

Carys wasn't perfect. She never once pretended to be or wanted anyone to think that she was. She had told him she would *give him* the throne, and he had turned against her anyway. Why? Because deep down he didn't believe her. Because if their roles were reversed, he couldn't be trusted to do the same.

The room spun.

Andreus laid his head back on the chair.

Spots of light danced in front of his eyes.

Lights.

He gasped for air and fought to breathe.

Everything he knew of Imogen's plot to steal the throne began and ended in one place. With the lights.

Wait—

He pushed himself out of the chair. His legs buckled, and he fell onto the thick carpet.

Tomorrow, he thought as blackness slowly pulled him under, he would find the person Imogen had worked with. He would use the lights and punish those working against Eden.

In doing so, he would find redemption.

13

Carys kicked upward and connected. Errik grunted. He loosened his grip and she rolled to the side, but not fast enough. Errik grabbed her cloak and yanked her back onto the cold ground.

"Stop," he hissed.

"Not as long as I draw breath."

She ignored the muttering of the wind and fumbled for the fastening of her cloak. The garment came free. Errik flew backward, and Carys scrambled to her feet. She drew the second stiletto from her pocket as Errik pushed her heavy cloak off him and got to his knees.

She cocked her arm back, prepared to do what she should have done when he first revealed his identity as a Bastian. His eyes latched on to hers. One eye was swollen with a gash underneath it. But despite the injury, his were the same eyes that had made her want to believe in him.

Whom could she trust?

Errik had betrayed her.

Just as her brother had betrayed her.

Just as everyone in her life betrayed her.

The wind gusted.

She cocked her arm back, but couldn't throw. Not yet. "What did you do with Larkin?"

"What do you mean?" Errik blinked.

"Where did you take her? Is she still alive? Did the Bastians you turned her over to kill her or are they hoping I will surrender myself to them in order to secure her freedom?"

"Carys." Errik looked directly into her eyes. "I didn't take Larkin. I would never turn her over to my uncle or anyone. She's here with me. We've been looking for you since you and Garret disappeared from the cave. Larkin refused to believe you'd been captured by the guardsmen we saw that night—"

"What guardsmen?" Carys asked.

"Larkin heard voices during her watch and woke me up. The two of us went out to see where the voices were coming from. We spotted Captain Monteros and two dozen members of Eden's guard to the west of the cave and had to take a circuitous route back to avoid being discovered. Only, by the time we returned, you and Garret and all of our belongings were gone."

Carys shook her head. "But we looked for you. Garret and I searched . . ."

Shouts rang in the distance. The sound of them was closer than below.

Errik pushed to his feet and slowly stood with his hands raised in front of him. "I don't know what Garret told you, but we should probably talk about it later. When we arrived, Kiara met us just outside the entrance to the Village of Night. She assured us you would be arriving soon and that once you did we should gather your belongings and your horse and meet you here. After all her effort, I doubt she would be pleased if we didn't get safely away."

Hope leaped. A shadow of doubt followed. She lowered the stiletto, but held it at the ready in case she needed to strike.

"If you don't believe me, will you at least believe Larkin?" Errik asked quietly. He leaned down, picked up Carys's discarded cloak, and winced. "She's waiting for us."

The shouts grew louder.

Errik pointed toward the large rock formation.

Carys took a step backward, then another, still wondering if this was a trick to get her to lower her guard. She wanted to believe him, but she couldn't. Too much had happened for her to trust.

Carys spotted a figure near three horses. Her black hair was woven into a haphazard braid. The woman was holding a notched bow pointed toward the darkness on the other side of the rocks, and she looked as if she knew how to use it. The woman shifted. Moonlight struck her face, and Carys had to stop herself from yelling her friend's name.

Larkin pivoted at the sound of Carys's approach, lowered the weapon, and smiled. It was the grin that had teased Carys to laughter all her life. The one she had feared, since leaving the cave with Garret, that she would never see again.

"You're here! We saw Captain Monteros arrive this morning, and I wanted to come find you, but Errik said we had to trust Seeress Kiara," Larkin said, the bow falling limply to her side as she took several steps as if to embrace Carys before stopping herself short and giving an embarrassed smile.

Carys blinked, then smiled back as she closed the ground

between them and wrapped her arms around her friend. They had only hugged once, as children, before Larkin was told it was inappropriate for a commoner to hug a princess.

"I found the markings you left for me. I knew you would try to make it here, but I wasn't sure if Garret would interfere. Errik said you would make it. He said that no matter what Garret tried, there was nothing he or anyone else could do that would stop you."

"He said that?"

"I did."

Larkin stepped back with a smile, and Carys turned toward Errik.

"Once again, I find myself returning what you have lost." His eyes held hers as he flipped the stiletto in his hands and presented it to her. "I appreciate you not throwing it at me."

The wind feathered the hair on the back of her neck, and Carys wrapped her fingers around the silver hilt. "I thought you had taken Larkin to your uncle. When I woke and you and Larkin were gone from the cave. Garret said—"

Voices called in the night. Some were behind the wall, but there were others that sounded closer. Carys shook her head. "You're right. We can talk about the rest once we are away from here."

"This way." Errik unfurled Carys's cloak and threw it over her shoulders, then pulled the pair of jeweled slippers she'd dropped out of his pocket and handed them to her. "The seeress said you would have the information you sought once we were reunited. But if you need more . . ."

"No, I have what I need," she said, first looking at Errik and Larkin, then down at the slippers in her hand. Kiara had claimed the information she provided was the key Carys needed. The only way to figure out what the information Carys had gained unlocked was to walk up to the door—and the two people standing at her side would help her do that.

Errik's uncle's forces were gathering. The Xhelozi were growing bolder as the imbalance of the virtues grew. There was only one way to deal with both. The time had come to face her brother again.

"We must return to Garden City."

The uneven terrain meant they had to let their horses slowly pick their way through until finally they reached a dirt road that led west. Carys could swear she heard her name carried on the breeze as she urged her horse to a gallop. The others did the same.

She glanced at Larkin several times to make sure her friend wasn't falling behind, but while Larkin looked uncomfortable, she was steady in her seat, her bow at the ready. Days ago, Larkin hadn't known how to notch an arrow, let alone hold a bow. Carys wasn't the only one who had traveled far to reach the Village of Night. Larkin had traveled much farther.

Errik leaned over the head of his chestnut mount. She had believed the worst in him and still he was here at her side. Larkin said he had never faltered. He hadn't turned against her even though Carys had stopped believing in him.

Garret had said he wanted her trust. He had deliberately separated her from Larkin and Errik so he could be the sole person she leaned on. According to Kiara, he had arranged the ambush at the Village of Night to solidify her belief in him. All because he wanted control of the power she had inside her.

Instead, Captain Monteros had double-crossed him, and now the men who betrayed Garret would be coming after her.

They pushed their horses, but eventually they had to slow their pace to a walk or risk injuring their mounts. Carys's nerves danced as their horses plodded up a hill.

She glanced over and saw Larkin's eyes flutter closed. Her friend tilted to the left as exhaustion tugged her under. Carys pulled on her reins, but Errik had spotted the problem and reached her first. He pulled his horse to a halt next to Larkin's and kept her from falling as Larkin's eyes snapped open. Her expression of surprise was so comical, Carys laughed as she urged her horse to the top of the hill. The laughter died on her lips as her mount headed downward and she rode into horror.

Dismembered bodies scattered around a low-burning campfire. Severed legs—some stripped of flesh. Torsos slit open and emptied on cold ground, stained with their lifeblood. And heads cut free and tossed into a pile near the raw, bloody remains of what was once a horse.

"Merciful Gods!" Larkin gasped from behind her. "What could have done this?"

Carys shook her head and nudged her horse forward. "It was Xhelozi."

"But—the Xhelozi never come this far out of the mountains," Larkin insisted, her voice pitched high with fear, tears thickening her words. "It is too long a way for them to get back to their dens before dawn."

"Garret and I outran the Xhelozi the night the four of us were separated, and I heard them in the distance several times when we were traveling," Carys said as Larkin turned her face away from the gore. "The Seeress Kiara said the monsters grow in number whenever the virtues are out of balance. They thrive in all kinds of darkness, not just the kind that envelop us when the sun sets but also the darkness that we create with our actions." Carys gasped as she understood the full implications of the seeress's words. "Soon, the lights on the walls of Garden City might not be enough to keep the Xhelozi from attacking."

Larkin blinked aside her fatigue. "My father! He and the others in the city will never know the attack is coming unless we warn them."

Carys nodded. "It is one of the many reasons we must hurry."

A rock skittered and Carys whipped her head toward the sound.

A hand moved from under a small bush near a fallen horse. She slid off her mount and hurried across the bloodstained ground, Errik keeping pace beside her.

Errik pushed aside the branches of the bush. Wide eyes stared up at them through a coat of gore. "Coming . . . ," the man whispered.

The fact that the man was alive was a miracle. His legs were pinned beneath the gutted horse. Claw marks ran from his shoulder downward.

Errik squatted down next to the man and shifted the ripped cloak. "He's part of the Bastian force."

"Coming," the man whispered. "Must meet."

"Meet for what?" Errik asked.

"The battle," the man wheezed. He struggled for air. "They won't see our number."

"How many?" Carys demanded. "How many are coming? When? When are you meeting?"

"Thousands. Soon. It's time."

Thousands of Bastian men. These few would not make it to the meeting point—but others would. And with Bastian traitors aiding the army from inside the walls, Garden City could quickly fall. She had to . . .

A shriek cut the air.

Carys stiffened. Errik stood beside her as she scanned the horizon, looking for the source of the sound.

Nothing. Carys's heart pounded as she held her breath and waited.

Another cry echoed. This one sounding nearer still.

Carys whipped her head to the north and that's when she saw them. Over a dozen tall shadows—more than the three of them could hope to fight—coming out of a distant grove of trees and running toward them.

"Come on!" Errik grabbed her arm. Side by side, they raced for their mounts. Her horse danced under her and shot off behind Larkin's horse before Carys was settled in her seat.

Larkin's and Errik's mounts pounded the frozen ground just ahead of hers. She urged her horse to go faster. Behind her—*Oh Gods, they sound closer*—a chorus of Xhelozi screams raked the night. Fear swelled. She clutched the reins tighter and willed her horse to keep running.

"They're gaining on us," Errik shouted.

Carys looked over her shoulder. The wind roared in her head. The Xhelozi were closing the distance—almost bounding over the ground on their long, fur-coated legs. Despite her insistence, Carys's fatigued horse was already starting to slow.

The Xhelozi screamed again. Carys clenched the reins tight as the wind howled. Her heart pounded in her ears as her fear bubbled and pushed to break free.

Larkin's horse stumbled and Carys watched her friend slip from the saddle.

"Carys! Keep going," Errik shouted as he leaped off his mount to help Larkin.

With the mauled, dismembered bodies flashing in her mind, Carys did the only thing she could do. She leaped from her own horse, balled her hands into fists at her side as she faced the creatures that were racing toward her with their hooked claws extended, and gave in to fear.

"Carys!" She thought she heard Errik yell, but he sounded distant compared with the pounding of the voices in her head.

Her cloak flapped as the wind around her swirled. Sweat dripped down her back. She dug her nails into her palms. Her muscles clenched and her stomach churned as the wind grew stronger, pulling dead leaves and branches and dirt into its embrace. Then, as if fired from a catapult, the wall of air surged forward.

Xhelozi cries echoed.

The wind roared and the monsters flew back with such force they were lifted off the ground.

Satisfaction pulsed inside her.

The wind whipped again. The air rang with shrieks of pain. Bits of fur and scales fell from the tunnel that churned and pulled at the monsters who dared try to harm her and her friends. The wind filled her and begged for more. More pain. More destruction. More vengean . . .

"Carys!"

Something yanked her backward. She crumpled to the ground and gasped for air. The howling of the wind faded as Larkin's and Errik's concerned faces swam in front of her.

"You're bleeding." Errik pulled a scrap of fabric from the pocket of his cloak and wiped under her nose. She started to rise, and the world tilted. Errik put a hand on her shoulder as she settled back onto the ground and he pressed the fabric into her hand. "Lean your head back and apply pressure to make the bleeding slow. Larkin, stay with her while I gather the horses. We don't want to stay here too long. Not with so many bodies near to draw predators."

Before Carys could object, Errik stood up and strode toward one of the horses.

"You scared him," Larkin said quietly.

"I should have told you what I was going to do or that I knew I could, but there wasn't time." It hurt to speak. Carys's voice sounded raspy to her own ears as she rose to her knees and felt a trickle run down her lip. The taste of blood filled her mouth, and she pressed the fabric against her nose. "I'm sorry the wind scared you."

"It wasn't the wind that frightened us, Carys," Larkin said. "We watched the wind take the Xhelozi, and then we turned and saw you. You stood so still even as blood ran down your face. Errik and I fought through the wind to get to you, and when we did . . ." Tears sparkled in Larkin's eyes. "You didn't seem to hear us or see us. Not until Errik grabbed your arms and shook you."

"I'm fine." The words grated. Carys touched her neck, and Larkin gasped. "What?"

"There are bruises on your neck."

To surrender to the wind in anger or fear is to unleash a power that can destroy not only your enemies, but yourself. There is no virtue when you lead with fear. There is only darkness and destruction and death.

The throbbing in her throat grew as the seconds passed. Carys pulled away the scrap of fabric to see if the bleeding had eased. The fabric was drenched with the blood that still dribbled down her face.

Carys shivered. Larkin tore a piece from her hem and Carys pressed it hard against her nose as fear filled her anew. Using her terror—her anger—was the only way she could make certain the wind responded to her. She had done what she had to do. But could she do it again and survive? Could she take her throne and destroy her enemies without it?

The bleeding stopped by the time Errik returned leading the horses. "We should find somewhere to hole up and rest for a few hours," he suggested, glancing at Carys, who nodded. The Bastian army was getting ready to attack Garden City, but the horses would give out soon, and so would they. "Did you and your father happen to stay in any caves near here?" he asked Larkin.

There weren't any caves, but after several leagues, they spotted a barn next to a partially collapsed cottage. The old barn was missing boards in the walls and tilted to the right in an alarming way. The structure creaked and shuddered as they opened the door and led the horses inside. Debris from above rained down on their heads when it closed behind them.

Holes in the ceiling that would be less than helpful during a rainstorm allowed slivers of moonlight through on the clear but cold night. Larkin waved them into a small room in the back corner of the barn. "We should sleep in here."

Errik and Carys agreed. The room was no less rotting than the rest of the building, but the extra set of walls blocked some of the chill from outside.

"I don't think we should post a watch. We all need sleep if we are going to keep up this pace," Errik said, settling onto the ground. "The horses will alert us to danger, and dawn will be here before we know it."

Larkin didn't need to be told twice. She curled up on the ground next to a crumbling hearth and closed her eyes. Errik did the same.

Every muscle in her body ached with fatigue, but when Carys closed her eyes sleep refused to come. Instead, the memory of the power she wielded returned, as did the triumph she felt when she unleashed the wind and allowed it to destroy. She had embraced her fear and anger and the wind had answered. It had also exacted a price.

Touching the tender flesh at her throat, Carys sat up. She glanced at Errik and Larkin to make sure they were asleep then pushed to her feet and headed into the main, open section of the barn.

A nicker and the soft blowing breath of the horses greeted her. Their presence was reassuring as she moved across the barn to the far wall. Several boards were missing here, which gave her a clear view of the horizon.

Seeress Kiara had told Carys it was possible to safely wield the wind. She just had to stay in control of her anger.

Trust.

Calm.

Carys closed her eyes and pictured the windmills atop the Palace of Winds. The pulsing of the blades was as much a part of her blood and life as her twin. The wind lit her world. It had kept away the Xhelozi. Without the churning of the blades, her kingdom would not be the same. If the windmills faltered . . .

The whispering returned. Hay swirled around her.

Carys released the fist she had unknowingly clenched and pictured the tunnels beneath the Palace of Winds. The hay settled and the knot of anger that was so quick to burst into flame faded.

She took several deep breaths and reached out her mind to the wind. Calm. Trust.

I'm surrendering! Answer me!

Nothing.

She shook her head.

Her stilettos went where she aimed. She knew the damage they would do when she unleashed them on her enemies. But her blades could only do so much. There were thousands in the Bastian forces amassing now to seize the throne. And the Xhelozi might soon be strong enough to overcome the wind-powered lights. The darkness in the kingdom was growing, and that darkness was adding to their strength. Carys had to put a stop to them and help restore the balance of virtue in the kingdom.

Only, without the wind, she had no idea how.

Something snapped behind her. She reached for a stiletto, swung around, and let out a relieved burst of air as Errik stepped from behind a beam.

"I thought you were sleeping," she said, sliding the blade back into its sheath.

"I thought we should talk."

She took a deep breath and nodded. "I owe you an apology. I should never have believed Garret when he said he woke and found you and Larkin missing. I—"

"That was not what I was referring to." Errik crossed to her side. "However, since you mentioned it, I'd like to say that considering my blood-tie to Imogen and the Bastians, what happened was not a surprise. It's understandable you would think the worst when you were told Larkin and I had disappeared. Only a fool would have trusted me under those circumstances. And you, Princess, are not a fool."

"Those who believe they cannot be fooled are perhaps the greatest fools of all."

"True," he conceded quietly. "Your brother did not believe he was capable of being fooled."

"And I trusted him. I trusted Garret," she admitted. "So what does that make me?"

"Human." He smiled, and her stomach fluttered. "You are allowed to make mistakes. We both have made them. We both are sorry for them and now we are here together again." He held out his hand and waited.

"I was going to kill you."

"Yes." He sighed and lowered his hand. "I wish you would stop doing that."

"I wanted to trust you, but I was scared to let myself. I don't think I'm capable of trusting the way I need to—the way Seeress Kiara told me I must. The blood and the bruising . . ." Carys touched her still-tender neck. "If I am scared or angry when I use this power . . ."

"You cause harm to yourself."

She nodded.

"You've survived all these years with the power inside you. Surely, you can . . ."

"I didn't know I had power before the Trials. The drink my mother gave me masked the talent," Carys admitted. "But there is a way. Kiara said I had to learn to trust the winds. That to control them, I had to first calmly surrender to them. That's what I was trying to do before you startled me."

Errik raised an eyebrow. "You, Princess, have never surrendered to anything in your life."

A laugh tripped out of her, and Errik responded with a lopsided grin.

"Well, this is one problem I might have a solution to. But first, you have to close your eyes."

"What will . . ."

He placed a finger gently over her mouth. "You said you have to learn to trust before we get to Garden City. So the two of us are going to practice trust. You can't ask any questions and you can't open your eyes until I say you can. Now, do you trust me?"

She wanted to.

Carys closed her eyes and Errik slipped his hand out of her grasp. Her heart pounded. She itched to move as she waited.

Leaves and hay crunched.

A horse nickered.

The barn creaked.

And nothing was happening.

In a few days, she would see her twin again. A few days and her brother would once again move to kill her if she didn't stop him or maybe kill him first. And she was just standing here.

Calm, she reminded herself. She unclenched her fist and waited.

Errik's footsteps came closer. His hand touched hers. Slowly, he interlaced their fingers. She felt his body no more than a breath away. Then Errik rested his forehead against hers.

She could hear his heart beating. Or maybe it was hers. Her breathing joined with his. The hair on her neck fluttered. The whispers returned. No. Not whispers. The sound was less insistent. Almost as if it, too, was waiting.

Errik's lips grazed her temple. Warmth spun from her stomach down to the tips of her toes. Then the warmth was gone as Errik stepped back.

"Do you trust me?"

She had only to think of the safety she felt when their hands were joined to nod.

More leaves crunched.

"Carys, would you please turn around," he requested.

She did as he asked and waited for him to put his arms around her. Instead he quietly said, "Now fall backward. I promise you won't hit the ground."

Her heart pulsed hard against her chest.

Calm.

The whisper of the wind seemed to echo the word in her mind.

Trust.

Surrender.

Could she?

Errik had risked his life to save hers. If she couldn't trust him to catch her, whom could she trust?

Carys released the breath she was holding, let go of the fear and the doubt, and leaned back, not caring if she hit the ground.

She never did.

Hands cradled her as she knew they would. They were gentle. Soft. Warmth flooded her. And after several moments, she was lifted up until once again she was standing on her feet.

"Turn and open your eyes."

Carys spun then froze when she spotted Errik several lengths away standing near a splintered beam.

"How does it feel to float on air?" Errik strode forward. "The wind caught you. You trusted and it came."

Carys put her hand to her nose. No blood. "You said you were going to catch me."

"No, I said you wouldn't hit the ground. I was ready to leap forward and break your fall if I was wrong."

Carys wanted to be angry at the deception, but it was hard

considering the hope swirling through her now. She had called the wind. It wasn't deliberate. She had simply thought of not wanting to fall and she hadn't. Just as when she had seen Larkin in danger. She had wanted to keep her friend safe, and the wind snapped the arrows before they could plunge into Larkin's chest. Carys hadn't thought about destroying the arrows. The wind had chosen that path. She had just wanted to keep Larkin safe.

The seeress had said the wind was not hers to command. But it could listen. *If* she stayed calm and trusted it to do what must be done.

"Carys?" Errik asked. "Are you okay?"

She looked around the barn as the wind whispered expectantly. The door to the building was open a crack. It was creaking slightly, she thought, which would make it hard to sleep because every movement of the unlatched door would make her think an attack was coming. She pictured it latched.

The horses nickered. There was a gust, and the door swung fully closed.

"It worked!" The door closing wasn't a big thing, but it was a step toward using her power safely. She would need that power if she was going to keep the thousands of Bastian soldiers from taking the Palace of Winds. "Thank you for helping me," she said, turning back to Errik.

He had stood by her from the first—saving her mother and supporting her during the Trials when almost everyone else had cheered for Andreus. And even when she had only seen the worst in him, he had seen the best in her—not a royal twin or a vessel of the wind or a potential ruler like Garret had. Errik saw *her*.

She stepped toward him and he met her halfway. His mouth

slanted over hers and she pressed herself tight against him to feel the beating of his heart. Everything inside her shimmered, and when she stepped back and looked into his face, she felt something deep take root. Not trust just in Errik, but in herself. She still did not know exactly how she was going to stop the Bastian army or eliminate Elder Jacobs and all who might be working with him inside the Palace of Winds, but she knew she would. With the help of Errik and Larkin, she would find a way. She just had to make sure they never saw her coming, until it was too late to defend against her.

It was time to return to the living and claim the crown that was hers. She must scale the walls that she hated and face her twin, who wanted her dead. She would uncover the traitors who were lurking in the shadows determined to destroy her family and take her throne.

She would return to their game—and this time she would be the one to end it once and for all.

14

Madame Jillian watched with narrow eyes as Andreus walked to the full-length silver mirror on the far wall. His leg still ached, but the weakness from the attack had finally dissipated.

Two days had passed since Max had found him unconscious on the floor and had run for Madame Jillian's help. When Andreus woke, he was certain the secret of his curse had finally been unmasked. But the palace healer had blamed the episode on the inflammation of his still-healing Xhelozi wounds, instead.

Council members visited with assurances that they were handling the business of the kingdom and that due to the unrest over news of Andreus's illness, the Council instructed the Masters to keep the orb shining. To do otherwise would cause further panic and possibly rebellion in an already-anxious city.

Andreus let them believe he was convinced by their argument as he plotted to unmask the traitor in his midst. In secret, he had already taken the first step toward that goal in the swirled snow atop the tallest tower just after the sun had risen. Soon it would be time to let the rest of his plan unfold.

Andreus bent his leg to test the flexibility of the new brace Madame Jillian had constructed for him.

"The infection seems to have passed quickly, Your Majesty," Madame Jillian said from behind.

"Thanks to you." He smiled into the mirror and in the reflection saw Madame Jillian let out a pleased chuckle. "I am lucky you are so skilled. Without you, Max wouldn't be tormenting the palace cooks, I might not be walking, and my mother would certainly not be recovering as well as she is. You are to be commended for all your work." He turned. "Have you seen my mother today?"

Madame Jillian sighed. "I have not been able to tend to her as much in recent days as I would like. I bring the remedies to aid her mind and body, but she prefers her chamberlain's company over my own. After losing so much, I am not surprised she is only comfortable now in the presence of someone she has known since before coming to Garden City."

He frowned. "My mother always said Oben was assigned to be her chamberlain when she arrived here at the Palace of Winds. I assumed my father or one of my grandfather's heads of household placed him in her service."

Madame Jillian shook her head. "I was an apprentice then and remember the day the Queen walked up the white steps of the plateau on your father's arm. She wasn't Queen then, but she held her head high as any queen I've ever seen. And she was so beautiful most people didn't look at anything else. But I saw Oben at the back of the guard. I used to enjoy watching the men on the practice fields and knew he had never been to Garden City before."

Her cheeks flushed with color, and for a minute Andreus could see her as a girl cheering on the guardsmen, hoping to gain their attention. "That doesn't mean my mother and Oben knew each other before they traveled to Garden City." Oben had once told Andreus that he had trained in a minor lord's household before using his sword for the High Lord of Derio and coming to the attention of the King.

"Perhaps I am mistaken, Your Majesty," the healer admitted. "It is just a feeling I get of a shared history. That, and he rarely if ever leaves her side. All know that Chamberlain Oben is fiercely devoted to the Queen. None would ever try to do her harm knowing they would have to go through him."

Of that Andreus was certain. The chamberlain's bulky robes did little to hide his strength. He had always seemed stronger to Andreus than almost anyone in the palace, except maybe Andreus's father.

The healer dropped into a curtsy, then eyed him sharply. "Take care to rest that leg as much as possible, Your Majesty. I know it is pointless to tell you not to walk on it at all."

When the door finally shut behind her, Andreus stepped into the bedroom doorway and called, "You can come out now, Max."

The wardrobe door swung open, and Max came bounding into the room. "I don't see why I had to hide from Madame Jillian."

"If Madame Jillian had seen you, she would have asked questions about the crumbs on your clothes and scolded you for eating too many sweets." It was an easier answer than the truth. Andreus needed both he and the boy to draw as little scrutiny as possible before he had a chance to unmask the traitor—something he would need Max to help with.

Max swiped at his mouth as Andreus warned, "There are things happening here in the Palace of Winds right now. Dangerous things."

Max's expression turned solemn. His eyes looked so much older than his eight years as he nodded. "I know, Your Majesty."

Was the boy recalling the hands that grabbed him and threw him over the battlements? Could he feel the terror of nothingness as his hands clutched the stone—as he held on for his life?

"Not everyone is happy to have me as King of Eden."

"But you are King. They can't do nothing 'bout that."

"Some people think they can. I need your help to stop them."

Max's little face grew fierce. "What do you need me to do?"

After everything Andreus had done, he knew he didn't deserve such loyalty.

When he had awakened, alive, from the curse's attack, Andreus held the scrap of parchment his sister had left for him and considered what his twin would do to find the answers he sought. Carys was not patient. She would not wait for the traitors to reveal themselves. Instead, she would create her own web and watch whoever was lurking in the shadows walk into it.

Which is what he decided he would do. And after all he had learned, he knew what to bait his trap with. The orb.

His sister had questioned the sabotage to the lights—and whether it was part of a larger plot—from the first. Almost immediately after his sister and he talked about her concerns, his father's and brother's bodies were dumped atop the entrance steps of the palace. Another night atop the battlements, Max had spotted people lurking in the shadows, and discovered the meeting of the Masters of Light. Moments after he spoke of that to Andreus, Max was thrown over the battlement walls. Add to that the fact that Andreus had commanded the orb be darkened, yet someone had convinced the Masters to disobey his wishes. The orb still shined because the orb wasn't just a symbol to those who were attempting to betray Eden. Andreus now realized that to them the orb was a beacon.

Perched high above the ground on the tallest tower, its light could be seen for miles on a clear night. It was a fixed point—like the stars—and was used to help navigate a traveler to safety.

Or to lead an attacking force across miles and miles to war.

Andreus crossed to the ornately carved King's desk and took two notes off the top. He handed the first to Max. "Give this order to whatever captain is in charge at the gates today." Andreus had commanded Graylem to avoid his chambers while he was recovering from his illness. Had the guard been seen, he might have aroused the suspicions of the Council. The Council had too many informers within the palace walls waiting for the chance to gain rewards for whatever information they gathered. "Once the captain gives Graylem his new orders, follow him and let him know I will require his assistance on the battlements."

Max took the first paper and gave a solemn nod.

"And then . . ." Andreus picked up the second piece of folded parchment marked by the golden wax seal of the Throne of Light. "I need you to deliver this to Master Triden." He was the one Master Andreus believed could be trusted. Andreus hoped he was not wrong in that faith. "Go with him. When he has finished the task I requested, come to the Hall of Virtues so I know it has been done." And that the trap was ready to be sprung.

"Max," Andreus said, stooping down to look the boy in the eye. "If you think you've drawn someone's suspicion, don't wait around to make sure. Run and hide."

"Should Graylem run, too?"

"Graylem is too big to duck into wardrobes." Before Max could come up with another query, Andreus said, "I will be meeting with the Council of Elders soon, so you have to move fast. First Graylem, then the Masters, then to the Hall of Virtues."

Max half bowed and bolted for the door before Andreus could warn him to be careful. He would just have to trust that the survival instincts Max learned on the streets of Garden City would keep the boy out of trouble.

He called his attendant to help him dress even though he would have preferred to be alone. With his valet's assistance, it took little time to get ready, although Andreus's heart beat harder to mark the passage of each second. Black fitted trousers. Polished black boots. Silk golden-yellow shirt and a deep-blue velvet vest trimmed to match the shirt. As his valet handed him the sword to buckle around his waist, he found himself wishing he could appear in the Hall in a mail shirt without raising suspicions. When his valet was reaching for the fur-lined robe, Andreus quickly slid two bejeweled daggers into the belt at the small of his back. Just in case.

Once the robe was slung over his shoulders and fastened, Andreus turned toward the full-length silver mirror and reached for the heavy woven gold-and-sapphire crown. Carefully, he placed the crown on his head, thinking of all the times his father had done the same thing and of how Micah should have been standing here had he not betrayed their father, or been betrayed by someone he believed was standing by his side. It struck Andreus that he had only come to stand in this exact spot, preparing to sit on a throne that represented light in a hall that celebrated seven virtues, because he, too, was willing to betray.

Andreus stared at his reflection, marveling at how almost nothing had changed about his appearance. Same dark hair. Same chin and forehead. Only one thing was different, and he was counting on the Council of Elders never noticing it. He felt regret. He felt a calling—a duty to make things right. To restore the seven virtues for his kingdom and to once again bring light to the people of Eden.

He nodded for the guards stationed outside the King's rooms to flank him as he strode toward the Hall. Had Max made it to the Masters yet? How fast could the boy track down the young guard who Andreus was trusting with so much?

The torches burned bright as he approached the two-story-tall, massive gold doors that led into the Hall of Virtues.

The throne gleamed. The seven members of the Council of Elders, dressed in black robes, stood at the bottom of the dais, each studying him with various expressions of concern, consternation, or disapproval on their faces as he approached.

Elder Cestrum strode forward, the missive Andreus had sent to the Council for this meeting clutched in his clawed metal hand.

The voice of the imprisoned woman rang in his head.

Iron for blood. Iron for heart. Clawing for summer when winter does start.

Was Elder Cestrum the one behind the treachery? Andreus wondered as he stared at the claw. Or was it one of the others who looked to unseat him?

"It is good to see you up and around, Your Majesty." Elder Cestrum nodded. "Your illness caused a great deal of concern in Garden City, and, as we have reported, we have done our best to make sure everyone believes the throne and thus the kingdom are completely secure."

"The throne is absolutely secure," Andreus said. He walked by the Elders and deliberately climbed the steps to his place in front of the throne. "And now that I have recovered, I require news of the petitions you heard in my absence."

"Surely, there is no need to bother you with minor matters." Elder Jacobs stepped forward. "After all, you have already been updated on the condition of the lights. The rest of the items are things your father found little interest in and trusted the Council to handle when he could not."

"I am not my father," Andreus said, taking a seat on the throne. He looked down at the men standing on the ground beneath him and insisted, "And I am interested in everything that happens in my kingdom."

The Council members glanced at one another. Elder Ulrich turned his one eye on Andreus and smiled. "We shall be sure to remember that, Your Majesty."

It was clear to Andreus that the members of the Council of Elders thought he would grow bored with the petitions quickly. Perhaps on any other day he would have. But he needed to keep the Council occupied and away from their informants until the final pieces of his trap were set. So he pushed the Council to discuss requests from lords and ladies for additional guards to protect them, from women who came to see if there was word of their son's or husband's fate on the battlefields to the south. He demanded more detail, questioned decisions, and watched the Council chafe at being forced to stand as additional torches were lit and night began to fall.

Finally, as Elder Jacobs spoke of the Council's concern over the need for more guardsmen, Andreus spotted Max at the edge of the main entrance of the Hall. He met Max's eyes across the wide space, then nodded ever so slightly to acknowledge the unspoken message.

The trap was set. It was time to add the bait.

"When Captain Monteros returns to Garden City with the new seer," Elder Jacobs explained, "he will train new . . ."

"I'm sure he will." Andreus stood. One by one, he studied the faces below him. "And I appreciate you doing what you feel is necessary for the Kingdom of Eden and Garden City when I fell ill. While I am certain you made choices my father would have approved of, my father is no longer King. I *am* the King of Eden now, and my orders will be followed."

"Your Majesty," Elder Cestrum said quickly, "we don't . . ."

"You have made your arguments. You have schemed and exerted your influence on the Masters to disobey their King. To disobey *me*. No more!"

Confusion and insult filled their faces as Andreus stepped to the edge of the dais and looked down on the Elders. None of them understood they were seeing the real Andreus now.

"The city is being alerted that I will speak to them after darkness is fully upon us. I expect all of you to stand with me when I demonstrate to the court, the guard, and those in the city that not only have I recovered from my brief illness, but also that *I* am the one who is in charge of this kingdom. I am King, and I will do whatever is required to keep my people safe. Because, as of tonight, the orb of Eden *will* no longer shine in the sky."

He strode down the stairs and past the gaping Elders. Elder Cestrum asked for him to reconsider, but Andreus didn't stop. He crossed the room, headed out the door, and then hurried down the hall to meet Graylem atop the battlements. He had to be in position before the traitor arrived.

Whoever was plotting against him would try to subvert his order.

If Andreus was correct, the traitor needed the light to help guide the Bastian forces to Eden under the cover of darkness. And in the desperate attempt to keep his treacherous plan from falling apart, the man who had worked with Imogen to take his crown would unmask himself. Once that happened, Andreus would expose the traitor to the city and end the plot once and for all.

He drew his sword when he reached the top of the tower stairs that led to the battlements. Then he pushed open the door, stepped into the gently falling snow, and hurried across the battlements to the alcove nearest the tall tower, where Graylem was waiting.

"Has anyone come yet?" He slipped beside the guard and squinted into the early night.

"Not since the sun began to fade, Your Majesty."

"It won't be long," Andreus said quietly. "Keep your eyes open. I need you to be able to swear to what you will witness in front of the Council, the court, and the city." As he was a sworn member of the guard, Graylem's words and his earnest manner would resonate with everyone in the city. Andreus would have the man seized, proclaim the man a traitor, and perform the execution himself.

"The orb is already dark!" an unfamiliar voice called.

Three shadows appeared in the falling snow, all with their hoods up and their backs to him.

"The Masters must have done the work before the King announced his decision."

"Or he did it himself." Another man appeared, and Graylem sucked in air beside him as Elder Ulrich pushed aside his hood and looked up at the tower with his one good eye. "And now Andreus plans to tell the kingdom what he did because he wants them to think he's a good King. Well, he will only be King for so long."

Graylem reached for the hilt of his sword. Andreus placed a hand on the guard's arm and a finger to his lips as Elder Ulrich paced toward them. If the Elder looked at the snowy ground, he would see their boot imprints that were slowly filling with snow.

Ulrich turned back as his men said something that was muffled by a lone creak of the windmill above. The blades were barely turning, which was the only reason Andreus could make out another asking if there would be a delay and something about riding out.

"No." Elder Ulrich's voice rang clear, and Andreus held his breath as the Elder strode closer to their position. "Tell our men to take the watch at the southern gates."

Their men. How many men did Ulrich command?

"Then someone find our Master friend so he can get the orb to shine. After all these years, the Bastian King is ready to return, and I will not keep him waiting."

Elder Ulrich looked up at the orb, then turned and headed to the stairway with his men at his heels.

"Follow Lord Ulrich's men," Andreus hissed.

"But, Your Majesty, you said . . ."

"Plans change."

Elder Ulrich had sprung Andreus's trap, but unless Andreus could make sure *all* the traitors working with him were caught as well, the threat from inside would continue. The guard within the walls was not powerful enough to take on an attacking army that was being helped from the inside. "Find out who they are and who else they are meeting with."

Graylem nodded and followed discreetly in the snowy footsteps of Elder Ulrich and his men. Andreus waited out of view for several minutes, then sheathed his sword and strode to the closest stairwell to get out of the snow.

Frustration and anger simmered, and beneath both he felt a sense of helplessness.

Most would think that foolish. After all, he was King!

Yet he was a king who could not trust the allegiance of those in Eden's guard or the loyalty of the Council of Elders. Without those, the crown's effectiveness was diminished.

If he was to succeed, he needed the people of the kingdom on his side. The people had power. He had lost their admiration to Carys during the Trials of Virtuous Succession, but if they saw him as the King they needed him to be, he could gain it back. He wasn't sure they would fight on his behalf if the army appeared at the gates, but maybe he could convince them to fight for themselves, their neighbors, and all of Eden.

Andreus strode through the torchlit halls of the palace determined to find the right words to bring Garden City to his side. Snow still fell as he stepped into the courtyard. Members of the court were speaking in small groups or walking toward the entrance. He spotted Elder Jacobs talking to Oben in the shadow of the gate. Both fell silent as he passed through the arching entrance. He could hear the nobles taking up places behind him as he crossed to the edge of the steps and looked down at the throng of people standing at the base of the steps in the city below.

The lights on the walls that rimmed the city shone bright. Here at the top of the steps, torches flickered in the falling snow. A small platform had been placed atop the steps as he had directed in the missive he sent to Master Triden. The coned amplification system Andreus had last used atop the walls during the Trial of Strength had been set up to make sure his words would be heard.

As a group, the Elders approached him, each wearing the cloak marked with the symbols of the district they represented.

Elder Cestrum leaned forward and whispered, "Your Majesty, you should know that it appears none of the Masters of Light are here and they cannot be found in the palace."

"I was not aware the Council was tracking every movement of the Masters," Andreus said as satisfaction filled him. No one had seen Master Triden lead the Guild of Light into the city to the inn Andreus had stumbled upon the other day. The Master was under instructions to remain there until Andreus gave word they could return. They would not be able to keep their presence there a secret for long. Andreus could only hope it would be long enough.

Elder Ulrich stepped forward. "We thought you might want them standing with you as you speak about the wind power and the lights. Their presence could help reassure the people."

Clever. Andreus clenched a fist at his side. Had he not seen Elder Ulrich atop the battlements, he would not have heard the deceit disguised as concern.

"The Masters are doing their job," Andreus answered. And it was time for him to do his.

Turning from the Elders, Andreus adjusted his crown and stepped up onto the small platform.

Trumpets sounded.

People turned to face him. Some cheered. Not as many as once there would have been, but some. He could feel Elder Ulrich's eyes on his back—adjusting his plans to put a knife in it.

The trumpets faded. Torches crackled as Andreus stared at the faces that looked up at him from below.

He thought of the last time he had addressed the crowd. Then he had believed he was more worthy of the crown than his sister. He had spoken with arrogance. She had spoken with her heart, and the crowd had given her their love.

He touched his pocket where he kept the note Carys had left him beneath the loose step and thought of the honesty—what he now knew to be honesty—with which she spoke not long before he made the choice to take her horse and leave her to the Xhelozi.

"People of Eden, thank you for coming out in the snow," he said simply. The amplification system caught his words and sent them to everyone in the city. "The cold months are upon us. With them comes the concern we always face from the Xhelozi. The monsters have once again awakened in the mountains and I know this year your worry is great, as is mine."

He turned and looked up at the windmill blades that were barely moving against the sky. Beyond that was the darkness where there had always been light.

Looking back at his audience, he said, "The wind is unpredictable and the lack of its power has caused a great deal of anxiety. I know that was made worse today when the orb did not light in the sky. I want you to know that I commanded the change be made until the wind blows strong again." There was a rumble through the crowd. "Many told me not to," he admitted. "They said the orb is a symbol of Eden, and if it darkened, you would believe that meant Eden was defeated. They said that fear would overtake the city. But it has not. And I don't believe that it will."

Andreus thought of Graylem, who lost his sister and still risked his own life in order to to protect others, and Max, who had been left for dead because of an illness he refused to let beat him.

He pictured them as he said, "I understand the people of Eden are stronger than they give you credit for. The nobles, the Council— they underestimate you. You understand that the orb is dark, but that does not mean we are in darkness. You know that the orb is but a symbol. The true hope in this kingdom is not a light high above a palace. The true strength of Eden is you."

The cheers of the crowd filled him. "We must work together and conserve all the power we can to see us through the days to come. The orb will not light again until the winds return. And if the winds continue to deny us, I know you can be counted on to stand strong against any who come to our gates and wish to do harm."

The people screamed their agreement.

"If that time comes," he shouted, "I promise that I will be standing beside you."

The cheers grew louder. Chants of his name and "long live the King" danced on the air.

He turned toward the Council of Elders. Cestrum frowned. Jacobs grinned. Elder Ulrich nodded and joined the others in their applause.

Then the torches behind them flickered.

The still-falling snow began to swirl.

Cheers from below turned to gasps as people pointed at the battlements behind him. Andreus turned and looked up at the blades of the windmills as they slowly began to turn, then gained in speed. The creaks of the windmills echoed with the growing excitement of the crowd.

The blades spun faster. Fiercely blowing snow made it impossible to see.

A gust of wind pushed him off his feet and he stumbled to the ground as all around him he heard cries of "The wind! The wind has returned!"

Through the blanket of snow, the lights on the wall flared

brighter than ever before. Hot and bright, and then the lights faded to normal.

The gusting air vanished as quickly as it came.

Andreus climbed to his feet and turned back to the crowd. The snow settled and Andreus spotted a figure standing just a few steps below. He held his breath as the figure lifted her hands, pushed the hood back, and revealed a face he knew as well as he knew his own.

His heart leaped even as his legs trembled.

Gasps echoed behind him.

"It is not the wind that has returned," Carys said, looking up at him. The defiance that had saved his life was bright in her eyes. "I have."

15

Everything was silent. The crowd. The wind. It was as though someone had wiped away all sound save the pounding of her heart.

Carys looked up at her brother wearing the crown that he had been willing to kill for.

She fought for calm, wishing Errik were standing beside her now. For the past two days, his support and faith had bolstered her efforts to strengthen safe control of her power. When she surrendered with calm, she had gone so far as to coax the wind to lift Errik, Larkin, and the horses on a gentle wave, gliding above the ground as it passed in a blur underneath them, allowing them to travel more swiftly than she had believed possible.

But no matter how hard she worked to keep her emotions in check, fear about the assembling Bastian army or the Xhelozi's growing boldness was always a breath away, pushing against her defenses. When it broke through, the gentle wind changed into a swirling tunnel that pulled bushes out of the ground and the air from her lungs.

The first time it had happened, the horses tossed their heads and

Larkin screamed as the twisting air engulfed her and spun her off the ground.

Carys had tried to picture the hidden passages beneath the palace. She'd fought to imagine something that made her feel safe to stop the flow of air as Kiara had instructed. But no matter what she imagined, Larkin was turned and pulled in front of her and the memory of the man the wind broke into pieces filled her mind.

Her fear grew and the wind blew stronger.

Then she felt a warm hand engulf hers.

Errik—steady and calm and strong.

Suddenly, Carys could breathe again.

The tunnel faded. Larkin landed on the ground with a thud—scared but unharmed. Still, it was enough to make Carys unsure when Larkin urged her to try again.

"I'll just stand behind you, this time," she joked once the horses had been calmed and they all had a chance to rest. When Carys didn't laugh, Larkin dropped her smile, looked her in the eye and said, "I believe you can do this, Carys. I believe in you."

"As do I," Errik said, sliding his hand in hers.

Carys faced her power again. And that's how they traveled—with Errik's hand tight in hers as the wind swept them across the kingdom back to the entrance of the tunnels that they had used weeks ago to make their escape, back to the walls she had always hated and sought to break free of, and back to her home.

A home that had been taken from her. A home that she was determined to reclaim.

Anger simmered as she unhooked her cloak and let it drop in a pool to the snowy steps. The gasps in the night said the garment Larkin had hastily put together for this moment had been well worth it.

The ensemble was one Larkin had been working on when she had been forced into hiding during the Trials. After arriving back in the city, Larkin and Errik had stolen through the night to her father's shop to retrieve it. The deep-silver, skintight trousers and fitted white tunic were edged in both blue and yellow. In the torchlight, Larkin said, Carys would look like a candle against the darkness. From the belt at Carys's waist hung her two silver stilettos—the weapons with which they had seen her defend her brother with skill.

Murmurs came from the people in the city below. Members of the court stepped closer as if trying to decide whether their eyes were deceiving them. The cold seeped into her body, but she refused to shiver. Instead, she straightened her shoulders, clenched her hands into fists at her side, and waited for her brother to say something.

Frustration and anger churned. The wind whispered in her mind, and she yearned to lash out.

Then her twin smiled.

The smile was so familiar. It stole her breath and pushed her off balance because for a moment, in her brother's eyes she could swear she saw joy.

"Imposter!" Elder Jacobs rushed forward and pointed down at her.

"What?" Carys thought she heard her brother say over the din of voices repeating the charge.

"Guards! Seize her!" Elder Jacobs called. A dozen Guardsmen standing at attention at the top of the steps drew their swords and started down the snow-slick stairs. "Princess Carys is dead. This woman dares befoul her memory."

"I am Princess Carys!" she yelled, drawing her stilettos as the guardsman advanced. Anger spiked hot and fast. The wind howled in her mind, but she pushed the whispers back. "I was injured in the Trials, but I did not die. I am the one who saved my brother's life in the Trial of Humility and scaled the wall when you required me to show strength. I watched you allow an innocent boy to be killed in the Hall of Virtues because of your twisted view of temperance. And I was left for dead by Prince Andreus, my twin, during the Trial of Endurance."

Her words echoed in the night. All around her people gasped. Elder Cestrum moved to stand next to Elder Jacobs. The Chief Elder held up his iron claw and shouted, "Halt," which caused the guards to pause their advance. His eyes narrowed as he studied her—as they all studied her.

Anger pulsed in her chest, and she took the steps upward—eyes on the men in the Council, stilettos firmly clenched in her hands. "You have forced me to compete. You have bruised my body and pushed me near death, but you will not deny who I am." Carys spun and faced the crowd below. "I am Princess Carys, daughter of King Ulron, Protector of Virtue and Defender of Light. I promised that I would always stand for you, and I have returned to claim my throne."

From the back of the crowd came cheers that grew louder with every beat of her heart.

Carys turned toward her brother, who stood still as a statue on the platform in the center of the landing at the top of the stairs.

"Do you deny it, Andreus?" she demanded. "Do you deny it is I, your sister, standing before you now?"

A hush fell over the crowd. The Elders turned to face Andreus as the Guardsmen tightened their grip on their weapons. Carys held her breath. The wind howled in her mind, and she knew if the guards attacked she would set it free even if it meant destroying herself.

Elder Cestrum stepped forward and called, "King Andreus, what is your judgment?"

Carys waited for him to deny her, but her brother looked her in the eyes and said, "This is my sister, my twin. Princess Carys has returned."

The crowd roared anew.

Elder Cestrum strode forward and stroked his beard with his claw. He held up his hand and waited for quiet before saying, "The Trials of Virtuous Succession were declared to be at an end, and yet here Princess Carys stands, which places King Andreus's claim to the throne in doubt."

The court behind the Elders gasped. The crowd below seemed to hold its breath as Elder Jacobs pushed himself forward. "I beg to differ. The law on this matter is clear. Once the Trials of Virtuous Succession started, Princess Carys and King Andreus were bound by law to compete until one of them won the throne or the other was dead. King Andreus fulfilled his obligation. His claim to the throne is undeniable while you, Princess, fled. You committed treason against the crown. King Andreus, I recommend the Princess be locked in the North Tower until she can stand trial for her crime."

Guardsmen advanced again, and the crowd's rumbles of upset turned into a roar. People chanted her name. Guardsmen started down the steps to push them back, but the people weren't retreating at the show of force. They were coming to protect her.

And in doing so, they could die.

The whispers pulled harder, but Carys shook them away and called, "Leave them alone!" Snow swirled, and she focused on what she had come here to do. "The last Trial was that of Endurance. I was injured and wounded and yet I endured. For me the Trials never ended."

"But they ended here," Elder Cestrum said. Behind him several Elders nodded. "The Council declared the Trials ended and by law Andreus is King."

"The law stated that the Trials of Virtuous Succession must either be won or the other successors must be dead for a new ruler to be installed on the throne. I stand here as proof that the conditions of the law have not been met." She straightened her shoulders and called. "I demand the Trials continue."

Andreus met her eyes and gave a small shake of his head as sound exploded around her. Cheers. Shouts of anger. Waves of unrest.

Elder Cestrum gave a hint of a smile as Elder Jacobs shouted, "No! The Council of Elders has already decided this matter. Andreus is King."

"We thought Princess Carys was dead. We were wrong." Elder Ulrich stepped forward. His eye turned toward her, and he folded his hands in front of him. "Princess Carys, I speak for all of Eden as I welcome you home. We asked you to endure, and it is clear by you standing here today that you did."

Elder Jacobs shook his head. "Just because . . ."

"Not only that," Elder Ulrich continued. "But when Princess Carys appeared, the wind that abandoned us returned. The lights on the walls shone brighter. The windmill blades turn now as they have not in weeks. We cannot in good conscience ignore such a clear sign of our mistake. Our way forward is clear. The Trials must start again."

"I agree," Andreus announced.

Carys looked at her brother, who reached up and lifted the

crown from his head. Beside him, Elder Jacobs shook his head as Elder Ulrich pulled Elder Cestrum close and whispered insistently in the Chief Elder's ear.

"Your Majesty!" Elder Jacobs climbed the first step. Carys itched to use her stilettos. "I understand you are surprised by your sister's return, as are we all, but I believe we should wait until the next Seer of Eden arrives before any decision is made. Captain Monteros will appear with the seers soon, and he or she will help us make the correct choice."

Before Carys could speak, her brother said, "There is only one choice. Princess Carys is my twin and she is alive." Her brother handed the crown to Elder Cestrum. Then he stepped off the platform and slowly walked down the snowy steps that separated them. He picked up the cloak that she had discarded, and placed it over her shoulders, immediately chasing away some of the chill of the night. His eyes met hers and held them. If he was waiting for her to look away first, he would have to wait a very long time. It was then she saw the flicker of pain in their depths. Despite the cold, there was sweat on his forehead. Her brother must be currently waging war against his illness—*his* curse.

Then he turned so they were standing shoulder to shoulder, and in a voice thick from exertion or emotion, he called, "The Trials we thought had ended are not over, which means the throne is not yet mine."

Yet!

Elder Jacobs took a step up the dais. "But King Andreus, the kingdom needs a ruler. With the lights and the Xhelozi . . ."

"*Prince* Andreus has made his decision," Elder Cestrum said smoothly as he took the place on the platform that Andreus had vacated.

Her brother's breathing was harsh.

She could feel him tremble beside her.

Suddenly everything that had happened faded away as the instinct to aid him—to save him—pushed through the anger. Despite that instinct, she forced her eyes to stare straight ahead—to keep focused on why she was here. She had returned to save Eden from the forces that were threatening to take the throne and from the monsters roaming the countryside. It was no longer her responsibility to act as his shield. Andreus had severed that tie when he turned on her and left her for dead. He did not deserve her love or her loyalty. If he had his remedy with him, he could save himself. If not, then he had only himself to blame.

They were standing together as they always had done, but they were no longer a team. Andreus had made his choice, and they were now each standing alone.

Still, the anger and bitterness that had built a wall around her heart since she left the Palace of Winds began to crumble. When he had been standing above her wearing the crown he had coveted, Andreus had been easy to hate. This Andreus next to her was more like the one she had always known. The one she would have done anything for.

Elder Cestrum said, "With the return of Princess Carys, it is the decision of the Council of Elders that the Trials of Virtuous Succession will continue as the law decreed."

From behind the Elders where the court stood, Carys heard a voice scream, "No!" Which was drowned out by the roar of the crowd below.

Beside her, Andreus stiffened.

Elder Cestrum held up a hand for silence and then continued. "At the end of the Trial of Endurance, Prince Andreus returned with the crown in hand and a lead on the scoring board. But much has happened since then and those events must be considered. By her return, Princess Carys has shown the ability to endure during difficult circumstances. She has suffered her own Trial of Patience and in doing so has gained not only the respect of the Council of Elders, but has earned the right to additional points on the scoring board. Therefore, it is the decision of the Elders that Prince Andreus and Princess Carys are both equal in points for the Trials of Virtuous Succession."

Equal!

Now she did look at her twin.

His breathing came in shallow bursts that turned to smoke in the cold. His hands were balled into fists at his side.

"However, Elder Jacobs is correct. This is a dangerous time for our kingdom. We need a king or queen to lead us safely through the cold to the warmer months ahead. After conferring with Elder Ulrich and the others, I have decided that the Trials will begin again tomorrow, and the winner of one contest will be declared the winner of all."

Cheers roared in the night.

Her name was shouted again and again. Here and there, she heard her brother's name called, but it was hers that rang above it all. They had not forgotten her while she was gone. They did not know of the danger that was coming, just that they were happy she had returned.

Slowly she turned around and faced those who called for her. She placed her hand to her heart and lifted it toward them and in the flickering torchlight saw hundreds return the salute.

She lifted her eyes to meet her brother's so he could see her triumph. So he would know that while she had agreed to allow him to win the crown the last time they faced the Trials, this time she was going to win.

His cheeks glistened with sweat. He swallowed hard against the pain of his illness, and she lifted her chin as if daring him to ask for her help. Part of her wanted him to ask so she could walk away and see him fall as he had done to her.

Instead, he placed his hand against his heart. When he extended it to her, she saw tears in his eyes. It was tears, not sweat on his cheeks. And his eyes—they were filled with sorrow and love and a desperate desire for forgiveness.

They were the eyes of the brother who she thought was lost to her. One who she hadn't expected to see.

She stepped back even as her heart urged her to step forward. Andreus had betrayed her once to gain the throne. She could not weaken in her anger or resolve or he would betray her again. He had proven that the crown was the only thing he wanted. She could not— she would not—allow herself to forget that or this time it would not only be she that fell but all of Eden.

"Carys," her brother said as the crowd continued to shout its excitement.

She pushed away the wrenching ache in her stomach and looked up at the windmills—picturing them churning the still-falling snow.

Cheers turned to gasps.

Andreus called her name again, this time with a hint of fear.

The snow swirled around her and grew thicker as the wind pulled it from the ground and sent it dancing into the sky.

Gears creaked and rattled, and Carys hurried up the steps through the blinding snow—the wind hiding her from view while guiding her way to the arching entrance of the palace.

The snow settled. She heard Andreus shout her name. The lights on the wall flared as if on fire as she turned on her heel and headed into the palace, leaving her brother and the connection she had to break behind.

16

Carys was alive.

Andreus still had no idea where his sister had come from. One minute he was addressing the people, the next she was standing there with the snow swirling at her feet. The note she had left him under the step had given him hope that his mistakes were not irreversible. But it wasn't until seeing her that he allowed himself to believe it was real.

She was real.

Elder Jacobs had accused her of being an imposter, but Andreus didn't need to see the scars she bore from her North Tower punishments or hear her tell of how she had escaped death while leaving another body in her place to know it was his sister. He had just to look at the defiance in her face to recognize who she was.

The last time he had seen her she had been sweating and pale with barely strength to stand. Her body withering and in pain from the lack of the Tears of Midnight. Now . . . he couldn't remember seeing his twin look so strong. Her head had been high. Her shoulders were back, and her distinctive white-blond hair spiked from her head, making it look like she was wearing a crown—as if she were already Queen. It was the hair that had caused him to believe the disfigured body he had viewed after the Trials was that of his sister. Even weak and in pain from the lack of the Tears of Midnight her body had craved, Carys had found a way to use her most identifiable trait to feign her own death.

Now she was back and his sister thought she had convinced the Council to allow the Trials to resume. But Carys didn't know what he did. That Elder Ulrich had other motives for whispering in the Chief Elder's ear. He had other reasons for pushing Elder Cestrum to restart the Trials tomorrow night, and if he didn't warn his sister, she could walk right into a trap.

Andreus had caught a glimpse of her going up the steps through the gusting snow. Then the lights flashed and he looked toward the walls to make sure they weren't malfunctioning. When he looked back, Elder Jacobs was hurrying in his direction, and his twin had vanished through the gates. Andreus had avoided the Elder and spent the last hour moving through the palace in an attempt to locate his sister. She was not in her room or in the Hall of Virtues. When he went to his mother's chambers, he found the sitting room in disarray—as if a wind tunnel had swept through, upending the furniture and dashing mirrors and flower urns to the ground.

"The Queen will be glad to know you stopped by," Oben informed him as he picked up an overturned chair. The heavy ring the chamberlain wore glinted in the firelight. "She took some of her tea and is finally sleeping. News of Princess Carys's return has left her . . . unsettled."

"Carys has not seen Mother since her return?"

"If she had come here, your mother's concerns would have been addressed."

Which meant Andreus still had no idea where his sister had gone. The palace was vast. It would take until well past dawn for Andreus to search every room, alcove, and corridor by himself. With Elder Ulrich and his men working to take the throne, he didn't have that kind of time to waste.

Frowning, Andreus said, "Thank you for taking care of Mother, Oben. I'm sure Carys will pay her a visit soon."

"I very much hope she does," Oben answered as Andreus headed out the door.

He had to assume Carys was deliberately avoiding him. She had to be warned about Elder Ulrich and convinced to join forces to see that the Bastians did not take their throne. And since he was failing to find her on his own, he'd have to enlist help.

Andreus checked his sister's rooms one more time—they were still empty, although an industrious servant had stoked a fire in preparation for her return. But there was no sign his sister had stepped foot in the chambers down the hall from his since her dramatic appearance on the palace steps.

Where in all the virtues was she?

Frustrated, Andreus threw open the door to his room and jumped as Max barreled toward him.

"Is it true?" Max demanded. "Is Princess Carys really come back from the dead like Graylem said?"

Graylem stood near the fireplace, censure etched in every line of the guard's typically earnest face.

"My sister never died. She just outsmarted the Council and me, something for which I will forever be grateful." He looked at

Graylem. "I thought Carys had betrayed me by killing Imogen. I didn't realize then that Imogen was using me as part of Elder Ulrich's plot." Or maybe it was Imogen who had enlisted Ulrich into the treacherous plan. Everyone always had an excuse for why they were convinced to turn against what was right. Andreus certainly had. "I made mistakes," he admitted. "But now Carys is back and if you are still willing to help, there is the chance to set things to right."

The fire crackled as Graylem looked down at Max and then back at Andreus. Finally, he said, "I followed one of Elder Ulrich's men from the battlements to the southeasternmost gate. He met with two other guards. I heard them tell him not to worry. They would assign men they trusted to man the three gates after dark."

If Elder Ulrich's men controlled the gates on the south side of the city, they could open those barriers when the Bastian army appeared. The enemy could be inside the walls and moving toward the palace before any alarm was sounded. A signal was all that was needed to let the Bastian army know the way was clear for them to proceed.

"I would recognize the men again if I saw them," Graylem said. "There are several who entered the guard at the same time I did. Give me the word and we could eliminate them."

Tempting. But while drawing blood would be satisfying, it would be akin to cutting off the tail of the snake. They had to remove the serpent's head. They had to remove everyone involved with the plot at once. There had to be a way to accomplish that, but Andreus couldn't see the moves he needed to make. He bet Carys would.

He had to find her.

He turned toward Graylem. "You said you followed my sister after the night the lights went dark. How often did you trail her?"

"Whenever I was not assigned to duty at the palace entrance or at one of the gates," Graylem said.

"She's not in her rooms or anywhere in the palace that I have looked. Do you have any idea of where else she might be? A place you followed her to that seemed unusual to you?" Andreus asked.

Graylem frowned and looked into the fire. Finally, he said, "I don't know if it's unusual, but there is a room on the next floor she visited several times. I hid in the staircase nearby, and the first time she went there I saw you . . ."

"The nursery!" He should have thought of the hidden room behind the tapestry that led to tunnels beneath the palace. If Carys wanted to stay out of sight, she would go where no one else in the palace would think to look for her—somewhere none of them knew existed, save him.

"We will draw notice if all of us go to the nursery together. Graylem, I think the two of you should leave here first. Make it look like you are heading to another part of the palace then use the servants' stairs to reach the nursery. I'll meet you there."

As Graylem and Max headed out the door, Andreus heard Max yell something about going to the kitchens for a snack. When the door closed behind them, Andreus paced the room, trying not to think about the hate he saw in his sister's eyes. When enough time had passed for Max and Graylem to have gotten downstairs and then doubled back, Andreus strode toward the door and headed to the third floor.

He passed the doors to Micah's rooms and continued down the hall toward the nursery where he and his sister had spent so much of their childhood. Their nurse had always marveled at how insepara- ble he and Carys had been. She said twins were like two sides of the same mirror—reflections of the same heart and soul. He had shown Carys the worst of their hearts during the Trials of Virtuous Succession. Now, their very lives depended on him showing her the best.

"No one's here," Max said as Andreus stepped inside.

Graylem stood next to Max, holding a flickering candle. "Perhaps I was wrong about where she went during the Trials."

"No, Carys has most certainly been here." Andreus walked toward the two-hundred-year-old wall hanging that stretched from the ceiling to the floor and covered almost three quarters of the wall on the far side of the room. He pulled aside the tapestry to reveal the door he had discovered years ago. As a child, he had pried one of the iron masonry nails that fixed the corners of the mountain scene out of the wall in order to hide from his sister. That moment had changed their life.

"A secret door!" Max danced next to him.

Andreus pressed his ear against the door and held his breath. Not a sound. "There's a small room beyond this door and a ladder that leads to a series of tunnels."

He took the candle from Graylem, pulled open the door, and shone the light inside the small room. There was a rickety table sitting just inside the entrance. The oil lamp that had sat on it only weeks before—the last time he and Carys came to this place—was gone, and the rug had been rolled up and the trapdoor raised revealing the ladder that led several stories down to the tunnels beneath the Palace of Winds.

As he put his feet on the iron rungs and started the downward climb, he thought of the times he had brought his sister here to try and shake her dependence on the Tears of Midnight. She had wept and sweated and screamed and shaken until he was scared she would die from the withdrawal and would give in to her craving for just one taste of their mother's drug.

Those memories had made him certain that emptying the red bottles and forcing his sister to go through the pain of unfulfilled need would tip the balance of the Trials of Virtuous Succession in his favor.

His leg was stiff, but he had climbed the rungs hundreds of times before and quickly made his way down as Max scurried along, sure-footed, like one of the stable chipmunks, with Graylem bringing up the rear. The tunnels must have been carved into the base of the plateau when the palace was built. His father hadn't ever shown an awareness of them. No one in the palace had, which had made it the perfect place for him and his sister to practice archery and throwing knives when they were children. It was the perfect location for Carys to ensure her safety now.

"Do the tunnels go somewhere outside of the Palace of Winds?" Max asked as he jumped off the ladder onto the dirt-packed floor.

Andreus placed a finger to his lips and whispered, "My sister and I searched for an exit for years, but we never found one."

Holding the candle high in front of him, Andreus walked to the end of the tunnel. He turned the corner and saw the glow of firelight coming from the next passage.

A breeze ruffled his hair and the candle in his hands went dark.

"It's okay," Andreus whispered as Max whimpered behind him.

The edge of steel dug into his side as his sister's voice floated on the dark. "Hello, Andreus. I had a feeling you would find me here. Give me one good reason why I shouldn't follow your lead and claim my crown right now."

"No!" Max yelled, and bumped against Andreus's side. "You can't hurt Prince Andreus. He wants to help you."

"I see you've found other shields in my absence," Carys said quietly. Andreus was careful not to move. He knew how sharp his sister's blades were.

"Who is the other one?" his sister asked.

"Guardsman Graylem, Princess Carys," the guardsman said in a tremulous voice. "You . . . you took my knife."

"Graylem helped save Max when someone threw him over the battlement walls."

"Someone threw the boy over the wall?" Carys gasped.

"It's true!" Max shouted. "It was the doom."

Andreus took a deep breath. "I know I did things . . ." There was so much he had to say. "You have no reason to trust me. But there are dangers here inside the palace. Enemies are ready to strike, and I need your help to stop them. Please, Carys. You have always been able to tell when I'm hiding something. You could always hear it in my voice. You *know* me. I am not lying now. You have no reason to put your faith in me, but if you want to help everyone in Eden, we need to talk."

He held his breath. The point of the blade dug into his side.

Then the pressure of the stiletto eased.

Andreus let out a relieved breath. It was a start.

"Walk toward the light," Carys instructed. "I'll follow behind the three of you. You thought you killed me once. I'm not going to give you the chance to try again."

Fair enough.

The light was coming from the part of the tunnels where he and his sister used to practice his guard drills. He turned the corner and stopped dead in his tracks as he spotted a fire crackling in the middle of the open space and the two people standing behind it with their bows drawn and pointed at him.

He recognized them both. The Trade Master who had stood on Carys's platform and danced with her at the ball held one bow. Larkin, the daughter of the tailor who they had played with when they were children, clutched the other.

Carys stepped around all of them and slowly walked to the fire to stand beside her friends. "You said there was a danger you wanted to warn me about. This would be the time."

While pacing his rooms and climbing down the ladder to the tunnels, Andreus had considered what to say. Now the explanations about his mother's plot to assassinate their father and the trap sprung by Elder Ulrich faded from his mind. Only two precious words remained. "I'm sorry."

His sister didn't move. Her eyes were hidden in shadows. If he could see them, he might know what she needed to hear. But maybe it was better this way.

Shame washed over him. He swallowed the knot tightening his throat as he thought of what he had done and what he had thrown away. "Words will never be able to fix what I broke between us. You helped me keep my secret even though doing so often meant pain for you. You stayed by my side through everything. Even when no one thought you were nearby, I always knew you were there."

In an alcove on the battlements when he was working on the windmills.

Appearing to be lounging under a tree near the practice fields, eyes alert.

In the North Tower, face-first against the wall as the whip cracked against her flesh.

Two sides of the same mirror. Only Carys never had a chance to see what her reflection looked like. She had been too busy watching his.

He wasn't sure if he would have done the same for her. She had never had the chance to make that kind of request. His secret had tied her to him, and he had taken that for granted. Maybe the only way forward now was to cut that cord and set her free.

Andreus dropped to a knee beside Max and turned the boy to face him. "Max, your family didn't want you to live with them when they realized you sometimes struggled to breathe."

"Mum said I was cursed by the devils." Max's voice was tight. His chin lifted as if daring anyone to think he might cry. "They said they'd all be cursed if I stayed with them. Even my sister."

"My sister, Carys, never said that. She told me she would love me no matter what." He looked up at Carys. His chest tightened—this time from a curse of his own making. "You see, I'm cursed, too. I have an illness that attacks my heart and makes it impossible to breathe."

Max's eyes widened. From the other side of the fire, Andreus heard Larkin gasp.

"You didn't tell them."

Carys shook her head, and Andreus closed his eyes. Even after all he had done, she had kept her promise to guard his secret.

"Carys helped me keep my secret. The old seer predicted that when the two of us were born one would be cursed and that child would need to be destroyed or the kingdom would suffer."

"There is no curse, Andreus," Carys said. "Seer Kheldin was a fraud, as was Imogen. The Bastians arranged for her to come to the Palace of Winds and help her family retake the throne they believe is rightfully theirs. She was never in love with you!" Carys hurled the words at him. "She only wanted power."

"I know," he said quietly. "I wanted to believe everything she said because then I wouldn't need you. Everything she said was a lie." Andreus swallowed. His words hung in the air. "I've needed you my whole life, and I didn't want to need you anymore. I was tired of being tied to you—of having no success that was just my own. And after you killed her, I didn't want to see the truth because then I would have to admit that nothing about me had changed. That no matter what I did, I would always need you." He looked up at the ceiling of the tunnel and clenched his jaw to ward off the tears as he admitted, "I still do. More now than ever."

He pushed aside the regret and forced himself to focus on now. "There is an attack coming by the Bastian army. I don't know how many or . . ."

"There will be thousands," Carys said. "We found a camp where the Xhelozi had attacked. One soldier had yet to die. He said they would be coming and they have help from inside the palace. Elder Jacobs . . ."

"No. It's Elder Ulrich."

"I traveled to the Village of Night. You did not," Carys shot back. "I spoke to a seer who told me that Elder Jacobs paid them a visit that none here in the Palace of Winds was informed of. He was the one that requested Imogen be selected as the new Seer of Eden. He is the reason she was here. She had to be working with him."

Andreus shook his head. "I don't know why Elder Jacobs went to the Village of Night to pick a new seer." He thought about the way the dark-braided Elder had been speaking to Oben outside the palace gates before Carys arrived and the way the emaciated woman in the North Tower described the man who poisoned the King's Guardsmen, and realized he might know. "He might have been helping Mother with her plot to make Micah King. You know how Mother believes in the power of the seers. Mother would want to make certain whoever was assigned to the Palace of Winds would not have the skill to foresee her plan to kill our father and put Micah on the throne."

"Kill our father? Do you have proof of her plot?" Carys asked.

"She confessed it all to me along with her desire to see me on the throne."

Elder Jacobs had actively given Andreus advice during the Trials to further that goal and since then had even gone so far as to express that the Queen would never have allowed Carys to take the throne. Then tonight, Elder Jacobs pushed to deny Carys had returned and worked to keep Andreus on the throne. Andreus had no proof, but he was starting to believe that the smooth, snakelike Elder had been a coconspirator with the Queen all along.

"Elder Jacobs is up to something," Andreus admitted. "But whatever his true motives and loyalties are, I am certain his intent is to keep me on the throne."

Carys might not like hearing that, but it was the truth as Andreus knew it. "It is Elder Ulrich who is working to give the throne to the Bastians. I heard him say as much tonight atop the battlements just before I addressed the city."

"I heard him, too, Princess," Graylem said quietly.

"Elder Ulrich was the one who told us we needed to be in the Hall of Virtues after Mother rejected her claim to the throne." Carys frowned as if trying to remember every word he spoke and every inflection in his voice. "He was the one that pressed Elder Cestrum to restart the Trials today."

"And Imogen was the one who made sure the throne was not given to Garret, and revealed the need for the contest between us.

The Trials made certain the entire city was focused on us, instead of on questioning why and how our father and brother were killed." And he had fallen for the ploy because he had loved Imogen.

Carys cocked her head to the side and frowned. "And with the final Trial happening tomorrow night, we will once again be following whatever plan the Council has for us. Meanwhile, the rest of the city will be focused on watching to see who wins the crown. No one will be paying attention to what is happening outside the walls."

"No one will see the Bastian army coming until it is too late to stop them," Andreus said, finishing his sister's thought.

The fire popped and crackled.

"So what are we going to do?" Max asked. "We can't just let an army take over Garden City."

"We aren't going to let them, Max," Andreus said, looking at his sister. "But we will need to work together in order to stop it. I cut the power to the orb so Elder Ulrich won't be able to use it to signal the Bastians, but if he doesn't find a Master to repair it, he'll find another way to put the final phase of his plan into motion. Thanks to Graylem, we know at least part of that plan."

Quickly, the young guardsman explained what he had already told Andreus about the guards at the gate.

"They have more guards than you can identify." Carys looked at Graylem, who nodded. "Which means there is no way to eliminate everyone involved before tomorrow night."

"We could try to warn the other Elders about the Bastian army," Andreus said. "But without proof . . ."

"They will question Elder Ulrich and no doubt warn whoever is plotting with him. That won't work." Carys sheathed her stilettos and paced. "If we are going to stop them, we need them to think their plan is unfolding as they wish. We need the Trials to start as scheduled so they believe we are distracted. That's when we'll strike."

"You have an idea of how to get around us participating in the Trials?" Andreus asked.

"No." His sister smiled. "But if the trial takes place in the city, I think I have an idea of how to use Elder Ulrich's own plan against him. We are going to need a lot of luck and some extra help if it is going to work. Right now, there are only the five of us."

"Six," Max said loudly. "I can help. No one really pays attention to kids unless they have to."

"Max followed Garret for me during the Trials and was never spotted," Andreus assured Carys.

"And there are several who entered the guard with me that I can vouch for," Graylem said. "If we are going to eliminate the traitors manning the southern gates, there will be a need for extra swords."

"My father and his friends will give aid," Larkin offered. "They aren't trained guards, but they will fight."

"Even if we remove the traitors inside our walls, everyone inside the city might be called upon to fight," Carys said.

"They will," Andreus assured her. "The people are scared, but they are proud of Garden City and their lives. They'll fight for them if need be. But they won't be able to hold off the Bastian army if they get inside the gates."

"If we do this right," Carys said, "they won't need to. We will lead the guards Graylem trusts to eliminate the traitors manning the gates. Once they have taken over the duties of those men, Andreus and I will remove Elder Ulrich from Eden before he has a chance to signal the Bastians to attack. With the Xhelozi roaming the countryside, the army won't be able to hold their position for long. A smart leader will understand something has gone wrong and retreat."

"And if he doesn't," Andreus said, "he will reach the gates expecting them to open for him and realize that Garden City will not allow him entry without a fight."

"But how are you going to know if the Trial will work for what we have planned?" Larkin asked.

Carys looked at Errik then down at her hands before saying, "I think I know a way."

At the same time, Andreus stepped forward and said, "Leave that to me."

17

"You?" Carys asked.

Andreus nodded and gave her the smile she knew was designed to charm. How many women had he enticed into his bed with that grin? How many promises had he made that he always intended to break?

Carys shook her head as Andreus said, "Elder Jacobs wants me to win the Trials. During the Trials, he gave me advice on how best to win the temperance challenge. Since I took the throne, he has been working to gain my trust and help me secure my position. He even went so far as to recommend that I marry an Adderton princess as Father had once agreed to do in order to end the war and bring peace to Eden."

"Whoever is working with my uncle to retake the Throne of Light for the Bastians wouldn't want to end the war," Errik said, stepping next to her.

Carys turned. "We don't know that Andreus is telling the truth." She turned back to face her brother. "And even if you are correct about Elder Jacobs, how do you expect me to trust you to alter the Trials to benefit the kingdom instead of yourself?"

"Because I'm not going to win the Trials of Virtuous Succession this time." Her twin's dark eyes met hers. "You are."

The words rang loud and true in the dirt-packed corridor. Andreus once again sounded like the brother who she had loved and protected before everything had changed.

She stepped back—away from the pull of emotion that bound them together. Trusting him would be a mistake. She had made that error before. She could not afford to make it again.

Will you forgive? She heard Kiara's words in her head.

No. Not yet. Maybe not ever.

"You don't believe me. I don't blame you." Andreus sighed as he ran a hand through his dark hair. "Carys, the last time we faced the Trials of Virtuous Succession, you told me we could control our own fate by working together. I cared about wearing the crown then. I thought I needed it to prove that I could stand on my own. I was wrong." Tears shimmered in his eyes. He blinked them away and straightened his shoulders. "I can't change the past, but I can set things right from here forward. Elder Jacobs saw how much I wanted the throne before. He won't question my words when I tell him I want it just as badly now. If I tell him I have a plan to win the Trials, he will listen. More important, I believe he will do whatever it takes to make sure the Council listens. And he will report back to me when the final plans for the trial are decided."

If she could believe Andreus, her brother's plan made as much sense as the one Carys intended to embark upon. Maybe more. And yet . . .

"How can you be certain Elder Jacobs will continue to support you?" Carys asked. "Or do you believe he chose your side because of your wit and charm?"

She saw her brother's hesitation, and the doubt wedged deep in her heart grew. "You can't expect me to trust what I don't . . ."

"Mother," Andreus snapped. "Elder Jacobs has told me he is working with Mother. He's supporting me because our mother does not want you to sit on the throne."

And in those words, Carys once again heard the ring of truth.

Carys closed her eyes and took a deep breath. The whispers inside her head grew at the thought of the woman who had from the first insisted that Andreus must be protected at all cost. That it was Carys's responsibility—to keep him safe even if it meant putting herself in harm's way. The woman who put the Tears of Midnight in her hand and encouraged her to stay under the drug's thrall.

"Carys, I . . ."

"It's fine." She shook away the whispers and opened her eyes. "You have always been the one mother preferred."

"Which is why it will be doubly rewarding when she has to watch you sit the throne," Andreus said. "Trust me, Carys. I can make Elder Jacobs push for the type of trial we need to take Elder Ulrich *and* the Bastians down."

Andreus had already shown willingness to do what was necessary to win the Trials. If Elder Jacobs was on his side, Carys didn't doubt the man would aid her brother now.

Could she trust him not to betray her again?

Doubt swirled and a single whisper echoed in her mind.

Will you forgive? Seeress Kiara had asked.

I don't know, Carys thought. But she could try.

"Go to Elder Jacobs now, before the Council of Elders have a chance to finalize their plan, and see if you can get him to push for the trial to be outside," Carys said before she changed her mind. "Graylem, pick a handful of the most skilled and loyal-to-the-crown guards to aid us. Larkin . . ."

"I will go talk to my father," her friend answered. "Then I will return to work on our disguises. Max," she said with a smile, "I could use some help carrying the things I need. And maybe some extra food for all of us."

Max smiled like the sun.

Graylem bowed. He and Larkin headed down the corridor with Max skipping ahead.

"I won't fail you, Carys," Andreus said quietly before turning to follow them. "Not this time."

She wished she believed him as he faded into the shadows.

"Do you want me to follow Andreus?" Errik asked, stepping to her side.

Her mind said yes. Instead, she answered with her heart. "No. If this plan is going to work, I have to trust him." She walked closer to the fire Larkin had built to chase away the cold and the darkness. "I thought I knew how I would feel when I saw Andreus again, and I'm still angry and hurt. But—"

"He's still your brother."

She nodded. "It was easier to push that to the side when I didn't have to face him. But just because I still feel connected to him doesn't mean that I trust him."

"Which is why you didn't tell him about your ability to call the winds and why you didn't mention the part of your plan that you are going to ask me to participate in now."

She should have known he would guess what she was thinking.

Slowly, she turned and reached for Errik's hand. "I still hadn't decided if I was going to ask you. With the Xhelozi roaming in the dark and no way to know where the Bastians have set up camp . . ."

"You need to learn how close the army is and find out when they plan on attacking. As a member of the Bastians, there is a chance I can get close enough to discover the information you require."

"And if your uncle learns of your presence?"

"He will either consider me an ally and welcome me with open arms or realize I am a spy and have me killed on the spot."

She shook her head. "We are almost certain the attack will come tomorrow night. You don't need . . ."

Errik gently touched her arm. "We both know you cannot make choices based on what you might personally want. You aren't just Carys now. You are the Princess of Eden, and you have to keep your kingdom safe."

She had never been just Carys.

Sister.

Shield.

Princess.

Now would-be Queen.

Errik stepped closer to her until there was almost no space between them. "The Bastian army is assembling now," he said quietly. "We know they are going to attack with the intent of putting a new King on the Throne of Light. If my uncle has his way, he will celebrate your death. I would rather die at the hands of my uncle or in a fight with the Xhelozi than live knowing I could have done something to prevent that from happening."

She placed a hand on his chest. Beneath her fingers, his heart beat strong and true. "If anyone can get to the Adderton camp and learn what their plans are without raising alarm, you can. If you ride out tonight, you can find the army and return before the Trials restart." Before Elder Ulrich had the chance to call forward the Bastian army.

Carys wound her fingers through his and squeezed tight as the wind whispered in her mind. Between the Xhelozi and the Bastians, the danger was great. He could fall, and she would never know how.

They could succeed without the information he could glean. But with it, they had a better chance of victory.

"You are not a subject of Eden," Carys said, looking down at the fire. "I can't order you to leave these tunnels."

"No, I am not a subject of Eden," Errik said. His fingers brushed her cheek and gently turned her face toward his. When his eyes looked into hers, he said, "But I *am* in love with its Queen."

Love. Her stomach jumped. She shook her head, knowing if she answered with what was in her heart, she would never let him go. So she put those words that she could not speak into her eyes and hoped he understood them as she said the only thing she could. "I'm not Queen. Not yet."

Errik smiled. "You have fought for people you have never met. You have run toward danger when you would rather flee and you are willing to sacrifice your own heart to see that others keep beating. A crown only bestows a title. It cannot change who and what you are." He leaned close. His lips gently brushed over hers, and tears lodged deep in her throat and stung her eyes. She wanted to hold him. Instead, when their lips parted, she stepped away.

"Be careful," she warned.

Errik picked up a small pack, a bow and quiver, then turned toward her. In the firelight, his olive skin glowed. She memorized the set of his strong jaw and the way his dark hair fell across his fore-head. Then he smiled. "Don't misplace your stilettos until I return."

His smile still bright in her mind, Carys watched him disappear down the corridor heading to the secret entrance that allowed them to flee from these tunnels just weeks ago. Then he was gone. The whispers in her head grew stronger. She paced the corridors and tried to ignore that the one method she had of safely controlling the winds had left her side.

The walls grew thicker and taller with every minute that passed as she thought of Errik, the Bastians, and the Xhelozi. Of the brother who she remembered during the Trials and the one who had faced her tonight. Of the mother who had enlisted her in protecting Andreus and preferred that he become King.

The wind whispered as she thought of Errik riding through the dark and things that could not be. And when the others returned, she pushed those thoughts to the side as she prepared for whatever tomorrow would bring.

Errik had yet to return.

The sky was clear and the air crisp as Carys stepped through the arching entrance of the palace in the last light of day. Music and sounds of celebration echoed from the city below. High above, the windmills were still. All around her, members of the court fell silent as they spotted her moving toward the platforms of blue and yellow that had been placed at the very top of the glistening white stone steps.

She looked behind her as she had dozens of times since leaving the tunnels—hoping Errik would appear. He might still be roaming the countryside, looking for the army. He might have lost his horse and been unable to ride. Or he could be dead.

Fear tugged at her heart. The wind whispered inside her head and she forced herself to take a deep breath and remain calm.

She looked up at the battlements, at the giant scoring board that the Council had created for the original Trials of Virtuous Succession. Once again it had been affixed to the exterior of the palace walls. An equal number of blue and yellow pegs marched across the board—blue for her, yellow for Andreus—providing a visual reminder to everyone in the city that the last trial would be the end of this exercise. The return of the scoring board would help build the excitement. It would have guaranteed that everyone in Garden City was talking of nothing else today. And tonight, everyone would be watching Andreus and Carys to see who would win the crown. Even the guards *not* part of Elder Ulrich's scheme would find it hard to concentrate on their duties.

Carys looked past the exterior city walls to the land to the south and the forest beyond. Was the army out there now? Had Errik fallen to them because he had the misfortune to entwine his life with hers? If so, how many more would die before the night was over? And would she be seated upon on the Throne of Light when the sun rose again?

Pink and purple streaked the sky as she waited for her brother to appear. He had returned to the tunnels last night, long after Max had curled up next to the fire on a pile of fabric scraps and fallen asleep.

"The Trials will take place in the city," Andreus said. "The Council is still working out the final details. I'll try to find out more from Elder Jacobs and get word to you before the Trials start."

But Carys hadn't seen Andreus since then and he had not sent

Graylem or Max with word. She just had to hope that her agreement to work with her brother was not a terrible mistake.

The wind whispered, mixing with her anxiety as the seven members of the Council of Elders filed through the gossiping court. Several of the Elders spotted her standing to the side and nodded. Elder Jacobs's face was calm as he twisted his long dark braid and spoke intently with Elder Ulrich. The one-eyed Elder's hands were folded in front of him as he listened to whatever point Elder Jacobs was pressing. A small smile played on his lips as he looked over at Carys and nodded.

"Are you ready, Princess?"

Carys whirled and Elder Cestrum gave a ghost of a smile.

"I apologize for startling you. I looked for you yesterday after your dramatic entrance, but you disappeared, almost as if by magic."

Magic. He knew about her powers. Garret must have told him what he suspected, and yesterday she confirmed her talent.

"I went to bed early," Carys said, feigning calm. "I wanted to make sure I was rested for whatever it is you have arranged for us today."

Elder Cestrum nodded and looked toward where the other Elders stood. "Many had strong opinions about what tasks you should perform. It seems your brother has made many friends in the Council in your absence."

Carys smiled. "My brother has always been charming."

"And you have always been the prickly one." Elder Cestrum smiled back. "Your father was proud of your strength."

"My father had me beaten for it."

"Did he?" Elder Cestrum asked. "Or did he follow the advice of one he trusted."

Carys went still.

"After all, you should know more than anyone what lengths a person will go to for someone they love."

He was just planting seeds of worry, she told herself. He was trying to make her doubt so that he could convince her to share the throne with Garret. She knew what Elder Cestrum wanted, and she wasn't about to let him unsettle her. There was too much at stake for her to lose focus.

"Your brother has a lot of friends on his side. You would do well to make your own friends. There is still time before the trial starts. But you would have to hurry."

"I'm afraid I'm not very good at friendships," Carys answered.

"I told my nephew that more than once. But he refused to believe me." His eyes narrowed. "Have you seen Lord Garret recently?"

She considered her options and decided on the truth. "Last I saw him, Garret was fighting Captain Monteros at the Village of Night. The captain you thought loyal to you was bought by another."

She waited for shock to widen the Elder's eyes. Instead, there was a gleam of delight. He knew that Captain Monteros betrayed Garret, and he approved.

"You set up your own nephew?" she asked. "Why?"

Elder Cestrum stroked his beard and looked up at the once purple-and-pink sky that was quickly fading to gray. Darkness was coming. "It is always smart to make friends who can help you gain what you seek. I make it my goal to secure the friendship of many. It is the only way to guarantee that even when a loss is suffered, I still win."

Fear flared. Of all the Elders, the Chief of the Council was the one whose motivations she had been certain of. Garret said his uncle wanted the power that came with the throne. She had assumed that meant Elder Cestrum had not been working with Elder Ulrich and the Bastians. But what if she was wrong.

"Your nephew would want us to be friends . . ."

Trumpets sounded. The music from the city disappeared. Carys turned as Andreus walked through the gates. The court stopped chattering.

In the quiet, Elder Cestrum whispered, "It is a shame that my nephew will have to live with disappointment. Good luck, Princess. Considering who your brother is and who he is working with, you *will* need it." He turned toward the Council and announced, "It is time for the final Trial of Virtuous Succession to begin."

18

Striding through the palace courtyard, Andreus pulled the white-and-yellow-striped cloak Max had delivered to him not long ago tight around his shoulders. The cloak was edged with the shimmer of silver and lined with snow rabbit fur. He stopped under the arching entrance of the palace and searched the crowd for his sister. He spotted her standing next to the Chief Elder, wearing a cloak of similar design, only in her colors of blue and white. Against the darkening sky, the cloak stood out like a beacon. Just as it was intended to do. Larkin was skilled and very clever. He would owe her a debt beyond gratitude for both if tonight was successful.

Trumpets sounded.

Elder Cestrum strode toward the other Elders. Andreus's sister followed the Chief Elder's movements. Then she turned and strode toward the blue and yellow platforms.

All eyes shifted to Andreus as he stepped through the archway and onto the steps where his father and brother had once lain in death. Killed by those who wanted the crown that he once again was supposed to compete for.

The trumpets sang again as his sister and he stepped onto their designated podiums. Carys looked straight ahead, never glancing his way. Never hinting that they had agreed to work together.

Elder Cestrum strode to the front of the steps to speak to the crowd that had, despite the cold, assembled below. Almost all were waving or wearing banners of blue. *As they should*, Andreus thought. His sister would make a strong and fair Queen. He would stand by her as she ruled just as she had stood by him all these years. She hated him now. He hated himself. But maybe if they survived the night, he would find some way to balance the scales between them. Maybe one day he could again earn the trust he had taken for granted.

But first they had to make sure there were more days beyond this one and a throne for Carys to sit upon. He'd been careful when talking to Elder Jacobs last night. With Max and Graylem's ability to move throughout the palace with little notice, Andreus was able to learn the Elder had left the Hall of Virtues and paid a visit to the Queen. Andreus waited on the stairs until he heard the Elder leave and then made it appear as if the meeting was by accident. Then he used the skills that he had learned from the ladies of the castle— only instead of being the predator, he pretended to be the prey. He'd feigned frustration at seeing the Elder and spun on his heel to leave only to have the Elder call his name and beg him to wait. From there it was easy. Elder Jacobs apologized for the new trial. He assured Andreus that the majority of the Council was interested in keeping Andreus as King. When Andreus lamented how his sister's appearance had ruined his chance to prove himself in front of the people of Garden City and earn back their support, Elder Jacobs was quick to point out that a public trial would provide another opportunity.

He couldn't appear too eager or ask too many questions and he was careful not to make suggestions. But he could see the gleam in Elder Jacobs's eyes.

When Elder Jacobs came to his quarters hours later, it was to tell Andreus that the Trials would take place in the city streets that his sister would struggle to navigate, and to suggest Andreus prepare to move as quickly through the city as he could.

"As you all know," Elder Cestrum announced, "the Princess Carys has returned to us and the claim to the throne is again in doubt. So tonight, we will once and for all determine which of these two successors becomes your King or Queen."

A cheer went up from the crowd assembled at the base of the steps. Anticipation shimmered in the cold air.

Elder Cestrum continued, "Charity and Chastity are two virtues that all rulers must have to wear the crown and today Princess Carys and Prince Andreus will show their dedication to these virtues by journeying to the seven shrines throughout the city."

Andreus smiled. Elder Jacobs had delivered the trial he had promised.

Elder Ulrich moved to the front of the cluster of Council members and looked up at the still-darkening sky.

"We have seven offerings for each of our successors to be delivered in the order of Charity, Chastity, Patience, Endurance, Humility, Temperance, and Strength. A signal representing Princess Carys or Prince Andreus will be launched into the sky after each offering is made. The one who makes it to the altars and then reaches the Hall of Virtues will not only win this challenge, they will win the crown."

And take down those who wished to steal their throne.

"But first," Elder Ulrich called, and stepped next to Elder Cestrum, "I believe it would be fitting if both the Prince and Princess address everyone assembled here. After so much that has happened, I am sure they have feelings they would like the opportunity to express."

Elder Ulrich's eyes flicked to the land beyond the walls even as he smiled his acknowledgment of the people's cheers of agreement.

"Prince Andreus? Would you like to start?"

The Elder was stalling. His forces could not attack until they were under the cover of darkness, and twilight was still upon them.

Andreus looked at his sister and then down at the hushed crowd below. He needed to be brief, but there *was* something he very much wanted to say. "Yesterday I regained my sister and lost a crown. I have no regrets. The Trials have not always been easy. I have learned a great deal about myself, but I believe I have learned even more about my sister. As have you. Princess Carys has shown her strength. She had demonstrated that she is loyal. And by returning to this city after being betrayed by someone she loves—by me—she has demonstrated that she is both resilient and brave. Tonight we shall compete for the throne, and tomorrow, no matter who wears the crown, I will be honored to stand by her side."

Approval roared from the crowd below.

He looked at his sister and saw the glint of tears in her eyes before she stepped forward.

His sister held her chin high. Her cloak fluttered. When everyone fell silent, she said, "I, too, have learned a great deal about myself and my brother during these Trials. I have learned that just because we live in a palace doesn't mean we are much different from you. We celebrate our triumphs, we weep when we despair, and when people threaten what is ours, we fight. Tonight my brother and I will continue that fight and we do it for you. Members of the Council, we are ready for the final Trial of Virtuous Succession to begin."

Carys's message was clear. No more speeches. No more stalling. The time to fight for their kingdom had come.

Elder Cestrum smiled. "Very well," he called over the shouts from below. "The trial will start when the trumpets blow."

One of the Council of Elders' pages handed a yellow satchel to Andreus. When he looked at Carys she was holding one of blue. Inside were seven wrapped packages marked with the symbols of the virtues that the contest dictated be delivered to the shrines.

Banners waved.

The crowd murmured with anticipation.

Elder Ulrich smiled at Carys and said something to her as Elder Jacobs approached Andreus, blocking his view.

"I have arranged for difficulties to befall your sister during this trial."

Andreus shook his head. "If the people think I cheated . . ."

"The people don't matter. If you love your sister, you must regain the throne." Elder Jacobs grabbed Andreus's arm and held tight. "Don't you understand yet? The Queen and her chamberlain will never let Princess Carys wear the crown. If she wins, she will die."

"There is nothing they can do."

"If you don't know different by now you are a fool," Elder Jacobs hissed. "People will do what they must to guard their secrets and gain the power or revenge they seek. If you want your sister to live, you must triumph. Her life is in your hands."

The trumpets sounded.

The Elder turned and hurried off.

"Wait," Andreus yelled, but Elder Jacobs didn't turn back. And there was no time to chase him.

If she wins, she will die.

Carys turned. Her eyes were clear. Her shoulders straight. Her white hair and pale eyes gleamed in the dim light before she lifted the hood of her cloak and settled it on her head.

His heart beat fast as he studied the streets that were getting darker by the moment as the sixth and final trial began. He started down the steps, side by side with Carys, Elder Jacobs's words trailing him.

He couldn't get those words out of his head.

He had promised Carys that she would rule. But if Elder Jacobs was right, she might never have the chance.

Andreus looked over his shoulder at the palace and those assembled on the landing above. Elder Jacobs nodded to him from the side of the stairs. Elder Ulrich's pale scalp caught the moonlight and appeared almost to glow as he turned and headed back toward the palace gates.

The final trial had begun, and Andreus had to move.

He pulled up his hood and continued after his sister. Her blue-and-white cloak billowed behind her. The sky was still a pale gray as he navigated the steps to the city below. His leg ached, but it would not slow him down.

"Carys," he called as she raced in front of him.

She didn't turn.

"Carys!"

The cheering of the crowd was too loud for his words to reach her. Clutching the yellow bag in his hands, he forced himself to go faster. He had to warn his sister of Elder Jacobs's plan to slow her down before she headed into the city streets.

His sister paused near the bottom as she searched for Larkin. The seamstress was supposed to be standing under a banner of blue. But there were dozens of banners supporting Carys, which made it hard to tell them all apart.

There. He spotted the tailor, Goodman Marcus, waving a blue banner edged in white and there was Larkin standing beside him wearing a dark cloak with the hood pulled high on her head. A banner of yellow waved not far from her and while the banner bearer was in the shadows, Andreus knew Graylem was beneath it. The faithful guard met his eyes, nodded, and then disappeared into the crowd. When Andreus looked back to the blue-and-white banner, he saw it was now gone, too.

Their allies had moved into position. Now it was their turn.

"Carys!" he yelled above the cheers, and was relieved when Carys paused and looked back at him.

He reached her side, and they stepped onto the cobblestone in tandem. "Be careful. Elder Jacobs does not trust me to win on my own."

"What do you mean?"

"He means to delay you so that I will win," Andreus shouted over the din. People pressed close waving and shouting encouragements.

"How?"

"He didn't say."

He could see her weighing his words. Doubting them because of all he had done. Finally, she nodded and the doubt in her face cleared. "I'll be careful. We will all need to be careful until it is done."

Tonight, above all nights, the two of them needed to be the team they had been since they were born.

"Are you ready?" she asked as they pushed through the crowd toward the street.

Andreus took a deep breath, pushed Elder Jacobs's words from his mind, and nodded. "Let's go."

Andreus grabbed a torch and followed his sister through the exuberant crowd to the south side of the square. People on both sides of the street shouted their names in the middle of the cold night. Somewhere from the darkness Andreus heard music. The city was celebrating. Those not near a shrine would look to the skies for signs of who was leading in the Trials. Few would be paying attention to what was happening on the streets or on the walls. Elder Ulrich would be pleased—but not for long.

They wove their way through the crowd to the south and headed down the city street. The first shrine they were instructed to visit was the Shrine of Charity located to the southeast—the closest of all the structures that had been erected to honor the seven virtues and as a place to plead for the winds to blow strong in the city.

Andreus rarely paid attention to the shrines when he was in the city, but he did know the city streets from his work with the lights on the walls almost as well as he knew the hallways in the Palace of Winds, so he took the lead as they ran to their first stop.

"Princess Carys! This way is faster!"

"We love you!"

"Let the Princess win."

Andreus glanced back at his sister to see if she had heard the cheers. Her head was high. Her eyes focused. There was no pleasure or satisfaction on her face at the calls of admiration and love. Instead, he saw the same steely expression she always wore when faced with a difficult challenge.

Finally, he spotted the glow from the torches and the shadow of the large tree that stood like a guardian at the entrance to the first shrine. He slid on the icy cobblestone, but kept on his feet as the crowd cheered his arrival and that of his sister, who was right on his heels.

The stone table of the shrine was carved from a slick, white stone. It was several lengths long and decorated with etchings of hands stretched out in kindness. A smaller version of the Tree of Virtues that stood in the center of Garden City grew behind the altar—sheltering it. A large stone bowl was carved into the center of the table. Wavy lines were etched on the sides and into the center of the bowl.

He glanced around at the people assembled nearby, searching for any sign of the traps that Elder Jacobs had spoken of. Seeing nothing obvious, he reached into the yellow bag and pulled out a small burlap sack tied with twine. He placed the small sack in the bowl, then tipped his torch to the offering hoping for once the Gods were listening. The small package began to smoke then all at once burst into flames—the offering to the Virtue of Charity would be complete when the flame in the bowl extinguished.

Everyone held their breaths as the last of the flame flickered and died. A streak of yellow sparks shot high into the air, signaling his completion of this part of his task. The crowd shouted anew as he handed the torch to his sister and hurried around the courtyard to the next street, stopping to listen to the cheers.

His sister was just touching her torch to the offering as he heard the call of "Long live the King" coming from his right. He watched his sister step away from the shrine, and waited for her to head down a different street toward the sound of a faint cheer of "Long live the Queen" before he turned and started to run.

Blue sparks lit the sky as he hurried down the street. A few well-meaning youths chased him, but when he turned down another narrow block where the call for the King came again, there was darkness. He reached under his cloak and drew his sword as he scanned the night. Snow and ice crunched under his feet. Each breath seared his lungs and was released like smoke as he crept along the alleyway.

"Prince Andreus!"

He turned and smiled as Graylem and a dozen guards he had recruited stepped out of the shadows. They looked younger than he did, but their faces were etched with resolve. They would need it soon, he thought as he unhooked his yellow-and-white cloak and swapped it for the black cloak that Graylem handed him. He slung it over his shoulders and studied the lanky, dark-haired guard who now wore the one that marked him as a prince. It was a ploy inspired by his foray to the North Tower disguised as Graylem. Somewhere in the darkness, Carys was swapping her cloak with Larkin.

"I always wanted to know what it feels like to be royalty," the guard said with a smile.

"It will feel like people are watching you," Andreus said, passing over the yellow bag. "Keep your hood up and when possible stay in the shadows." As long as no one had reason to believe differently, everyone would assume he and Carys were participating in the Trials. And once they were done removing the traitors from Eden, they would switch back with no one the wiser.

He hoped.

Graylem handed him a bow and quiver. He slung both over his shoulder and raised the hood of his black cloak over his head as the guard pretending to be him headed off to complete the Trials. When the yellow-and-white cloak disappeared into the darkness, Andreus looked at the others and said, "Let's go."

He could still hear cheers and music in the distance as he crept through the darkness with his sword in his hand. Graylem moved at his side. The wind-powered lights atop the walls grew brighter the closer they got to the southern gates. Finally, he spotted someone in a black cloak coming out of the shadows.

Carys pushed back her hood and stepped into the moonlight as a blue streak lit up the sky. Behind her, several men holding bows appeared—merchants who had been recruited by Larkin's father—ready to do battle for their city.

Andreus frowned and looked up at blue sparks bright overhead. "Larkin moves quickly. We will need to be faster. Did you warn her?"

"Goodman Marcus and several of his friends stayed with her instead of coming with us. They'll guard her back from Elder Jacobs and his traps until she returns to the palace steps."

Good. He hated to lose fighting men, but they had to cover all their bases. "Then let's go."

Graylem quietly gave out orders. They split up into two groups, Graylem leading one from the right with Andreus and Carys fronting the one that would approach the first gate from the left. Graylem would give the signal and the two sides would move in to eliminate Elder Ulrich's guards. Their own men were wearing bands of blue and yellow on their arms so none were mistaken for foe.

Yellow sparks filled the sky. His double had made it to the second shrine and was now on his way to the third. Time was ticking away. His heart beat hard as he stood with his back to a stone wall around the corner from the gate.

A whistle pierced the air and he raced around the corner with his sister keeping pace beside him—a bow notched and drawn in her hands. From the other side of the street Graylem and his men raced out of the darkness, swords flashing in the light of the wall.

Andreus slowed as he spotted two guards seated near the gate with their helmets low on their foreheads. From a distance they might look like they were sleeping, but Andreus could see the bloody gashes in their throats and the pool of blood staining the ground.

The guards he had come to the gates to kill were already dead.

19

They were dead. The two guards here at the gate. Two others with their throats cut just around the corner. The streaks of blood on the ground next to them had yet to dry.

Someone had killed them and left the gate unmanned. And Carys had no idea why.

Yellow sparks colored the sky.

"The locks on the gate have been broken," Graylem reported. "And there are two more dead guards in that alcove."

"We have to check the other gate," her brother said.

Carys turned to Graylem. "Leave the men you assigned to guard this gate here. The rest of you come with us."

Blue sparks shined above as they raced through the snow-filled streets to the next gate. It, too, had the chains that locked the lifting mechanism broken. Eight men in the uniforms of Eden were dead.

"I don't understand," her brother said.

Graylem squatted down next to each of the dead guards, studying them. His face was sickly white when he admitted, "The men I followed aren't here. They weren't among the dead at the other gate, either."

"Then where are they? And who killed these men?"

"Someone must have learned of the men's treachery and killed them," someone offered.

Carys shook her head. "The locking mechanisms are broken. The Bastian army can still gain entry without resistance."

A set of blue sparks went up. The trial marched on even as they stood here.

Carys looked down at the dead men. "Elder Cestrum spoke to me before the Trial," she explained. "He said something about making lots of friends so that even when he loses he still wins."

"I thought he wanted to put Lord Garret on the throne. Do you think Elder Cestrum has thrown his lot in with Elder Ulrich?" Andreus asked.

"I don't know." Maybe he had, but she doubted he would give up his ultimate goal and allow the Bastians to win. But he wasn't one to stand to the side while others were looking to take away his power. "But I know a way to find out." It was time for the Elders to pay for all they had done.

It took time to decide which guards would stay and which would go with Graylem to the next gate to make sure it was secure.

"Do what you have to in order to keep the gates closed," Carys said.

"On my word," Graylem said quietly, "while I am living no one shall pass."

More sparks flew into the air—once again of gold—as Carys followed her brother through the dark city streets. He led them down narrow alleys and around the backs of stables and taverns. Despite having grown up in the city, she would have been turned around and lost if not for her brother's sure-footed guidance and the sight of the Palace of Winds growing closer with every step.

Gold streaked across the sky again. Carys stumbled as a knot formed in her chest. "Have you seen blue sparks recently?"

Andreus stopped running and put his hands on his thighs. Breathing hard, he looked up at the sky and shook his head. "The last two have been yellow."

"Something has to be wrong." Elder Jacobs had said that he was going to make sure Andreus won. Carys tried to remember how many sets of blue sparks she had seen launched into the sky. Three? Four?

"Larkin will be fine," Andreus insisted. "Even if Elder Jacobs set a trap, she has her father and his friends to protect her. They won't let her come to harm."

Clinging to that thought, she followed her brother toward the Palace of Winds. Even if she knew where to look for her friend, there was no time, she told herself. She had to trust Larkin and those with her to see that she made it through the trial safe.

Still, worry cut deeper with every step. Carys clutched a stiletto tight in one hand and the hood of her cloak with the other as she followed her brother's lead to a winding path south of the main palace steps that led to the royal stables.

Finally, sparks of blue shimmered above. Relief burst from her lungs and evaporated into smoke in the cold air. Andreus gave her a grim smile as they reached the slope that wound up the plateau to the stables. There they found their palace lookout waiting for them.

"Prince Andreus!" Max called, then clapped a hand over his mouth as he raced toward them. His eyes were wide with excitement and fear. "I followed Elder Ulrich like you told me. After the trial started, he went up to the battlements. Then Elder Cestrum came with two guards and they had one of the Masters of Light with them."

"Elder Cestrum was there with Elder Ulrich?"

Max nodded. "I heard him say something about Elder Ulrich owing him. I couldn't hear what Elder Ulrich said to him, but before Elder Cestrum left he said that he wasn't worried because he always got what he had coming to him."

"Where are they now, Max?" Andreus asked.

"Elder Ulrich stayed on the battlements. Elder Cestrum went back inside the palace. I would have followed him, but I had to come tell you."

"You did good," Andreus said, starting toward the palace. "If Elder Cestrum helped find one of the Masters, I'm betting they are working on reattaching the orb."

Carys pulled her hood tight around her face as she raced beside her brother and Max. High above, the orb flickered with light, then went dark just as quickly. Fear lodged in her throat. With the locks broken, the Bastian army would not face opposition when they lifted the gates and entered the city.

But the Bastians might not have seen that quick flash of light, she told herself as they ran. There could still be time for them to prevail.

They raced up the steps she had climbed hundreds of times before—Andreus breathing harder and limping a bit more with every step. His face was glistening with sweat when they reached the top.

"Are you okay?" she whispered as they stepped out onto the

battlements and looked up at the North Tower where the orb now blazed with light. They were too late.

"I'm fine."

The raspy sound of his voice told a different story.

"Andreus . . ."

Blue sparked against the black of night. The Trials continued. The orb was shining, and an army could at this very moment be marching toward them.

Carys drew her stilettos and ran across the snow-caked stone beside her brother. His breath was still labored, but he was keeping pace beside her.

The torches inside the stairwell were lit, making the steep stairs easier for Carys to climb, but with every step her brother slowed a bit more. The stress and the cold and the exertion of the night had triggered one of his attacks. If Andreus pushed himself any further, the curse could overtake him. And without his medicine or time to rest, her brother could die.

Fear and anger burrowed deep in her chest. The Elders had taken enough from them. They had taken their family and their trust. They were not going to take her brother's life.

"Stay here," she said, drawing her other stiletto.

"No." He pushed away from the wall and lifted his sword. It was steady in his hand. "We will do this together."

Before she could object, he pushed the door open and together they raced through.

She heard the footsteps before she saw the guardsman's blade. Andreus lifted his sword, and steel clanged against steel. Another guardsman raced toward her. He slashed at her with his sword. She ducked, pivoted, and dragged her blade across the back of the guardsman's calf. His scream rang loud and the guard stumbled to the ground. She didn't hesitate before plunging her blade into the man's back. Seconds later, Andreus's foe fell to his knees onto the cold stone.

Together they turned toward the wide stone pedestal in the center of the tower. Atop the pedestal, the orb shone bright.

She spotted an older man in a gray Masters of Light cloak huddled on the ground on the other side of the tower. Blood streaked his pale cheeks and beard.

"I didn't have a choice," the man called.

"Of course, he did." Elder Ulrich stepped out from behind the wide pedestal. The light from the orb high above glinted off the knife in his hand.

The wind grew louder in her mind as she faced the man who had plotted against her family—had killed her father and brother— had destroyed her mother's mind and had shattered everything she had believed in. There was no question of his guilt now. No one else would seek to restore the orb's glow. No one else would have a reason to do so.

Her cloak fluttered.

The windmills creaked.

Inside her head, the wind howled.

Her brother lifted his sword. Carys cocked her stiletto back and Elder Ulrich grinned. "Go ahead and kill me. You overcame death once, Princess." He shifted the gaze of his one eye onto her brother. "And you, Andreus. You wanted so badly to be King that you fell into Imogen's hands. Micah had to be convinced, but you were easy. Imogen laughed at how simple you were to seduce. You were so ready to turn on your own sister and so willing to turn the entire kingdom against you all for the promise of a throne and a woman who would never really belong to you."

Snow started to swirl.

"I was a fool," Andreus yelled. "But you are a traitor."

Despite the cold, heat built inside her.

"I am loyal to the true ruler of Eden," Elder Ulrich called. "The Bastian King is returning, and there is nothing you can do to stop it. The orb has signaled them forward, and when my men finish you won't see the army coming. Stop fighting me, and I will convince the Bastian King to allow you to live." He stepped forward. "Elder Cestrum says you are both too stubborn to save yourselves. So filled with your own importance. He doesn't see that his nephew is the same. That you are all worthless as leaders. You are all like your father."

Rage bubbled. The wind pulled at Carys's cloak.

"Micah was even worse," the Elder taunted.

Her heart pounded. She clenched the stilettos in her fists as the wind howled.

"I was glad to have a part in seeing him dead."

Carys couldn't breathe.

Then the Elder lifted his knife and charged.

Andreus raised his sword, but Carys cocked her arm back first and let the stiletto fly. The wind raged. The blade punched into Ulrich's stomach, lifting him off his feet and then sending him crashing backward into the stone column. His eyes went wide as he slid down the stone pedestal to the ground below. The wind gusted again, angrier than before, and something cracked.

"Carys! Look out!"

Tunnels of air pulled at the pedestal. Bits of stone broke free and crashed to the ground.

"Carys!" Her brother shook her, and she tried to breathe. "Carys!"

She gasped for air and stumbled back as her brother pulled her into the stairway just in time.

For a second, the orb—Eden's beacon of hope and virtue—seemed to float in the circle of air before it fell on top of Elder Ulrich's unmoving body and shattered.

20

The orb was broken. Elder Ulrich was dead, and his sister . . .

"I couldn't stay calm," Carys whispered as they hurried down the steps. She stumbled at the bottom, as if her legs had given out. Andreus steadied her as they stepped out onto the dark battlements. It was then he saw the blood running down her face.

"I-I couldn't control it," she stammered as they started across the battlements. The wind was calm again. The windmills no longer churned. The gusts that had appeared as if by magic . . .

Magic. "You . . ."

Andreus pictured her standing with the wind swirling around her. She had been still as death itself as the tunnels of air appeared and lashed out with their power.

The air had attacked. Like in the stories. At the very moment his sister had thrown the stiletto, the wind had struck. Just as it gusted when she appeared on the steps to reveal she was still alive, and swirled again when she vanished from view.

He stopped in his tracks. "You caused the wind?" It seemed

impossible. He knew his sister, and yet he could not deny what he saw then and now. "How?" How could he have not seen this part of her? How could she have not shared it with him, especially now when they needed all the strength and power they could muster?

"The Tears of Midnight," she said as she pressed a piece of her cloak to her nose and shivered beside him. "Mother knew what I could do. The Tears erected a wall between me and the wind. Once I stopped taking them, I could hear its call, but I am still learning to control it. It's dangerous when it is done wrong. I have to be careful or I could . . ."

Yellow streaks of light brightened the sky. He and Carys turned, and his heart stopped as one by one the lights on the wall went dark.

"Elder Ulrich said no one would see the army coming," Carys whispered.

"One of his men must have cut the lights."

Crowds in the city cheered. They were focused on the Trials. No one in the streets was looking for trouble from beyond the walls.

"Carys . . ." He pointed to the darkness beyond the city. Men with banners riding and marching in the dim light of the moon. Thousands of them. Right toward Garden City.

"We have to sound the alarm."

He held fast to his sister's arm as they raced down the steps and across the battlements.

"Oh Gods, no!" his sister cried. Andreus went still and followed her gaze toward the mountains to the east. Long shadows were racing down the mountains and through the foothills. Dozens and dozens of them, moving like an avalanche. They must have been watching the walls of the city. Waiting. And now Elder Ulrich's people had cut the lines to the light. The Xhelozi had seen the darkness. It called to them, just as the orb had called to the Bastians. Now, both were coming.

"Come on!" Andreus yelled as the wind kicked up again. He tugged at his sister and they both started once again to run. "We have to fix the lights."

The lights wouldn't stop the army from coming to the gates, but they would slow the Xhelozi's attack. If he was fast enough, maybe the Xhelozi would turn on the attackers moving toward Garden City instead of moving on the city itself.

Side by side they raced down the uneven stone stairs. Pain shot up his leg and grew worse with every step. His chest tightened. Every breath was less deep, but he refused to let the curse slow him down. His sister knew how to fight, but she didn't understand how to reconnect the lights. The city needed both him and Carys to use their skills if everyone was going to survive, and he wasn't about to let them down.

He fought to pull air into his lungs. As they reached the main floor, he asked, "Do we go to the Hall or the courtyard?"

The end of the Trials was in the Hall of Virtues. The court and the Council of Elders would be assembled there. Elder Cestrum would be there.

Carys looked down the corridor toward the throne room. "We don't have time to deal with the Council. We have to alert the guards and the city."

"I can help," Max called, running down the hallway toward them. In everything that had happened, Andreus had forgotten the boy, who had been instructed to hide in an alcove until their return. "If the bad people are coming, I can sound the gongs."

Yes, he could. "Go! If there are others nearby, have them help you. Sound the alarm and don't stop."

The boy turned and bolted in one direction, and Carys and he raced in the other.

Their leather boots pounded against the stone floors. Servants jumped back against the tapestries that hung against the palace walls as he and his sister flew by—Andreus lagging farther behind his sister with every step. He gritted his teeth, clenched his jaw, and fought to keep up. But it was no use. Carys disappeared out the door to the palace courtyard and he limped after her into the bitter air.

The rumbling of cheers from the city below sounded in the quiet of the night. Underneath it all, there was the sound that made him shiver and move faster. It was the sound of a rusty screech like a portcullis that needed greasing. The sound of the Xhelozi.

"Carys!" he heard someone call.

His sister turned as a woman came through the entrance of the palace in the white-and-blue cape—hood still pulled high on her head.

Larkin had made it through the Trials safely. She had returned.

His sister hurried toward Larkin.

He saw it too late. The outline of a man stepping from an alcove. A bowstring being drawn back. The arrow that flew through the air.

Andreus called out a warning. He raced forward, biting back the pain in his leg as the man notched another arrow and sent it flying into the center of the blue-and-white-striped cloak next to the first.

Larkin stumbled. The hood slipped from her head onto her shoulders as his sister caught their childhood friend in her arms.

"It's not her!" a woman screamed.

The man with the bow advanced several steps then reached for another arrow. Andreus slipped on the ice as the attacker notched the arrow in the bow and took aim. Fighting to keep his feet under him, Andreus lifted his sword and swung.

The blade sliced through flesh. The bow, along with the attacker's hand and forearm, thudded to the ground. Blood spurted warm onto Andreus's legs and the white snow.

Andreus raised the sword again, and buried the blade in the attacker's neck as his mother screamed, "Oben! No!"

"Larkin!" Carys saw her brother race toward the man with the bow. She caught the glint of the sword in the moonlight before dropping to her knees next to her friend. "You're going to be okay," she said desperately as she clutched the stiletto in her hand, ready to kill any who came near.

Larkin looked up at the sky with her deep brown eyes. Carys had always thought her friend had the most beautiful she'd ever seen. They were wide and dark and so often sparkled with laughter. Only now those eyes shimmered with pain.

"Someone get Madame Jillian!" Carys screamed even though she knew what the arrows buried deep in Larkin's chest meant. The healer was skilled, but there was no denying the gurgling sounds Larkin made as she fought to take in air.

The wind hadn't stopped the arrows this time, because Carys hadn't seen the danger. She hadn't known, and now . . .

"You can't die," Carys insisted. She reached for her friend's hand—slick with the blood that drop by drop was draining Larkin's life. "I command you not to die! Please, Larkin! Please, don't die."

"Carys," Larkin whispered. "I . . ."

"Shhh. Don't talk." Carys squeezed Larkin's fingers. They were so cold. Too cold. "Save your strength. Madame Jillian will make you better and you can keep telling me that I'm not a lady."

"But you are," Larkin whispered. "You always have been. Just a different kind. Free." A shudder rippled through Larkin. She coughed and blood stained her mouth.

"Please," Carys begged. "I can't lose you."

"Never lose." Larkin's eyes fluttered shut. "I'm here. Like the wind. Always . . ." Larkin's breath gurgled. Her chest shuddered. Her friend's pale lips parted and the air around them went still.

Larkin—the girl who had taught Carys that there were more important things than crowns and jewels and power—was dead.

Carys held tight to her friend's blood-streaked, always-capable hand. She didn't want to let go. Larkin was supposed to get married. She was supposed to leave the city walls and find happiness. Instead she died pretending to be Carys all because she was determined to fight for Eden. Larkin had wanted those she loved to be safe. Only they weren't. Not yet.

The Bastian army was approaching the walls. The Xhelozi were coming from the mountains. Larkin would insist Carys get up off the cold ground. She would want Carys to continue to fight and protect the city and her father, who didn't know his daughter was dead.

Carys's mother shrieked.

Andreus shouted back as Carys slowly released her friend's hand, pushed to her feet, and turned.

"Mother, no!" Andreus yelled, grabbing their mother, who was standing over the chamberlain's body.

"She was supposed to die! She has to die!" their mother screamed. The words punched into Carys as if they were the dagger the Queen raised high over her head.

And in that moment Carys understood why Larkin was dead.

The white-and-blue cloak. Larkin's newly short hair that she had bleached pale to swap identities. The bow next to the fallen chamberlain's body. The arrows hadn't been meant for Larkin. They had been meant for her.

"Kill her, Andreus! You have to stop the curse. The curse is real. I've seen it in my dreams since I was born. People will continue to die if the curse continues. She is the curse!"

"Mother," Carys called as the wind began to whisper in her head again. Hurt. Anger. Fear. "You . . ."

"Don't call me that!" The Queen whirled. "I'm not your mother! He insisted that I lie and I did, but I have never been your mother!"

The white dress billowed. Dark hair whipped around the Queen's face, framing eyes that were clear and determined and far too sane for the words that she spoke.

"Ulron's mistress and I became pregnant at the same time." Carys's mother held the dagger in front of her. The blade gleamed in the moonlight as the Queen shifted back and forth. "He thought Andreus was his child just as he believed Micah was. He didn't know that I never intended him to have a child. The curse of his line—the curse his family began when they took the throne—was supposed to end when Micah became King. Ulron's bloodline would have been removed from power even as others thought it lived on."

"Mother, you're not making any sense," Andreus said, his eyes flicking toward the arching entrance of the palace gate toward the city. The Bastians and the Xhelozi were still coming. "Micah was our brother."

"Micah was *your* brother." Carys's mother turned back to Andreus. The dagger still tight in her fist. "He was like you. He was Oben's son."

The gong began to sound.

But it was her mother's words that rang in her head. *Oben's* son?

Carys looked down at the chamberlain's body. Micah and Andreus, with their richer skin tone and darker hair, had always looked different from her. Everyone said they favored their mother, and that Carys took after her father. But . . .

Her stomach churned.

The single gong grew into a chorus. The war starting outside the walls echoed in the night, but the only battle she could focus on was right here. Carys unclenched her hands and fought for calm. She had to stay calm. "Andreus and I are twins, Mother."

"I'm not your mother!" the Queen screamed. Rage twisted her beautiful face. "I learned I was pregnant with Andreus just before Ulron told me his mistress was with child. The woman said she had the power of the seers, and Ulron believed her. He had hoped my visions meant his children might have true powers like the rulers in the past used to vanquish their enemies. He claimed you would help him conquer Adderton and any that would rise against him. He wanted you and insisted I owed him my cooperation for making me his Queen."

It couldn't be true!

"Mother," Andreus said, taking a slow step forward. "You're confused. Carys and I are twins. We were born on the same day."

She and Andreus were two halves of the same whole. Two faces in the same reflection. Her life was as it was because she had lived it for him.

Their mother laughed. The ugly, bitter sound cut deep into Carys's heart. "Ulron hid his mistress in the city while she was pregnant and snuck her back into the palace when it was Andreus's time to be born." The Queen looked adoringly at Andreus. "The midwife delivered you, my son, then with Oben's help cut the King's bastard free. At her birth Carys proved the curse of her family's bloodline. It was her life that led to her mother's death."

Carys shook her head, even as something inside her clicked. It was as if a key had slid into a lock and a door opened. Her mother had never cared when Carys had been beaten to protect Andreus. She had never flinched or wept when Carys was scarred or was in agony. She didn't care what the Tears of Midnight did to Carys. Never did she encourage Carys to break free of the drug that kept the whispers of the wind and the hurt at bay. Their mother had simply insisted Carys take more because she didn't want Carys to know the truth. Carys wasn't a twin. Andreus had never been her brother.

She was the King's child.

The heir to the throne.

The last of her father's line.

Yet now more than ever, she felt as if she was nothing.

"You murdered the midwife," Andreus said.

The woman's disappearance after their birth finally made a horrible kind of sense. No witnesses could be left alive to tell the King's secret. With her dead none would be left alive to know that Carys was not birthed by the Queen. Except the Queen herself and the man she said fathered Andreus and Micah.

The Queen smiled. "The King believed Oben slit her throat on his order, but the King was wrong. Oben did it for love of me and to keep our secret."

A secret that led here—to the death of her father and Micah, the start of the Trials, and now the war that was about to be waged for a throne Carys had never wanted and yet was truly hers by blood.

Her father was dead. As was the mother she had never known.

Seeress Kiara said the jeweled slippers were the key to setting her free. The slippers that belonged to the Queen—a woman who had used Carys's love for Andreus and the Tears of Midnight to hold her life hostage.

Her brother turned to look at her.

No—not her brother. Andreus—a man who did not share her blood.

She stared into his eyes that were as dark as hers were pale. That was but one difference between them. Now she looked for them all. His dark hair. His tanned skin. The weak heart that she fought to hide because hers had been born strong.

She saw those things that divided them now.

They weren't two halves of one whole. They were never meant to be each other's reflections.

"Kill her, Andreus!" The Queen seized Andreus's hand and pressed the dagger into it. "You were meant to be King. Your father lost his parents when Carys's family seized the throne. He bore scars so you wouldn't have to wear them. He sacrificed everything including his own life for you."

Andreus took the dagger and shook his head. "No. It doesn't matter what you say, Mother, or what blood runs in my veins . . ." He turned toward Carys and let the blade fall to the ground. "Carys is my sister and you, Mother, are nothing."

Andreus met her eyes again and she understood the question she saw in their depths.

The wind howled in her mind. Their mother raged.

Carys looked down at Larkin and put her hand on her heart and then lifted it to the sky, and the whispering of the wind faded.

Larkin hadn't been born in a palace and she had not shared a drop of royal blood, but she had been Carys's sister.

Carys looked back at her brother and nodded. She and Andreus weren't siblings by birth. They didn't need to share the same parents to be connected, because they shared a heart.

Carys saw the tears in Andreus's eyes as he understood without words what she was saying. Dreus was her twin. He was her brother, and they would stand together not because blood dictated they should, but by choice—tonight and always.

His stomach was like lead. Each breath felt as if he were inhaling glass. Nothing was the same. So many secrets. So many lies.

Larkin dead. Killed by Oben—his mother's chamberlain. The man who was his father. The man he had known all his life and had barely known at all. His father—the man Andreus had just killed.

Andreus looked at Carys again. Her light-colored eyes met his. Steadfast. Resolute. And filled with love. He didn't need to hear the words to know what was in her heart and mind. She was his sister no matter what his mother said. No matter what he had done. He had made mistakes, but he had learned from them and he would stand by Carys. He would fight for Eden beside her. She *was* his family.

The gongs continued to ring.

The cheers that had filled the night turned to shouts and screams. In the distance, he heard the sound of metal striking metal. The fighting had started.

"We have to fix the lights and arm the gates."

Everything was different, yet nothing had changed.

He let out the breath he was holding and turned toward the arching palace entrance.

"Andreus, you have to stop her." His mother clawed his arm. "The curse . . ."

"If there is anyone cursed, it's you!" He shoved his mother away from him and walked away with her screams chasing behind him.

"Graylem is at the gates," Carys said, falling into step beside him. Her stiletto was raised and ready. "He will do what he can to hold them until reinforcements arrive, but I'm not sure how long our forces can hold out against the Bastians and the Xhelozi. If we had more time . . ."

He knew what she was thinking. With more time they could order anyone who couldn't fight to take refuge within the palace walls. They could arrange those ready to defend the city in places where their fighting could do some good. But there wasn't more time.

"I have to get to the walls of the city to fix the line Elder Ulrich's men cut." The Xhelozi had grown bolder—attracted to the darkness that wasn't just from the night, according to the seer Carys had talked to. The lights might not be enough to push them back, but he had to try.

His leg burned and threatened to buckle, but the sound of the gongs, his sister running next to him, and the shadows he could see beyond the walls kept him upright. Carys held his arm as they went down to the stables for the second time that night. They rode to the base of the steps where Graylem was directing guardsmen, merchants, and common citizens to the southern gates.

The sound of rusty cries brought everything to a standstill. All eyes turned toward the southern walls. The shrieks clawed the air again followed by the faint sound of human screams.

The Xhelozi had arrived and had met the Bastian forces.

Dozens of people on the city streets shouted in fear. They pushed at one another and raced into the darkness for their homes. But there were others, like the men Larkin and her father and Graylem's guards had recruited, who stood their ground, waiting for orders. They would do what they could to defend Garden City.

He dug his legs into his mount and galloped down the street. His sister kept pace on her horse next to him. The high-pitched cries of the Xhelozi grew more frequent and sounded closer now.

Andreus urged his horse to go faster. The lights had appeared to darken first on the southeasternmost section of the wall. The Master working with Elder Ulrich must have told him it was the logical place to strike if one wanted to sabotage the lights without damaging the entire system. It would also be the easiest to repair, something Elder Ulrich would have wanted to do quickly after his plan was complete.

Doors slammed as the people of Eden took to their houses. Andreus raced down another street as the hooves of his mount and that of his sister clattered on the cobblestones.

The shouts and screams and shrieks from beyond the walls grew louder. The crash of metal rang loud in his ears. Something crashed against the gates and the ground beneath him seemed to shake as he and his sister turned their mounts down the road that led to the light connection he had to repair.

Andreus yanked on his reins and slid from the horse when it came to a stop. His sister was right beside him—guarding his back as she had always done. They reached the walls, and Carys lifted a torch as he scaled several rungs of the ladder. The sight of the two mangled cuts that had removed a section of the line kicked him in the gut. He had hoped whoever had disabled the lights, knowing that the city would need the lines for safety after this night passed, would have taken more care.

"It won't be perfect, and it might not last long, but I will find a way to give us some light."

The gongs continued to crash.

Screams and sounds of swords striking swords clashed in the air.

"What do you need?" Carys asked.

"Twine or strips of fabric. Something I can use to attach whatever conductors I come up with together." If he stripped the tar off the line wire and used the silver on his belt . . .

Carys reached down and grabbed her hem. Her stiletto flashed in the torchlight. Seconds later, she handed him several long strips of black fabric.

The Xhelozi screams mixed with human ones. His sister looked toward the wall. She shifted her weight and looked back at him. He knew Carys wanted to see what was happening—but she wouldn't leave him alone. After everything he had done, and everything they had learned, she was still acting as his shield.

"Go!" he insisted. "I don't know how long this is going to take. Graylem and the others need a leader. They need you."

His sister shuffled her feet. Indecision warred on her face.

"We need to use both our strengths," Andreus said. "Mine is here with the lights. Yours is on the walls."

He saw the shimmer of tears as Carys straightened her shoulders and nodded.

"I'll find you on the walls when we're done," he said. "I promise. Go!"

She took two steps backward, then his sister turned and ran.

21

Dreus was right. There was nothing she could do to help him fix the lines. She knew little about the workings of the lights or the windmills and would only get in his way. She had to go where she could help those screaming in the night. So she ran toward the sounds of war and the crash of something that made the city shake.

The outside forces were ramming against the gates to break them down in order to get in.

Her heart pounded.

The whispers returned.

The gongs went silent and only the sounds of battle remained.

Screams.

Metal crashing.

Cries of death as men and women fought for life.

And the voice of the wind grew louder with every beat of her heart. Anger warred with the need for calm. The controllable force fighting against the many whispers that were desperate to break free.

"Graylem said we have to hold the gate!" men yelled as she rounded the corner.

Torches blazed. Dozens of guardsmen and merchants hefted a large beam to bolster the gate against the onslaught. Everything shook as the enemy on the other side slammed their battering ram against the iron barrier, trying to break through.

Fear filled the air. She could taste it as she pushed her way through the crowd of fighters.

A shudder traveled up her spine as the Xhelozi raked the night with their calls, followed by desperate shouts.

The raging whispers grew louder, begging for vengeance.

Something cracked against her head. Carys stumbled backward, and the wind howled its upset. She shoved someone aside and squeezed her way to the rungs embedded in stone that would take her to the top.

The wall shook as a battering ram slammed hard against the gate.

Men shouted.

Something cracked.

Flakes of stone rained down.

They wouldn't be able to hold the gate for much longer. And if the gate broke—there would be nothing to keep the Bastian army or the Xhelozi from the people of Garden City.

The whispers urged her to set them free. They would fight for her. They would destroy her enemies.

The wind whipped her cloak.

Swords clashed near the gate, and Carys began to climb. She put one hand over the other, almost losing her grasp as the wall shook again. She heard the whoosh of a catapult. Sparks rained as a mass of burning tar flew through the night sky over the wall to the other side. Screams of pain and fear and death echoed, and she kept climbing.

She reached for her bow as she crested the top, willing the lights to come back on. To her untrained eye, the damage had appeared to be unrepairable, but she knew Andreus. If anyone could make the walls blaze with light, it was her brother.

She kept low as she hurried across the wall, so as to not draw the fire of the men on the ground below.

"What's happening?" she yelled to the guards who were launching arrows into the Bastian forces. The men below fell atop others who had already met their deaths. The soldiers with the battering ram raced forward. At the flanks of the attacking force, hooked claws and long teeth slashed. Bastian men swung their blades and fired arrows into the Xhelozi while the monsters threw soldiers to the side like rag dolls as both forces advanced on the city.

Another group of Bastian guards charged toward the gate farther down the wall. The battlements shook, and the crack of the stone was louder this time. The gates would not hold for much longer.

The Xhelozi screeched.

The whispers howled, and she shook her head. There was something not quite right.

Far in the distance, she saw most of the Bastian army was retreating. Xhelozi coming from the mountains were angling toward them. Those below—some were ramming the gates, but the rest weren't firing their arrows at those guarding the top of the wall or over it to hit the men holding the gate against them. Their weapons were aimed at the monsters still coming in packs from the mountains. The Xhelozi's fangs and claws bit deep and split open the flesh of guardsmen around them, as they fought for their lives.

"Hold the catapults," she screamed, scanning the chaos. Guardsmen relayed her commands. The whispering in her head returned with a renewed fury.

A monster stumbled. Dozens of arrows were sticking out of the stringy white fur and scaly hide when it fell not far from the walls to the east. Another volley of arrows launched toward the monsters and that's when she saw them behind the bowman.

Yelling orders from atop a rearing mount was Errik. Next to him was Garret. Both firing arrows toward the Xhelozi instead of the defenders of Garden City. Beside them a bannerman held a pike aloft . . . the symbol of the Bastians flew from the pole and atop it was a severed head.

Errik hadn't come back to warn her about the size of the army. Instead, he had killed the would-be Bastian King.

The lights flared to life.

Andreus had done it!

Cheers floated up from the city streets. Carys blinked against the blinding white. The screams beyond the walls increased in number. The Xhelozi cries were closer. The spots in front of her eyes cleared, and she saw one of the monsters charge the wall, dig its claws into the white stone, and start to climb.

The lights were on, but none of the monsters were fleeing.

The bloodlust was too strong or the imbalance in virtue too great. The lights were no longer enough to drive them away, and soon the men outside the walls fighting for their lives would be dead.

Carys turned, pulled the bowstring taut, and let the arrow fly.

The Xhelozi screamed as the point pierced its eye. The monster lost its grip on the wall and slammed onto the frozen ground on its scaly back. For a second, Carys thought she had killed it. Then the Xhelozi moved. A clawed hand yanked her arrow free from its flesh and the massive creature let out a rusty scream.

The battlements below shook. Men cried out, and the monster

charged the wall while several more Xhelozi followed close behind it.

The wind tugged at her cloak.

Carys fought for calm as she looked around at the guardsmen atop the walls. Two or three dozen guardsmen were armed with bows. There were at least that many Xhelozi fighting below, and in the shadow of the mountain, she could see more coming. They didn't have enough men to defeat them, and the lights the city had always counted on weren't pushing them back.

"Fire at the Xhelozi, not the men!" she commanded.

She saw Errik charge one of the Xhelozi near the wall. His sword speared its flesh, and just as quickly, he yanked the blade out and raced his mount away.

Her heart tightened. The whispers grew louder, but one was louder than the rest and Carys heard its meaning clear and strong. There was only one way to save those she loved. She had to give in.

Errik's horse raced toward the gate and disappeared into the masses below.

Waves of arrows hit the monsters illuminated by the lights atop the wall.

Some stumbled, but none fell.

The wind pounded in her head. Fed on her fear. Pulled at her anger. Compelled her to surrender to its call.

She thought of Larkin, dead. She pictured Errik fighting for his life and then thought of her brother—who would always be her twin.

Men screamed as they slashed open throats and sliced across backs, and the Xhelozi continued to advance as the wind whispered that she was ready. She needed to surrender. It was time to set herself free.

* * *

The lights still shone.

The gongs went silent.

Triumph fueled him as he hurried toward the sounds of death and fighting to help his sister.

The city still held, but for how long?

Andreus stepped around a bloody man stumbling away from the melee and squinted at the top of the wall. In tandem, bowmen sent a volley of arrows into the darkness. The city trembled as a battering ram crashed against the gate that Graylem and the men he directed were trying to hold. He stumbled, grabbed hold of a broken cart to stop his fall, and realized the cries of the Xhelozi that grated above the fighting were louder than before. The lights were on, but the monsters weren't retreating.

Dozens of torches flickered in the breeze as he rounded the corner. Men used their backs to bolster the trembling iron gate and shouted as the battering ram struck again. Stone trembled and cracked. Andreus was about to turn toward the ladder to join his sister atop the wall when he saw Errik's face appear behind the iron grid. Blood dripped down Errik's forehead as he dodged a spear from a Garden City guardsman. He shouted and Andreus shoved men aside to get close enough to hear what the man was saying.

"The Bastian King is dead!" Errik shouted again. "The men that remain from his army answer to me. We're here to help."

Lord Garret appeared at Errik's side. The Xhelozi roared beyond the walls. Men screamed, and Andreus looked at the battered man his sister trusted from the first. If she trusted him, Andreus would, too.

As much as Andreus wanted to lash out at Garret, the man was not his uncle. Elder Cestrum would pay, but not yet. For now, the city needed all the skilled swords it could get. "Open the gates and fall back!"

The guardsmen looked startled, but every one of them followed his command. The beam barring the door was hefted off. The men on the other side pushed at the gates and poured in through the opening. Once inside, Errik shoved his way to Andreus.

"The Xhelozi aren't retreating and it appears that more are coming from the mountains and beyond the plains!" Errik said. "There's no way we can defeat them all. I don't know . . ."

Wind gusted.

Errik's attention snapped to the top of the wall. He pointed to the men coming down the ladder, bows clutched in their hands. "Carys must be sending them down."

"She can't," Andreus yelled. "We need them to drive the Xhelozi back."

"They aren't going to retreat. She must think calling the wind is the only way. But if she does it wrong . . . I have to get to her."

"Why?" Andreus grabbed Errik's arm. "What will happen? Carys said she was struggling to control the magic. What will happen if she does something wrong?"

"The wind will choke the air out of her lungs. She'll die."

No. That wasn't going to happen. "You deal with the men down here. As soon as they are through the gate, bar it shut and get them ready to hold the gates until dawn."

Heart pounding, he ran toward the ladder. Andreus shoved the last of the men off the rungs and started up. He gritted his teeth and held tight as the wind pulled at his cloak. *You don't have to do this, Carys. You don't have to stand in front of me this time.* With the

Bastian guard now on their side, they would find another way to drive the Xhelozi back. They would do it together.

He reached the top, pushed to his feet, and for a second couldn't breathe as he took in the scene on the other side of the walls.

Hundreds of Xhelozi streamed toward the city while Errik and Garret's guardsmen stormed through the southeasternmost gate. Dozens more elongated shadows were approaching from the south and west, getting closer with each heartbeat. The Xhelozi nearest the wall screamed as if in pain when they stepped into the light. But they retreated only a few feet before surging forward again.

The wind whipped around him.

Andreus pulled his eyes away from the monsters and caught sight of his sister near one of the lights. Carys stood completely still. Her black cloak fluttered behind her. The stiletto he had commissioned for his sister was clutched in one of her hands and her eyes were wide as she looked upon the horror below.

"Carys!" He lowered his head and leaned into the wind that was gusting harder with each step. The lights shined bright. "Carys! Errik took over the Bastian army. He and Garret are assembling the men inside the walls. They're going to fight with us, and we'll keep the Xhelozi back until the sun comes up. You don't need to call the wind."

His sister turned. Resignation and resolve shone bright from her eyes. "The sunlight will only slow them down. They will always be drawn to the darkness inside Eden. You will have to find a way to balance the darkness with light."

A tunnel of air appeared in the sky.

The Xhelozi howled as they raced toward the open gate where the Bastian army was still streaming inside the city walls. Claws dug into the flesh of men bringing up the rear. Spears bit the leathery skin. And still more Xhelozi were coming from the mountains.

"You have to go, Dreus," Carys shouted. "Get everyone away from the walls. I don't want to hurt them or you."

"I'm not leaving you," Andreus yelled. "Not this time."

He had left her to face the Xhelozi by herself so he could take the throne. He would rather die than leave her alone again.

"You have to leave, Andreus. You have to survive and become King." The tunnel split into two, then split again as more tunnels appeared.

Andreus pushed against the churning wind, determined to reach his sister. He had to stop this before it was too late. "The throne doesn't belong to me." Curse or no curse, he didn't deserve to rule. "I have no right to be King."

"Which is why you will make a good one." The wind shoved him back. He stumbled and his sister turned to face him. Her eyes were clear. "Don't you see? You are neither from the line of Ulron or the Bastians. Both had legacies of darkness. You will have a choice of what your legacy will be. You can make it one of light." She stepped toward him, cloak billowing, and held the hilt of her silver stiletto out to him. "Give this to Errik. He will understand why."

A gust shoved him back another step. The tunnels in the sky looked like fingers as they started to descend.

"This is wrong," he yelled. "You shouldn't have to do this. It should be me." He wanted it to be him. He had earned the right to finally be the one who got to be strong. He wanted to make the sacrifice.

"I don't belong behind these walls, Dreus. I never did." Carys turned to face the horror beyond the walls and shouted, "It's time you let me go. It's time for me to be free."

Andreus clutched the silver stiletto tight in his hand and took a step backward. A weight settled in his chest as he looked at the face of the sister who shared not his blood, but had always shared his heart. She was tired of fighting. He could see it. He could feel it. And he had to let her go.

Swallowing tears, he yelled, "May strong winds guide your steps, sister."

She mouthed something to him that he couldn't hear. But in his heart, he understood as he dropped to his knees. He crawled to the ladder, the wind whipping round and round, faster and faster, pulling at him like greedy hands desperate to gain hold. He slid his legs over the side of the wall and climbed down the rungs as the tunnels of air roared above. Stone and branches and bits of the city dropped on top of him as his feet hit the ground and with each gust he pictured his sister standing atop the white stone. Head high. Shoulders straight. Heart strong.

The lights grew brighter. Pulsing with the power of the wind. The power of his sister.

The blast sent him to his knees. Sparks flew in the air as the light above him burst. The next light down the wall exploded. Then the next, as bright, shimmering white sparks launched into the air and circled the city.

When the last glimmer faded into black, the gusts of wind had calmed and were now a gentle breeze.

All around him people stood. Some cried. Others shouted questions as Andreus once again slowly climbed the rungs to the top of the wall, bracing himself for what he would see.

Only there was nothing.

The lights were gone. All evidence of the battle beyond the walls had been swept away. The remaining Bastian soldiers, the bodies of the fallen, and the Xhelozi with their hooked claws and long, pointed teeth had disappeared. As had his sister.

After being trapped for so long behind these walls, his sister had left them for good. Through his tears, Andreus looked upon the countryside of the kingdom he and his sister had fought for and hoped she was finally free.

22

"An Adderton messenger arrived, Your Majesty," Lord Errik said, executing a low, almost mocking bow. "Princess Xaria and the rest of the Adderton court will arrive tomorrow." Lord Errik smiled. "I think your sister would approve of your betrothed and everything else you have done."

Andreus's heart tightened even as he smiled. "The fact that I have agreed to marry a woman sight unseen would amuse her the most." Errik had negotiated the betrothal as part of the treaty that ended the war between the two kingdoms. King Ulron had caused the war by taking Andreus's mother as his queen and now Andreus had ended it.

Andreus just hoped Princess Xaria was as appealing as Errik claimed. More important, Andreus hoped she wouldn't mind the time he spent at the walls or on the battlements working with the Masters of Light. There was still much to do in order to restore all the lights and the lines that Carys's powerful wind had carried away. The Xhelozi were gone for now. He was working on restoring the balance of virtues, but men could not be counted on to keep their oaths. The Council of Elders and their schemes had proven that as had Elder Cestrum's trial, which was held on the steps in full view of the city.

The Elder had denied all claims and counted on his nephew to speak on his behalf. Lord Garret proved him wrong, instead revealing Captain Monteros's treachery on his uncle's behalf at the Village of Night and how the captain was under instructions to keep Garret from the battle until all claimants to the throne—Andreus, Carys, and Errik's uncle—were dead. Elder Cestrum had been playing all sides against each other in the hopes of eliminating them and clearing the path to the throne for his own blood.

As King, Andreus wasn't sure he could ever trust Lord Garret, but he did appreciate how the man insisted on wielding the blade that severed his uncle's body from his traitorous head. Garret had in a small way helped Carys return in time to save Eden. Andreus would not forget that.

He squinted up at the northern windmill as it churned against the sky. The wind had blown steady since the end of the Trials. The lights inside the Palace of Winds and down in Garden City glowed, and Andreus was busy working with the Masters on creating new wind power storage devices to aid them the next time the wind refused to blow. The people of Garden City had faced the darkness once. He didn't want them to have to face it again.

"I hear the Queen is busy making preparations for the wedding," Errik said quietly. "And that you've assigned Graylem to serve as her new chamberlain."

More like her jailer since Andreus did not have time to watch his mother every minute of the day. The madness that had started when Micah fell in her treacherous plot had only grown worse since Oben's death. Everyone had assumed it was the loss of the Princess that had sent the Queen into fits of weeping. Andreus did not correct them. Then suddenly, his mother had appeared in the Hall of Virtues looking calm. She was dressed in a bejeweled golden gown, her crown nestled in intricately woven hair. She spoke quietly to members of the court. She laughed at the entertainers who juggled apples and wedges of cheese. She had even smiled at Max when Andreus asked the boy to bring her a goblet of wine.

He did not mention Oben or the secrets his mother had revealed on the last night of the Trials, and she acted as if none of it had happened. Part of him had been relieved, and pushed away the niggling concern he had when he saw her smile as Elder Jacobs offered his arm and asked to escort her to her rooms. Elder Jacobs was found the next day in the chapel on the stone floor—his throat slit into a wide, bloody smile.

Now Graylem escorted the Queen through the castle and watched for the telltale sign of her toying with the ruby-crusted dagger on her belt while members of the court whispered about the rumor of a scorned mistress who killed the Elder out of revenge. Not the most original story, but it was better than revealing the truth of Elder Jacobs's allegiance to the Queen and the secret of Andreus's birth.

"Lord Graylem doesn't seem to mind his new position," Andreus said.

And Errik laughed. "Neither do the Queen's ladies in waiting. I hear they find him quite charming."

"Are you jealous, Lord Errik?" Andreus asked.

Errik's smile faded and he touched the stiletto at his side. He'd worn it every day since Andreus had climbed down the walls and presented it to him along with his sister's final words.

"You don't believe she's dead," Andreus said, hoping Errik could confirm what deep in his heart he believed. He knew it was foolish. He had checked the loose stone in the staircase to the battlements and found it to be empty. He had stood over Larkin's body in the Tomb of Light in his sister's stead. Carys was gone. And yet he doubted because every day he waited for the emptiness in his heart to appear in the space his sister currently filled. The emptiness never came.

Errik looked beyond the walls at the land beyond the battlements and smiled. "No, Your Majesty," he said quietly. "I don't believe she is dead. She's out there somewhere, and I will find her. You see, I have something of hers she wishes me to return."

Carys's hair fluttered as she placed a coin into the hand of each man who manned the sails and oars of the small water vessel. They closed their greedy fists over the gold even as they cast nervous glances at the dock. A gentle mist hovered over the shore, making it hard to see what lay beyond.

"Are you sure this is the place, m'lady?" the older of the two men asked, shoving the coin deep into a grimy pocket of his thick, well-worn sea coat. He ran his tanned, wrinkled hand over his gray-streaked hair as he looked at the shore and then back at her. "Strange things happen here, they say. Not that I believe the stories, mind yeh."

Carys looked back at the dock and sent out a question to the voice of the wind. The air stirred, revealing a white bridge beyond the docks and a path that snaked into a grove of squat trees.

"I thank you both for your service," she said with great sincerity.

"And I wish you safe passage on your return." With that, she picked up her skirts, climbed up the narrow, rickety stairs that led to the edge of the small vessel, and stepped onto the gray stone dock.

The sailors untied the boat and the air around her danced, pushing the two men away from the dock without them ever having to pick up an oar. The journey to the island had been faster than they had expected. Carys was certain their voyage back would be equally as quick and that they would fail to find the island again if ever they chose to attempt to return.

Carys reached into her travel bag and pulled out the jeweled slippers the Seeress Kiara had handed to her weeks ago. Inside was the slip of paper—the map to this island—that had been tucked inside. These slippers would unlock the walls that had defined her for so long.

Princess.

Daughter.

Sister.

Defender.

Carys looked toward the Fire Sea and wondered how long it would take for Errik to make his way to this island. He had said he would always find her, and he had made it a point to place the stiletto in her hand whenever it went astray. She was counting on him to do it again.

Turning her back on the water, she walked toward the bridge, thinking of her brother, wishing she could stand by him as he became the kind of king that she hoped he would be. But she knew it was time for him to fight his own battles just as it was time for her to do the same.

The wind tickled her neck, and in the distance several figures appeared. She saw a familiar woman in a white gown step onto the bridge and beckon Carys forward. With a smile Seeress Kiara held out her hand and said, "Welcome to the Isle of the Seers, Carys. Are you ready to take your place among us?"

Carys returned the seeress's smile. The voice of the wind rang with excitement as Carys said, "Yes, I believe I am."

The walls were gone. Carys's life was hers, and it was finally time to find out who and what she was truly meant to be.

ACKNOWLEDGMENTS

Writing a book is a lot like climbing a mountain. It is a long process that's fun, exhausting, intimidating, scary, and exciting. Thankfully, I never have to climb the mountain alone.

As always I owe a huge debt of gratitude to my family, especially my Skittles-providing husband, Andy; my enthusiastic son, Max; and my pun-loving mother (and assistant), Jaci, for putting up with my late nights and my fits of doubt. I'm not sure how you deal with it, but I am glad you do.

I also owe a huge group hug to the HarperTeen team. I am so honored to work with you all! To Kristen Pettit, thank you for your emails filled with exclamation points and enthusiasm for gruesome deaths. I also owe a huge shout-out to PR person extraordinaire Ro Romanello, who makes sure I never feel alone when I am on the road. Also, big thanks to Elizabeth Lynch for her attention to detail and her ability to always be near her computer. (How do you do that?) And I would be remiss if I didn't give my most heartfelt thanks to Jennifer Klonsky, production editor Emily Rader, copy editor Chris

Fortunato, designer Jenna Stempel-Lobell, and artists Toby & Pete, as well as the entire marketing, publicity, and Epic Reads teams. You are all amazing.

No matter what story mountain I decide to climb, I am beyond honored to have the incomparable Stacia Decker right beside me making sure I don't fall. You are my agent, my friend, and my literary rock. Thank you for always being there to brainstorm at all hours of the day and night, and for not ignoring my crazy texts and emails. I honestly am not sure what I would do without you.

To all the booksellers, librarians, and teachers who dedicate their lives to giving readers the love of stories—thank you! When you give someone a book, you aren't just giving them a tale of adventure or love or magic. You are helping them look at the world from other points of view and opening their hearts to new possibilities. The world is a better place because of all of you.

Finally, I want to thank every reader who has opened the pages of one of my books. With so many worlds to explore, I am so grateful you have chosen to spend time in mine.

READ ON FOR A SNEAK PEEK AT
JOELLE CHARBONNEAU'S NEXT
THRILLING PAGE-TURNER

ONE

My stool creaks in the slate-gray silence. I stretch, then turn once again to stare at the partially finished canvas.

A single desk lamp bathes the picture in a soft light. Shadows dance outside of the light's glow as I attempt to imagine what my mother was creating when she placed the geometric lines on the canvas over an ash-black background. Some of them, around the edge of the canvas, are thick and strong. Others move at a diagonal and seem to fade into the empty white area in the center of the work, as if disappearing into some mysterious place that only an artist could understand. Some lines at the edge are silver. The ones in the center are a burnished gold. Small red stars in the corners of the image make me believe there would have been more color had Mom had more time.

Now it is up to me to take the next step.

Looking down at the screen in my hand, I pick up my stylus and begin to draw on the copy I made of my mother's work, just as I have done every single day of the last eleven weeks and six days. I extend the lines—add detail. Match the color of red she used with one from my palette and begin once again to draw.

Sunlight creeps through the windows of my mother's studio, telling me that the time to get ready for school is approaching. But I don't move. Not yet. I stay seated on the rickety stool my mother had set up for me years ago when I begged to be allowed to watch her wield her brushes against canvas—a medium no longer used by artists but one my mother refused to completely abandon for electronic screens and the high-tech accessories that could do everything the tools on her desk did.

They can't do everything, I remember her telling me as she frowned into my eyes. *The things on the screen aren't real. What we can touch—that's real.*

Maybe I should have asked what she meant. Or maybe she should have just told me why she was spending so many late nights in this room using tools the rest of the country had discarded to create images that are impossible to understand. If she had been clearer, maybe I wouldn't be here right now trying to finish this painting for her.

I push a strand of hair that has escaped my ponytail out of my eyes and return to my sketch, working from the edges inward. I add a door in the empty space my mother left in the center of the work. The door is partially opened, as if waiting for someone to push it and walk through.

Over half my attempts have this door. Although until now the entryway has been closed. This time, without thinking, I painted it open. Does that mean something?

Streams of golden sunlight through Mom's studio window chase the rest of the shadows away. I layer color and shading until finally, I cock my head to the side and study my efforts.

The image is . . . interesting. If I brought it to my art class today, Mrs. Rudoren would certainly praise my talent, something my mother rarely did. In the middle of the other geometric lines, the entryway seems almost otherworldly with the slight arch I have added at the top and the light coming from somewhere inside. The picture is the most compelling of the dozens upon dozens I have created thus far, with the red patch on the side acting almost like a warning to keep someone from walking through my door.

And still, I know it's wrong.

I punch the erase feature on the screen. My part of the image disappears in a blink. As if it never existed. But my mother's work remains. She's gone, but that is what is left of her, and that's all that's left to me.

I rub my eyes, pick up my stylus, and touch it to the center of the screen to begin again. Wait. . . .

Damn it.

A persistent beeping sound echoes from above me. I slide off the stool and hurry through the door of my mother's studio, into the hall, and toward the stairs. I've been so busy working on the puzzle of Mom's painting that I lost track of the time.

The beeping gets louder with each step. The fact that it doesn't stop before I reach the landing tells me exactly what I will find as I step across the threshold of my parents' room.

My nose wrinkles.

The wailing of the alarm continues.

I step on a crumpled shirt and kick aside a pair of wadded-up gray trousers as I pad across the light blue carpet toward the nightstand.

A push of a button and the room goes blissfully silent, but a look at the clock's display tells me I have spent far more time in my mother's studio than I'd intended. My father isn't the only one who is going to be late at this rate.

"Dad," I say, turning toward the bed to where my father still sleeps. His breathing is raspy. His dark, normally wavy hair is plastered against his head. The mouth that once so quickly curled into smiles is mashed against a dark blue spot on the pillow, and a large, empty go cup rests next to one of his hands.

"Dad! Get up!" I snap.

He doesn't move.

"You slept through your alarm," I say louder. "If you don't get up now you're going to be late for work." And it wouldn't be the first time.

I stalk across the room and tug open a window to let the fresh, almost-summer air chase the heat and stale smell out of the room.

"Dad!" I yell.

When he snorts and rolls over, I head into his bathroom and turn the shower on. Then I grab a slightly stiff washcloth, run it under ice-cold water from the sink, and stomp back to drop it on his face.

The cold washcloth does the trick. Dad yelps, sits up, and snatches the wet washcloth from his forehead with one hand while knocking the to-go cup off the bed with the other. The cup rolls under the bed. Dad blinks his puffy red eyes several times before shifting them to look at me.

"The shower is already running. You can't be late," I say as I wait for him to swing his legs over the edge of the bed and plant his feet on the floor. If I leave now there is a good chance he'll just lie back down. It's happened before.

"I'm sorry, sweetheart," he says, running a hand through his hair before pushing to his feet. I wait for him to sway, but he's steady, and despite the swollen redness, his eyes are mostly alert. It's an improvement over last week. Maybe I should find hope in that. But I'm not ready for hope.

"Be downstairs in fifteen minutes," I say, heading for my room so I can get myself ready for another day. It takes me half that time to yank on the pair of navy-blue pants and pale yellow shirt that make up my school uniform. I used to hate it, but now I'm grateful for the required sameness. Figuring out what clothes to wear is one less decision I have to make.

I brush my hair, start to pull it neatly back into a ponytail as is my typical style, but one look at my eyes in the mirror has me leaving it loose. Hopefully, the fatigue won't be as obvious that way.

The smell of coffee hits me as I hurry downstairs and walk into the cozy yellow-and-white kitchen. My father gives me what I'm sure he thinks is a cheerful smile, but it comes across as more than a little desperate. His hair is still wet from the shower. His face is shaved and he's dressed in a blue shirt and gray jacket that I picked up from the cleaner yesterday after school. His eyes still look a little tired, but they are way clearer than they have been in the past few weeks. If I didn't know better, I would think that he was back to the dad I used to know.

He holds out a green apple—my usual choice for breakfast. A peace offering. I shake my head and grab a banana, even though it has brown patches on the skin.

My father sighs, turns back to the counter, and pours himself a steaming mug of coffee. In an upbeat voice he says, "Only one day left of class and two days of finals before summer break. Has the City Art Program made their decision yet?"

"I don't know," I say, taking a seat at the butcher-block table. "I didn't apply." I frown at the banana, knowing that picking the thing up means I'll have to eat it.

"Wait a minute." Dad sets his mug down on the counter. "Why didn't you apply? You worked so hard on your portfolio pieces. What happened?"

"You know what happened."

Mom died and my dad started to drink.

We did what we had to do in order to get from day to day. Those things did not include essay writing and portfolio development.

Before he can try to initiate some kind of father-daughter-heart-to-heart thing, I shove back my chair, spring to my feet, and cross to the garbage. "It's okay." I drop the overly ripe banana into the can with a thump and shrug as if it couldn't possibly matter. "There's another project I'm working on. I'll have plenty to keep me occupied this summer without being a part of City Art. And I can always apply next year if someone drops out. So it's fine," I lie. "Look, I've gotta go."

"I can give you a ride to school," Dad offers.

No. He can't. Not without being late for work. It's an empty offer and I can see from the slump of his shoulders that I'm not the only one who knows it. More than anything I want to call him out. But I bite back the angry words and instead say, "Rose said she might wait to walk with me. She'll never forgive me if I don't show up." I shift the bag on my shoulder and make a beeline for the back door.

My hand is on the knob when my father says, "Meri, I'm sorry. I should have asked before about City Art. I know your future is on the line and I—I'm screwing it up. I'm trying to do better, it's just..."

I glance over my shoulder. My father looks down at the coffee in his hand so I won't see the tears. But I see them anyway, and even if I couldn't I can hear the sorrow thickening his voice when he quietly admits, "I miss her."

Everything inside me freezes. The red-hot anger I stoke like a life-giving fire suddenly extinguishes, leaving me cold and weak and raw.

I can't breathe.

I can't speak.

It's like the moment I relive every night when I try to fall asleep—the one where the police officers come to the door with their serious, rosy-cold faces and stiff words, telling us about the vehicle that slid on a patch of black ice and couldn't stop in time.

They were sorry. Everyone was sorry. My friends. My teachers. Our neighbors. The guy behind the counter at the market two streets over. Everyone told me first with their words and now months later with a shake of the head how *sorry* they were that the person who drove the vehicle too fast during a spring snow was alive and well and my mother, who had simply been standing on the sidewalk in front of a potential new design project, was dead.

We're all sorry. So what? It doesn't change a damn thing.

"I'll see you tonight." I yank the door open and head outside, clinging to the anger that once again sparks inside me. I hate the pain my father is in. I hate that I understand why he drinks, and I hate knowing that if I didn't force him out of bed every morning he would drink himself into oblivion to forget what we have lost.

His work gave him two weeks off after the accident, and people looked the other way for the month after as Dad showed up late or in the same clothes he'd worn the day before. Finally, Dad's boss came to the house with a warning that he had to do better or he would lose his job.

The drinking continued, but little by little, day by day, Dad seemed to be doing better. Surrounded by more grays and dark blues than shrouded in empty black. He didn't have to reach for something to add to his morning coffee in order to face a world without my mother's lopsided smile and observant gaze.

I hurry down the steps and around the house, toward the street.

A gray squirrel darts across the sidewalk in front of me and bolts under the moving van parked in front of the house two doors down. I used to watch every new person moving into a house on the block for signs of kids my age, especially in the last few years when so many older folks moved away for work or retirement—or just because they wanted something new. Now I was glad not to see any signs of teenagers in the back of the van.

Robins chirp in the branches of the fairly young trees lining the street. The city's gardeners planted them only two years ago. Between the golden sunshine, this being the final week of school, and my dad's less glassy eyes, I should be feeling positive about the day. Maybe if Dad hadn't brought up the City Art Program I would find it easier to be happy about the little things, but thoughts of all the work I had done—the time wasted—what I had wanted so badly until my mother's death—made it hard to find the good in anything.

I'd worked for months on my portfolio so that I could be one of the four sixteen-year-olds chosen to intern alongside the city's design and beautification team for the next two years. Being chosen isn't just an honor. Being chosen gives a student the chance to work with the very best imaginations in the city and maybe even assist in designing one or more of the city's ongoing projects. It's one of the sure ways to gain a coveted slot as a visual arts major. Without a visual-arts degree it's impossible to secure a job as a working artist here in Chicago's City Pride Department or in similar departments in other cities across the country.

Of all the government jobs, the City Pride Department's were among the most important and prestigious. Years ago, a pilot program spearheaded by the best artists in the country was launched here in Chicago under the theory that people who lived in beautiful surroundings felt better about themselves and their futures, thereby causing them to make positive choices that would benefit not only themselves but the community they were so proud of. It was a radical idea, but the new City Pride Department was determined to make every part of the city beautiful—especially those most touched by neglect and crime, because the people living on those streets needed to see that they were worthy of beauty.

And it was working. Bit by bit. Block by block. The citizens here blossomed under the inspiration of the city's new beauty. But the project is never ending, because the city is large and always changing. So often my mother worked long into the night to create the perfect mural for the side of a neighborhood market or select the ideal color palette for a sign intended to draw the community into embracing a new park. She had even received a silver plaque last year to celebrate the work she had done. She was one of the top designers. The work she uploaded into the National Elevation through Arts database was some of the most often downloaded for use around the country.

Was it any wonder that I wanted to capture beauty in an image the way she did?

Everyone assumes my mother wanted me to submit to the summer program. That she encouraged me to walk in her talented footsteps. I've let them think it because it's easier than talking about the way, in the months before she died, she pursed her lips whenever I asked her opinion about my work.

Are you sure that's the color palette you want to use, Meri?

Is that really what you want to work on or just what you think you should be working on?

Then finally the one I'll never forget. When she fastened her hair at the nape of her neck with a long-handled, tapered paintbrush and turned to me, eyes shimmering with disappointment.

Maybe you should think about doing an internship at Gloss instead. Designing layouts requires a sharp eye and there's a lot less competition for those positions than there is for government jobs.

Those words made it clear to me that she thought I wasn't good enough. Maybe if I hadn't shut myself off from her from that moment on, maybe I would have found out why. Maybe—

"Hey, I almost gave up on you."

I look up and spot my best friend, Rose, standing in the shade of an old elm tree.

"Isaac decided you weren't coming and went on ahead. He's going through a self-important phase because Dad got him a summer job with city security. I'm not sure what is so amazing about filling in for security officers who are spending the day at the beach, but what do I know?" Rose rolls her eyes, which tells me everything I need to know about her opinion of her older brother's plans. Then she frowns. "Actually, it's good Isaac left, because you look terrible."

I shrug. I could take offense, but she's just telling the truth.

"Well, you look perfect," I respond. "So we balance each other out." The thing is, I'm not kidding about the perfect part. With her thick black hair twisted into a French braid, her glowing brown skin made even more flawless by makeup applied with a skilled and light hand, Rose looks more like one of the models in the fashion e-zine her mother edits than a sixteen-year-old high school student on her way to class.

"I'm not kidding, Meri." Rose steps toward me. Her intense brown eyes narrow as she studies my face. "You didn't sleep again."

"I slept." Sort of. When Rose purses her lips and gives me her don't-mess-with-me frown, I add, "Okay, so I woke up extra early and couldn't get back to sleep. It's no big deal."

Rose sighs and slides the straps of her yellow backpack off her shoulder. She unzips the front pocket and pulls out her purple-and-white-swirled makeup kit. "You keep saying that it's no big deal, but when was the last time you slept for an entire night?"

I wish I could answer that, but it's been too long for me to remember.

"I've had some bad dreams," I say.

Pity swims in her eyes, then vanishes almost as quickly as it appeared. She gives a no-nonsense shake of her head as she flips open the lid of one of her dozens of makeup compacts. "Lucky for you I have just the thing to fix you up."

There's no fixing me. Even if I slept for a week, I would never look like Rose. Boring dishwater-blond hair, pale hazel eyes, and average height are not model material. "You don't need to go to the trouble."

Rose grabs my arm as I try to sidestep her. "If you don't want your teachers calling your father out of concern for your well-being or, worse yet, sending you down to the counselor, you'll stand still and let me work."

"We're going to be late."

"Not if you keep still and follow my instructions," Rose says. "And if we don't get to class in time for the second bell, a call from either one of my parents will get us out of trouble. Deal?"

I sigh, knowing there really isn't much of a choice. When Rose has her mind set on something, there is little chance of changing it. Besides, I don't have the energy or the time to put up a fight. "Deal."

"Good. This won't take long. Hold this." She hands me the makeup kit, and I can tell from the colors that half of what she has with her has been brought specifically for me. Knowing that Rose has been worried enough to go out of her way to get these things ties my throat into a knot. Tears prick the backs of my eyes. The world blurs and I blink to chase it all away.

"Stop moving," Rose chastises. She dabs a sponge under my eyes and on several other spots on my face. I stare at a light green leaf on a tree in the distance and try to clear my mind and my heart the way I can with my tablet. Rose attacks my eyes with a pencil and eye shadow and actually growls at me when I try to move away before she puts the finishing touches on her design. Finally, she gives a satisfied smile and holds a mirror up to my face. "There is no denying that I'm a genius. My mother and *Gloss* editorials have taught me well."

She isn't lying. My skin is no longer blotchy. The peach shadow she used on my lids is almost translucent, but somehow makes them appear less sleep deprived. I seem almost normal—as long as no one looks too hard. The anger and fatigue and distrust in my eyes cannot be smoothed away with powder and lip gloss. Those are beyond even my best friend's ministrations.

But when I look away from my image and see Rose's grin, I can't help but smile back. After so many years, all the changes in our lives, and the bitterness and hurt I have waded through, the thing I am most grateful for is Rose's friendship. "Thanks," I say, lifting my eyes to hers. "I owe you."

"Real friends don't keep score." Rose shoves the makeup case back into her bag. Once it's stowed, she shrugs the bag onto her shoulder and we start walking. "So what happened this morning?" she asks.

"What do you mean?" I wait for a red sports car to pass and cross the street with Rose beside me.

"Meri, I yelled your name three times before you noticed me. That's not like you."

I take a deep breath and say, "Dad asked about my submission to the City Art Program this morning. It's the first time he's brought it up since . . . before." I walk faster, as if I can escape the ache that comes with the reminder of my mother's death. "He was disappointed when I told him I didn't finish my submission. I guess I thought in some way he would be relieved."

"Why would you think that?"

"He never goes in Mom's studio. He took her award off the shelf in the living room. He can't bring himself to look at her art or talk to anyone she used to work with. And whenever I start sketching or even talk about one of my assignments for art class he goes into another room."

The things that keep me going drive him to search for a way to forget. The award lives on the shelf next to my bedroom window. I draw for hours every day. A nicer daughter would give those things up to help him. Clearly, I'm not that nice.

"Your father's hurting," Rose says quietly. "But he knows how important your art is. He's not like my dad—determined to make everyone just like him. Your dad would never want you to give up something that makes you happy. Speaking of the City Art Program, I know you said your portfolio wasn't finished, but—"

"The submission deadline was two weeks ago." I walk even faster as our school and the dozens of cars and buses navigating the street in front of the redbrick building come into sight. "It's over, Rose."

Maybe I'd still get into one of the college art programs, but my chances of becoming a City Art Program designer now were low. And I had only myself to blame.

"Nothing is ever over until you admit defeat. I talked to—"

"Can you just drop it?" I ask. "Please? I haven't had a chance to ask you about whether you convinced your dad to let you work at *Gloss* instead of at City Hall this summer."

"Did you see the new issue? Mom said she sent one to your account. She wanted to know if you have ideas for the logo redesign. She wants something more youthful and striking and thinks a younger designer's point of view will help." Rose shakes the smile off her face and settles back into a frown. "But no fair changing the subject. We can talk about me and my summer job later. After you—"

The first bell rings, which cuts off whatever Rose was going to say because in order to make it to our class before the second bell sounds, we have to run. Side by side, we race across the street and down the sidewalk, dodging the other stragglers and the large outdoor screens that flank the front door entry like sentries. The one to the right is dedicated to a running display of times and dates for school- and student-appropriate city events. The other is set to local news, as are the two screens in the cafeteria. As Principal Velshi has said in every assembly, the only way we can be sure what we want to do when we go out into the world is to first understand what is happening in it.

The truth, however, is that no one really cares what the chirpy anchor with the plastic-looking hair is saying about the stepped-up recycling effort as students shove their way to the front entrance. Assistant Principal Schmidt is near the door, shouting over the din for everyone to hurry up.

Breathing hard, Rose pushes her way forward. I'm about to follow when a bus pulls away from the curb. Out of the corner of my eye I catch the flash of red lights. I turn, thinking the light must be from one of the announcement screens, but it's not. The flashing is coming from atop a police car in the distance. I stop walking as men in charcoal-gray suits shove a struggling person with magenta-and-black-streaked hair toward an open police car door. One of the suits backhands the man he's escorting across the cheek. I flinch and hold my breath as I keep watching. The suit yells and points toward the street. He's too far away from me to make out what he said, but several navy-blue-uniformed officers nod and race toward some bushes near the edge of the street.

"Meri, come on!" Rose tugs on my arm, and I start moving again toward the front entrance. I glance back in time to see the suited men shove the cuffed, shouting perpetrator into the police car and slam the door. Just before I step into the school, a uniformed officer pulls something out of a bush.

As I race down the hall trying to beat the next bell, I picture the scene from across the street and the item the officer waved in triumph at the suits.

It wasn't something anyone used anymore.

Obsolete, but not illegal.

So why, I wonder as the bell rings just as I am sliding into my seat, did the police arrest someone over a piece of paper?

**TURN THE PAGE TO READ
THE DIVIDING EDEN NOVELLA**

1

The blade sliced the air. Graylem ducked then pivoted in time to swing his own sword. The impact of metal against metal sang up his arm. The lord he was facing was better than most Graylem sparred against for his employer. The man was strong and faster than he looked, but Graylem was quicker. He leaped over the broadsword that aimed for his knees, hit the ground, rolled, then bounded back to his feet with his blade already flying toward his opponent.

His sword clanged against the larger, dark-bearded lord's weapon. The lord's eyes narrowed as he swung again with both hands. His attack was a fraction too low, which pulled the man just a hair off balance. Graylem zeroed in on the opening. One pivot and twist of his own blade and the fight would be over. He could end this now.

Instead, he held his ground and met the forward motion of the broadsword with a defensive parry. Grunting, he took a step back. Triumph flashed in the lord's eyes. The bearded man swung again. Graylem reacted a second later than he normally would, met the attack successfully, but stumbled back again. When next the blades connected, Graylem allowed his own to slip from his grasp. Slowly, he put his hands up in surrender and panted for air.

"You gave me a good fight," the lord said, lowering his blade—victory bright in his eyes. "There was a moment where I thought you would emerge victorious from our exercise."

"You are far more agile than you appear, Lord Havershire," Graylem said, making the burly lord laugh. "And," he nodded at the shining broadsword in the man's hand, "you have a far superior blade."

"The balance and workmanship exceed my expectations." Lord Havershire turned toward the thick-chested, gray-haired man in a black smock who was standing nearby. "If anything, my friends understated your talent. You have earned your price and a bit more." Lord Havershire pulled a small leather pouch from his belt and lobbed it at Goodman Bryant, who caught it with a wide smile.

"I am flattered, my lord." The blacksmith bowed his head before untying the purse to glance at its contents. "This is most generous."

"I believe in rewarding skill and efficiency. You have demonstrated both. As has your young friend." Lord Havershire turned toward Graylem, and the smile disappeared. "You have skill, boy. If you ever have interest in trading your hammer and apron for a banner and shield and learning how to win a fight, I would be happy to have some of my men work with you."

"I'm honored, my lord," Graylem said quietly, sheathing his sword as heat filled his cheeks. Between the red hair, freckles, and the now-red face, he most certainly looked like the strawberry his sister always claimed him to be.

Behind his bushy beard, the lord's smile grew. He reached into his pocket, pulled out his hand, and extended it toward Graylem. When the lord opened his fist there were three silver nicks in his palm. "There is no shame in losing to an older and more skilled foe."

Especially when he had never intended to win. One day he would win. Once he had fulfilled the promise he made to his mother he would enter Lord Blackthorn's annual summer tournament and do his best to win not only his fights but the attention of Lord Blackthorn or one of the other lords that would be in attendance. He had heard of several lowborn men who had been given a position of respect and authority in a prestigious household's guard after a strong tournament showing. He intended to do the same.

But not just yet.

Lord Bryant flipped the coins to Graylem, who caught two but missed the third. Lord Havershire chuckled as Graylem scurried to grab the coin as it rolled into the mud next to the wheel of Goodman Bryant's rickety old cart.

No. That wasn't mud.

Graylem dug the silver out of the splat of manure then ducked into the sweltering smithy to wash the grime off his coin and the sweat from his face while Goodman Bryant and Lord Havershire finished talking.

The fire burned hot in the wide stone hearth along the side wall. The most experienced of Goodman Bryant's apprentices gave him a fleeting glance before picking up his hammer and setting to work at the anvil, creating music with the steady clangs that transformed lumps of metal into weapons and tools. Something Graylem never had much luck doing no matter how much patience Goodman Bryant showed. The blacksmith, with his bulky build and thick muscles, looked as if he had been created and dropped down in Eden for the sole purpose of working in a smithy. Graylem—well, he looked more like what his father had tried to train him to be, a thief.

Graylem placed the cleaned coins in a small leather pouch and tucked it safely into the pocket of his vest. Three silver nicks meant nothing to a lord, but to him they were priceless. Every day he added more to the pile he had stashed with the letter that had arrived a month ago from his mother's childhood friend. She had moved to the other side of Eden when Graylem was small, but she had responded to his mother's deathbed request and agreed to a match for Deevana. He just had to get enough coin together to make the journey. Then he'd break the news of the betrothal to his sister.

"A good day's work, I'd say." Goodman Bryant's thick frame filled the doorway.

"Has Lord Havershire gone?" Graylem shouted over the ringing of hammer against iron.

Goodman nodded. "Back to Lussuria. But he'll be back in a month and has requested two daggers and a battle-ax be waiting for him when he returns." Goodman pulled a gold coin from the pouch and smiled as he pressed it carefully into Graylem's hand. "Much of that is thanks to you. I can stick someone with a sword if need be, but I'm not skilled enough to give someone like Lord Havershire a true contest. You made him think he was a better swordsman than he is, which makes my weapons look even better than they are. I counted three times you could have easily won that fight."

"Eight," Graylem said quietly. The first several openings came because Lord Havershire had taken one look at his freckles and lean frame and automatically assumed he was young and inexperienced and lacked the strength to be any competition. That incorrect assessment would have been enough for Graylem to take the man in a tournament. But this wasn't a true contest and winning wasn't the point.

Goodman Bryant clapped Graylem on the shoulder and laughed. "You should enter one of the High Lord Wynden's tournaments. You're old enough now. I could make a lot of money wagering on you, and you could stop pretending to have any interest in being a blacksmith."

Heat that had nothing to do with the smithy fires crept back into his face, making Goodman Bryant laugh harder.

"I know you try," Goodman Bryan said. "Your mother was a good woman. I know you asked for this job because of her, and you do serviceable enough work when you aren't demonstrating the quality of my swords or keeping that sister of yours out of trouble. I heard she had some trouble with Mistress Suzanna recently."

Graylem winced. "Deevana has very firm opinions about how much day-old bread should cost."

"Mistress Suzanna seemed to believe that your sister was hoping to leave her shop without paying at all."

Their father had taught Deevana the same skills that Graylem had learned. Graylem often thought she had learned them better than he because she enjoyed the challenge of outwitting others far more.

"Your sister has always wanted more than she has. She gave your parents a great deal of trouble before they passed, and her impetuousness has only grown as she has gotten older." Goodman Bryant mopped a line of sweat from his forehead and turned his now-serious eyes on Graylem. "You're doing your best to honor what your mother wanted for both of you, but I know from experience that you can't change someone who doesn't want to be changed. You can lose yourself in the trying."

Graylem shook his head. "Deevana is just restless since our mother's death. She misses the freedom our parents allowed her." Not to mention she despised working in the kitchens at Blackthorn Keep. "She'll be happier once we get to the District of Irae." Although she might not be all that keen on the idea of her younger brother arranging that happiness for her.

"For your sake, I hope you are right." Although the way Goodman Bryant shook his head said he had serious doubts about that plan, he didn't voice whatever worries he had. Instead, the blacksmith asked, "Have you decided when you and your sister will head south?"

He thought about the coins in his pocket and those he had secreted away. "In a few weeks. Maybe before that." He had answered the letter weeks ago, agreeing to the terms his mother's friend had laid out and promising he and Deevana would, as requested, arrive before summer did. Spring had finally broken the back of winter, but it had yet to completely chase away the chill, so he felt they still had some time before they had to set out. But they would have start the journey soon, which meant he couldn't put off telling his sister any longer.

"Well, I for one will be sorry to see you go."

"Because I make your swords look good?"

"Aye, there is that." Goodman Bryant laughed, but his eyes were serious as he put a large, calloused hand on Graylem's shoulder. "You're a good boy who is growing into a fine man. Your mother and that father of yours would both be proud."

The pride in the steady blacksmith's eyes warmed Graylem and pulled all words from his head. His face heated again, but this time he didn't dip his head to hide it.

Goodman Bryant awkwardly patted Graylem on the shoulder, cleared his throat, and said, "Well, since you're still here yet, I guess you should get to work."

The work—even the minor smithy jobs of making wall hooks and hinges—was hot. By the time the sun was shifting downward, his shirt and hair were soaked with sweat. Waving farewell to Goodman Bryant, who was still sweating at the fire, Graylem stepped into the chill of the late afternoon and headed down the dirt road to the very edge of the village.

The squat, two-room cottage looked small and tired in the fading light, but in another month the grounds around it would be blooming with the flowers and herbs his mother had planted and nurtured, first under the guidance of her father and then on her own after she took over as the village herbalist. It was among those flowers that his father first saw their mother. "Hair as red as the blooms she tended and a face far more beautiful than any flower could hope to be" was how he told the story that never failed to make his mother blush.

Perhaps it was the love his parents shared that made him see the best in the cottage that despite his best attempts had was falling into disrepair. Deevana, however, only saw the roof that leaked and the latch on the door that stuck more often than not. Ever since they were kids she had coveted the expensive fabrics and decorations on the gowns the ladies wore. She envied their smooth, unblemished hands that never had to scrub a pot or sweep a floor or get singed by a spark as they stirred soup over the fire.

"With what father taught us, the two of us could do far better than this cottage and this village," she'd said more times than he could count since their mother passed.

She wasn't wrong, even if he knew it wasn't right.

He lit a fire in the hearth and set a pot with potatoes and carrots and water on the hook so his sister would see dinner was already under way when she arrived. He hoped that would put her in a cheerful mood.

Knowing Deevana should be home soon, he quickly washed away the sweat from the day and changed into a fresh tunic and trousers. He untangled his wet hair with his fingers and walked to his cot in an alcove not far from the hearth.

With a quick glance toward the door, he climbed onto the cot. The beam above it had warped, leaving a small gap between it and the roof thatching. Carefully, Graylem slipped the folded parchment and the small leather purse from the hiding spot and pocketed it. Deevana had sharp eyes and a curious mind that made it hard for most people to keep things from her notice. But his sister had some blind spots—one of which was that she never looked up.

He was adding some rabbit he had hunted yesterday to the pot over the fire when the front door opened. His sister was breathing hard. The auburn hair that she pulled into a knot at her nap during the day had partially come free and her deep brown eyes were filled with alarm. Instinct had him crossing the room for his sword as Deevana stared at the road for several long heartbeats before closing the door and latching it.

"What's going on?" he asked.

"I have no idea what you are talking about." Deevana waved him off but glanced at the small window that faced town.

"Deevana," he said, sword lowered but still clutched tight in his hands.

"I feel like taking a walk. How about you?" She shifted the satchel hanging from her shoulder, lowered her gaze, and headed for the bedchamber that she had moved into after their mother's passing. "I think maybe—"

"Deevana." Graylem stepped in front of Deevana, blocking her retreat. When she finally lifted her eyes, he said, "Tell me. What's wrong?"

She pursed her lips and fisted her hands at her sides. "A few items might have gone missing at the keep."

Now Graylem looked toward the window. "Might have? What happened?" When she said nothing, he asked again. "Deevana, what did you do?"

"I was careful, Gray," she said quickly. Too quickly. Dread twisted his gut. "They shouldn't have noticed anything. I don't—"

"Do they know it was you?" he asked, wishing he could shake her for being so foolish. The penalty for theft in the village was three days in the square's stockade. Stealing from a lord or lady would result in the loss of a hand or worse. "Deevana," he repeated when his sister said nothing. "Do they know?"

"I *was* careful. But I saw Mistress Lillian look at me funny, so I followed her. She was talking to the captain of the guard and I heard my name. She couldn't know—"

"Pack your things," Graylem said, feeling everything he had ever worked for slipping away—the tournament and the position in the guard and his life here in Blackthorn surrounded by the memories of those he loved—all because of his sister. "Get ready to go." And when his sister hurried to the back bedroom that their parents once shared without a word of complaint, he knew there had never really been a choice for him to make. The guards would be coming, and whatever Deevana had taken would mean more than the loss of a hand. They had to move, and quickly.

As the wardrobe door banged in the room next door, he hurried to his cot and pulled his father's leather travel bag from beneath it. Quickly, he threw in several trousers, tunics, undergarments, and socks. He grabbed his father's old pair of boots from beside the hearth and shoved those in then pulled on his own. He then rolled the blankets from his cot and tied them with string. Onto the cot next to those items he added bread, cheese, dried fruit, and jerky from the larder while trying to decide what else to take.

He glanced out the window.

The sun was setting, but there was still enough light to be certain there was no one coming down the road to their cottage.

Yet.

Deevana had snuck out of Blackthorn Keep before anyone was aware she was gone or had been alerted to their suspicion. The guards would sweep the Keep first before extending their search here. He and Deevana had to be gone before the guards turned their sights on this place.

Heart pounding, Graylem stood in the center of the small room he had slept in, played in, sat on his mother's lap learning to read in, trying to decide what else to take. His father's bow and cloak. The handkerchief his mother made for their father with his initials on it—a subtle reminder that it, unlike the others he had acquired, belonged to him. The first pot he made in the smithy. A small leather bag of what had been his mother's favorite tea.

That was all, and his father would say it was too much. The lighter a thief traveled, the faster he could run.

Graylem shoved the items into another bag, fastened his cloak, and strapped on his sword. Slinging the bags and the bow over his shoulder, he hurried to where the soup bubbled, pulled a stick out of the tinderbox, and wrapped a rag around the top of it.

Clutching the makeshift torch in his hand, he yelled, "Deevana, it's time for us to go."

"I'm almost ready."

"Be ready now!"

Deevana appeared in the doorway of her room, her red hair almost as vibrant as the scarlet cloak slung around her shoulders. Her blue eyes were bright despite the weight that she was juggling. A number of bags were slung over her shoulder, and still she held several more in her arms.

"You can't take all of that," he warned. "It's going to slow us down."

"The horses can carry this without a problem."

"We won't be taking the horses." Swallowing hard, he touched his torch to the fire and watched it smolder until it too was caught by flames. "I'll meet you behind Cartrace Mound. Leave what you can't carry quickly, because I'm not going to carry it for you. Make sure you aren't seen."

"Graylem, we can—"

"No horses," he repeated, looking toward the window again. Night was almost here, and he knew in his gut that with the darkness would come the guards. "We will find mounts once we are safely away. Now go!"

His sister looked at the lit torch in his hand, then lifted her eyes to meet him. Slowly she nodded. "I know how to move without being seen, brother. I will be waiting for you." Without putting down a single bag, his sister hurried out the door.

Turning, Graylem walked into the room Deevana had claimed after their mother's passing—just a month after their father had toppled over with blood oozing from his ears. Poison. His mother knew plants enough to diagnose the cause, but never did they learn the culprit. And a month later, his mother died of what the Keep's healer called falling disease. But the healer was wrong. His mother had died of a broken heart in the bed she and his father had shared for eighteen years. He was glad she wasn't here for her heart to break again now.

He saw the miniature his father had done of his mother with Deevana in her arms. His chest ached as he looked at their father's best shirt that still hung on a peg behind the door.

Taking a deep breath, Graylem lowered the torch to the bed and watched the fire take hold. He kicked over the small night table. The candles Deevana had lit toppled.

Coughing, he backed up as the flames began to consume the things his mother had tended and the bits his father had stolen. He stepped back and touched the torch to his father's shirt. Then he turned and walked out to set the rest of his life on fire.

He left the front door open and threw his manufactured torch into the opening. Then, heart racing, he set off toward Cartrace Mound. Cries rose up from the village behind him. The tolling of bells filled his ears as he darted through pine trees and wintergreen bushes to the hill where he and his sister and the rest of the Blackthorn village children had spent countless hours sledding in the snow.

He was thankful there was no snow now, though he could smell it in the air. There were no white prints in the ground to give evidence that the cottage fire was not from a clumsily overturned candle. The barn was far enough from the cottage that it would not catch fire—at least not before those in the village came to rescue the panicking horses—horses that anyone attempting to flee Blackthorn out of guilt would certainly take.

Standing next to a pine at the foot of Cartrace Mound, he turned and looked back at the glow of the fire in the distance and the smoke rising against the backdrop of the night. The bells still tolled. The light of the fire was brighter than before. The fire burned hotter. Graylem could almost see Goodman Bryant running from the smithy toward the fire, trying to get it under control. He could imagine the faces of those who brought food after their parents' deaths whispering in the smoke of the curse the house was under—that while terrible for the children, it was right that all traces be burned away. The curse would be rendered to ashes, just like the life he had been hoping to build for himself.

"You burned it." Deevana appeared next to him. Her hands, free of their burden, rested on her hips as her eyes reflected the flames.

"There was no other choice, Deevana. Not unless—"

"Brilliant!" His sister's lips bloomed into a smile. "The best way to not be caught is for no one to be looking for you in the first place. Father always thought you weren't paying attention to his lessons."

"I paid attention well enough."

"And now we are no longer tied to this place or what we were here. We can go anywhere and be anyone we wish." She looked back at the smoke circling up to the heavens. No sorrow or regret. Only joy as she said, "Everyone who ever knew us or our parents will think we are dead."

No. Not everyone.

Graylem slid his hand under the cloak and felt for the leather pouch and the letter. "We need to get going."

"Where—"

"At the moment where is less important than when. And when we are finally safe, we are going to talk about the why," Graylem said.

"Of course." Deevana's eyes lowered, but not before he saw the flash of resentment at the reminder of her part in this.

To lighten the mood, he added, "I'm still not going to help you carry all the stuff you brought with you, no matter how much you beg." His sister's head snapped up, and he turned on his heel and headed around the hill to the road that would take them south.

They would get away and then they would have the talk he had been planning before her arrival and their dramatic departure. Because there was one person who would know them and would not have heard of their death. Their mother's friend would never know about the fire. No one would remember the connection or think to contact a lady from a southern district about the death of an accused thief and her brother. To her, they were still alive and there was an agreement in place. He would see to it that their mother's wishes were honored and that his sister would get what she claimed to have always wanted. Then he'd worry about what to do with his own life.

Glancing over his shoulder, he took one last look at the place where he had learned to be who he was, then turned back to his sister who was struggling to balance all of her packages in her arms.

With a smile, he walked toward the road and called back, "I really hope you wore comfortable boots."

2

"We need to talk," Graylem said as he placed the pot back into his travel bag and fastened the bag shut. They had walked for hours last night—Graylem carefully listening for sounds of rock wolves or any Xhelozi that might not have gone into hibernation yet.

The monsters of the mountain rarely ventured this far west. There were enough villages and keeps between this part of the district and the mountains to entertain the Xhelozi until the creatures retreated to their caves for the warmer months, but he had heard stories of them roaming farther afield as of late. While he didn't often believe stories, he wasn't about to discount them. So he had chosen where they made camp with care—in the center of a grove of pine trees—and had been equally careful to bank their fire so they had protection from the cold and whatever animals might be prowling the night.

Both he and Deevana had been too tired from their flight to do more than curl up next to the warmth of the flames and sleep. He'd awakened first. Not a surprise. So he'd found water and made tea and was well aware of his sister's eyes following him even when she continued to feign sleep. Now that she was officially awake and they had eaten, it was time to discuss the future as well as what they had just left behind.

"Deevana," he said louder as his sister busied herself with her bundles. "Did you hear me? We have to talk."

She flashed him the overly delighted smile that had never failed to make their father laugh and their mother sigh. Her bright hair shone in the morning sunshine, making her look as if she were surrounded by a cascade of copper. They both had been born with their mother's red hair and their father's reflexes, but that was where the similarity ended.

"You're right," Deevana said breezily. "We can't just wander around aimlessly waiting for a new life to find us. I vote we acquire some horses and ride to the northern mountain pass. I've always wanted to see the kingdoms Father told us about. Now is our chance!"

"Snow will still be falling in the mountains for at least another month. Maybe more," he said. "If you had listened to Father as well as you often claim, you would know it is still too dangerous to pass even if the Xhelozi stay in their caves."

Deevana shrugged, but he saw the insult in her eyes as she asked, "Then where do you think we should go? Is this the part where you tell me that you have come up with a better plan?"

"No," Graylem said, careful to keep his voice level even as he felt the flush that was always so quick to color his face. "This is the part where you tell me why I was forced to burn our home in order to keep you out of the guards' hands."

"I didn't tell you to burn anything," Deevana shot back. She paused, waiting for him to speak, but he forced himself to stay quiet.

Finally, her shoulders slumped as the defiance Deevana always led with was chipped away by the lack of resistance, and she reluctantly said, "I guess I should say thank you."

"You guess?"

She swallowed hard. Her chin lifted, and her brilliant blue eyes met his. "I am grateful. It's just hard for me to admit that I needed help. I still don't know what I did wrong. No one was around. I did everything right."

"What did you steal?"

His sister flipped her hair behind her shoulders. "Nothing important. Things they didn't care about."

"We wouldn't be here if they didn't care about what you took from them."

"I liberated a few things."

Liberated. "What things?"

"A few odds and ends Lady Blackthorn disliked. A pair of boots she said pinched her toes. Nothing she appreciated. She has so much. They all do. None of them cared about the things that I took."

"All evidence to the contrary," he said with a sigh. His sister straightened her shoulders, as if daring him to tell her she didn't deserve the things she had taken. The things that others always had and their father had constantly spoken of and that she desperately believed was her due. Maybe this blow to her pride and the loss of their home would make her understand there was another way. Their mother's way.

"Deevana . . ."

"I know," she said, crossing her arms in front of her chest. "You're disappointed in me. We were doing fine. We didn't need what I took."

How many times had they heard those muted words coming

from underneath the bedchamber door of the home they no longer had? How many arguments had been had when their mother and father had thought he and Deevana were asleep? He didn't want to argue now. Deevana was the one who liked to slash away with words. Was it any wonder he preferred a sword? The damage done with steel was cleaner and in his mind far less painful.

"I know you hated working in the Blackthorn kitchens," he said quietly. "You have always dreamed of a kitchen in a keep of your own."

Deevana turned away and shrugged. "It's stupid to dream of things bigger than what you can slip in your pocket and smuggle away. Even the smallest keep is too big for my pocket."

"Perhaps, then, it is time for you to get bigger pockets."

His sister turned. "Is that your idea of a joke? Because it's better than your normal fare."

He shook his head, reached into his cloak, and pulled out the letter. "There is the son of a lord in the District of Irae who is interested in getting married. His mother was friends with ours back when they were girls. After Mother died, a letter arrived from Lady Venia saying that she would be delighted to have you as a daughter."

"There is a noblewoman who actually wants me to marry her son?" Deevana asked. Then her eyes narrowed. "Is there something wrong with him?"

"It's a minor noble house." Blackthorn's chancellor had been able to look up their lineage and give him an idea of their lands. They weren't one of the great houses of Irae. They weren't even one of the medium power bases. But they were steady. "And he's the youngest of three sons," Graylem said, careful not to look his sister in the eye. Hoping the heat of the lie didn't show on his face.

18

"Third sons, even those of minor lords and ladies, don't have to look to a far northern district to find a bride." She took a step forward. "What's wrong with him, Graylem? If this is something you wish me to agree to, I deserve to know. Because there *is* something you're hiding."

"There might be, but I don't know what it is," Graylem admitted, knowing his face would give away any lie he told. "When Lady Venia's letter arrived, I looked for others she had sent Mother. From the sounds of this one, they had been exchanging letters for months. Mother must have worried that you would find them before she had gotten Lady Venia to agree to the match. She either hid them extremely well or destroyed them."

His mother knew his sister well.

"But there is something in the letter you hold that makes you think there is more than a possible match Mother was hiding."

He sighed. "Lady Venia mentions being glad that you were willing to become her son's wife." He opened the letter and scanned it until he found the words. "She said 'Deevana clearly has the same heart as you, my dear friend. I am grateful to hear you say she has your ability to see beauty in places others might not. It will not be easy for Deevana to leave all she knows behind for something so different from what maidens dream, but I promise she will never regret the choice or her kindness in joining your family with mine.'"

Deevana pursed her lips and nodded. "So he could be a monster."

"Mother would never suggest you marry a monster."

"Mother wanted to be free of the problems I caused."

"She knew you wanted to be a lady and that there was little chance of that ever happening." He held up the letter. "This is your chance, Deevana. Mother found you a way to get everything you wanted."

"By marrying a man that I have never met and might find repulsive?" Deevana bit her lip and looked down at the ground. "What about love? Does that not matter?"

She looked so vulnerable in that moment. Her eyes shone with tears. Her shoulders slumped, making her look small and fragile. His heart tightened even as he put his hands together and applauded her performance.

Four long, slow claps, each louder than the next.

Deevana gasped. "You're mocking me?"

Then he smiled. "I know you. You don't care about falling in love."

She lifted her chin and her lip quavered. "All young maids care about love."

"And after all these years you want me to believe that *you* are like all young maids? That as long as a handsome man came along and won your heart you would happily scrub pots and wash linens for the rest of your life?" Graylem shrugged. "Very well. At the next town, I will send a message telling Lady Venia you have changed your mind about being the next Lady of Green Valley."

He made a move to rip the parchment in half, and Deevana's hand snatched the letter from his hands.

"Don't." His sister blinked the tears away until her eyes were sharp with purpose. "You're right." She shrugged. "I don't care about love. Love ties a person down. It clouds the brain and limits what can be achieved. It makes you forget what you want."

"And you want to be a lady."

She smiled. "It *is* a step up from being a kitchen maid." Deevana looked down at the parchment in her hand, and the smile faded. "Mother did this without telling either of us. And you kept her secret after she died."

"Mother wanted you to be happy, Dee," he said quietly. "*I* want you to be happy. I was going to tell you over supper last night. I was making soup."

"Well, I can't say I'm sorry to have missed your cooking." She laughed. Then the laughter faded and her eyes grew serious. "And I *am* sorry. The house. Your apprenticeship. You liked life in Blackthorn."

Graylem thought about Goodman Bryant, the others in the smithy, and the friends he held dear. He would miss them. They had made his life better. He would have been content to someday, perhaps, have his own family in the cottage.

Only, the cottage no longer existed.

Pushing aside the disappointment, he grabbed his travel bag off the ground, shrugged it onto his shoulder, and said, "I guess it is lucky I like you better. But still not enough to help you carry those bags."

Later in the day, Deevana pointed to the horses near a rundown farm. "Brother, our journey on foot appears to be over."

The horses in the still-brown pasture looked tired, and with no one in sight it would have been no work at all to lead them away without raising an alarm. Their father had always said it was easier to steal from those who had the least because they assumed the worst would happen and accepted it. They never called for the guards because the guards had no reason to care about their loss. They were not important enough to warrant care.

He shook his head. "Those horses will give out in a matter of hours."

"We can steal others when they do."

"And risk being caught with each attempt."

"I won't get caught."

"I'm sure you said the same yesterday. Let's go."

A light, chilly mist began to fall as they trudged up the next hill. They used the river to guide them south. As they traveled, he could feel his sister brooding behind him. He knew with each glance over her shoulder she was regretting leaving the nags with the family who would certainly have suffered greater hardship with the loss.

Deevana wouldn't have noticed the smoke coming out of the crumbling cottage chimney or the rock wolf pelt drying on a porch support peg because neither of those things were items she wanted. But he noticed. Whoever owned the horses had had a hard winter. They had suffered at least one animal attack already. He would not add to their troubles even if it meant walking for another day. But the two men he spotted in the distance an hour later, framed by the light of the almost-set sun, well, they were a different story.

He turned to Deevana and hooked a finger toward the men who had turned off the road and were headed west. "Follow me."

Soundlessly, he hurried toward the trees. Despite the bundles weighing her down, Deevana's tread was light and fast and she kept pace behind him as they moved through the shadows of the early night toward the men, who had dismounted at the bank of the river. The horses lowered their heads to drink while the men took the packs off their mounts' backs and set them on the damp ground.

"See those trees over there?" he asked, pointing to two large oaks that were to the south not far from the road. "That's where I'll meet you. Be ready to ride."

"Gray . . ."

He didn't wait. Deevana could argue with him later if she liked. But for now he kept on the balls of his feet and carefully stepped around twigs and leaves as he hurried through the shadows toward the river where the two riders were setting up camp for the night. Their laughter was ruckus and their steps just uncertain enough to suggest they were slightly impaired by drink. Their inattention, combined with the damp ground, made it easier than it otherwise would have been to slip behind a large oak tree not far from where they sat on a fallen log. From here, Graylem could see the men weren't much older than he was. Perhaps three or four years. They passed a skin between them as one lamented traveling in the damp cold.

"Yes, but it's better to be sleeping on the cold ground up here than for all of us to be forced to march to war in the south."

"I'd have stayed in Garden City if I'd thought Captain Monteros would send me to the battlefields. At least then you know who the enemy is. I'm glad we left. Especially now when they can't spare the men to look for us."

Graylem held his breath. The men were deserters of Eden's Guard, which explained the quality of the saddles and horses. It made him doubly glad he had chosen these mounts to steal. After all, was it technically stealing when you took what didn't rightfully belong to another? It would serve them right to have to walk to wherever they were going. They had broken their oath to serve the kingdom and keep the people in it safe. They deserved to suffer a bit for that crime.

He watched the men drink from their skins and waited for the moment he knew would eventually come. Finally, one pushed off the log and unfastened his britches as he staggered toward the water. The other laughed and followed behind. That's when

Graylem bolted toward the horses.

"Stop!" There was splashing behind him as Graylem swung himself onto one of the mounts. He leaned over, grabbed the reins of the other, and tightened his grip with his legs to urge the horse to run.

His heart thudded with the pounding of the hooves. Still, he grinned at the calls of "Thief! Stop!" knowing they would never catch him, even if they did get their pants fastened.

The horses thundered through the trees as he looked for Deevana. There. She stepped out from the shadows, and he brought the horses to a stop next to her. Angry shouts echoed in the distance. They were far, but not far enough to render them little threat.

"They weren't happy to be relieved of their mounts, so you're going to have to hurry." He slid down, grabbed two of her bags, and fastened them to the back of the horse as his sister climbed on. He passed the rest of her things up and started to tell her to just hold onto them and secure them later, when the sound of hooves rang from behind him.

"Graylem!" Deevana called as he pulled his sword from its sheath and spun in time to see two mounted men racing toward them.

"Thief!" The calls from behind were closer. "Greckor! Tyson! Stop him!"

"We've got him!" One of the mounted men yelled back as both men on horseback reached for their swords. "And his lady!"

"Run, Gray!" Deevana yelled.

Not unless he wanted a blade in the back.

He cursed his stupidity as the first horse bore down on him. *All of us* one of the men by the river had said. These were the others those words referred to.

He drew his sword as his sister screamed. *Focus on what's happening now*, he thought as he took deep breaths. The hooves grew closer, and he knew the man would swing his weapon as soon as he got in range. Graylem had one chance to get this right.

Wait for it. Set. *Now.*

He slashed out. The blade sliced through the leather strap of the saddle, and Graylem dove to the side as the other man's sword whistled just overhead. He heard the man shout. There was a thud. A horse neighed. And then the approach of more thundering hoofbeats as he scampered to his feet and turned. He struck out with his blade as the deserter from the guard brought his sword downward. Metal struck metal. Graylem deflected the blow and spun. The other man's weapon was bigger than Graylem's, but as with Lord Havershire, the weight of the broadsword meant it took longer for the man to recover from his swing. The deserter was just pulling back his blade when Graylem stabbed the man deep in the thigh and yanked the blade downward.

The man screamed. Blood spurted. The broadsword dropped to the ground as the man leaned forward to clutch the wound. The horse darted forward at a dead gallop, disappearing with the bleeding man into the night.

"Watch out, Graylem!"

He turned and raised his sword just in time. The man he had unseated from his mount was big. The guardsman's sword crashed against Graylem's blade and sent him staggering backward. The guardsman swung again. Another block. Graylem's feet slipped on the wet leaves as he retreated once again, making the oath-breaking guardsman smile.

"Gray. The others are coming!"

"It's no matter. Because I'm going to kill you first," the burly guard yelled. He raised his sword and ran forward. Only this time, Graylem didn't block. He ducked and lunged to the side. Then from one knee he thrust his sword upward into the attacker's stomach. The man screamed. Pain and death swam in the deserter's eyes as Graylem yanked his sword free. The man toppled, and Graylem raced toward where Deevana and their horses waited. He grabbed his mount's reins from her hand and yelled, "Ride!"

Her horse started forward as he swung up on his own and urged him to follow.

"Stop!"

He glanced over his shoulder as the wet deserters came running into view. One of them leaned over their fallen friend while the other pulled back his bow. The arrow didn't come close. Knowing they could never catch him or his sister, Graylem turned forward and galloped behind Deevana.

3

Several times Deevana shouted his name and asked for them to slow, but he insisted they keep riding—first to the road and then south for as long as their horses could gallop. Finally, he slowed his horse and called, "I think we are far enough away now to make camp. The horses need rest."

They left the road and found a small pond where the horses could drink. In the distance beyond he saw the steady glow of dozens of wind-powered lights against the night.

"That's a lot of lights," Deevana said, coming to stand next to him. "Do you think it could be Temperance Hold?"

He shook his head. "We haven't traveled far enough to reach the District of Miluina yet. It must be a large village near a keep."

"If it is, they have a lord more generous than Blackthorn was," his sister observed. Graylem nodded. Blackthorn Keep used wind power to light its halls and power the village water pumps and the mill. The rest made due with torches and candles to chase the shadows. Their father used to tell stories of windmills the size of

27

mountains and cities that glowed like the sun even when the moon shone. Maybe they weren't exaggerations after all.

He tethered his horse to a squat bush next to the pond then reached for the reins of his sister's mount.

"I didn't know you could fight like that," she said.

He felt Deevana's eyes on him as he stared at the lights in the distance. "You saw Father teach me how to use a sword."

"Not like that. Father had quick hands and quicker feet, but he couldn't fight like that."

"The sword he used was heavier. I started using a lighter one when I began working with Goodman Bryant." A few weeks after he'd started at the smithy, there had been a tournament held by the Blackthorns. The son of a neighboring lord had fought with the same kind of blade Graylem now carried. The lord was of lean build, just like Graylem, and appeared as if he would be at a disadvantage next to all the bigger, stronger fighters. Graylem had never seen anything like it.

It took him weeks to convince Goodman Bryant to help him make a similar sword. Once he did, Graylem practiced what he remembered seeing on the tournament field—alone, and then with whatever apprentice was willing to face him. He'd lost more than he'd won to start. Then one day he started winning.

"And you kept it a secret."

"It wasn't something anyone needed to know," he said, glad the moon wasn't bright enough for the blush of his half-truth to show. His father would have pushed him to use the skill to aid his thieving. His mother would have endlessly worried for him. So he had kept his secret and waited for the day he could prove himself with his blade.

He never imagined that the first time he did so, he would cause men to die.

"I wonder what other secrets you are keeping," Deevana whispered. "What else can you do?" Before he could think of an answer, she turned toward her packs to set up camp. For a change, she said little as they ate and only complained of his unwillingness to let her use his blankets when it was time for sleep.

"You should have thought to pack your own instead of bringing along—" He glanced at the bundles next to his sister. "Whatever it is you brought with you."

Deevana sighed. Graylem refused to feel guilty when she settled into her cloak and he into his blankets, but he failed when she shivered in her sleep. Carefully, he placed one of his blankets over her and wrapped himself in the other. He watched as some of the lights in the distance darkened as he waited for the screams of pain and the gurgles of death to fade from his mind.

"I had the most wonderful dream," Deevana said when the pond glistened with the early morning light. "I dreamed of hundreds of lights like the ones we saw last night. And the orb shining high above the Palace of Winds."

"It sounds as if you slept well."

"You didn't?" she asked, turning toward him. Whatever she saw in his face made his sister frown. "What's wrong?"

"Nothing," he said, not wanting to give voice to the images of death that had haunted him through the night. He reached into his travel pack, pulled out a roll, and threw it to his sister. "It's time for us to ride. The farther south we go the farther we will be from the men we relieved of their horses." The men might want their horses back, but they wouldn't risk traveling closer to Garden City where they could be recognized as deserters.

"Do you think we could see it?" Deevana asked once they were on the road again.

"See what?"

Deevana rolled her eyes and laughed. "The lights of Garden City. The orb of Eden. I want to know if they are as bright and beautiful as everyone says."

"Knowing you," Graylem said, "I'm sure you'll find a way to convince your husband to take you there. Maybe you'll even see the Hall of Virtues and the Throne of Light."

"Or I could see it before then." She smiled. "After all, we are riding south to Irae. Garden City is on the way."

He had planned on giving Garden City a wide berth. The last thing they needed before Deevana was safely married and assured her new life was a city full of items that could tempt her. "There's no time. We don't want word of your supposed death reaching Lady Venia and her son before you do."

"There is little to no chance of that happening, Graylem. And the way your face currently matches your hair tells me you know that to be true. So why can't we stop in Garden City? Lady Venia and my soon-to-be husband can't be expecting us to arrive anytime soon. If they were, you would have talked to me about the marriage prospect before yesterday."

"You'll see Garden City once you are married," he assured her. "If you just wait . . ."

"But if I wait, I won't see it with *you*." Deevana yanked on her reins and brought her horse to a stop. "I won't be able to picture you there. And that's where you intend to go after, isn't it?"

30

His horse danced underneath him as he urged it to stop. "What?"

Deevana sighed. "You kept your skill with the sword a secret for years. I'm guessing it's because you wanted to enter one of the Blackthorn tournaments and take all the other swordsmen by surprise. If you won, you would have been given enough coin to live on for years and offered a position as one of the ranking members of some northern district lord's guard."

Graylem shrugged. "And now they think I'm dead."

"Which is why you have to do something else. And really, this is better because *you* are better than that life."

"I'm not our father, Deevana. I don't need more."

"Maybe not, but you deserve more than what being in the service of Lord Blackthorn would offer. Now you can set your sights higher. What higher place could there be than Garden City and the Palace of Winds? You could be a defender of the Seven Virtues and slay the King's enemies."

Graylem looked off in the distance.

"You didn't like killing those men. It haunts you." It wasn't a question. Like it or not, just as he knew his sister's heart, she knew his.

"I never took a life before," he said quietly. "I always knew I might have to as a member of Blackthorn's guard, but so rarely does that happen. I guess I just told myself it would never happen."

"You know you didn't have a choice. They attacked us. They would have killed both of us had you not defeated them."

Defeated.

A nice word to cover unpleasant things.

"You told me you thought they were deserters of Eden's Guard."

He nodded.

"What would happen to them if they were caught and brought back to Garden City?"

"They would be put to death," he said, feeling some of the pressure inside his chest release at the truth Deevana offered. The men had earned their deaths long before they had met him. And yet . . .

"I know you've always been frustrated with me," Deevana said. He lifted his eyes to meet hers, and she smiled. "You've always liked to follow the rules that I felt chained by. You believe in earning what life gives you. There is no one I can imagine making a better King's Guardsman because you do what is right. It's why you feel responsible for my happiness."

"I care about your happiness because I love you. You're my sister."

"And what of your happiness?" she asked, her eyes ablaze with feeling. "I know you don't think that I worry about you, but I do. It's an older sister's job to worry about her younger brother."

"You are only ten months older, and you don't have anything to worry about."

"Of course I do. You have ensured my future. You burned everything we owned to make sure I could live that future. And now it is my turn to make sure you don't give up on yours." Deevana nudged her horse closer to his, and she reached over and took his hand in hers. "It's my fault that you lost a chance to gain the life you wanted to live. Let's go to Garden City now so you can see whether a better life might be waiting for you there. I can be there for you the way you have always been there for me. And when I start the life that you have worked so hard to give me, I will be able to do so without regret."

Warmth and relief flooded him. Despite living in the same house and seeing each other every day, Graylem had been isolated from his sister as he planned for the future and worried about what she might think of those plans. Now . . .

Something glinted in Deevana's eyes, and he noticed the way she leaned forward on her horse. The way she held her breath as she waited for him to agree. He had seen that anticipation before.

"And that's the only reason you want to go to Garden City. For me. To help me decide if I should try to become a member of Eden's Guard?" he asked.

Deevana's eyes narrowed for just a second, and the knot inside him tightened. "No, that's not the only reason," she admitted with great sincerity. Then she gave him an impish smile. "It's also because it will be fun!"

His sister's sense of fun lasted two days. The sun shone as they slowly made their way south through their home district of Orgo to the very northernmost part of the kingdom of Eden, toward Miluina. Then sleet fell from the sky and the food Graylem had brought with him began to run low. He had to stop their travel in order to set traps and hunt—two things Deevana chafed at.

"Why don't we go to one of the farmhouses or get food in a village?" she asked.

"Because winter has just come to an end and the farmers will have little enough food for themselves. They won't have extra on hand, and unless you have a wealth of gold that I don't know about, we don't have the coins necessary to pay for food and still have enough to stay in Garden City for a handful of days."

His sister frowned each time they stopped early so he could tread through the trees and over the hills, putting his father's bow to use, but she was full of effusive praise when he arrived back at their camp with a gray rabbit or a grouse, and, on their second week of travel, a hill deer who must have recently joined the male herd Graylem had stumbled across. The animal had not been quick enough to sense danger before the arrow found its heart.

It took time to skin the deer as well as cook the meat and dress its fur. But for once Deevana didn't mind helping with the chores or the delay since it meant gaining a warm ground cover for her to sleep on and enough meat to allow them to travel for days without needing to waste time on finding more. Graylem also used the time to practice with his sword and work out the kinks from sleeping on the ground. All the while he slashed at imaginary foes and ducked away from the blades he could picture coming toward him, he could feel his sister's eyes watching. Though every time he turned toward their campfire, she was looking away.

The sleet and rain disappeared as the days passed. Green buds appeared on the trees. They saw more travelers on the road, and one night he and his sister camped with a Garden City merchant and his daughter. While Deevana discussed the jewelry the merchants made and the lords and ladies who purchased their wares, Graylem asked the only question he had need to have answered.

"How many days will it take for us to get to Garden City?"

"My daughter and I have been traveling for just over a week, but you are traveling without a cart. You should arrive sooner."

Less than a week. And according to the merchant, it would take about that much longer to reach their final destination and Deevana's new home. They could spend several days in Garden City and still be able to travel south in plenty of time.

Still, he couldn't help worrying when his sister changed the subject each time he spoke of her upcoming wedding.

Her smile grew wider with every farm and village they passed, and three nights later, when Graylem spotted the distant but steady glow in the sky where no star had shined the night before, he couldn't help his own spurt of excitement. Their father had told stories on wintery nights with Graylem and his sister sitting in front of the fire. He spoke of the enormous orb that had been placed on a pedestal at the top of the tallest tower of the Palace of Winds. Its light was a symbol of the purity of the virtues the Kingdom of Eden had been founded upon and was meant to guide those who were searching in the dark to the safety of the great white walls. It was the walls, the virtues, and that light that the King and his guard were sworn to uphold.

Humility. Charity. Temperance. Patience. Endurance. Strength. Chastity.

Justice was not among the virtues. Neither was honesty, as his father was quick to point out. Therefore the virtues were also important for those who were successful thieves. It was Deevana's lack of humility that no doubt raised suspicions in Blackthorn Keep and set them on the road south. In just a handful of days he and his sister would stand inside the walls of the city that exemplified those virtues. And there, Graylem would learn whether he belonged.

"What are these?" he asked. He pulled a pair of black trousers decorated with silver thread on the cuffs from his travel bag and looked for his sister. Despite being close enough to see the walls of Garden City, she had insisted they camp near a river so they could both bathe before they entered.

He pulled out another pair of brown trousers, these edged with threads of gold, and ran a hand through his still-damp hair. "Deevana, where are *my* clothes?"

"Those are your clothes," his sister called. The bushes nearest the river rustled, and Deevana stepped out wearing a dress he had certainly never seen before. "So," his sister said as she smiled. "What do you think?"

He scrambled to his feet, the trousers in his hand forgotten.

The dress his sister was wearing looked richer by far than any he had seen Deevana wear before—richer than any girl in their village had ever hoped to own. It was a green color that matched the winter tree needles they had in abundance up north, cut with pale blue and edged with gold. The brush in Deevana's hand was silver. Also something he had never before laid eyes upon. But she had clearly used it to brush her hair until it fell like a crimson waterfall around her shoulders.

"Is that what you stole?" he asked. "Clothes? Brushes?" Was this for what they burned everything their mother had loved?

"Lady Blackthorn looked terrible in this dress. She said so herself and insisted that it be carried away. I just waited until there was no one around to notice when I took it farther than she anticipated."

"And those?" He pointed down at the clothing in his pack. "Were they unflattering as well?"

She lifted her chin, and her eyes flashed. "No one notices when a few trousers or a dress go missing. Not when they have so many. I wanted to leave you a gift that you could use on a special day so you would think of me."

"Because you were always planning on leaving Blackthorn." It made sense. The dress. The bulky items that she must have already had packed in bags ready to take with her when she made her escape. "You planned on leaving me behind."

The realization didn't surprise him. Neither did the hurt.

Deevana walked toward him. Sunlight gleamed off her hair as she said, "We are not children anymore, Gray. You were making plans for the future, and I was as well. I knew you would disapprove of the methods I used to secure what I needed on my path, so I didn't tell you. I didn't want to risk losing the love of the only family I had left."

"You didn't want me to put a stop to whatever it is that you had planned."

She reached down and plucked her red cloak off her bags. Shrugging it over her shoulders to protect her from the chill, she admitted, "Perhaps that was part of it, too. But that's behind us now because here we are ready to ride into Garden City together and see the Palace of Winds and everything we have ever been told about. Is it wrong that I want to do so in clothing that isn't stained by dirt and sweat and the blood of the men you killed?"

Guilt surfaced again, just as he knew his sister had intended. Straightening his shoulders, he asked, "What else did you take, Deevana?"

"Things to sell," she admitted. "Which I intend to do once I get to the city. Do not worry, Graylem. I am Father's daughter. I avoided taking anything with the Blackthorn crest or markings that would show they are from a noble house in Orgo. No one will know they were not ours in the first place, especially not when I am dressed like this and you are dressed in those." She nodded at the trousers in his hand.

"Deevana . . ."

"And," Deevana added, "members of the guard will be far likelier to answer your questions and introduce you to their captain if you appear to be a noble of skill looking to serve your king instead of a peasant seeking out a place to sleep and three meals a day."

Graylem frowned and looked back down at the trousers in his hands. As much as it bothered him, there was nothing he could do about the items his sister had *liberated* now. That was in the past. And if he balked at Deevana's ideas it would make the future far more problematic.

Despite wanting to throttle her, he kept his voice calm and said, "I'll wear these, but only if you promise that once we are inside Garden City you won't cause trouble. I need you to promise that you won't steal—not silver or clothing or anything—not even if you justify it by saying it will help me because it is better than what I have." He looked into her eyes. "Do we have a deal, Deevana?"

"I promise that I won't steal, Graylem," Deevana said solemnly. "And if it makes you feel any better, the shirts I took for you had holes in them. I mended them myself."

He couldn't stop his lips from twitching. "Then maybe they have blood on them after all."

The brown trousers were the least decorative, so he chose those and went behind a bush to change so his sister couldn't laugh at him as he fumbled with unfamiliar closures. He wasn't sure why lords needed crisscrossing ties and then a flap with a buckle at the top and more ties at the bottom of his legs when just one simple tie to keep the britches from falling down would do.

It took him a good quarter of an hour to properly get into them, and he made a vow not to drink much of anything until he was sure he could unfasten them with haste if need be. He then unfolded the light blue tunic and smiled at the uneven stitching on one of the cuffs before slipping it over his head. After checking the fastenings again to make sure his pants wouldn't fall, he walked back to where his sister waited with her hands clasped in front of her and a gleam in her eye. Their bags were already stowed on their horses, the fire extinguished.

He grabbed his cloak from the branch of a tree and shrugged it over his shoulders. "Are you ready to go?"

The smile his sister gave him was wide and filled with delight. "I've been waiting for this day my entire life."

The sun shone brightly as they rode. The grasses got greener and the air warmer the farther south they went. Billowy white clouds dotted the brilliant blue sky. Then the clouds shifted and Graylem felt his breath catch as in the distance he saw what could only be the Palace of Winds. He knew the Palace was sitting atop a plateau, but from where they were it looked as if it were floating with the clouds. In the glare of the sun, he couldn't see the orb, but he could make out eight windmills churning atop the battlements.

They urged their horses to go faster as the Palace of Winds grew larger and higher and the walls around Garden City came into view, only slowing when they reached the main gates where carts and people went in and out. Graylem couldn't help but stare. The walls surrounding the city were taller than Blackthorn Keep by double, perhaps triple the height and they were smooth as glass. His father said walls were made for thieves to climb, but these walls—only thieves with more recklessness than sense would consider scaling them with hope of success.

He studied the guards standing at the gates in their mail shirts with cloaks of blue and yellow—their hands resting on the hilts of the broadswords hanging at their sides—as he rode beside his sister into the city that was home to Eden's King and Queen.

"We should first find a place to stay," Graylem said, trying not to gawk at the sheer number of people roaming the wide street. It seemed to stretch from the gate straight ahead into the heart of the city, which was bustling with activity. "The merchant, Goodman Tyrelle, suggested the Red Stag. Perhaps we should stop and ask one of the guards for directions."

His sister shook her head. "Let's wait until we get closer to the center of the city," she said as she nudged her horse forward.

Kids laughed and ran in and out of narrow streets. Other people shouted as they sold their wares. The smell of so many people mixed with baking bread and the soot of torches and fires was almost overwhelming. He wasn't sure how far they rode into the city. It was impossible to gauge when all the buildings looked much the same.

Eventually, Deevana pointed into the distance with delight at a large tree in the middle of an open square. A man in a yellow and blue cloak with the seal of the Seven Virtues stood with three other guardsmen near a low wall. The seal, Graylem realized, marked him as a member of the elite King's Guard. Beyond the wall, closer to the tree, were a group of richly dressed women. One, standing a little bit apart, wore a snowy white cloak. Her head was bowed in contemplation or prayer.

Excitement filled his sister's face as she nudged her horse forward and yelled, "Follow me!"

Before he could ask for an explanation, she turned her mount toward the buildings at the northern side of the square. She stopped in front of one with a symbol of an in-bloom rose often used to represent the virtue of Chastity and the District of Lussuria hanging on a plaque over the door.

His sister slid off her mount and handed the reins to a young, brown-cloaked boy who stepped out from the stable beside the building. Before Graylem had a chance to dismount, she tossed her hair and in a firm, haughty voice said, "My brother and I are here to see Lord Nigel and Lady Ariella of Justice Hall."

"Lord Nigel and Lady Arielle aren't here, m'lady," the boy explained.

"But they *will* be?" she pressed. When the boy just stood gaping at her, she asked, "This *is* the inn where they stay when they come to Garden City? Or do I need to tell Lord Nigel and Lady Ariella that they are not remembered by this establishment?"

"Excuse me, my lady!" A man with a neatly trimmed dark beard and a frown for the boy appeared in the inn's doorway. "My apologies for my son's confusion. The lord and lady of Justice Hall do often stay here when they come to Garden City. But they are not in residence now."

Deevana's eyes flashed as she walked toward her brother. "I know they told you they would be here by now, but I am sure there is a good reason for their delay. You will send a messenger after this man shows us to our rooms." She turned toward the inn's owner and lifted her chin. "If we have to wait for them to arrive, we might as well wait here."

"Yes, my lady," the man said with a nod to his son. "It would be our honor to serve you, my lady. And we have two of our best rooms available."

Before Graylem could say anything, his sister winked and swept through the inn's open door, leaving him with no choice but to follow.

4

"What do you think you're doing?" Graylem hissed as his sister closed the door to her chamber. The room had windows that looked onto the tree she had admired—the Tree of Virtues, according to the innkeep—and boasted rich fabrics on the chairs and a bed overflowing with pillows and draped with silk. "You promised you wouldn't do anything foolish while we were in Garden City."

"Actually, I promised I wouldn't steal, and this isn't foolish," she insisted as she walked to the window. "We have a place to stable our horses where they will not be stolen, clean rooms to sleep in, and by telling him that we are familiar with Lord Nigel, I ensured the innkeeper will not charge us more than he charges them or ask for coin in advance, since that would be an insult to both us and our highborn friends."

"And when it is time to leave and we can't pay his price?"

"I told you, I have things to sell, which we will do as soon as we find a reputable merchant to haggle with, so stop worrying. While you were talking to the jewelry merchant, I learned a great deal from his daughter."

"Information about Lord Nigel and Lady Ariella?"

"And places where I can sell a few items that remind me of sad times that I no longer wish to remember." Deevana grabbed a bag from the foot of her canopied bed, opened it, and pulled a deep blue dress from its depths. "As long as you don't give us away with your stricken looks . . ."

A knock came at the door.

"Enter!"

Graylem stepped away from the door as it opened and a girl, perhaps twelve, with deep brown hair appeared.

"My father thought you might like assistance, my lady." The girl curtsied. "I often serve as Lady Ariella's maid when she is here."

"If Ariella finds you acceptable, I am sure I will, too." Deevana glanced at him. "I hope you can help me do something with my hair. Is there a popular style, one worn by Princess Carys perhaps, that would suit me?"

"Princess Carys is not interested in hairstyles, my lady," the girl said. "But the new seeress of Eden, Lady Imogen, has just become betrothed to Prince Micah, and she is known for her beauty and style." The young maid took the dress Deevana was holding from her and hung it in the wardrobe.

"The new seeress of Eden sounds intriguing. Do you see her often?" Deevana said, walking across the room to the window.

"She visits the Tree of Virtues at least once a week, my lady. I believe she is there now."

"Well, I look forward to meeting her," his sister said with a toss of her hair. "But I want to be presentable when I do. If you don't mind, brother, my maid and I have much to do. I'll see you at dinner."

His sister nodded toward the door.

"So you'll be here in your rooms until then?" he asked.

"Of course," she said quickly. "Where else would I go?"

The door shut behind him. He heard his sister laugh and headed to his own rooms next door, which boasted darker colors than his sister's but a bed just as big, and a separate space with a table and chairs near a window that also had a view of the square and the tree.

Keeping his cloak on, he pulled a chair next to the window and waited. He would have preferred to watch the door from the stables, but while he wasn't sure how exactly a lord was supposed to behave, he doubted many made a habit of hiding with the horses. After half an hour had passed, he wondered if maybe he had misjudged his sister's intent. Then he spotted the fluttering of a red cloak below and his sister hurrying down the walkway with the innkeeper's daughter at her side.

When he stepped outside, the red cloak was approaching a small gate that led to the courtyard where the tree stretched toward the sunlight. Her head was high and her shoulders straight. He wove through the people hurrying about the city until he reached the low stone wall that circled the tree's grove. Now that he was closer, he could see the sides of Deevana's hair had been braided and wrapped around the back of her head in an intricate pattern, which explained why it had taken her so long to venture into the city. His sister said something to the girl, who nodded and stayed by the gate while Deevana moved forward.

Raising the hood of his cloak, Graylem moved to where he had a better view of his sister as she approached the enormous tree. She placed a hand on the gnarled bark then knelt next to a group of women who had been there for some time.

After several minutes, a woman stepped out of the center of all the others. It was the woman in white. When she removed the hood, he could tell her long dark hair was styled in the same fashion as his sister currently wore. That was no coincidence. And it was certainly no accident that when his sister rose, she lost her balance and drew the attention of the woman who could only be the new seeress of Eden.

"Excuse me, guardsman," said Graylem as he approached the four men in mail shirts. The one wearing the mark of the King's personal guard had streaks of gray winding through his dark beard and a small scar on his forehead. The other guards behind him looked to be barely older than Graylem's sixteen years.

The older guard nodded. "Is there something we can help you with, my lord?"

"The lady in white near the tree. Do you know her name? She is quite beautiful." The woman had turned her head to speak to Deevana, giving him a clear view of deeply tanned skin that almost glowed, high cheekbones, and dark eyes that narrowed just a bit at the edges.

The guard laughed. "You must not be from around here."

"My family hails from Orgo." His sister had claimed they were from another district, but Graylem didn't feel right about lying to a man who wore the seal of the King's Guard. "This is the first time I've had the chance to visit Garden City."

"Even if you had visited before, you would not have seen Seeress Imogen."

His heart sank as the King's Guardsman confirmed what Graylem had suspected. His sister had been in Garden City for just a handful of hours and she had managed to meet the Seeress of Eden.

"And you aren't the only one who finds her attractive, my lord."

The King's Guardsman smirked. "She arrived at the end of winter and is already betrothed to Prince Micah."

Prince Micah. The heir to the throne. Graylem sighed at his sister's brashness. "It figures."

The older guard laughed as he watched the woman by the Tree of Virtues—the white cloak of the seeress making her stand out like a rose in the midst of a group of weeds. "If you came to Garden City to look for a potential wife, my lord, it is better to choose one who doesn't claim to read the future or set the wind after you."

Graylem grinned, although he couldn't help noticing the look in the guard's eyes when he spoke of the seeress's skills and the way the younger guards shifted or rolled their eyes.

"If I wanted a wife, I would have stayed in Orgo," Graylem said. "I came because I am curious about what it takes to become a member of the King's Guard."

The older guard turned to study him. "I assume your noble-born father told you stories filled with the glory and honor of defending the King and the Council and encouraged you to come?"

"My father told me there was little glory in fighting for honor, and this is the last place he would want me to be."

"So . . ." The man nodded. "You're here as a rebellion against your family, my lord? Could you be the younger son who will not inherit the title or the land and is looking for something for himself?"

"I am the youngest in my household, and I was taught that the only way I would gain anything in life was to seek it out and take it." It was their father's philosophy that his sister lived by.

"My father told me the same," the King's Guardsman said as Graylem's sister tilted her head to listen to whatever the seeress said.

"And my older brother was not one inclined to share."

"I, too, have a sibling not inclined to charity," Graylem admitted.

In the distance, Deevana dropped into a low curtsy. The seeress smiled and said something, which made the other women nod before they started toward the courtyard's gate. The guards snapped to attention. The older guard sent the other three to meet the seeress and then turned back to Graylem.

"That sword is lighter than most that the King's Guard typically uses. If you can't swing something bigger, you should go home."

"If I swing something bigger, I wouldn't win the fight. I've worked hard to make sure I can win. I figure in a fight winning is what's most important. You must think so as well." Graylem nodded to the blade at the man's side, which was almost the same length and width as his own.

Now the King's Guardsman smiled. "Those of us searching to make our own fortune have to do what we think is best. Are you serious about wanting to know if you have what it takes to become a member of Eden's Guard?"

Graylem nodded.

"Then come to the Palace tomorrow morning and ask for Roddick. I admit, you have made me curious to see if there are more similarities between us than our swords."

The guard walked to the gates and fell in step beside the seeress. One of the younger guards flanked her on the other side and the other two walked behind her as she traveled around the stone wall then down the street past where Graylem stood. Her eyes were lowered and her hands clasped in front of her as people on the street called for the blessing of the wind and the light. As she passed Graylem, she looked back at the tree for just a moment. A satisfied smile tugged at the corner of her lips, transforming her face from one of fragile loveliness to a beauty as strong as a blade. He saw his sister talking to several of the other women at the tree, and when he looked back at Lady Imogen, the iron strength was gone as she headed, flanked by the guards he had spoken with, to the Palace of Winds.

"You told me you were going to stay inside," he said when the door to Deevana's rooms opened and his sister appeared.

His sister didn't bother to feign contrition. After unfastening her cloak, she threw it on the end of the bed and smiled as she dropped into an ornate armchair. "Sasha, my maid, suggested I visit the Tree of Virtues to ask the Gods for a blessing. She said it is the first thing most ladies do after arriving in Garden City."

"And what blessing did you ask for?"

"It is not polite to ask a lady to reveal her heart's desire. At least that is what some of the women at the tree were saying when I arrived." She stood up and walked the length of the room. "Besides, you already know what I want. I want this." Deevana spun in a circle with her arms extended. "The curtsies and the ladies and the beds that are as fluffy as clouds and—"

A knock came at the door. "Lady Deevana, I have the supper you requested for you and your brother."

Deevana winked at him. "Enter!"

A handsome woman entered carrying a large tray. The girl, Sasha, trailed behind her carrying another. The smells of simmered meat and potatoes and some kind of spice that he wasn't familiar with filled the room. His stomach rumbled as the two placed both trays on the table, took covers off the bowls of thick, brown soup, and arranged a jug of wine and a pot of tea and cups for each at each place setting.

Once everything was arranged, the woman Graylem assumed was the innkeeper's wife asked, "Is there anything else I can get for you, my lord and lady?"

Graylem rose and bumped the table. A goblet fell to the floor with a clang and started to roll. He reached for it and bumped the table, sending a spoon flying. Heat flooded him as the dark-haired girl scurried to retrieve both the cup and the spoon.

"I will send my daughter back with a clean cup and spoon, my lord," the innkeeper's wife said.

"No need," he said, at the same time his sister snapped, "Please do, and bring more bread. After so much travel, my brother and I are both hungry."

The woman nodded. "Yes, my lady. Ring the bell when you wish the trays to be taken away." She and her daughter curtsied and headed out.

The minute the door closed, his sister whirled around to face him. "Are you trying to get us caught?" she hissed, stalking toward him. "Lords don't stand when servants come into the room, and whatever you do, don't thank them. Do you want to ruin everything for me with your bumbling? No wonder Father always said you would never be able to survive outside of Blackthorn."

Graylem turned, hating the disappointment shining in his sister's eyes and the disdain in her voice. "We will be gone in a matter of days, and the next time you come to Garden City you will be married to a lord and you *will* be a lady."

"Are you simple, Graylem? Do you not understand that people question what is different? If you act like you aren't a lord, they will start to question whether you are."

"As long as we pay them, it won't matter—"

"Of course it matters. You need to act as they expect or they will start to ask questions that cannot be asked. They expect you to stay seated and to be served. They expect you to be arrogant."

"Look," he said, pushing away the embarrassment. "I understand how much you have always wanted rooms like these and to have people wait on you instead of you serving them. But we aren't important to anyone. They won't care—"

A knock came at the door.

"Enter!" his sister snapped. The door opened. "Be quick," Deevana said as the girl hurried inside, placed the new cup and spoon on the table, bobbed a curtsy, and hurried out.

When the door clicked shut, Deevana paced to the other side of the room and placed her hand on the stone hearth. "I have been invited to the Palace of Winds, Graylem!" She looked down into the fire. "Or I guess I should say that *Lady* Deevana is requested to visit with the seeress at the Palace of Winds, because a kitchen maid would never have dared enter the gate and pray at the Tree of Virtues while the seeress and other ladies of the court were there. The Seeress of Eden, who will one day be the Queen of Eden, spoke to *me*. She will allow me to see the wonders of the Palace of Winds and listen to the musical performance that is set to entertain the court ladies tomorrow. If anyone were to question who we say we are . . . if anyone whispered in the wrong ear . . ." Deevana turned. "What do you think the Crown Prince would say if word reaches the Palace that I lied to his betrothed—to an advisor to the King and the Council of Elders—about being a lady?"

It was a punishable crime for a commoner to lie to a member of the nobility. At Blackthorn, those whose lies were exposed were flogged once for each lie that was told—painful, but lenient compared to the stories his father shared of what happened to those who were imprisoned in the North Tower of the Palace of Winds.

He thought of his own invitation to the Palace gates. After having his skill questioned by the older guardsman, he wanted a chance to pit his blade against those who were the very best. While the deaths he had caused gave him pause as to whether he could kill on command, he still wanted to know whether he was good enough to gain the right to serve. Whether he might have a future beyond the one he had lost.

Shaking his head, he said, "We should ride for Irae tomorrow . . ."

"No." Deevana dropped into a chair and took a piece of bread from the tray. "No lady would refuse an invitation from the next Queen and current Seer of Eden. If I left now, it would draw even more notice and cause questions should I return." She popped a bit of the bread into her mouth and sighed with contentment. "And none of this will be a problem if you just try to be more like the kind of lord they have come to expect."

She poured a cup of tea and held it out to him. "Please, Gray," she said with a catch in her voice. "We won't be here for very long, and after this week is over, I promise you won't have to worry over me ever again."

"Somehow," he said, taking the cup of tea and wishing he could swallow away the knot of worry lodged in his throat, "I doubt that will be the case, sister."

But he could dream.

He was standing at the door of the stables the next morning when his sister slipped out of the side door of the inn. Her hair was twined into what looked like fancy ropes and wrapped around other parts of her hair that had been curled. It was probably considered attractive here in Garden City. To him it just looked complicated.

"Going to the Palace of Winds?" he asked, falling into step next to her.

To Deevana's credit, she didn't flinch and her eyes didn't widen with shock, but the catch of her breath told her his presence caught her unawares. "I did not see you come out of your room."

Not a surprise since he'd assumed she'd have set her maid or someone else watch his quarters after they rose at dawn. Which is why he slipped outside before the sun started to creep into the sky. "And you were hoping if I was watching from my window I wouldn't see you leave."

"I guess I should find it comforting to have a brother that knows me as well as I know him," she said lightly. "I knew you would want to escort me to the Palace and that your bumbling could cause me trouble."

Embarrassment curdled in his stomach, but he held his ground. His sister might not want him to be a part of her plans, but he wasn't going to let her get into trouble if he could help it. "You said you wanted me to act like a lord. While I'm not always sure what you think that means, I am pretty sure a lord would not allow his sister to wander around a strange city alone."

Deevana frowned then nodded. "Very well, but once we get there . . ."

"You don't have to worry about me hovering," he said. "No one has to know we are together."

"You don't think they'll wonder who you are while you are

waiting around for me by the gates?"

"Who says I'll be waiting outside the gates?" Then he smiled. "You aren't the only member of this family with an invitation to enter the Palace of Winds. Yesterday, while you were meeting the Seeress of Eden, I met with a member of the King's Guard."

Surprise filled his sister's eyes, and she gave him a look filled with pride. "Good for you, Graylem! You've been busy!"

Since their horses and saddles were originally stolen from the guard, Graylem insisted they walk through the city streets to the Palace. The air was cool and crisp. Scents of baking bread, simmering spices, and people living in tight quarters hung in the air. The streets seemed endless, but with each step the Palace of Winds and the windmills atop the battlements grew closer. As did the people inside the Palace.

"I have been busy since we arrived," he said, glancing at his sister. "And I've heard some things about the Seeress Imogen whom you are going to be visiting today. It is said that she has mostly avoided spending time with the women of the court and instead can most often been seen on the battlements looking up at the sky or traveling back and forth through the city to the Tree of Virtues. She always leaves an offering there."

Her eyes flicked to him then returned forward.

"They also think she was chosen as seer because King Ulron wanted her as his mistress and cared little of whether she could call the wind or read the stars."

"You seem to have heard a lot," his sister commented.

He had made a point of venturing into several taverns and inns when Deevana was asleep to listen to the local gossip and to voice the occasional question. Fatigue was not as important as understanding what his sister was getting herself—and dragging him—into.

"Lady Imogen is betrothed to Prince Micah," his sister added. "And the King doesn't need a mistress since he already has one."

"You seem to have *also* heard a great deal."

"Young Sasha is happy to answer the questions of her lady. As is the innkeeper's stable hand. After all, a lady must see her horse is well cared for." She smiled.

Leave it to Deevana to find her own sources of information. Graylem could almost see her mind turning as she contemplated how her knowledge combined with his could help her gain whatever she wanted. Because she wanted something more than just seeing the inside of the Palace of Winds and playacting as a lady. He just hoped his sister wasn't contemplating trying to become one of the King's conquests. From what the merchants in the inn said, His Majesty was always on the lookout for another and save one who mysteriously disappeared they were all well rewarded for their attentions. Jewels and coin would not make her the lady she had wished to be, but perhaps she had changed her aims?

They turned a corner and stepped into a large square, and thoughts of his sister's plots disappeared as he saw the white steps— dozens of them—maybe hundreds—cut into the side of the plateau leading up to the Palace. The windmills . . . The steps . . . The white walls . . . The orb waiting to shine again in the darkness . . . All were exactly as the stories described. Suddenly, it was as if he were five and sitting next to his sister as they listened with rapt attention to the Harvest Festival storytellers.

They climbed the steps side by side, his sister nodding at the guardsman they passed.

"Lady Imogen said there is a path cut into the plateau to the south," Deevana said when they stopped at one of the landings so she could catch her breath. "I am to present myself to the guards at the main gate, and they will take me to the gathering I have been invited to attend."

"Remember what you promised, Deevana," he said quietly. "No stealing. Especially not here, where the King could have you thrown in the infamous North Tower and leave you to rot or worse."

"*Lady* Deevana, brother," she corrected under her breath. "And stealing is for commoners. Ladies simply have to make an impression to get what they want." With that, she gathered her skirts and started up the last set of steps.

"Just be careful," he said.

Deevana paused. "I am not the one who will be facing battle-trained men with swords. So it is I who am asking you, Graylem, please take care. This place is so far everything I have ever dreamed of, but it won't be if I lose the only person left that I love."

They climbed the rest of the stairs in silence, Graylem trying to ignore the knot of nerves growing deep in his gut. He had killed the deserters who had attacked them, but he had no idea whether they had been well trained. And while he *believed* he could have defeated the lords he fought in the yard outside the smithy, he had never actually beaten them. If he truly wanted to be a member of the elite King's Guard, this could be the only chance he had to convince anyone of his skill.

"You go first," Deevana said when they reached the top. "I want to have the memory of you entering the Palace of Winds."

"And you'd rather no one see us enter together and ask either of us questions about the other."

"Like I said, it's nice that we know each other so well. I would wish the light of luck shines on you . . ." Deevana gave him an impish smile. "But I honestly don't think you'll need it."

He tried to smile back, but anxiety tickled his stomach as he turned and walked toward the high archway entrance of the Palace of Winds, which was flanked by members of the guard.

One guardsman stepped forward, hand on his broadsword, when Graylem reached the open gate. "My lord."

The distinctive clangs of metal against metal sounded from somewhere inside the walls.

It took several tries for Graylem to find his voice before he finally said, "I was told to come to the gates and ask for Roddick. He's a member of the King's Guard."

"I know who Roddick is." The guard nodded. "Follow me."

They passed benches and trees and people speaking in clusters or standing in alcoves, but while Graylem knew they were there, he barely saw them as he followed behind the guardsman. The sounds of fighting and men shouting grew louder as they walked through the main courtyard, down a path, and into where the men of Eden's Guard trained.

There were dozens of them in a large practice field covered with trampled grass that had yet to turn green. Their mail shirts, shields, and helmets glistened in the sun. Men charged and slashed with blades, while in another part of the practice field others launched arrows into targets.

"Lord Roddick, this lord came to the gate asking to see you!" His escort shouted toward a small group standing next to the fence at the edge of the practice field.

The King's Guardsman turned. When he spotted Graylem, he threw back his head and laughed. "I guess you meant it when you said you were looking to find your own opportunities. Either that or you are one of the lords that comes here thinking they'll make the women sigh and end up in a traveling minstrel's song if they join us. No one has yet made up a song about walking the battlements on a windy night, and most women prefer men who aren't likely to end up dead. Of course, you could be the first."

The men standing with Roddick laughed—at him.

Heat filled his cheeks as Roddick yelled, "Get back to work," to the men. When they did as he bade, he crossed the grass toward Graylem. "You can go back to your post," he instructed the escort. Roddick waited for Graylem's escort to leave before saying, "I was curious if I would see you again, my lord. It takes courage, cunning, anger, or sheer desperation to walk through those gates."

"Which one describes you, my lord?" Graylem asked, then shook his head. "Sorry. That was rude."

Roddick studied him, then answered, "Truth be told, I'm no longer certain which describes me best. Ask me again in a few months and I might be able to answer."

"What happens in a few months?"

"I hope the end of the war. If it doesn't end before that."

"Do you think it will?" Graylem asked.

"What do you think, Lord—?" Roddick smiled. "I fear I never got your name."

"Call me Graylem."

"Graylem, is that right?" Roddick's grin dissolved as the older guardsman slowly walked around Graylem, making him aware of the rich gold stitching on the cuffs of his blue pants resting above the scuffed, almost worn-through boots he'd had resoled twice since he bought them.

He straightened his shoulders. "Yes, my lord."

"Well, Graylem, normally Lord Bolton handles signing up new guardsmen and does some basic training with them before Captain Monteros evaluates their worth. Both Captain Monteros and Lord Bolton are traveling back from the war right now."

"Do I have to wait for their return before I can learn if I'm allowed to serve?" he asked.

Roddick reached across his torso and pulled his blade with a metallic hiss out of its sheath. "Funny you should ask."

5

Graylem drew his own sword. "It would be my honor, my lord Roddick."

"There are no lords on the training grounds," Roddick said. "Fighting makes all men equal, and there is your proof."

He pointed to where a smooth-faced man with dark hair wearing a deep blue cloak stepped out of a doorway and strode toward the practice grounds. Men bowed as he passed. Several girls appeared in the doorway and followed behind, but it wasn't until he saw the woman with long, almost white hair striding purposefully through the others toward the tall, wooden fence, that he realized the identity of the man in the blue cloak.

Prince Andreus removed his cloak and draped it on a post. Then in a smooth move, he vaulted over the fence and drew his sword. He was dressed in a mail shirt like all the others, but his gleamed brighter—as did his weapon. A man with gray-streaked blond hair saluted with his own weapon before he charged. The swords clanged, separated, and then flew toward each other again. The Prince was good. His grip . . . his balance. The blades came together again.

The white blond woman could only be Princess Carys.

"Well?" Roddick yelled. He was standing in a different section of the field not far from where the Princess leaned against a fence, watching her brother fight with great intensity.

Graylem glanced back at Andreus, who shoved the older man back and was stalking him in a circle waiting for another attack. Then he hurried across the brown grass to where Roddick waited. "I assumed you would want to wait until Prince Andreus was finished."

"Like I said before, Graylem, there are no lords once you step onto this field. Let Prince Andreus worry about his fight. I suggest you worry about your own."

Roddick's blade lashed out, and Graylem stumbled back as it whistled through the air where his torso had just been.

"I wasn't ready!" Graylem yelled as he fumbled for the clasp on his cloak.

The other swordsman swung his sword in a lazy circle with a smile. "Do you think the enemy on the battlefield is going to wait until you are ready?"

Graylem let his cloak drop to the ground and kicked it to the side, then began to circle the guard.

"Lords like to fight with honor," Roddick said over the shouts and clangs coming from the other parts of the field. "Anyone in Eden's Guard does whatever it takes to win."

Roddick charged forward, and his blade cut the air.

Did the King's Guardsman want him to win or lose? Graylem wondered as he swung his own weapon and held tight to the hilt as the two swords clashed and his arms vibrated with the force of the strike. Had the blade struck him, it would have cut him in two. But the power Roddick had used for such a blow made it harder for the guard to recover his balance.

His heart slammed hard as he stepped back, pivoted, and slashed. It wasn't a full swing. It wasn't meant to be a striking blow, but one to force a reaction from Roddick. Which it did. The older guard turned to block the attack. Graylem pulled back his own weapon just before the guard's struck it. He could swear he saw Roddick grin as he stumbled forward and that he laughed when Graylem hooked his foot onto the man's ankle and sent him flying to the ground.

Roddick glared up at him, and Graylem lowered his sword. "I didn't mean . . . I didn't think . . ."

"You didn't try to finish me off while I was on the ground." Roddick planted his sword in the ground and used it to climb to his feet.

"Well, no," Graylem said. "I mean, this isn't . . ."

He heard the footsteps—the swish of the weapon—and dropped to the ground. He rolled to the side and jumped up as a battle-ax hit the patch of dirt he had just stood upon.

Graylem rolled again, flipped up to his feet, and swung his blade as the ax whistled toward him. The two weapons crashed together. A hulking, dark-haired guard with a missing tooth put all his weight behind his weapon and pushed Graylem's sword so it inched toward his face.

Graylem clenched his teeth. His arms shook as he pushed back, stopping the forward motion of the ax, but he couldn't keep it up for long. His heart thundered. He held his breath and yanked his sword away as he dove to the side. The guard flew forward. With Roddick's words about finishing the fight in his ears, Graylem advanced. Out of the corner of his eye, he saw a movement and swung his steel barely in time to connect with Roddick's blade. Roddick pulled his weapon back and struck again. Graylem moved backward as he matched the King's Guardsman strike for strike.

Sweat poured down his neck. His breathing came in fast, short bursts—when he could breathe.

He swung again and felt the blow resonate through his body. Roddick's dark eyes met his and held them. Victory was clear in the man's eyes. The blade headed for him again. He slashed his own to meet it, only Roddick changed the angle of his swing at the last minute. It was just a few inches, and Graylem altered his own swing to match it. Roddick smiled, then pulled his blade back, and Graylem registered the sound of footsteps too late.

Something kicked against his back. He lost his footing, and his chest hit the ground. Breath burst from his body. A boot pressed down, pushing away any chance of gasping for air. He turned his head in time to see the point of the sword bury into the ground an inch from his nose.

A calloused hand appeared in front of his face. "That could have been worse for you," Roddick said. "You move faster than most lords who step onto this field, Graylem, and you don't seem to end up with as much grass in your mouth when you hit the ground. Nevertheless, you lost."

Graylem pushed up from the ground with his sword still clutched in his fist and clasped Roddick's hand. "I thought I was going to be fighting you."

"You did fight me," Roddick said.

"Yes, but . . ."

"But having other men fight you as well wasn't fair?" Roddick mocked. "If you want fair, stick to tournaments and duels where there are rules that everyone agrees to follow. Here, we do whatever it takes to gain our objective. We create a plan when we fight, but we know that it is often necessary to break the rules in order to win. If you can't do that, you don't belong here."

As if to articulate the point, across the field Prince Andreus elbowed the man he'd been fighting in the side and then jammed his knee into the other man's crotch. His fighting partner sank to the ground and dropped his weapon. Prince Andreus had won.

"You didn't lie about knowing how to use that sword. With some work, you might learn enough to become a member of the King's Guard. Or you might come to your senses before you decide to take an oath to walk the battlements and fight the King's wars." Roddick looked over at where several young guardsmen struggled to hit the center of the targets with their arrows. Then he glanced to where the man who had been fighting Andreus rose to his feet.

"I can learn, my lord," Graylem said, picking up his cloak where he had dropped it on the ground. "If I can come back tomorrow, I can prove it to you."

Roddick shook his head. "Proving yourself will have to wait. I am leading a hunting party outside the city in the morn."

"When will you return?" Graylem asked.

"We are scheduled to be out a few days. The men at the Palace gate will know when I've returned." The King's Guardsman sheathed his sword. "I'd recommend that you take that time to practice. And if you're smart, you'll think about whether you truly wish to take an oath, and what you are willing to sacrifice in order to fulfill that oath."

Roddick strode toward the other side of the training grounds and yelled, "Prince Andreus, Crown Prince Micah requested that I put my sword at your service for today's training session."

Prince Andreus pushed away from the fence he had been leaning on and turned toward Guardsman Roddick.

"Training Master." The Prince nodded. "I didn't see you on the field."

"I was giving instruction to someone who is interested in petitioning to join the guard."

"I am fascinated that whoever this new guard might be rated your attention before that of your prince," Princess Carys called as she swept over to stand on the other side of the fence, just behind her brother's shoulder. Her head was high. Her pale hair was pulled back at the sides to keep off her face, but the rest hung free of the twists and curls his sister had worn. And her voice . . . There was something familiar about the edge to her words and the set of her jaw.

Everything on the practice field stopped as the guards turned toward Carys, who was staring at Roddick as if she wanted to be the one to fight him instead of her brother. She paced several feet away from her brother and all eyes followed her.

"Perhaps," she called, "your neglect is something I should mention to Captain Monteros when he returns. Or maybe I should mention it to my father."

"Your father believes Prince Andreus should take more of an interest in working with the guard than with the windmills, Your Highness. We all know King Ulron would not mind Prince Andreus putting in extra work."

Her eyes flashed. "But my father would mind one of his guardsmen and trainers putting a commoner's training above that of royal blood."

Several men flinched, but Graylem stepped closer, compelled by the familiar set of the Princess's jaw and the belligerent tone. His sister—the Princess reminded him of Deevana at her most defensive, when she was doing her best to hide that something was wrong. But what could be wrong?

"You are correct, Your Highness," Roddick said with a bow, then started to turn. "I apologize and—"

"As well you should." Princess Carys cut off Roddick's words, and the guard turned back toward her. But Graylem didn't because he finally understood.

The Princess said something about having the man sent to the battles to the south and stalked farther down the fence. Keeping all eyes on her, which meant they weren't on Prince Andreus, who had rested his heavy broadsword against the post he himself was now leaning on as he fumbled for something in his pocket. Even from this distance, Graylem could see the sheen of sweat on the side of the Prince's face.

It was cool out. The fighting had been over for a while. Yet the prince was sweating, and, unless Graylem was mistaken, Prince Andreus was pulling whatever he had taken from inside his cloak to his lips.

Something was wrong with the prince, but no one noticed because they were all watching Princess Carys as she berated Roddick.

But Graylem was watching Prince Andreus as he took several deep breaths before wiping his forehead and turning toward the others. "I don't see any reason we should tell the King about this."

Carys spun toward her brother, and while her expression was one of irritation, Graylem saw the uncurling of her fists and the easing of the tension in her shoulders as she walked back toward her brother.

Roddick bowed. "Very well, my prince. And the training your brother requested?"

"The next time I train, I will seek you out," the Prince said with a small smile. "I guess I should be glad that you are training men now instead of Lord Garret. Otherwise, I might have something to worry about."

With that, Prince Andreus walked toward the path that led away from the practice fields, his sister trailing behind him. No one else seemed to find it strange that the Prince had left his heavy broadsword behind.

Crossing to where Roddick stood with his fist clenched, Graylem asked, "Does that happen often?"

Roddick glanced at him then back to the path the Princess and her brother had taken. "Noblewomen don't throw tantrums in Orgo?"

"Not like that," Graylem admitted.

"If you truly decide to join the guard you will learn to get used to it. Most of us have."

"Most?"

Roddick shook his head and unclenched his fist. "Clear out, boy. I have training to see to. Rhyden! Julien! Get those men shooting straight or I'll send you all to the North Tower to be flogged."

Graylem went to the other side of the fence. But his mind wasn't on the dozens of men he watched fighting with swords and pikes and axes. Instead, he thought of the sharp-featured Princess with pale hair who he was certain had fought just as bravely as the men on this field. He was still thinking of her when he went to the gates to wait for his sister. She might not want him to be there, but he would do what he must to keep her from harm.

* * *

"Did you spend much time with Lady Imogen?" Graylem asked after his sister finished gushing over the grandness of the Palace, the beautiful dresses the women of the court wore, and the delicious food that was served after the musical performance she had been invited to attend.

"Not much at all," Deevana admitted with a frown. "She came to the solar, greeted me, and stood on the side of the room as I introduced myself to some of the ladies. It wasn't long after that she excused herself from the festivities to go to the battlements and study the winds. The rumors seem to be correct. Lady Imogen doesn't appear to have many friends."

Graylem gave his sister a soft smile. "You sound almost as if you feel sorry for her."

"Lady Imogen is the Seeress of Eden, advisor to King Ulron, and one day, after she marries Prince Micah, she'll be Queen." Deevana laughed. "It's impossible to feel sorry for someone who has everything I could ever dream of and more. But maybe after listening to the other ladies whisper about how much time Lady Imogen spends atop the battlements and away from the members of the court, I feel like I might understand her better than they do."

"I'm sure the other women understand her. After all, they are all ladies."

"Lady Imogen lived for years in the Village of Night with people who spend all their time staring at the skies. She might be betrothed to Prince Micah and live in the Palace of Winds, but when you think about it, she is just as new at being a lady as I am."

Graylem put his hand on his sister's shoulder and stopped walking. "The difference is the seeress really *is* a lady, Deevana. Just as you will be when we ride south. You've seen the court now. I've had a chance to speak and fight with a member of the King's Guard. He told me I could be good enough to join Eden's forces, but that I should think about whether I am ready to make that commitment. We have both gotten what we came for. It is time for us to go."

"No!" Deevana's eyes flashed with anger. Several nearby women carrying baskets glanced over, and Deevana quickly looked down at the ground and lowered her voice as she said, "I'm sorry. I didn't mean to snap, but I can't go just yet, Graylem."

"You've seen the Palace," he said. "You've enjoyed playing lady. It's time to make that a reality. Once you have, you can return."

"I won't be able to return if I leave now," she insisted. "Several of the ladies from important houses asked me if I had visited the Shrines of the Seven Virtues. When I said I hadn't, they made me promise to go with them at the end of the week. They had already planned to go, and now they have invited me along. They said it was unlucky for a lady, especially one who was yet to be married, to visit Garden City and not make sacrifices at the shrines. I know we had planned to leave the city before then, but I didn't feel like I had a choice. I had to tell them I would go. If I leave now, they will take offense. They won't forget the slight. I don't want to become a true lady only to know that I will be shunned if I come back to court."

As much as Graylem wanted to tell his sister that she was being foolish, he had heard Lady Blackthorn rage more than once at Goodman Bryant over hooks he had made years ago that she had found less than satisfactory. If she invited a local lady to a special event and the lady failed to show up, Lady Blackthorn would remember and be vicious about it if they met again.

"Fine. We will stay until you have visited the shrines. But this will be our last delay."

His sister's eyes gleamed, and he felt the knot of anxiety tighten like a hangman's noose. As they reached the inn, he said, "Deevana, I need you to promise me that after you have finished that obligation we will leave Garden City and go south. And I need you to mean it."

His sister turned to him and smiled. "Of course we will, Graylem. A few more days and I will finish what I came here for. I wouldn't lie to you."

But of course, she would. That's what worried him.

6

"I thought we would explore the city together today," he said as his sister pulled from her wardrobe a light blue gown he could swear hadn't been there yesterday.

"There's a storyteller coming to the Palace today. Some of the younger ladies my age invited me to attend."

"And you couldn't turn them down?"

Deevana laughed. "I didn't want to. Besides, I thought you would want to spend your time on the practice fields."

In all truth, he would, even if Roddick's warnings about the oath he would have to take and the faces of the men he had killed still echoed in his memory. He wasn't sure what he would do yet about the guard, but he wouldn't have to make that choice until Deevana was safely married and living as the Lady of Green Valley. "Well, at the very least I can escort you to the Palace and maybe see some of the wonders Father used to talk about."

Deevana bit her lip, and he sighed. "What is it now?" he asked.

"You can't come in to the Palace." Deevana looked out the

window toward the courtyard and the Tree of Virtues. "You haven't been invited."

"I'm sure your new friends won't mind extending the invitation to your brother."

"They would, but they don't think I'm here with my brother."

"There is no way they believe a highborn lady came to Garden City alone."

"They don't. They think I am being escorted to my aunt Venia in Irae by a skilled swordsman from her guard."

"And how did they come to believe that?"

"Because I told them." Deevana gave him a bright smile. "I did it for you, Graylem. That way on the chance you do decide to join Eden's Guard you won't have to lie if anyone questions your family line. I'm looking out for you, little brother."

He was sure that this was how she fooled herself into believing her deceptions were warranted. He just wished he didn't know his sister so well.

The rest of the walk was mostly done in silence with his eyes on his sister while hers were raised to the top of the plateau and the impossibly high white walls of the Palace of Winds—desire and excitement shining bright on her face.

"You *will* be careful," he said quietly, taking his sister's arm as they reached the top of the steps before she could head for the gates. "You won't steal anything."

"I told you, Graylem . . ." Deevana yanked her arm away. "A lady doesn't steal. She has other ways of getting things she wants, and here in Garden City, I am a lady. Don't worry about waiting to walk with me back to the inn. I will have one of Eden's Guardsmen escort me home." His sister turned on her heel and, with her head high, strode toward the gates, where after a quick discussion with the guards she was allowed entrance.

He walked to the gate and watched a guard escort Deevana through the main courtyard before disappearing into one of the dozens of doorways—into the dream she had been holding onto for as long as he could remember. Since he didn't have an invitation into the Palace, there was little he could do by remaining, but he couldn't bring himself to go.

"Do you have business at the Palace?" one of the guards stationed at the gate asked.

"Not today," he said. With one last glance at the walls, he turned and headed back to the inn. While his sister was playing lady inside, he would do what he had to in order to honor his mother's wishes and ensure Deevana became a lady outside.

He hurried back to the inn and up to his sister's room, where he dug through the bottom of the wardrobe for the satchels she had insisted on bringing with her from Blackthorn. There were two that had yet to be opened. He undid the fastenings on the first and emptied the contents onto the bed.

A small leather pouch, a small white fox pelt, four spoons, and three dining forks—all of silver—fell out of the first satchel. The pouch contained at least four dozen coins of bronze and copper. Not enough to pay for their rooms, but it would help.

He tied the pouch to his belt and opened the second bag. Inside were four silver candlesticks, two goblets of gold decorated with etchings of vines on the stem and roses on the chalice, and three gold chains. All made him shake his head at his sister's audacity. She had stolen so much from those who would happily punish her for her actions. But it was the necklace with ropes of gold and silver entwined with an orb of yellow hanging from the center that made him want to grab his sister and shake their father's influence out of her. Graylem had seen the jewel gracing Lady Blackthorn's neck at tournaments and public events. People whispered that it had been a gift from the High Lord Wynden and Lady Rivenda.

As reckless as his sister was, he had a hard time believing she would have dreamed of stealing the necklace from Blackthorn Keep and surviving the escape. Had she created a plan to take the necklace, she would have left the Keep immediately and been long away from Blackthorn before anyone noticed the jewel was missing. The fastening hook made him believe his sister had acted on impulse and had almost paid a high price for her folly. That setback should have made her more careful, but from what he had seen his sister had only exchanged one plot for another.

He packed the cups, the candlesticks, and the fancy dining forks and spoons into one of the bags to take with him. The jeweled necklace and the other items he shoved into the other satchel, which he placed back in the wardrobe.

He found Sasha getting water from the pump behind the inn.

She turned and almost spilled her pail as she spotted him staring at her. He frowned at the recent bruise coloring her right cheek as she gave an awkward curtsy and asked, "Is there something I can do for you, my lord?"

"I need a favor," he admitted. "My sister and I are from a place far to the north where there are more rabbits and pointed-horn deer than people. I am aware of the dangers of the city, but my sister sees only the excitement of the buildings and the shrines and the court." He reached for the pouch at his side. "Since the Lady Deevana balks at my desire to always be at her side to protect her, I am hoping you will help me keep watch over my sister and let me know when she returns to her rooms and if she leaves without my knowledge."

Sasha set the pail down with a slosh. "I do not want to upset Lady Deevana, my lord. She has already complained to my father about my slow service."

Which explained the bruise on her face.

Graylem pulled several copper nicks out of the bag, then looked around to make sure no one else was near. "My sister is often displeased with me as well, and your father should know that there is no pleasing some people no matter how fast or slow you are. I will make sure to speak to my sister to make sure she is aware how lucky she is to have such a capable maid to assist her."

The girl gave him a shy smile. "Thank you, my lord."

"Will you help me as well?"

The girl glanced around and nodded.

He pressed the copper into her hands, wishing his face looked as attractive when he blushed. "If the Lady Deevana asks, we never had this conversation. Those of us who anger my sister need to stick together."

He left the girl to her chores and went in search of her father, who was quick to recommend a shop where Graylem might ask about some items that he claimed had been stolen from his family.

"I need someone who has a good eye and a fair heart," he explained.

"Goodman Yarrow is the best and the most discreet merchant I know, my lord," the innkeeper assured Graylem, then provided him with directions through the complex network of streets that wound through the city. "Look for the red door and the sign etched with a swan."

Armed with that information, Graylem set out with his sister's satchel on his shoulder and a hand on the hilt of his sword. The day was warmer than normal for so early in the spring, and it seemed as if everyone in the city was moving through the streets.

Old women with thick, woolen shawls draped over their shoulders clutched them with wrinkled hands. Young children dashed in and out of alleys, whose laughter and sweaty faces belied the cold around them. Highborn in fine clothing. Commoners in worn cloaks and drab colors. Then two members of the King's Guard in their cloaks of blue and yellow and another dozen guardsmen passed by.

All eyes on the street turned to the men riding under the banner of King Ulron. One man slunk into an alley—clearly worried the guard might be looking for him—but almost everyone else looked at the men with respect. Graylem had noticed the commoners here rarely wore swords at their sides. They couldn't afford the cost of a blade. Not here where coin was so dear and the blacksmiths had no interest in wasting their work on those who could not pay large sums for it. But he spotted dozens of men with daggers on their belts as he turned down streets hoping he had not taken a wrong turn.

Graylem fingered his own weapon as he walked, thinking about what he would do different if the opportunity to fight Roddick ever came again. He still wasn't sure if he was ready to take an oath and live in a city so large and so far away from everything he had known. But last night, when the faces of those he had killed faded from his dreams, the image of Princess Carys appeared, and once again he watched as she protected her brother from those who were sworn to see him safe. The only reason for such a deception was distrust of the men whose oaths were made to her family and to Eden. He found himself wondering if that distrust was well placed and what it would take to earn it back.

Still thinking of the Prince and Princess of Eden, Graylem spotted the mark of the swan over a red door. Straightening his shoulders, he pushed open the door, strolled in, and frowned as if the place was not what he had expected. After all, he was supposed to be a lord.

The scent of cinnamon and flowers greeted him, as did an incredibly tall and equally rotund man dressed in black velvet pants and a frothy green shirt. The man limped forward and smiled a greeting that made the wide, jagged scar that slashed across his face and mouth appear almost as if it were alive.

"Lady Imogen and Lord Roddick both claim I can count on discretion in this shop," Graylem lied as he shut the door behind him. Being recommended by the Seeress of Eden and a member of the King's Guard was a greater incentive to be honest than if Graylem mentioned the true source. If the innkeeper asked, Graylem would say he hadn't found Goodman Yarrow and none would be the wiser.

The merchant's grin widened. The large body rocked with silent laughter and Graylem caught a glimpse of the emptiness inside the man's mouth and understood why the merchant had called Goodman Yarrow discreet. The man could not speak of what transpired inside these walls because the man had no tongue. But he could write with long, fluid letters as he bartered over the value of the silver and gold Graylem had to sell.

Graylem had a basic knowledge of the value of the pieces in the northern district and suspected they would fetch even more coins here in a city where there were so many more with the wealth to pay the price. Still, he was stunned when the merchant offered him double what he would have asked and amazed when he received triple that offer after their lengthy negotiation was complete. The coins should be more than enough to settle their debts and allow them to leave Garden City in good standing. Now if only he could convince his sister to do nothing untoward before it was time for them to go.

"You went through my things?" Deevana stormed to the hearth and put her hand on the mantel next to a scarred wooden box. "Did you find what you were looking for?"

"I did what you said you wanted—I sold most of the items you *liberated* from our old life to pay for this one." He took a deep breath and pulled back his anger, knowing it would only push her away. "I didn't sell the necklace. It's still in your bags. I thought you might want to wear it once before you sell it. Although it might not be so lucky to wear it when you go to visit the shrines."

A reluctant smile tugged at the edge of his sister's lips. "Perhaps not. Or maybe the Gods have a better sense of humor than you do."

Graylem let out a relieved sigh as his sister's resentment faded.

"And it's not like I have need of candlesticks on the battlements or in the Palace of Winds," Deevana admitted.

"The battlements?" he asked.

"The view is amazing up there. And the turn of the windmills is so loud you could swear they were going to pick up the Palace and fly it away. You should see it," Deevana said, then shrugged. "I guess you will see it if you become a guard. I saw several guardsmen when I went up to pay my respects to Lady Imogen. Most of the ladies don't like going onto the battlements, although many men do, including Prince Andreus."

Which meant she was drawing attention by scaling the steps and stepping out onto the top of the Palace.

"You didn't go up there to try and meet the Prince, did you?"

"Of course not." Deevana laughed with obvious surprise, making him breathe easy for a moment. Then she gave him the familiar smile that made everything inside him tense with fear. "I found exactly what I was looking for on the battlements, brother. You can relax."

No, he thought as she answered the knock that came at the door and young Sasha entered with water for Deevana's bath. He would not relax. Not until he had his sister safely away.

The next day, the skies were muted with gray clouds and still darker ones on the horizon as he walked with his sister on the now-familiar route to the Palace. The subdued skies did not dampen his sister's mood as they walked or the gleam in her eye as she disappeared inside the Palace entrance. She did not see the storm coming or notice the way a guardsman stepped out of an alcove that she passed by. Maybe it was a coincidence, but he didn't want to take the chance.

"We should leave today," he said the next morning when his sister finally unlocked the door to her room dressed in a green and gold gown—the glitter of Lady Blackthorn's jewel dangling between her breasts.

Deevana had slipped into the inn long after the wind-powered lights had illuminated the city. Now she held a satchel filled to bursting with offerings of food for the shrines in one hand while the wind outside howled. Storms were approaching.

"We've talked about this. The ladies are waiting for me to visit the shrines. I have to go."

"Deevana," he said, grabbing her by the arm as she tried to sweep out of her room past him. "A guard followed you after you entered the Palace yesterday. What have you done to draw his attention?

What have you taken?"

"Nothing!" she snapped, although he could hear the edge of concern in her voice. "I have listened and watched, but I have taken nothing. Just as I promised. You constantly think the worst of me. Do you know how that makes me feel?"

"I think the worst? How can you say that after everything that has happened?" He took a deep breath and shook his head. "It doesn't matter. Right now you are safe, and I promised Mother I would keep you that way. We are leaving for Irae and Green Valley today. There is a life waiting for you there. The life of a lady . . ."

His sister yanked her arm free. "Yes, a lady married to some sort of cripple who can barely speak, let alone come to court."

"You don't know that."

"And *you* don't know that I'm wrong," she hissed. "I won't leave with you. You can't make me. Just because you are too scared to break the rules to gain what you want or too uncomfortable showing off your skills doesn't mean I have to be."

Heartache burned his throat. "This isn't about me . . ."

"No." She lifted her chin. "It's about me. Unlike you, I am taking control of my life. I'm finding a way to get what I want. What I *really* want—not the scraps that you or Lady Venia or anyone else bestows upon me."

Fear spiked inside him. "This is not Blackthorn Keep, Deevana. You don't know what you're doing."

"You are the one that doesn't know, brother. You have never seen the world for what is really is. You think you are so much better than Father and me, but what you really are is weak."

Hurt churned in his gut. He could feel her slipping away. "Deevana . . ."

"It's *Lady* Deevana, Graylem," she said sharply. Stepping close to him, she said quietly, "No one born to our station gets what we deserve in this life unless they take it. Father taught us both that. So you can crawl back to the life we had before and beg people to let you earn their respect. Meanwhile, I will do what Father told me to do."

"At least let me watch out for you," he said as she started out the door. "Mother would want—"

"I don't care what Mother would want," she sneered. "And I don't need your protection. Don't follow me today. Don't try to be the hero in the stories because you will never be one. And I'll order one of the ladies' guards to arrest you and throw you in the North Tower if you try."

"Deevana . . ." He stepped toward her. "I'm your brother."

For a second he saw something soften in her eyes. He saw the sister who had laughed with him when they were little and cried with him when they buried their parents in the ground. Then it was gone, and the hardness was back. Straightening her shoulders, his sister said, "I'm Lady Deevana, and Lady Deevana doesn't have need of a brother."

With that she swept out the door, down the stairs, and, if she had her way, out of his life.

7

A knock startled him, and he sat up straight in the chair he had dragged to the window to watch for his sister's return. He had called himself a fool for still caring when his sister clearly wanted nothing to do with his protection, but still he had sat there and kept watch.

Only he had fallen asleep.

The knock came again.

"Lord Graylem!" Sasha's voice whispered as he leapt out of his chair and hurried across the darkened room. The girl stood in the doorway, holding a candle that illuminated her dark eyes. "I am sorry to disturb you, m'lord, but you asked me to keep watch for your sister."

"She's returned?"

Sasha shook her head. "She's gone to the Palace. I was in the stables when I saw two men from the King's Guard stop her on the street. I was too far away to hear what they were saying, but one handed her a sealed scroll and a small box. Once she came inside, she called for me to help her fix her hair then asked me to heat water for washing and to bring her soup and bread. I was only gone for fifteen minutes. Maybe twenty. But when I came back the box, the note, and your sister were gone."

He thought about the time it would take for the young girl to get the water from the pump, heat it over the fire, as well as make the soup, and he knew the time that passed had probably been far longer. His sister hadn't wanted anything she had ordered. She must have suspected Graylem had enlisted the girl's help and had wanted her spying eyes out of the way.

"How long ago was this?" he asked, grabbing his cloak and striding to his sister's door.

"I came here as soon as I saw she was not in her room, my lord," the girl said as he stepped into the richly appointed space that had so delighted his sister when they first arrived. The room that now stood empty.

"You said the men she spoke with were members of the King's Guard?"

"They were wearing blue and yellow cloaks, m'lord, and had the seal of Eden on them."

Which meant the men and the note they brought must have come from the Palace. "If my sister returns before I do," he said, headed for the stairs, "tell her . . ." He stopped and shook his head. "Just tell her that her brother will be back soon."

He hurried to the stables for his horse, no longer caring who might recognize the markings on the saddle, and pushed the horse to go as fast as he dared through the city streets that were illuminated with torches and the wind-powered lights that spilled over from the windows of the buildings. In the distance, the Palace walls almost glowed white against the darkness. The orb shined bright over the tallest as if beckoning him forward. His heart pounded in concert with the clatter of his horse's hooves on the cobblestones.

He told himself Deevana was right. He was being an alarmist. But his sense of dread only grew.

She would be furious with his interference if he was wrong. She had vowed to never speak to him again. She—

A woman's scream clawed the night. A flurry of red streaked down against the background of the bright white walls as the scream grew louder. In the distance he saw the flurry of red hit the ground. The scream vanished but still echoed in his head.

He urged the horse forward, leapt off at the base of the steps, and raced up the white stone staircase. A lone gong sounded—once—twice. Then it, too, went still.

Guards raced out of the Palace gates. Others spilled out as well as he reached the top. The world spun. Voices swirled around him as he pushed his way through the crowd until he could see the familiar bright cloak, the shining hair still twisted and curled slowly being coated by the ooze of red blood that was spreading against the white of the Palace stone.

"Turn her over," someone shouted.

Graylem's knees trembled. Bile seared his throat as her body flopped over and the face that he had loved was broken beyond recognition. But there was no mistaking the jewel that still hung around her neck.

"Was it an accident?" he heard someone ask.

A familiar guard leaned forward—Lord Roddick—and pulled a small box, just like Sasha described, out of the cloak's pocket. He opened it to reveal a silver ring set with a gem that resembled the orb in miniature. "The guards caught her stealing. I'm told after they chased her to the battlements, she jumped rather than facing punishment."

No. Graylem stepped back and shook his head. That wasn't Deevana. She always believed she would win no matter the odds. She would *never* have jumped.

The box was the one that Sasha had described to him. Someone had given it to the King's Guard and had it delivered to Deevana along with a note.

"Does anyone know her name or her family?" someone asked. "Ask the members of the court if they know anything about her. She might not be working alone."

Slowly, Graylem turned. He forced himself to walk away from his sister's broken body . . . down the staircase that seemed to have gotten longer than when he had raced to the top and to the horse that was grazing on a patch of brown grass. Tears thickened his throat as he rode. The weight of loss pressed on his chest.

When he returned to the inn and walked in to what had been Deevana's room, Sasha leaped out of a chair and asked, "Did you find her, m'lord?"

"She's gone," he answered. "She won't be coming back."

He opened the wardrobe, grabbed a satchel, and then looked at the gowns his sister had looked so beautiful in. "You can keep the dresses," he said, turning to the young maid. "Sell them. Wait until you are old enough to wear them. My sister will no longer have need of anything in this room. It's yours."

"What about this, m'lord?" the girl asked, holding out the small wooden box that had been atop the mantel. Slowly, she crossed the room and placed it into his hands. "This was your lady sister's as well."

The girl gave a quick curtsy. "I will be in the hall if there is anything else you need."

Graylem's hand shook as he unlatched the box. Inside was a small stack of letters. Six to be exact. The first four in a shaky handwriting that he recognized from his correspondence with Lady Venia, all addressed to his mother and describing her worry about her two older sons who had gone to fight in the war and her dedication to caring for her youngest son since the tournament accident that left him unable to walk, scarred on the back of his head so that hair could no longer grow there, and reduced to the mind of a cheerful child. But one that could still produce an heir and carry on the family name.

He had thought his mother had destroyed the letters. Instead, Deevana had found them.

The next page was still curled at the edges; the script was formal and the words simple.

Come to the Palace. Your silence will be rewarded.

The note had no identifying seal or signature. No way for him to know who Deevana had met and who had sent the invitation or the gift that was used to brand her as a thief before they forever silenced her.

Deevana knew something. His sister had gleaned information and planned to use it for her own gain. Did they recognize that necklace and realize it would be easy to paint her with the brush of a criminal? He wasn't inclined to think so. Deevana hadn't worn the jewel until after the gift and the note arrived. To Graylem, it was the irony of the Gods that saw his sister die—accused of the crime she had freely committed for years and was utterly innocent of here in Garden City.

Swallowing hard, Graylem picked up the last page, which was covered with the beautiful handwriting Deevana had spent so much time perfecting to make it look as close to Lady Blackthorn's hand as possible. One she must have written before she went to the Palace. Was it in case she didn't come back, or because she wasn't sure she would have time to write it upon her return? He wished he knew which. Then he realized it didn't matter.

> *Gray,*
> *I am sorry, but I cannot go south and accept less of a life than the one I had before. Not when I've found a way to be promised all that I ever dreamed. I hope you can forgive me for my harsh words. It was the only way to guarantee you would not interfere. I am and will always be your sister. Promises have been made to me. When we meet again, I will truly be—*
> *Lady Deevana*

He climbed the bright white steps to the Palace of Winds with his bag on his shoulder. The handful of silver left on the inn's table and the horses that remained in the stable should more than cover any debt. When he arrived at the gates, he spoke to the guards on duty and then waited for Lord Roddick to appear.

When he did, Graylem said, "If you think I am skilled enough, I would like to join the guard."

"Are you sure you don't need more time to think about it? The oath of a guardsman is for life," Lord Roddick reminded him.

"That's a long time. Perhaps you want to discuss it with your family or find something else you'd rather do?"

"My family is too far from me to talk to," he said quietly. "And I have nothing else I need more."

His sister had used anger to push him to lower his guard and avoid his protection. He had fallen for the distraction—the same one Princess Carys had used on the guard. He had failed his sister, and his sister had died.

Whatever Roddick saw on his face must have convinced him because he clapped Graylem on the shoulder and escorted him through the gates, saying, "Very well. But don't say I didn't warn you. Palace life is not what the storytellers claim it to be."

"I know, my lord." Graylem glanced up at the battlements and nodded. "Trust me, I know."

He had lost his sister because of whatever lurked in this place. As much as he wanted to alter that, there was no changing the past. And if he was honest with himself, there was nothing he could have done once they rode into this city. But while the past was set, the future could still be made better. *He* could do better. And maybe he could use what he had learned and what he had lost to protect another who needed it.

This time he would break the rules as Roddick told him a guardsman must. This time he wouldn't let anyone he wanted to protect push him away.

HOW FAR ARE THEY WILLING TO GO TO WIN THE CROWN?

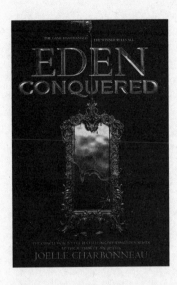

Delve deeper into the world of Eden with these novellas!

IN A POST-KNOWLEDGE WORLD, WHAT CAN ONE GIRL DO TO UNCOVER THE TRUTH?

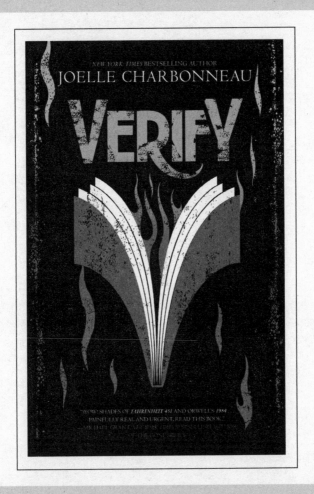

"Wow! Shades of *Fahrenheit 451* and Orwell's *1984* . . . Painfully real and urgent. Read this book."

—Michael Grant, *New York Times* bestselling author of the Gone series

JOIN THE

Epic Reads

COMMUNITY

THE ULTIMATE YA DESTINATION

◄ DISCOVER ►
your next favorite read

◄ MEET ►
new authors to love

◄ WIN ►
free books

◄ SHARE ►
infographics, playlists, quizzes, and more

◄ WATCH ►
the latest videos